Taylor sighed and closed her eyes as she held Jen in her arms. Something wonderful had happened. Jen had come into her life and filled a void, a void Taylor didn't think she would ever fill. Until now, she had been satisfied with the lust-driven one-night stands that sailed in and out of her world. But she couldn't deny it. Jen was different. She was special. Jen's body could start a flame burning in Taylor with just a toss of her silken blond hair. Even the sight of Jen napping with Picasso on her lap brought a smile to Taylor's face. As surprising as it was, Taylor knew she would never look at love and commitment in the same casual way again. She wanted her arms around Jen, protecting her and keeping her safe. She wanted Jen to find comfort in her arms and to rely on her for everything she would ever need.

"I can't wait for these casts to come off." Taylor sighed, kissing Jen's softly.

"I know, sweetie. Me too."

Visit

Bella Books

at

BellaBooks.com

or call our toll-free number

1-800-729-4992

BRAGGIN' RIGHTS

Kenna White

Bella
BOOKS
2007

Bella Books, Inc.
P.O. Box 10543
Tallahassee, FL 32302

Printed in the United States of America on acid-free paper
First Edition

Editor: Anna Chinappi
Cover designer: LA Callaghan

ISBN-10: 1-59493-095-3
ISBN-13: 978-1-59493-095-9

This book is dedicated to Annie, my beautiful daughter, for her steadfast courage and her infectious sense of humor as she battles cancer. And to Ron for standing beside her in the darkness and in the light. I want you to know you do not face this battle alone. You are my hero and I love you with all my heart.

ACKNOWLEDGMENTS

A big thank you to Dr. Osborn for his support and medical advice with this book. Thank you also to Pat, Patty, Sonnie, Dave, John and Ann—the coffee klatch crew who keep me inspired, laughing and writing.

About the Author

Kenna White lives in a small town nestled in Southern Missouri where she enjoys her writing, traveling, making dollhouse miniatures and life's simpler pleasures. After living from the Rocky Mountains to New England, she is once again back where bare feet, faded jeans and lazy streams fill her life.

Chapter 1

Taylor Fleming stood outside the corral, her arms draped over the top rail of the fence. It was spring and the Texas sun was already hot. She removed her cowboy hat and ran her fingers through her hair then settled it back on her head, pulling the front down low to shade her eyes. Tiny white streaks marked her frown and smile lines through the layer of dust that covered her face. Taylor had a pure and classic beauty about her lean body. Her brown eyes and chestnut hair framed a golden tanned face. Her leather chaps were burnished to a well-worn gloss and were speckled with mud, blood and sweat. Her Appaloosa stallion, Coal, was tied to the fence next to her, munching on a flake of hay. The cinch had been loosened, a reward for his hard morning's work.

Grier Fleming, Taylor's father, stood next to her, also dressed in jeans, chaps, western shirt, boots and a Stetson hat. He was a tall man with a square-set jaw and a keen eye for the action inside the corral. It was roundup and the air was thick with dust and the smell of manure. The vast herd waiting to be processed mooed like a constant concert.

"Good looking group, if I do say so myself, Taylor," Grier said, adjusting his hat to the back of his head. His face was dirty and weathered, the look of a Texan working his cattle. Even his bushy moustache was covered with range dust.

"T-bone sired some good young 'uns. I'm glad we kept him," Taylor replied, taking a drink from a water bottle then handing it to her father. He took a drink then handed it back.

Inside the corral, the calves were being roped, branded, inoculated and castrated. The work was dirty, smelly and disgusting at times but Taylor loved it. This was what a Texas rancher did to produce restaurant quality prime beef, and the registered Black Angus raised on the Cottonwood Ranch were some of the best Texas had to offer.

Grier had inherited the ranch from his father, Drew Fleming, who had inherited it from his father, Bull Fleming. Taylor knew her great-grandfather had to have been given a name other than Bull but it was a constant source of family speculation as to what it was. Since he signed his name with a squiggle and an elaborate 'F,' even the deed to the ranch was no help in settling the guesswork. Any important documents that might have held the secret to Bull's real identity were lost when a grass fire swept across the prairie in 1934, consuming 10,000 acres of pasture grass and the family home. Any cattleman would explain that good pasture grass during the Dust Bowl era was far more valuable than the house. Bull, his wife Sabrina and their two children were forced to live in a one-room sod hut until the home could be rebuilt—a new two-story home considered one of the most modern ranch houses of its time in southern Texas. In spite of the Depression, or perhaps because of it, Bull built his wife her dream home, employing local out-of-work craftsmen and feeding them prime beef while they worked. The house had two full bathrooms, a large efficient kitchen with a mudroom, fireplaces for charm and beauty as well as function, walk-in closets (a luxury at the time), a big and wide covered back porch and an upstairs screened-in sleeping porch that allowed cool breezes to flow through on hot summer nights. Air-conditioning wasn't added until Grier took over the house when his father died at the age of forty-eight. The ranch house was built with traditional wood-framed construction and white clapboard siding. Taylor thought it looked like a sugar cube with windows but she loved the old house so much that she insisted she be allowed to move into it after her parents built their new five-thousand-square-foot home at the far end of the ranch, the end that offered a dramatic view of Rio Mesa. Taylor's home was a twenty-minute drive from her parent's house, a feature she appreciated as a thirty-six-year-old independent woman.

By the time she started high school, Taylor realized she found cowgirls more attractive than cowboys. It was to her advantage to be a rancher's daughter since jeans, boots and horses were just part of everyday life. She didn't have to hide anything. She couldn't anyway.

Taylor had always been a strong-willed woman, not above getting her hands dirty in the everyday workings of the ranch. She worked for her father and it was no secret he expected her to take over the operation some day, something she was well capable of doing. As an only child, Cottonwood Ranch would someday be her baby.

"I don't agree with the count," a woman said, trotting her pinto over to the fence.

Lexie Tate was a grizzled, hard-working ranch hand. She was something over fifty but refused to confess how far over. She could ride a horse, rope a steer, buck a bale of hay and pull a calf as well, if not better, than any man on the place. But so could Taylor, for that matter. Lexie was hired more than twenty years ago to help with the newborn calves, her specialty, but she was soon doing all the jobs the other ranch hands were asked to do. Some joked that Lexie had been a poker-playing gunslinger in a former life. She had a long gray ponytail and tanned face that never knew a drop of makeup. Her eyes were dark and piercing and often cut through a cowboy who thought he could slack in her presence. She could snap a fly off a fence post with a whip at ten paces and could stitch a heifer's torn vulva without batting an eye. She had the respect of every person on the ranch and earned it through years of hard work. It was assumed that Lexie was a lesbian. She never dated, at least not that anyone ever saw. On her days off, she drove her battered pickup truck down to Del Rio, a small town on the Texas Mexico border. When she returned she wore a coy smile for a few days, a smile the ranch hands assumed was due to the sweet Texas air around Del Rio. Lexie had seniority over the other ranch employees, everyone except Cesar.

Cesar Reynos was half Mexican, half Cherokee Indian and all Texan. He had thick gray hair, a skinny little moustache, a scar over his right eye from the kick of an angry bull and had been wearing the same brown cowboy hat for ten years. He had been with the Flemings since he was a fifteen-year-old rough-talking rabble-rouser. He was now head wrangler and oversaw Cottonwood Ranch's sperm bank. The Fleming's registered Black Angus bulls contributed some of the most sought after sperm in the state. Selling sperm from prizewinning bulls was a cash crop that brought in a handsome profit above and beyond the vast herds that were trucked to market. Cesar's son and grandsons also worked for the Flemings, something Cesar took great pride in but something he was quick to criticize if they failed to measure up.

"How many off are we?" Grier asked, swatting at a pesky fly.

"I counted the ones in the holding pens and we're still missing about eighty head. Did you move any out of this pasture?"

4

Lexie asked, her horse fighting against the reins to turn back to work.

"Nope. Did you, Taylor?" Grier asked, fishing a plug of chewing tobacco from his vest pocket. He bit off a corner and began chomping it into shape.

"Nope. Are you sure the pasture was cleared? They get up against that row of trees by the stream and they are hard to flush out."

"I thought we did. I'll go take a look after lunch."

"Taylor," one of the ranch hands yelled, pointing at a calf that had slipped through the partially open gate and was scampering merrily across the open pasture. "That one ain't been done yet."

"I'll get him," Taylor said, tightening the cinch on the Appaloosa's saddle and untying the reins. "Time to get to work, Coal," she said as she grabbed the saddle horn with both hands and jumped, catching the toe of her boot in the stirrup.

"Just send Coal after the dang thing, Taylor," Lexie called with a robust laugh. "He does all the work anyway."

Taylor swung her leg over as she steered the stallion in a circle. She reached over the fence and knocked Lexie's hat off then headed Coal for the runaway calf.

"Sorry about that," Taylor yelled over her shoulder then cackled triumphantly.

Taylor urged Coal into a full gallop as she leaned forward, tugging her hat down tight. She took the rope from around the saddle horn and formed a loop, rotating it over her head. When she drew within reach, she broadcast the loop, catching the calf by the neck. She dallied the rope around the saddle horn, turning the calf around with a snap.

"Lucky shot," Lexie yelled then reached down and grabbed her hat without dismounting.

"Come on, young 'un," Taylor said, leading the calf back to the corral as it bucked and tugged against the rope. "You aren't ready to go out on your own just yet."

Lexie maneuvered her horse toward the gate and opened it for Taylor then closed it with her foot, giving the latch a kick. One of the ranch hands released Taylor's rope from the calf's neck and wrestled it onto its side. Three cowboys immediately descended upon the calf, injecting it from a stainless steel syringe, castrating the young bull and branding him with a mark that looked like a lollipop with a bent stem. That was the Cottonwood Ranch brand and it had been since Bull Fleming bought his first heifer. Grier still branded his cattle the old school way. Taylor had tried to convince him to jump into the modern age of ranching and inject the cattle with a microchip that meant a more accurate record could be kept of everything from age to how much they cost to feed. But Grier wasn't ready to change just yet.

Taylor steered Coal back to the fence from where Grier and Lexie were watching.

"I'll go check the pasture. I have a feeling I know what happened to the eighty head," Taylor declared then squinted off to the north.

Grier grunted, spitting tobacco juice at a horsefly that had lit on the fence.

"I hope Rowdy isn't swiping our cattle again. I don't have time for him."

"Unless aliens flew down and scooped them up, where else do you think eighty head have gone?" Taylor asked, watching the wayward calf climb to his feet after his ordeal. He seemed mad but none the worse for wear.

"Crazy old man," Lexie muttered, spitting a mouthful of dust.

"I'll go take a look," Taylor said with resignation.

"Call and let me know what you find," Grier said, checking to see if his cell phone was in his vest pocket.

Taylor nodded, taking one of the canteens strung over the fence post. She headed north at a comfortable pace, one that Coal could maintain all day. She had raised the big stallion from the time he was an obstinate colt, naming him for the black spots on his rump that reminded her of lumps of coal. He was considered too wild to be a good cutting horse but Taylor's patience paid off, his temperament no match for her stubborn determination to tame him.

The Cottonwood Ranch was divided into several sections to keep the vast herd into manageable numbers. It was more efficient to have holding pens, squeeze chutes and corrals in each section of range for processing the calves and for inoculating the adults. The north pasture was the farthest from Grier's ranch house but the closest to Taylor's. A corner of Fleming property touched Rowdy Holland's ranch, The Little Diamond. It was a small ranch with a house, barn, fencing, corrals and outbuildings all in need of painting. Rowdy no longer raised cattle and he had sold a chunk of his ranch several years ago, a spur of land that jutted out into Fleming property at the extreme corner of the north pasture. It was only sixty acres but Grier and Taylor were happy to buy it since it squared up their property, making it easier to run fence and keep track of cattle. But Rowdy had trouble remembering the sale, even when the sheriff repeatedly came knocking on his door with a copy of the deed transfer and a warning to leave the Fleming fence alone.

Taylor made good time. She knew all the shortcuts to the far reaches of the ranch. When she was satisfied there were no stray cows, she aligned herself with the fence row and the spot she thought most likely to be where Rowdy would have cut an opening. She crossed the creek and to no surprise she found all four strands of barbed wire had been severed. A nearly hundred-foot-long section was open, the wires in pieces and scattered across the pasture. She pulled out her cell phone and punched in her father's number.

"Fence is down," she reported, grinding on her teeth as she examined the ends of the wire.

"Yeah and I bet I know who did it," he snarled.

"I'm heading over to his place."

"Don't get too close, Taylor. Remember last time. I don't want him taking any pot shots at you. He's crazy as a loon."

"He couldn't hit a barn with a cannon," Taylor scoffed.

"Yeah, I know, but don't take any chances, you hear me?"

She ended the call and stuffed the phone in her pocket. It was only a few miles to Rowdy's house and she couldn't wait. They had been making excuses for his eccentricities long enough. She urged Coal up to a trot, hoping her anger would fade before she got to Rowdy's corral where she had a strong suspicion Cottonwood Angus were being held captive. When she caught sight of his house, she eased Coal to a walk. A man was standing at the corral gate, a rope in his hand. The corral was filled with cows, Black Angus cows, all with a bent-stemmed lollipop brand on their rump. Taylor pulled Coal to a stop and wiped the sweat from her forehead as she gazed across the field.

"Well, well. What do we have here?" She urged Coal onward. As she approached, the man shaded his eyes from the sun and stared at the rider.

"What do you want?" he growled. "This here is private property. You better get off my land."

Rowdy Holland was seventy-four and thin. He had a perpetual three-day beard and wore suspenders and a belt to hold up his worn jeans. He stared daggers at Taylor through beady little eyes.

"Nice bunch of cows you got there," Taylor said, trying not to sound suspect.

"Yep. I raised 'em all myself. They're Texas longhorns," he said proudly.

"I thought they were Black Angus," Taylor said then wished she hadn't.

"They're longhorns. That's all we raise down here," Rowdy argued.

Taylor noticed Rowdy had his boots on the wrong feet. She

8

caught a whiff of his body odor as Coal moved closer and it took her breath away. She coughed and gave a tug on the reins, making the stallion back up a few steps. It was obvious Rowdy had no idea who she was and identifying herself might do more harm than good.

"What brand is that, Rowdy?" She pointed to the cows in the corral.

"They don't have a brand yet. I haven't had time. Too many things to do on a spread like this. Fence is always down somewhere and I can't keep hired help."

Taylor nodded, not wanting to raise Rowdy's anger or his suspicion any more than necessary. Rowdy hadn't had anyone working for him in years and the last cow he took to market was eight years ago but arguing over these details would serve no purpose. Like every other time, he had been the one who cut their fence and lured Fleming cattle into his holding pens. And like every other time, he seemed oblivious to reality. Taylor certainly didn't want to be the one to force the issue. It wouldn't do her any good to move the cattle back through the fence since it would take several hours to mend what he had destroyed.

"You wouldn't happen to know who cut some of our fence, would you Rowdy?" she asked carefully.

"No," he replied with a frown. "I haven't seen anyone cutting no damn fence. Bet it was rustlers," he added, as if it was a secret.

"No doubt," Taylor said, nonchalantly circling the outside of the corral so she could see if the cows looked all right. She noticed they had several bales of hay and a galvanized tub of water so at least she didn't have to worry about them going hungry. A few of the cows hadn't calved yet but she recognized them as experienced mothers so she didn't press Rowdy about where they came from. This was a matter for the sheriff, especially since Taylor noticed an old double-barreled shotgun leaning against the corral gate just out of his reach. He may have been a crazy old man but she didn't want to test his marksmanship.

"I've got work to do," he grumbled, latching the gate and propping a board against the latch as if it was a lock. He picked up his shotgun and walked to the house, mumbling to himself as if he forgot Taylor was there. She waited until Rowdy was inside and had closed the door before punching in her father's number on her cell phone.

"He's got about eighty head of our stock in his corral. Looks like about twenty calves too."

Grier gave a long string of cuss words, yelling loud enough so everyone working in the corral could hear. "You sure it's our brand?"

"Who else has our circle-stick brand?" Taylor replied as she steered Coal for home.

Taylor suddenly heard a shot then another from the direction of the house. She looked back and saw two puffs of smoke rising from the shotgun in Rowdy's hands.

"What are you doing there?" Rowdy yelled as he crossed the yard and waved a fist in Taylor's direction. "You get off my land. You're trespassing." He stood in the clearing between the house and the corral gate then raised the shotgun to his shoulder and took aim at her.

"Crazy old man," she screamed at him. She knew he had shot both barrels of the rusty old gun and hadn't reloaded but she was taking no chances. "Put that thing away before you hurt yourself."

"Taylor!" Grier was yelling into the phone. "Taylor? What's going on?"

"Nothing. Rowdy's just acting like John Wayne." She urged Coal into a canter and moved out of Rowdy's range.

"I'm calling the sheriff. I'm tired of messing around with old man Holland. Where did he cut the fence?"

"Just west of Rattlesnake Pond. It's about a hundred-foot section."

"He has cost me money and aggravation for the last time,"

Grier announced, spitting angrily.

Taylor chose not to admit that Rowdy had shot at her again. He hadn't hit anything but Grier didn't need more fodder for his anger. Rowdy was just an old man with no family to speak of and was growing more senile with every passing year. He had been a good, decent rancher but that was before his touch with reality began to wane. This wasn't the first time Taylor had to retrieve Fleming Angus from Rowdy's corral and she knew unless something was done to stop him, it wouldn't be the last.

The day's work was drawing to a close and the ranch hands were loading their gear by the time Taylor returned. A line of pickup trucks followed the dirt trail to the county road and home. A hot meal, a bath, a night's sleep and they would be back tomorrow to finish working up the cattle on this section of range. Taylor loaded Coal into the trailer and hung a bucket of feed for him. She was bone-tired and hungry. All she could think about was soaking in a hot tub and forgetting the aggravation Rowdy had caused.

"I called the sheriff," Grier announced as he pulled alongside her truck. "I told him I want Rowdy Holland arrested for cattle rustling." Grier spit his wad into the dust and ground the stick-shift into first gear.

"He's not really a rustler, you know," Taylor said, stepping into the cab of her truck. She didn't like the extra work Rowdy caused but she wasn't sure he was worth arresting.

"The heck he isn't."

"It's your call, Dad, but he doesn't know what he's doing. He never sells them."

"You coming to dinner tonight?" he asked, ignoring the subject of Rowdy and the cattle.

"I don't think so. I'm beat. I'll grab something at home and see you out here tomorrow. Tell Mom I'll eat with you when we're working up the east and south sections."

Grier nodded then pulled away.

"I hear Rowdy has the missing cows," Lexie said, striding over to Taylor's truck. She had removed her chaps and draped them over her shoulder. Sweat marks stained her jeans where they rode on her hips.

"Yeah, cows and calves," Taylor replied.

"Your dad's calling the sheriff on him this time. He's mad enough to chew nails."

"We've got to stop Rowdy from cutting up the fence. Send a crew out first thing in the morning to fix that. Tell them it's about a hundred feet, all four wires. The posts look okay. Tell them to put in a swing section but don't advertise it. I want to be able to drive those cows back through once the sheriff gets there. And tell them no one goes onto Little Diamond property until the sheriff arrives. That crazy old man is liable to shoot someone."

"Did he shoot at you again?" Lexie asked, giving Taylor a hard stare.

"Yes." Taylor said it quietly. "But I don't want anyone to know."

"Taylor, the sheriff ought to know about it. You can't let him go around shooting at you. This isn't Tombstone, ya' know."

"He missed."

"Too bad his kid doesn't do something about him."

"What kid? He doesn't have any children."

"Well, not his by birth but he and his wife adopted one. At least that's what I heard." Lexie pushed her hat to the back of her head.

"When? I haven't seen anyone else around that place in years."

"Rowdy had a nephew or someone working on a ranch the other side of Harland several years back. I remember he said Rowdy and his wife couldn't have any kids of their own. About thirty or thirty-five years ago, there was a bad car accident that killed a young couple and left their baby girl a ward of the state so Mrs. Holland petitioned the court for custody. Within a year they adopted her. They were both in their forties at the time."

"I don't remember anyone that age living over there. She would have had to go to Harland schools."

"According to rumor, they split before she was school age. Mrs. Holland took the girl and ran off. They said Rowdy hasn't been the same since," Lexie added.

"In that case, she probably doesn't know anything about him now."

"I think she lives in San Antonio. I overheard the clerks in the courthouse talking about trying to get in touch with her."

"What's her name? She's probably married and has a couple kids by now."

"Let's see," Lexie said, scratching her head and squinting off into space. "I think I heard something like Janice or Jean or Jennifer. Something with a J. And I don't think she's married. They used the name Holland when they were talking about her."

"Sure would solve our problems if she'd come have a talk with her old man and get him to leave our fence and cattle alone," Taylor suggested.

"Maybe you ought to mention that to the sheriff."

"Maybe," Taylor replied, her mind already giving thought to contacting the woman herself, hoping to convince her to do the daughterly thing and talk to her father. All the efforts of the sheriff's department had done little to stop Rowdy from hacking up their fences.

"I need a bath," Lexie said, whacking her hat against the leg of her jeans. "See you tomorrow."

"Yep, tomorrow," Taylor said, giving a nod and pulling away just as the sun took an orange bite out of the horizon.

Chapter 2

Taylor was the first to arrive back at the corral just before dawn. It was a cool morning, full of fresh, clear skies and the sweet aroma of sage grass. This was her favorite time of the day, before sweat and noise blotted out the innocence of the prairie. She saddled Coal and tied him to the side of the horse trailer while she strapped on her chaps. By the time she finished her thermos of coffee and scrambled eggs rolled into a tortilla, the trucks started arriving. Cesar immediately barked orders to get the morning underway.

All the ranch employees had a good working relationship with Grier and Taylor. The Flemings were fair and kind employers, willing to pay a decent wage for a decent day's work. They were not above stepping in and doing the work themselves. Taylor always knew she couldn't be purely supervisory. She wanted to feel the rope in her hand and the horse between her thighs. It was in her blood. It was what woke her in the morning and accompanied her through the long days. Even after a sunup-to-sundown workday, her body might be exhausted but her soul still wanted more. Nothing put a smile on her face like the Texas wind in her hair and the open spaces stretched out before her. She developed her ranching skills at an early age and her dedication to the ranch grew as she matured. But it came at a high cost. With long days and year-round responsibilities, Taylor had little time for anything else. Living on a ranch meant socializing was limited to telling jokes and grabbing a beer from the ice tub with the hired help. But like Lexie, Taylor found her private life in occasional trips to Austin or San Antonio. She had exhausted all lesbian possibilities in Harland, a small cattle town in southern Texas. Lexie and Taylor never discussed what they had in common, although they both knew the other was gay. Lexie was too old for Taylor and Taylor was too stubborn for Lexie. Both wanted a soft touch and a no-strings-attached kind of woman. And that was only found behind the smoky haze of bars in distant towns.

Grier backed his horse out of the horse trailer. It was already saddled and eager to get to work.

"Did you call the sheriff?" Taylor asked, swinging her leg over Coal's broad back. "I don't want to go back up to Rowdy's to claim the cows until he gets there."

"You bet. He'll be there by nine." Grier stepped up on his horse and checked his watch. "He said he'll call when he gets there."

"I understand Rowdy has a daughter in San Antonio. I think maybe she should be contacted. If she is his only next of kin, she may have to handle things for him."

"I doubt she'll want anything to do with him. She's probably just as crazy as he is." Grier settled his hat on his head and turned his horse toward the holding pen, Taylor following along behind. "However, if she is his next of kin, maybe someone should talk to her. If Rowdy is as crazy as I think he is, she may have to be brought in anyway."

"I'm going up to San Antone tomorrow to pick up supplies. I think I'll have a talk with this daughter and see why she hasn't stepped in and done something," Taylor said.

"We need her help. Not more problems from the Hollands. So go easy with her, Taylor. Be nice."

"Aren't I always?" she said, pulling her hat down over her forehead and trotting off toward the day's work.

"Don't cuss at her, for Christ's sake," he yelled.

Taylor, Grier, Lexie and the rest of the wranglers spent the day cutting out the calves to be processed, worming and inoculating the adults and separating the ones who still hadn't calved. Lunch was coolers of meat, cheese, fruit, pies, pop and gallons of water. Grier even allowed a beer with lunch so long as no one let it interfere with their ability to do their work. By sundown, the north pasture had been finished and the cattle had been turned out to graze. According to the sheriff, Rowdy Holland had been taken into custody, cursing and complaining all the way to town. The Cottonwood crews had repaired the fence and reclaimed the hijacked cattle. As far as Grier was concerned, it was finished. He didn't care what happened to Rowdy as long as he didn't have to keep repairing his vandalism. Rowdy was out of his hair. Grier had forgiven his deeds for the last time.

Taylor talked with the sheriff to see if he knew anything about Rowdy's daughter. With limited information, she found an address in San Antonio for a J. M. Holland. It wasn't much to go on and the address was several years old but it was worth a shot. Taylor didn't want to call her and take the chance that she might just hang up. The only way she planned on meeting this woman was face-to-face. She knew Rowdy wouldn't be in jail for more than a few weeks or months at the most. The judge wasn't going to throw the book at this old man. It wasn't as if he was an ax murderer or something. At the very least he would be out and back to cutting Cottonwood fencing by fall. If bail was granted and he could pay it, he might even be out within a few days.

Taylor was up early and heading east on Highway 90 for the two-hour trip to San Antonio. She had a list of stops to make including the feed store, ranch equipment dealer and a few while-you're-in-town errands. But she didn't mind. She planned to stay overnight anyway, planned her weekend down to the last detail, in fact. She would finish her errands, eat dinner at Globe's Chicken Hut then check in at the motel before going to the Rainbow Desert nightclub. Tomorrow she would find J. M. Holland but tonight was hers. Once a month, Taylor drove to San Antonio for supplies and once a month she spent the night at the Capri Motel down the street from the Rainbow Desert. The Capri wasn't the Taj Mahal but it didn't need to be. It was clean and it was close enough to walk to the nightclub. It was also close enough to walk back in a hurry if she found a cute reason.

Taylor had been frequenting the Rainbow Desert since it opened six years ago. It had been a redneck rabble-rousing kind of place with more broken chairs and tobacco spit than Dodge City during the 1800s. When it was bought out of bankruptcy by a lesbian couple and converted to a gay nightclub, there was a certain smug satisfaction the gay locals found in adding a rainbow flavor to the once homophobic-as-hell atmosphere. It was now a thriving business, being one of the only gay–lesbian establishments on the west side of town. The neighborhood didn't mind. There were fewer fights, quieter patrons and a cleaner parking lot.

Taylor arrived at the bar just after eight. She had showered and changed into clean jeans and a fresh shirt before walking the four blocks from the Capri. Lucy, one of the owners, was bartending. She waved, tipping her white cowboy hat at Taylor. Taylor touched the brim of her Stetson, the one she wore when she felt like dressing up. She almost didn't wear it but the flavor of the bar cried out for her to follow her country western roots. It framed her face and showed off her big brown eyes. Her thick chestnut hair fluffed out around the back and a few bangs peeked out from under the brim. Taylor had a tight butt, long legs—the kind that were just made for lean fitting jeans—and highly polished cowboy boots. Her alligator skin boots had silver toe tips that matched her silver belt buckle. She stood next to the bar, allowing her eyes to adjust to the dim light.

"Taylor," a woman called from the darkness. "Over here, Taylor."

She squinted into the room and moved toward the voice as another song began to play. A group of women were waving at her from the far corner table, the one that had the best view of the front door, the dance floor and the bar. Taylor weaved her way through the tables, smiling broadly at the four women. Several of them jumped up to give Taylor hugs and kisses.

"Hey, you're looking good, Taylor," Nancy said, looking her up and down.

Nancy was a short Hispanic woman with a thick head of black hair, full lips and a pleasing figure. Her makeup was perfect and her body language demure. Nancy was a third-grade teacher and was a lipstick lesbian from the old school. She wanted a woman to open doors for her and buy her a drink. She wanted a relationship to last for years and grow better with time like fine wine. Her last relationship lasted six months. After spending hundreds of dollars on a woman who could talk the birds from the trees, she learned the woman had several girlfriends, most of them at the same time. Nancy had been part of Taylor's once-a-month group since the beginning. Her crush on Taylor lasted for over a year and ended only after they consummated their curiosity then decided they would be better off friends than lovers.

"Hey, Nancy." Taylor smiled and squeezed her shoulder as she slid into the corner chair. "How is everyone?"

"We're all fine. All but Sonny," Nancy said, bumping the

woman next to her.

"Don't start with me, Nancy," Sonny barked, her eyes drifting across the room.

Sonny was a baby dyke. She was over thirty but she had a cute round face with baby blue eyes, short blond hair and a come-hither look that melted women's hearts. What's more, she knew how to use them to her advantage. Sonny liked her women attractive, spunky and a bit naughty. She dated carefully but wholeheartedly when she did find a soft victim to her liking. She and Taylor often clashed over bragging rights to some new bar clientele. But it was good-natured rivalry. It had become a game for the women at the corner table to watch Sonny stalk her prey, like watching a hawk circle the prairie.

"What's up, Sonny?" Taylor said, giving her order to the waitress.

"Nothing," she said with a scowl, watching a woman at the end of the bar.

"Are you having trouble with the ladies?" Taylor asked with a glint in her eye.

"No. No trouble." Sonny's blue eyes were narrowed and stared accusatorially at the woman in the black skin-tight jeans.

"Sonny got dumped by the redhead with the big boobs," AJ offered from across the table.

AJ was a product of the Seventies. Her parents were Woodstock hippies and she was their love child. She was a free spirit and wore the bell bottom jeans and peasant tops to prove it. Her brown hair hung past her waist and was adorned with beads and odd pieces of jewelry, many of them found at local thrift stores and worn to make a statement against waste in society. Her lesbian lifestyle had been worn like a crown since she was in high school, something her parents found courageous and endearing. AJ was the oldest in the group but had the most fragile self-worth. She fell in love at the drop of a hat and fell hard, often with disastrous results. Her last relationship lasted two years and ended in a bitter battle over politics, religion and her partner's need for a little space. AJ was too blinded by love to realize that she meant space to see the waitress from the corner café on Thursday nights.

"I was not dumped," Sonny declared. "Dumped is what happened to Amber."

"I'll have you know I was not dumped, Sonny," Amber said, giving her Valley girl impression. "I was ceremoniously lowered from the pinnacle of love's pedestal." She flashed a sideways glance and batted her eyelashes then laughed a saucy laugh.

Amber was the youngest of the group at twenty-nine. She had round hips, small breasts, an energetic laugh and a big heart. An auditor for a large downtown bank, she often arrived at the Rainbow Desert from work in her slacks and blouse. For her first twenty-five years, Amber had been living an unremarkable life in a padded bra. She may have been gay when she was young but she wasn't even sure what a lesbian was until a woman winked at her in an elevator and asked her to lunch. Amber was innocent and the kind of woman everyone wanted to cuddle and protect. She had dimples in her pudgy cheeks and tears that flowed like water when someone was being thrown to the lions. It was hard for her to hide her crush on Taylor but she had learned to live with it, offering up small sighs and moans when Taylor accidentally touched her or, be still the heart, danced with her.

"Oh, damn, Amber," Taylor offered with a soft sigh. "I'm sorry to hear that. Who was it? That delivery driver?"

"No. That was Denise. She was toast weeks ago. This was Nicole, the unemployed." Amber cackled. "And don't be sorry. This ass-kicking I liked. Nicole dumped me because I wouldn't let her take my car to Chicago for spring break."

"Why did she want to go to Chicago for spring break? She's not in college." Nancy asked with a concerned frown. "Besides, no one goes to Chicago for spring break. You go to Galveston or Brownsville or somewhere in Florida. It's cold in Chicago that time of year."

"My point exactly. She wanted my car, a full tank of gas, my best leather jacket and my iPod," Amber reported, snapping her fingers like it was a done deal. "What she didn't want was me going along. I said screw it. So she said good-bye." Amber gave a small, reflective smile.

"Sorry anyway, kiddo," Taylor offered.

"Yeah, well, you know." Amber shrugged and sighed. "The sex was good, though."

"You let a good one get away?" Sonny teased. "What's her name? What's her phone number?" She grinned.

"You've got your own troubles, Sonny. You didn't need Nicole," Amber argued.

"Hey, the way it's been going, I may have to date you," Sonny teased.

Everyone laughed.

"We'll have to come up with signals so we can let each other know if someone is worth the effort, if you know what I mean," Amber said, pouring herself a glass from the pitcher of beer.

"What do you mean signal?" Taylor asked, taking a long draw on her draft.

"You know," she replied, winking deliberately.

"You mean if they are hot to trot?" Nancy suggested.

"Yeah, hot to trot," AJ added.

"How are you going to signal that?" Sonny asked doubtfully.

"I don't know. But we'll have to figure a way." Amber took a long slow drink, leaving a foam moustache on her upper lip. She smiled with it.

"You mean like rating them on a scale of one to ten?" AJ asked, giving the idea some thought.

"Well, not exactly. But something like that. It has to be something only we understand. A secret code," Amber said.

"Oh, God," Taylor quipped. "That sounds pretty schoolgirl to me." She leaned back in her chair to watch the people on the

21

dance floor.

"I have it," Amber said, sitting up straight and grinning with a jubilant revelation. "We'll use candy. I love candy." She winked at the table.

"Candy?" Sonny asked, grumbling at the idea.

"Let's hear it, Amber," Nancy said. "I'm willing to try anything."

"Okay. Remember that girl with the spike heels and the burgundy lipstick last month. The one you said looked too hard to ride," Amber said in Sonny's direction.

"Yeah."

"Well, I heard she was one of those great big lollipops."

"Big lollipop?" Sonny still wasn't buying it.

"Yes," Amber said, leaning in. "An all-day sucker." She smiled wickedly.

Nancy and AJ giggled at the comment.

"Woo, Amber. That good, eh?" AJ asked mischievously.

"In that case, we know what kind of candy Sonny likes," Nancy said, laughing in her direction.

"What's that?"

"It's simple. All it has to be is a Mounds," Nancy replied, giving Sonny a pat on the cheek.

"Well, I like anything round and sweet and soft in the middle," AJ offered.

A loud roar of laughter had risen from the tables across the room where a group of men were sitting.

"Then that makes them gum," Sonny said, nodding toward the gay men. "Juicy Fruits."

"Oh, that was bad," Taylor chuckled.

"How about you, Taylor," Amber asked. "What kind of candy do you like?"

Everyone looked at Taylor. She shook her head and grinned.

"They all give me a cavity," she replied, tilting her chair back against the wall.

"Come on," Nancy urged. "I bet you like *some* kind of candy."

She grinned at her, hoping to get Taylor to admit her preference.

"Something that melts in your mouth, not your hand?" AJ teased.

"Or something that sticks to the roof of your mouth?" Amber asked, as Taylor blushed.

"Taylor likes hard candy I bet." Sonny offered. "The harder, the better."

"I don't like candy. It's habit forming." Taylor stood up and headed for the ladies' room. She certainly wasn't going to admit she liked soft women with the patience to linger over a golden sunset or willing to lie in her arms all through the night. For all these women knew, Taylor liked a hot and fast thrill, nothing more.

"You do too like candy, Taylor Fleming. I bet you eat more candy than all the rest of us put together," Amber declared, patting Taylor's fanny as she slid past.

When she returned from the bathroom, Amber was waiting and jumped up to greet her. The dance floor was filled with women doing a line dance.

"Dance with me, Taylor. Please," she whined, taking her by the arm.

"Sonny likes to dance these things," Taylor said, trying to get back to her chair.

"No, I do not," Sonny replied. "I don't dance line dances. You can't touch your partner. Why not just stomp around the floor by yourself?"

"Come on, Taylor." Amber was pulling her toward the dance floor. "I love this song."

"Okay," Taylor grumbled and allowed Amber to pull her onto the parquet flooring. Within a few beats of the music, Amber and Taylor had joined in the parading, spinning and stomping. Amber was surprisingly light on her feet for a large woman. Taylor hooked her thumbs in her belt and moved with the music, graceful and agile herself. When the song ended, Amber locked her arm through Taylor's and walked her back to the table, preserving every moment of their time together.

"Thank you, Taylor." Amber gave her a kiss on the cheek and a hug for her effort.

"You should have danced with us," Amber said in Nancy's direction. "I love to line dance."

"I much prefer partner-type activities," Nancy said sardonically.

"We were talking about your candy thing," Sonny said, taking another look at the woman at the bar who had dumped her. "No doubt about it. Misty would have to be horehound."

Everyone laughed.

Taylor eyed a woman entering the bar.

"Oh, mercy," Taylor said with an exaggerated drawl, watching her cross the room.

"I don't know what kind of candy that is," Sonny said with a slow moan, also noticing the woman with the long blond hair and the jeans that hugged her body in all the right places. "But I hope that one is my flavor."

A tall woman followed the blonde through the front door and escorted her to a table where two other women were already enjoying a drink. The blonde smiled greetings to the other women and took her seat, facing Taylor's table. The tables were on opposite sides of the dance floor and meant Taylor and Sonny had to bob and weave to see between the dancers.

"I think the candy store just opened," Nancy giggled, watching Sonny and Taylor ogle over the woman.

"You two can't afford that one." Amber said, giving the woman's body a critical stare. "That's pure chocolate. You two need to stick with penny candy."

"No kidding," Nancy said, looking the blonde up and down as well. "Why can't my ass look that good in jeans?"

"Why can't my anything look that good in jeans?" Amber asked with a groan then propped her elbows on the table.

"I'm going to ask her for a dance," Sonny announced, finishing her glass of beer then pushing her chair back.

"She's with someone," Nancy declared, grabbing Sonny's arm. "She won't dance with you."

"She won't if I don't ask her." Sonny stood up and looked over at Taylor. "She who hesitates is s-o-l."

"Go for it," Taylor replied, being a good sport about it.

The rest of the women at the table watched as Sonny crossed the room and introduced herself to the blonde, smiling her best smile and touching the woman's shoulder softly. To everyone's surprise, the woman smiled and stood up. The tall woman she arrived with was deep in conversation with the ladies at the table, seemingly uninterested. Sonny took the blonde's hand and led her to the dance floor for a Texas two-step. Taylor was immediately judging the woman's height as Sonny guided them around the floor. Five-feet-six, maybe five-seven. A good dancer. Cute ass. Nice breasts. Radiant smile. Beautiful skin. Yep. Sonny had found the gold chocolate coin in the candy store. Taylor was sure of it.

When the dance was over, the woman smiled a thank you and headed for the ladies' room. Sonny returned to the table with the look of triumph equaled only by the Allies' march into Paris. Amber and Nancy were giving Sonny catcalls as she took her seat with a smile too wide to be ignored.

"What's her name?" AJ asked.

"What did she say?" Amber added with excitement.

"Is she with that other woman?" Nancy asked. All of them leaned over, anxious for Sonny's report.

"I just asked her to dance. I didn't ask for her personal history. I said would you like to dance. She said sure. You have to take these things slowly." Sonny leaned back and stared off where the woman had gone.

"Slowly? Since when do you do anything slowly? You mean she said thank you and walked away," Taylor offered with a wry smile.

"She had to use the ladies' room. What am I supposed to do? Go with her?"

"Didn't you get her name?" AJ asked.

"I don't remember," Sonny argued, happy with her victory even if the women at the table were not.

"Are you going to ask her for another dance?" Taylor inquired, watching the blonde as she stepped out of the bathroom and crossed to her table. The woman's escort paid little attention to her, the conversation at the table seemingly more important than politeness. The blonde sat down and looked around, smiling and sipping a strawberry margarita while the other three women talked. Taylor assumed she wasn't a beer babe. The woman unconsciously flipped her shoulder-length hair, exposing her ravishingly supple neck, something that sent a shiver through Taylor. Sonny and Nancy were too deep in a conversation to notice the woman looked completely and totally bored. But Taylor noticed. She hadn't taken her eyes off the blonde since she sat down and as fate would have it, she and Taylor finally made eye contact. Taylor quickly smiled as she noticed the woman staring at her. It was a spontaneous smile and Taylor was sorry it hadn't been more genuine. The woman looked away. Taylor sat staring in her direction, waiting for her to offer another glance if even for a brief moment. The woman's eyes found their way back to Taylor. They were blue and soft, or at least Taylor assumed they were from her vantage point across the room. They were full of emotion and tenderness. Taylor could tell. She could feel it. Even across the room, separated by a dance floor full of people, Taylor could sense this was the sweetest piece of chocolate she had ever seen. Taylor allowed a slower, more cautious smile to form on her lips as they studied each other.

"Are you going to ask her to dance?" AJ asked, nudging Taylor's arm.

"What?" Taylor hadn't heard a word she said.

"Are you going to ask her to dance? You've been staring at her long enough."

"Naw, I don't think so," Taylor replied, satisfied to watch the blonde from a distance.

Before anyone had a chance to say anything, Sonny was on her feet and on her way to ask the woman for another dance. Taylor kicked herself. But this time the blonde smiled politely and said no to Sonny's invitation. It was obvious Sonny was crushed.

"Wow, shot down," AJ said, rubbing Sonny's arm as she took her seat. "What did she say?"

"What do you think she said? She said no." Sonny poured a full glass of beer and downed half.

The woman did accept a dance with one of the women at her table and was immediately lost in the crowd on the dance floor. Taylor couldn't see her. For a fleeting moment she gave thought to asking Nancy or Amber to dance just so she could get close to the woman. Instead, she looked for the waitress. Maybe after another beer she would find the courage to ask the blonde for a dance, courage she usually didn't have trouble finding.

"I need a beer," Taylor said, going to the bar to order it herself. She leaned against the bar, waiting her turn and watching the dancers. She scanned the top of the crowd for blonde hair. With each momentary glimpse, she would stretch and crane her neck to see if it was her blonde, the one with the blue eyes and the angelic smile.

"Excuse me," someone said from behind her.

Taylor didn't realize she was blocking the path to the bar.

"Are you going to order or are you going to just stand there in the way?" the voice asked impatiently.

"Take a hike," Taylor said, standing on her toes to see over the growing crowd of dancers.

"I beg your pardon."

"I'm busy. Go around the other way." Taylor paid no attention to the woman trying to get through.

"I don't care what you are doing. You could move over." The woman behind her was getting angrier by the second. She gave Taylor a gentle push to get her to step aside.

Taylor held her ground, thrusting an elbow backward. She had lost sight of the blonde and was desperate to find her again.

"Are you stupid or something? Don't you understand plain English? I said go the fuck around," Taylor shouted above the music. She usually wasn't this rude. But her normally placid manner was taking a backseat to her need to find the woman with the breathtaking smile. She turned on her heels to confront the nuisance. She gasped and stumbled over the leg to a bar stool as she stood face-to-face with the blonde, her blue eyes glaring venom at her.

"You are the rudest person I ever met," she hissed, gritting her teeth at Taylor.

Taylor felt the blood instantly drain from her face and her chicken dinner did a swan dive in the stomach. Her knees became so weak she wasn't sure they would hold her up. Try as she might, no words would come. She stood staring at the woman, feeling more foolish than she could ever remember.

"Well," the woman said, perching a hand on her hip.

"Do you want to dance?" Taylor stammered, her mouth taking control of her brain.

"You have got to be kidding," the woman scowled. "Are you going to move or just stand there like you own the place? And by the way, I know you don't own it because no business owner would ever dare to be so impolite and offensive."

"I'm not impolite," Taylor heard herself say but she meant to say she was sorry for being impolite. Nothing was coming out of her mouth the way she meant it. This woman had tied her brain in knots.

"Your opinion, Annie Oakley."

The woman turned and went through the other doorway. Before Taylor could regain her senses, it was too late. The woman had gone outside, followed by the other three women from her table. She had vanished into the night without Taylor's apology. All Taylor could do was stand and stare at the door, wondering what had happened. She pushed her hat back on her head and ordered a shot of tequila, muttering to herself for being stupid.

"Hi, Taylor," a woman said, slipping her arm around Taylor's waist. "Long time, no see."

"Hi, Crystal," Taylor replied, her eyes still on the door.

"What was that all about?" Crystal was a thirty-something woman with plenty of nature's gifts and willing to share them with the right women.

"I have no idea what that was," Taylor said, throwing back the shot.

"I've never seen her in here before but I don't think she's a bar type." Crystal took a long draw on her beer.

"No, I don't think so either."

"Want to dance?" Crystal had worked her fingers into the waistband of Taylor's jeans.

"Sure," Taylor said, glad for something to take her mind off the blonde and her brain's general meltdown that kept her from apologizing. Taylor allowed Crystal to lead the way to the dance floor. It was a slow song, one that had most of the couples draped over each other and swaying close. When Taylor slipped one arm around her waist, Crystal immediately wrapped her arms around Taylor's neck and nuzzled against her shoulder. She was only a little over five feet tall but she used every inch of it against Taylor's nine-inch advantage to command her attention. Her ample bosom was pressed against Taylor's ribs and one of her tight-muscled thighs was nestled between Taylor's legs.

"Where have you been keeping yourself, Taylor? I've missed you."

"Working," she replied. She knew Crystal wasn't interested in a detailed description of her life. She wanted one thing and one thing only from Taylor and it had nothing whatever to do with being polite or curious.

Crystal allowed her hands to slide down Taylor's back, her nails carving their way down her shirt.

"It's too crowded in here," Crystal said as they were bumped by other dancers. She allowed her hand to linger over Taylor's firm bottom. It was obvious all Taylor had to do was suggest they stroll outside for a little fresh air and Crystal would be out the door like a shot. Taylor hesitated a moment, deciding if she wanted to do the outside thing with Crystal tonight. She hadn't really planned on it. She was open to the possibilities but not necessarily with Crystal. But why not? She had already made a fool of herself in front of the blonde. Why not redeem herself and her self-respect? One thing was certain, Crystal would gladly accept Taylor for who she was and there would be no strings attached. Tonight she needed that.

Taylor hooked a finger through one of Crystal's and led the way outside. The sky was full of brilliant stars and the air was clean and warm. The ear-pounding music could be heard in the parking lot but it was muted. Crystal took out a pack of cigarettes and offered one to Taylor. Taylor shook her head but took Crystal's lighter and lit hers.

"Oh, that's right. You don't smoke."

"Nope," Taylor replied. "I have other vices but not that one."

"Do you mind if I smoke?"

"They're your lungs. Suit yourself."

"I want to show you something, Taylor," Crystal said, pulling her by the hand to the back corner of the parking lot.

"What?"

"My new truck," she replied, pointing to the shiny new pickup in the far corner, its hood tucked under a large tree. It was protected by the privacy fence on one side and a metal dumpster on the other. Taylor wondered how long Crystal circled the parking lot waiting for this spot to become available. The only space more private would be in a garage. "What do you think? Nice, huh? Of course it isn't mine yet. It belongs to the bank. But I get to drive it and make payments."

"Then it's partly yours," Taylor offered, examining the bright red step-side body and chrome wheels. She had no idea why Crystal would buy a pickup truck that was so high she would need a boost from a cattle prod to climb inside. She was short, prissy and worked at the DMV. Unless, of course, the truck was meant to be bait for jeans and boot wearing cowgirls like Taylor.

Crystal smashed her cigarette out in the gravel and checked her looks in the side mirror, combing her fingers through the renegade strands.

"I just hate it when I can't get my hair to behave. It has a mind of its own."

"Looks pretty good to me," Taylor replied, knowing she was supposed to say that.

"Do you really think so?" Crystal asked with a hopeful smile.

"Yeah, I like it. I like long hair."

Taylor stood behind her as Crystal squinted into the mirror, the dim light from the Rainbow Desert's sign washing over the parking lot. She flipped her hair, the long cascades falling over Taylor's shoulder.

"You should have seen it a few years ago. It was down past my waist. You would have liked that, I bet."

"I bet I would," Taylor said, stroking Crystal's hair as she leaned back into her.

"It was so long it covered my entire butt."

"It would be a shame to cover a cute butt like yours." Taylor pressed herself tightly against Crystal's round bottom and folded her arms around her. Crystal responded with a soft sigh as she slowly massaged herself against Taylor's pubic bone. Taylor kissed her neck as she unbuttoned the top of Crystal's blouse.

"I'm glad you like my hair," Crystal whispered, leaning her head back, exposing her neck to Taylor's kisses.

"Uh-huh," she replied, as her hand slipped inside Crystal's blouse and cupped her breast. Her other hand found the bra hook in the back and released it with one quick flick. Taylor unleashed a wild animal when she touched Crystal's breasts. She arched her back, pushing her bosom up to Taylor's hands. Her dark nipples immediately hardened and stood erect as Taylor's nimble fingers massaged them.

Taylor opened Crystal's jeans and pushed her hand inside, sliding down her smooth abdomen. Taylor's fingers passed over her hairless mound. The idea that Crystal had shaved her pubic area gave her a sudden rush, the image of her careful strokes exciting something deep inside.

Crystal groaned as Taylor's fingers parted her folds and curled inside her. She began a deliberate and slow rhythmic grind as Taylor slipped in and out of her. Crystal covered Taylor's hand with her own, pushing it harder against her need.

"That's it," she moaned, closing her eyes. "Harder. Harder." Taylor obliged with deeper and firmer strokes. The night air had grown sticky. Taylor could feel sweat rolling down Crystal's cleavage and into her jeans, mixing with her own wetness. The music from inside the bar set a rhythm that matched the one directing Taylor's strokes and Crystal's moans. Taylor pinched her nipple and pulled at it as Crystal's uterus contracted, signaling her orgasm was near. Crystal's body pulsed with the music. She gave a muffled scream as she reached her peak, holding her hands over Taylor's, savoring the last precious moments of pleasure.

"Oh, baby," she sighed, leaning back against Taylor. "No one can do what you do."

Taylor kissed her neck and slowly pulled her hand out of Crystal's jeans. As the sound of talking came from across the parking lot, Crystal quickly buttoned her shirt and straightened herself. Nothing was said between them. No words of tender-ness, no insistence they would see each other the next time Taylor was in town.

"I better go back inside. My friends will wonder where I am." Crystal took her purse from where she had hung it over the side mirror and hurried away as if nothing had happened.

Taylor leaned back against the truck and closed her eyes. She was tired, tired of the endless parade of meaningless sexual part-ners. When was someone going to love her, not just lust after her? When was someone going to need her to love them? But Taylor didn't know how to ask for that. It wasn't her style. These casual, flippant liaisons required no thought and no emotional effort. They also represented no potential heartache. They were safe. They couldn't break her heart if the women didn't love her first.

Taylor went back inside, washed her hands in the ladies' room and ordered a beer. Tomorrow she would find Rowdy's daughter, give her a piece of her mind then go home to her own world and her own bed.

Chapter 3

Taylor was up early. She took a bagel and a cup of coffee from the motel's breakfast counter then checked out, anxious for her meeting with Rowdy Holland's daughter. According to the address she had, J. M. Holland lived just a few miles from the downtown Riverwalk. It was hard for Taylor not to prejudge the woman. From all the rumors and assumptions, this woman had to be indifferent, self-centered or downright strange. Taylor didn't care what the woman did. She could wear fish heads for earrings for all she cared, so long as she talked Rowdy into staying off Fleming property.

Taylor pulled up in front of a small stucco house obscured by huge trees. It sat back on the lot with a circlular drive that took up most of the front yard. The number 247 was painted on the mailbox in pink paint with a smiley face on the metal flag. Flower beds circled the base of the two large trees and were full of eagerly blooming annuals. The lawn was little more than several tufts of weeds but the flower beds and flower boxes at the windows were a cheery greeting. An old van was parked in the driveway, its paint oxidized to a dull green. The passenger door was a completely different color and had a dent in it that ran the entire side of the van. A girl's bicycle was propped against the corner of the house. A red plastic milk crate was tied to the back with several bungee cords and a large yellow plastic mum was taped to the handle bars like an antennae. Taylor pulled into the driveway, stopped near the front door and rang the doorbell. When no one answered, she knocked this time, hard.

"Is anyone there?" she called, pounding her fist on the door frame. "Hello?"

A black cat jumped up in the front window and stuck his head between the curtains, meowing a greeting. The cat arched its back and stretched then walked the full length of the window sill before jumping down and disappearing. Taylor knocked again.

"Tell your owner to come to the door."

She could hear what sounded like grinding coming from the backyard. The noise was interspersed with sharp tapping. After one more attempt at the front door, she went around to the side of the house and entered through the open wooden gate. A garage was wedged into the back corner of the yard. Its double doors were held open by gallon paint cans. A flickering light shone through the side window, a light Taylor suspected came from a welding torch.

"Hello," Taylor called, peeking around the corner of the door, careful not to stare directly at the welding arc. The noise of the welding machine drowned out her calls. A person in an army surplus flight suit and a welding hood stood on top of a stepladder, attaching a pair of iron horns to a statue of a bucking bull. A metal cowboy sat astride the bull, holding onto the reins with one hand and his cowboy hat with the other. It was hard to make out all the details but Taylor recognized the bull as a Braymer by the hump on his back. The metal statue was life-size and nearly filled the small garage. Taylor stood in the doorway, studying the sculpture. The bull almost seemed to snort from its nostrils, its eyes piercing and angry. The cowboy had a determined look on his face, his forehead furrowed with concentration. When the welder stopped for a moment, Taylor called again.

"Hello," she said, determined to finally get a reply. "I'm looking for Jennifer Holland," Taylor added, hoping she had picked the right name to try.

"I don't know anyone by that name," the welder said, keeping attention concentrated on the spot to be welded. "But I do know Jen Holland."

"Jen Holland, yeah. Where can I find her?" Taylor replied, surprised the welder couldn't at least turn around and look at her.

"Who wants to know?" The welder asked, finally taking off the hood and turning to look over her shoulder. Taylor gasped at the long blond hair that exploded from under the hood. The woman ruffled her hand through her matted locks then shook her head, the hair settling around her shoulders.

"It's you." Taylor stared awestruck at the woman she had seen at the bar, the woman with eyes bluer than Texas summer skies.

The woman looked down at Taylor and immediately frowned with disgust.

"Well, well. If it isn't the famous cowgirl from the Rainbow Desert?" She leered down at Taylor, the memory of their conversation at the bar fresh in her mind.

"What are you doing here?" they said in unison then scowled at each other.

"Did you come here to continue your barrage of insults and sarcasm?" the woman asked from her perch on the ladder. "If that is what brought you snooping around my studio I can tell you right now the door is that way and the circular drive leads right back onto the street." She pointed out the double doors emphatically.

"*Your* studio?" Taylor scoffed. "This is your studio?"

"Yes, it most certainly is. What of it?"

Taylor threw her head back and laughed wildly.

"What is so funny?" the woman asked with a deep scowl.

"You're Jen Holland," Taylor declared with a chuckle.

Jen straightened her posture defensively.

"Yes, I am. Let me guess. You are *not* Annie Oakley."

"I'm sorry about last night. No, I'm not Annie Oakley. I'm Taylor Fleming."

"Oh," Jen replied then narrowed her eyes as she recognized the name. "Taylor Fleming, as in the Flemings from Harland, Texas? As in the Flemings from Cottonwood Ranch?" There was an instant and unmistakable chill in Jen's voice.

"My father is Grier Fleming, yes. Does the name ring a bell?"

"That is the understatement of the century," Jen muttered then climbed down the ladder and busied herself with a pile of metal.

"So you know why I'm here?" Taylor asked, watching Jen sort through some pieces of metal.

"I have no idea," Jen said without looking up. "And what's more, I don't care." The more Jen forced her attention toward the stack of rusty metal, the more she furrowed her forehead. "I have work to do. This has to be finished by tomorrow and there's still lots to do so why don't you save your breath. I'm not interested in Harland, Texas or Cottonwood Ranch." She pulled a strip of metal from the pile that looked like a spur and held it up to the cowboy's boot to see if it fit.

"How about the Little Diamond Ranch? Are you interested in that, Ms. Holland?" Taylor asked, studying the woman's expression.

"No," Jen replied, tossing a caustic glance at Taylor.

"Maybe you should be."

"I don't think so. And before you say anything else, I suggest you keep your nose out of my business." Jen replaced the welder's hood over her head and positioned the spur into place. "Don't look at the arc. It'll damage your eyes," Jen offered in

Taylor's direction then turned her attention to welding. "Good-bye, Ms. Fleming."

Taylor smirked and turned around as the white-hot light from the welding tip showered sparks across the garage. She knew Jen expected her to leave but she wasn't going anywhere until she said what she came to say. After two minutes of noise and sparks, the spur was secured to the bull rider's heel. Jen took off the hood and looked over at Taylor, still staring at the wall.

"What's the matter? Can't you find the door, Annie Oakley?" Jen asked, going back to the pile for the other spur.

"Ms. Holland, I don't give a shit about your personal business but I came to San Antonio to tell you your father needs your help."

"My father doesn't want my help. That's for sure." Jen nearly laughed.

"I didn't say he wanted your help. I said he needed your help. You may not want to hear it but as Rowdy Holland's daughter, don't you think you have a responsibility to at least be aware of what is going on," Taylor couldn't help but sound condescending.

"My father is an adult. He can take care of himself. He doesn't need or want me to interfere." Jen intentionally dropped a piece of metal on the floor, sending out a loud clang. "If you have a problem with Rowdy, take it up with him, not me."

"We have. Repeatedly. Do you want to know how many times in the last year we've had to call the sheriff because of your father's actions?" Taylor asked.

"No, I don't. And why are you telling me this. Can't you and the sheriff's department handle one feeble old man without getting me involved?"

"Do you really want your father thrown in jail for cattle rustling?" Taylor declared harshly then shoved her hands in her pockets.

Jen looked over at her and raised the welding hood.

"Rowdy Holland is many things but a cattle rustler isn't one of them."

"Not according to the eighty head of Cottonwood-registered Angus I found on his property."

"Maybe your fence came down and they wandered onto his property."

"The fence was definitely down but how did they wander into his corral and close the gate behind them?"

Jen didn't reply. She stared at Taylor then pulled the hood down and went back to fitting a piece of metal into place.

"I've seen him, Ms. Holland. I've seen him cutting our fence and I've seen him luring our cattle into his corral."

"All this fuss for a few head of cattle? If I'm not mistaken, Cottonwood Ranch raises thousands," Jen said without looking back at her.

"Eighty this time. The total is three hundred sixty so far, including a dozen heifers with calf and a registered bull."

Jen hesitated but didn't look back.

"And in case you are wondering, that's four hundred thousand dollars worth of prime registered beef. And that, Ms. Holland, is a felony."

Jen slowly removed the hood. She kept her eyes down and heaved a heavy sigh.

"What do you want from me, Ms. Fleming? I certainly do not have four hundred thousand dollars to pay my father's debt to society. If you knew he stole the cattle why didn't you stop him before he sold them?"

"He never got a chance to sell them. We got them back before he did that."

"So he never made any money on what he stole?" Jen asked without looking up.

"No."

"What is it you want from me?"

"I want you to be a daughter. Your father has some problems

and you are the only one who can help him."

"I told you. My father doesn't want and won't accept my help on anything."

"When was the last time you saw him?" Taylor asked.

"I have no idea. A couple years ago, I guess."

"Harland is only two hours away. Won't that old van of yours make it that far?"

"I beg your pardon." Jen frowned at Taylor's judgmental tone.

"Do you ever call him?"

"He had his phone taken out."

"Thirty-nine cents. That's all it takes to buy a stamp and send a letter, Ms. Holland. You know what those are, don't you? It's a cheap way to keep in touch with loved ones."

"Don't patronize me. You don't know anything about my family and I do not appreciate your holier-than-thou attitude."

"A few years ago Rowdy wasn't a big problem. Only once in a while. But now it's every month, several times a month. Did you know your father has been thrown out of both cafés in town for cussing at the waitresses? Did you know he has been found driving around in circles on the high school parking lot until he ran out of gas? Did you know he was arrested for trying to break into an abandoned house in town? Did you know he was warned about urinating on the shrubs at city hall?"

"All right," Jen said loudly, disgusted with Taylor's tirade. She didn't need a stranger's help to make her feel like an ungrateful or indifferent daughter.

"Do you need more?"

"I said all right."

"So you'll come to Harland and have a talk with Rowdy?" Taylor asked hopefully.

"Life sure is easy for you, isn't it?" Jen said, her words dripping with sarcasm. "You think all you have to do is wave your magic wand and everyone jumps through hoops for you, right

Ms. Fleming? You think everything with my father is fixed now, don't you? You did the Good Samaritan deed. You came to tell me my father is succumbing to senile dementia and all I need to do is talk to him and it will all be fine."

"I never said anything about senile dementia," Taylor snapped.

"You didn't have to. All the signs are there. They have been for several years. Rowdy Holland is living in the past. He is losing his grip on reality and there is nothing I or anyone else can do about it. Even if there was some miraculous cure, my father won't accept it. Rowdy Holland is going to live his life the way he wants and no one is going to stop him. The best we can hope for is that he doesn't hurt anyone."

"How about himself? Doesn't he count?"

Jen looked up at Taylor and shot a fiery stare at her.

"What do you take me for? Some kind of monster? Do you think I'm glad my father is ill?"

"I didn't say that. But maybe Rowdy needs someone to intervene before he hurts himself. If he doesn't see danger, maybe somebody else has to do that for him."

"Have you ever talked to Rowdy, Ms. Fleming?"

"Yes. Two days ago. That's when I found the eighty head in his corral."

"And what did he say to you?"

"He said they were his and he insisted they were longhorns. He looked right at the Cottonwood brand and said they weren't branded yet. Then he chased me off his property with a shotgun."

"Did you think he was a rational man?" Jen asked.

"No and that is my point exactly. He isn't and someone has to help him. And that someone is you, Ms. Holland. Unless you have a brother or sister who can take care of him, it all comes down to you."

"I'm quite sure you know Rowdy has no other children and no wife."

Taylor took a deep breath and stared at Jen for a long moment.

"Why is this so hard for you? Why are you so afraid of coming to Harland to see if you can help your father?" Taylor couldn't help from displaying a disapproving frown.

Jen turned off the welder and hooked the hood over the handle.

"If I say I will come to Harland to talk with him will you leave me alone?" She looked up at Taylor with a plaintive stare.

"If you mean it."

"I don't lie, Ms. Fleming."

"You come to Harland and talk with your father, then yes, I will leave you alone."

"It won't be until I finish this project but I promise I will."

"You're doing a good job repairing it." Taylor looked the sculpture up and down.

"I'm not repairing it," Jen said adamantly.

"Oh. I just assumed you were putting stuff back on that fell off."

"My work doesn't fall off." Jen stared up at the cowboy.

"You made this?" Taylor asked with genuine surprise.

"Yes."

"You are a metal sculptor?"

"I am."

"May I ask what are you going to do with this?" Taylor asked, circling the piece and taking in all the details.

"The bull rider and the other pieces will be in the park outside the fairgrounds south of town."

"Other pieces?" Taylor asked, looking around the garage.

"They have already been picked up. Five in all. A bronc rider, a calf roper, a barrel racer, a clown and this bull rider."

"And you made them all?"

"Yes." Jen crossed her arms defensively.

"I've never met a woman sculptor before." Taylor reached up

and touched the cowboy's boot. Before Jen could warn her, she drew her hand back abruptly.

"That's still hot from the welding," Jen quickly offered.

"No kidding," Taylor replied, shaking her hand and licking her fingers.

"Don't do that. Here, let me see it," Jen said, reaching for her hand. "Come over here. I have some burn salve."

"It'll be all right. I don't need it." Taylor pulled her hand back and looked down at her reddening fingers.

"Don't be silly. Let me put some salve on it and it won't blister. It'll take the sting right out." Jen frowned at her stubbornness and opened a jar of cream. "Here," she said, coming at Taylor with two fingers full. She grabbed Taylor's hand, her soft touch completely capturing Taylor's attention. In spite of the smell of welding and sweat, Taylor caught the delicate aroma of Jen's perfume, encircling them in vanilla musk.

"I'm all right," Taylor said, pulling her hand away. She gave it another shake then shoved it in her pocket. She couldn't tell if it still hurt from touching the hot metal or the shock of Jen's delicate touch. "I have to go. I'm glad you'll be coming to talk with your father. Be sure you tell him he has to stop destroying our fence and taking our cattle."

"Yes, Ms. Fleming." Jen nodded. "I know what you want me to say. I'll do the best I can but I make no promises."

"I hope he listens to you," Taylor replied. She wanted to pull her hand from her pocket and check the burn but her stubborn streak wouldn't allow Jen to smear that goo on her fingers. Taylor turned and walked out of the garage. As soon as she was outside she looked at her burned fingers. "Ouch," she muttered, shaking and licking them again.

Jen stood at the garage door with the salve still on her fingers, watching Taylor circle the house. She could hear her truck start and roar away, leaving her with work and emotions coursing through her mind.

43

Chapter 4

Taylor was halfway home before she could put Jen Holland out of her mind. Her blue eyes and cascades of blond hair circled in her thoughts like an old record stuck in the groove. As much as she didn't want to admit it, Taylor knew Jen may have only agreed to talk to her father so she would leave her alone. It was quite possible Jen Holland would never set foot on her father's ranch or in Harland. But Taylor had done her best. She had talked to her. She had given her the cold hard facts about her father. And she had done it without raising her voice or cursing, for the most part anyway.

"I bet she doesn't do squat," Taylor mumbled, searching the radio for a country station. "She's too full of herself to help that old man."

Taylor tried to turn her thoughts to work. She had gear to mend, paperwork to finish and a mountain of laundry to do, not to mention help with the roundup in four more sections of range. She rolled down the window and patted the side of the door in time to the music. She would be home by two and in the saddle by three. She almost wished she hadn't gone to the Rainbow Desert last night. She only came away with frustration—and an angelic vision she couldn't put out of her mind. Too bad the woman attached to the vision was a bitch, she thought.

She delivered the supplies, ate a piece of her mother's pie and listened to her retell ranch gossip. Within twenty minutes Taylor had learned Cesar's oldest granddaughter had a boyfriend with a tattoo of a pirate on his back, the youngest granddaughter lost her first tooth, earning a new Barbie doll for her efforts, Aunt Francis had gallbladder surgery in Lubbock, Grier cut his thumb to the bone on a baler and Lexie's pickup truck had a new bed liner. Nothing earth-shattering but transferring the information seemed to please her mother. Sylvia was fifty-nine with salt-and-pepper curly hair. Her face belied the early wrinkles of age and her plump figure showed her hearty appetite. She was a jolly, kind and dedicated woman, full of energy and concern for her family and friends.

"How was your trip to San Antonio, honey?" Sylvia asked, refilling Taylor's glass of milk.

"The highway is being blacktopped between Spruce City and Twin Oaks. When you go to Uncle Jack's, go the other way so you won't get stuck in traffic. Other than that, it was fine."

"That's nice."

Taylor knew her mother understood why she went to San Antonio once a month. How could she not know? Sylvia accepted that her daughter was a lesbian. She didn't ask for details. She wanted Taylor to be happy and trusted her to find happiness in a safe and responsible manner. When she was younger, Sylvia assumed Taylor would ask if she had questions about sex but once she came out to her parents during her junior year in high school, Sylvia seemed to hold her breath, afraid Taylor might ask something she had no idea how to answer. Sylvia wasn't homophobic. She was just naive. Taylor could tell her mother she had gone to San Antonio to pick up babes at a gay bar but Sylvia would only wrinkle her forehead as she wondered how women could possibly have sex. The subject was better left alone.

"I heard you were going to meet Rowdy Holland's daughter."

"Yeah, I did." Taylor mashed the last crumbs of crust onto the back of her fork and licked them off.

"Your father is so mad about that. He was cussing and carrying on about cut fence and stolen cattle all day yesterday. And he about hit the roof when he heard that poor old man is back home again."

"They let him out?" Taylor scowled. "That was fast. Did he sleep with the judge or something?" Taylor took her plate to the sink.

"Taylor," Sylvia said with an irritated look. "That is a terrible thing to say."

"He had eighty head of our cattle in his corral, cut a hundred feet of our fence and he is only in jail one day. Somebody got paid off somewhere."

"The sheriff said Rowdy has a hearing before the judge next Friday. He's out on his own something or other for now."

"Recognizance," Taylor supplied, leaning against the counter with her arms folded.

"Yes, I think that is what he said."

"That's a joke. Being out on your own recognizance means the person has some responsibility for their own actions. Rowdy Holland doesn't have any of that. By Friday he'll have done something else stupid." Taylor went to the back door and looked out over the valley. "I better go, Mom. I've got things to do. By the way, I'm taking one of the horse trailers to town for tires tomorrow so let me know if you need anything." She gave her mother a hug and a kiss on the cheek.

"Drive carefully, honey." Sylvia walked her out to her truck, rubbing Taylor's back affectionately. "Come by for dinner one of these nights, sweetheart."

"I will, Mom. Thanks for the pie. It was great." Taylor started the engine and pulled away, her mother waving from the steps. "What am I paying my taxes for if they let Rowdy out in just one day? What kind of court system is that?" she muttered to herself, slapping the steering wheel.

Taylor headed home to do housework. She caught up on laundry, swirled a mop around the kitchen floor, burned a pile of trash in the pit and checked orders and contracts for the ranch. That evening she checked on the two heifers she had brought up to the corral. They hadn't calved yet and according to the calendar they were at least two weeks overdue. The expectant ones were worth too much money to ignore and hope nature would take over. If nothing had happened by morning, she may have to induce labor before the calves got so big they might injure the mother during birth. By ten o'clock that night, Taylor was helping one of the heifers, pulling her obstinate calf into the world. It was a strong baby heifer. It climbed to its feet and immediately tried to ram Taylor. She chuckled at the little black animal, not even dry behind the ears yet.

"You're sure an ornery little cuss," she chuckled, guiding it toward its mother's teat and the protective colostrum. The other pregnant cow seemed to have learned what was expected of her and gave birth as well, dropping a healthy baby bull. Taylor kept them in the corral, tossing out an extra bale of hay for the new mommies and their young.

The next morning she hitched the single-axle horse trailer to the truck and started for town, hoping to have the tires mounted and be home by lunch. The shortest route was the dirt road to Cactus Flats then the seldom used and pothole-riddled road to Harland, coming in on the north side of town. The better route was the paved road through Steelville then back to Harland on the highway. But that was thirty miles further and not necessarily faster. Taylor took the road to Cactus Flats. The empty trailer bounced along the ruts, rattling noisily as she crossed cattle guards and potholes. The highway department had recently graded the road, leaving a ridge of rocks and dirt along both sides. It made little difference as far as smoothing the road was concerned and Taylor often wondered why they didn't just apply a coating of tar and a layer of gravel. It would last longer and be easier on the vehicles.

"Hey, Dad," she said, answering the jingle on her cell phone.

"Didn't you say Rowdy's daughter was going to have a talk with him?" Grier said angrily.

"That's what she said." Taylor could tell by his voice something was wrong and something more than the normal problems.

"Well, either she lied to you or he's ignoring her. Cesar found a whole section down. This time he did more than cut the wire. This time he pulled a dozen posts out of the ground. Crazy old man knocked them over with his truck. You can see tire ruts where he rammed them. We've got cattle everywhere. On his place, some in the pasture with the hay bales and some roaming down the road. That old man has tested me for the last time."

"Where is the break? Same place as last week?" Taylor asked, envisioning the work they had to do.

"From Sweetwater Spring to the corner."

"Yep, same place. That's new wire."

"Not anymore it isn't," Grier snapped. "He cut it up in two-foot pieces and bundled them with baling twine."

"Sounds like he has been busy." Taylor had to laugh, thinking of the little old man meticulously cutting up four strands of barbed wire and tying them in bundles. She wondered how many times he cut himself.

"It isn't funny, Taylor. I've had enough. I'm suing him for

every penny he owes me. I've got a list of everything he has cost this ranch." Grier had worked up a head of steam and wasn't going to be denied his tirade.

Taylor couldn't help wondering if Jen Holland did as she promised and talked with her father. She had no reason to believe Jen would have lied to her but if Rowdy did indeed destroy another section of Fleming fence her words must have fallen on deaf ears. If Jen was right, if her father was succumbing to senile dementia, perhaps all the words, pleadings and warning in the world wouldn't have made any difference.

"I'm on my way to town. I'll have a talk with Sheriff Dunton. Tell Cesar not to touch the fence until he can get there to look at it. He'll need evidence to prosecute, again."

"Rowdy was standing right there. He admitted doing it. He said it was his fence. He said he didn't like it there. He wanted to move it to the other side of the river."

"What river? There's no river there," Taylor scoffed.

"Cesar said he was standing there in his old greasy straw hat and his worn boots. Do you want to know what else he was wearing?"

"What?" she asked, not really sure she cared.

"Not a damn thing. He was naked as the day he was born."

"You're kidding? Naked?" She chuckled at the thought.

"Yep. Bet he got one heck of a sunburn." Grier laughed victoriously as if it served Rowdy right for destroying his property.

"I bet he did." Taylor immediately thought of Jen. She must have been right. Rowdy had completely lost touch with reality and was beyond reason. Taylor couldn't help but feel sorry for Jen and for Rowdy.

"Gotta go," he said. "We're on our way to get the cows off the road."

"You need me to come up there?" she asked, suddenly sorry she hadn't been available.

"No. We'll take care of this. You go on to town. Cesar said

you better pick up a few more reels of wire if there are any left in Harland." Grier broke the connection.

Taylor tossed her cell on the seat and shook her head disgustedly.

"Well, Ms. Holland, sounds like you didn't do much."

Taylor pressed on the gas pedal, anxious to get to town. As much as she didn't want to prosecute a helpless old man, she knew the Cottonwood Ranch couldn't continue to excuse random acts of vandalism and theft. Perhaps her father was right. Pinching Rowdy in the pocketbook might be the only way to stop him.

She removed her hat and tossed it on the seat then ruffled her hair, something she did when she was mad enough to spit rocks. She roared down the road, slinging a plume of dust behind her. The ruts yanked at the steering wheel, making the truck swerve back and forth. She eased up on the gas pedal and brought the trailer under control. She heard a bang and the trailer pulled hard to the left.

"Now what?" she yelled, taking her foot off the gas and allowing the truck to come to a stop. She looked out the window, craning her neck to see the trailer tire. But she really didn't need to—the loud bang and the pull on the wheel meant it was flat. Disgusted, she climbed out and slammed the door hard. The trailer had come to rest against the ridge of plowed dirt and rocks, partially submerged in the soft stuff.

"I don't have time for this today," she grumbled, kicking the flat tire with the toe of her boot. She gave thought to calling Lexie and asking her to bring the portable air tank and a can of fix-a-flat but that would take longer than if she just changed it herself.

Taylor rummaged in the toolbox for the scissor jack and tire iron. She would have to remove the flat, unhook the trailer, take the tire to town for repair then return to the trailer. It didn't bother her to leave the trailer by the side of the road. It would be safe. The cottonwood tree painted across the side told anyone who happened by that this was a Fleming trailer. Besides, she hadn't passed a single vehicle since she left the house and she would probably be back before anyone drove by.

It took some doing but she finally found a spot that was level and solid enough to support the jack. She raised the trailer just enough to roll the tire off and tossed it into the back of the truck. She planned on wedging the bale of hay she was carrying under the axle for support but the weight of trailer had begun to sink it into the soft dirt along the edge of the road, too far to allow clearance for the bale. She needed to jack it up higher. As she raised the trailer it shifted toward the ditch.

"No, no, no," she muttered, trying to shove the bale under the fender but she felt the ground move under her feet. She grabbed the trailer to regain her footing but it was too late. The parched earth was too soft to hold her weight and it gave way. Not only was Taylor sliding down the ditch but the trailer was sliding down as well. The bale of hay was crushed as the axle gouged a trough through the rocks and weeds. She couldn't stop it. The trailer slid down the embankment, the torque of it straining at the trailer hitch and safety chain.

"Whoa, baby," Taylor called as she pushed against the wheel well but she was no match for it. She could hear the wrenching sounds of the hitch as the trailer tongue twisted the ball. She knew the hitch was capable of pulling the trailer down the highway but the breakaway action meant that in case of a rollover accident, the trailer hitch would release and not flip the truck with it. Taylor dug her heels into the dirt and leaned hard against the slow but steady sliding trailer. She was well below the trailer, standing at the bottom of the ditch. Suddenly the hitch snapped. The front of the trailer lurched toward the embankment, the sound of the tongue scraping across the road then digging into the dirt.

"Stop. Stay up there, you sucker," she muttered, gritting her teeth as she pushed against the side.

The axle dug itself into the dirt and came to a stop but the front of the trailer continued down the slope until the weight of it began to tip the side toward Taylor.

"NO!" she yelled as the trailer slowly tilted over her. She tried to get out of the way but her boots were wedged too deep into the soft dirt. The trailer fell over on her, pushing her back and pinning her to the bottom of the ditch. The valley was deep enough to offer her a protective well from the full weight of the heavy trailer but she could hear the distinctive sound of two snaps then a shooting pain rising from her legs, a pain that took her breath away and left her motionless. She screamed in agony as the metal side came to rest across her lap, mashing her into the hot dirt. She grabbed the trailer as if hugging it would ease the excruciating pain as the fender pressed across her lower legs. She felt the pain instantly sap her strength, leaving her helpless to move even her arms. She gritted her teeth and fell back, her head striking a small rock—and everything went black.

Chapter 5

"Taylor, wake up, honey. Open your eyes. Come on, it's time to get up now. You'll be late for school if you don't open your eyes right this minute. Taylor. Taylor. Open your eyes. Taylor Fleming, you answer your mother. Breakfast is on the table. Come on now." The school bus was waiting outside, honking and flashing its lights. A stream of children was climbing in and out of the open door, running around the bus, laughing at her for not opening her eyes. A cattle trailer was rolling toward her, its tires wobbling and clattering against the rocks in the road. Her mother stood on the porch, waving at the bus and the children as they continued to skip around it, laughing and playing. "Taylor. Open your eyes now, honey."

Taylor's mother's voice wafted in and out of her consciousness. Taylor wanted to reply. She wanted to open her eyes. She was trying but they wouldn't open. Someone was holding them shut. She also wanted to move. But someone was holding her legs down. She tried to move her hand but it weighed a ton. Nothing would respond to her efforts.

"Taylor, honey. Open your eyes." Her mother's voice floated toward Taylor through a fog, growing louder and clearer. "It's mother, honey. You're fine. It's all over now. You'll be fine, sweetheart."

Taylor could feel her mother's lips press a kiss against her forehead, the kiss she remembered from her childhood when she came running home with a boo-boo, tears streaming down her face. She struggled to open her eyes. A bright light blinded her vision and she closed them again.

"That's it. Open your eyes, sweetheart." Sylvia stroked Taylor's hair.

Taylor blinked and strained against the bright light to see her mother's face.

"There you are," her mother cooed, patting Taylor's hand gently.

Taylor rolled her eyes up to meet her mother's. She was leaning over her, smiling a cautious and concerned smile. Taylor raised her hand a few inches, a stabbing pain meeting her every move. She tried to speak but nothing came out.

"Easy now. Just rest," Sylvia said reassuringly. "I'm right here for you, honey." She patted Taylor's head and kissed her.

When Taylor woke up again she could hear voices, women's voices talking about things she didn't understand. They were technical things and they sounded like medical terms.

"Hello, Ms. Fleming," a friendly voice said. She was moving Taylor's arm and wrapping something around it. There was a squeezing sensation. Taylor tried to pull her arm away but the woman held tight to it. "You're fine. I'm just taking your blood pressure. Relax your arm, hon."

Taylor didn't understand what was going on but she did as she was told. She relaxed and closed her eyes. When she did, she realized her legs hurt and hurt bad. They felt like they were on fire. She opened her eyes again and tried to reach for them but she couldn't move. She wanted to scream out at the sudden explosion of pain but she couldn't speak or move.

"Are you in pain?" the woman asked, releasing Taylor's arm and placing it under the covers. "Do you need something for pain?"

Taylor nodded, her eyes pleading with the woman to take the pain away. The woman's face disappeared. Taylor wanted to call out to her and tell her to come back but she couldn't make a sound. She closed her eyes, the pain searing itself onto her soul. She tried to move away from it but her body wouldn't respond.

"This will help, hon," the woman's voice said, patting her shoulder. Within a minute Taylor could feel a warm fuzziness settle over her and she drifted back to sleep.

The next time she opened her eyes the room was dark. Taylor could hear the sound of a rhythmic beeping. She could smell something pungent. It reminded her of bleach and cleanser. She turned her head toward the sound and saw a maze of plastic tubes leading from a machine to her arm. The lights from the machine blinked and pulsed as liquid dripped from plastic bags into the tubing. The pain she had felt in her legs was still throbbing and burning, making her sweat. She wished she could remove the covers from her body. Perhaps she would be cooler if she could pull them off. She looked down at her legs and was shocked to see them both wrapped in bandages and suspended in slings, being held a few inches above the bed. Her toes were orange and swollen. A sheet covered her from the thigh to the neck. She tried to touch her legs and the bandages that covered them but she was too weak to reach them. She felt trapped in her body, aware she was in pain but unable to do anything about it.

"Hello, honey," her mother said, coming in the door. She had a pained expression on her face, one Taylor remembered from when she was a little girl and fell off her pony, scraping her elbow to the bone. Sylvia rushed over to the bed and kissed

Taylor's forehead.

"Where am I?" Taylor asked in a weak voice, surprised at how hard it was to speak.

"I can't hear you, honey," her mother replied, leaning closer.

"Where am I?"

"You're in the hospital, sweetheart. Don't you remember? You had the accident with the trailer." Sylvia stroked Taylor sympathetically. "We were so scared. Your father has been here all day but he had to go back to the ranch and take care of some things. He'll be sorry he wasn't here when you woke up." Her eyes filled with tears as she spoke soothingly to Taylor. "But you'll be okay. It will take a little while for your legs to heal but you'll be okay."

"Trailer?" Taylor still didn't comprehend what had happened to her.

"Yes, it rolled over on you. It landed on your legs," she replied, stroking Taylor's arm as if it would pacify the reality of the accident. "Cesar found you. That man was so upset about it he could barely talk. He and Lexie stood outside the operating room every minute you were in there. They wouldn't even sit down. They just paced, Cesar, Lexie and your father, back and forth."

"What happened to my legs?" Taylor asked, her voice still weak.

"They are broken, honey. You had to have surgery on the left one. The doctor put a plate in it and some screws. But he said you'd be fine. Don't worry. You'll just need some time to heal. They'll take good care of you, sweetheart. You'll be up and around in a few months. You are a strong person. I know you'll be fine in no time."

Taylor shook her head. She couldn't accept what her mother was saying. She didn't want to believe she had broken her legs. It was all a dream, a bad dream. She wanted to wake up and be back to her old self. She wanted to saddle her horse and go for a ride.

She wanted the fresh Texas wind blowing through her hair. Taylor closed her eyes tight, trying to force away her mother's news and the pain that consumed her.

"I'm so sorry, honey. But the doctor said you'll just need to rest and get better. When your legs heal, you'll take some physical therapy to get your strength back. You just have to be patient so your body can heal itself."

Taylor shook her head. She grabbed the sheet with both hands and stiffened her body. She didn't want to accept it. She couldn't accept it. There was no way she was going to be stuck in a bed with both legs suspended like this for months. She had things to do. There were calves to inoculate and brand. There were heifers to watch for their first calves and fences to mend. She couldn't be stuck in a bed. She couldn't.

"Tell the doctor I need to go home," she said through closed eyes.

Sylvia patted her hand softly.

"Honey, you can't."

"Tell the doctor I need to go home," she repeated, her forehead furrowed with determination.

"Taylor, listen to me," her mother started.

Taylor opened her eyes and fixed her mother with a demanding stare.

"I have to go home today. I have things to do." Taylor strained against her confinement. She tried to pull herself up to a sitting position, pressing her hands down into the bed. "Call the doctor. They need to take these things off my legs. I need to get out of bed." She reached down and grabbed at the bandages.

"Taylor, no. Don't do that. Don't touch those. Lay down, honey." Sylvia pushed on Taylor's shoulders, trying to ease her back against the pillow. When she couldn't do it, she pressed the call button. A nurse came into the room and immediately grabbed Taylor by the shoulders and pushed her down.

"You have to lay back, Ms. Fleming. Please don't do that."

"I have to get out of bed. I have work to do. Take these things off my legs," she said, frantically pulling at the sheet and reaching for the slings.

"If you don't stop that, I'll have to restrain you, Ms. Fleming," the nurse said harshly. "Now lay back and relax." The nurse grabbed Taylor by the wrists and pushed her back into the bed. Taylor was surprised at how weak she was. She considered herself a strong woman, able to defend herself and carry her own weight. But the effort she had exerted had completely exhausted her. She fell back against the pillow, her body spent.

"That's better," the nurse said, checking the IV and the slings. "Now just rest. Would you like something to drink?"

Taylor shook her head. She slept on and off throughout the night. She sipped a few mouthfuls of water but she wasn't hungry or thirsty. The hours were all the same, full of pain, fitful sleep and confusing thoughts of how she would deal with her strange imprisonment. Her mother slept in a chair next to her bed, occasionally coming to adjust her covers and pat her hand. Taylor tried once to convince her to leave but she couldn't make the words come out the way she wanted. She finally gave up, her mother's reassuring presence a comfort she came to rely on each time she opened her eyes.

"Ms. Fleming," a new voice said. Taylor opened her eyes. The light from the window grew as the curtains were parted. "Would you like a bath, Ms. Fleming?"

Taylor looked over at the chair where her mother had spent the night.

"Your mother went down to the cafeteria for breakfast. She said to tell you she'd be back in a little while. She has the sweetest smile."

"What time is it?" Taylor asked through cotton-mouth.

"It's nine thirty, sleepy head," the woman said happily. "Are you ready to meet the day?"

Taylor's eyes widened. She hadn't slept past nine since she was a child with chicken pox. She couldn't believe no one had wakened her. She had a headache and this woman's Pollyanna attitude was only making it worse.

"We'll get you a nice bath and then maybe you'll want a bite to eat," the nurse said.

"I take showers, not baths," Taylor said.

The nurse chuckled.

"You won't be taking showers for a while, honey. I'll get a pan of hot water and some towels. Be right back." The nurse disappeared into the bathroom. Taylor could hear the water running as the nurse hummed cheerfully. She returned with a plastic pan of water, several towels, a clean hospital gown, a toothbrush and toothpaste and a bottle of baby bath. She rearranged the bedside table and pushed the IV stand to the head of the bed.

"I think I have to use the lady's room," Taylor said, aware of her full bladder. She couldn't imagine this small woman was strong enough to help her out of bed and into the bathroom alone. The nurse didn't say anything. She kept humming and arranging the bath supplies. "I said—"

"I heard you, hon. But you don't have to worry about it."

Taylor didn't understand why she seemed so indifferent. This was one of the chores, as unpleasant as it was, nurses had to deal with. Taylor wished she didn't have to ask for help but she knew she couldn't get up and out of the slings without help.

"But—" she started. Suddenly the urge flowed out of her. She no longer had to go. "What happened?" Taylor's eyes got wide.

"You have a catheter, honey," the nurse replied and pulled back the sheet. "Let's get this gown off and get you cleaned up."

Taylor was still digesting the news that she had a catheter as the nurse removed the hospital gown, leaving her exposed to the world. Her first impulse was to cover herself with her hands but before she could move, she felt the comforting warmth of a washcloth against her chest. The nurse gently washed one breast then the other, the smell of baby bath soothing and familiar.

"I love the smell of this. Don't you?" the nurse said as she lathered Taylor's stomach. "I think everyone loves the smell of baby bath." She continued washing, drifting down Taylor's abdomen. As she approached her pubic area, Taylor closed her eyes. She didn't want to accept she was thirty-six years old and having to be washed by a perfect stranger. The nurse washed her, pulling her thighs apart and working the washcloth between her legs. Taylor gasped, her embarrassment growing as the nurse's exploration of her private parts increased. By the time she had rinsed and patted her dry, Taylor was sure her face was bright red.

"Can you pull yourself up a bit with the bar? I'll wash your back if you can."

Taylor opened her eyes.

"What bar?" she asked.

The nurse pointed to the trapeze bar hanging over her head by a chain and attached to the bed frame. Taylor hadn't noticed it before. She tried to reach for it but her arms felt like rubber. She lunged for it but missed and her hand fell back onto the bed.

"That's okay. We'll just do what we can," the nurse said. She helped Taylor roll as far as she could to each side, washing the part of her back that was exposed. After the bath was over, the nurse applied lotion, massaging Taylor's shoulders and arms with tender strokes. She dressed her in a fresh gown and covered her with a clean sheet. She put a clean pillowcase on the pillow and helped Taylor brush her teeth.

"We won't change the bottom sheet right now. We'll need a lift for that." The nurse dumped the water and rearranged the bed table, leaving Taylor clean but exhausted. She never thought a bath could be so strenuous.

"There's my beautiful daughter," Sylvia said with a bright smile as she opened the door and peeked in. "Did you have a nice bath, honey?" She rushed to Taylor's side and went about adjusting the sheet and pillow.

Taylor just looked at her. She couldn't possibly explain the humiliation of having a perfect stranger wash between her legs.

"What day is it?" Taylor asked.

"Wednesday, dear. Don't you remember? Of course you don't," she chuckled. "You slept away Monday and Tuesday."

Taylor stared out the window. She couldn't believe she'd lost two whole days.

"Ms. Fleming," another nurse said brightly, bursting into the room. "How are you feeling? Do you have an appetite yet?" She was carrying a tray of food. She set it on the bed table and rolled it in front of Taylor. She then pressed the button and raised the head of the bed. "You may not want much but see if you can manage a little." She removed the plastic plate cover to reveal a bowl of broth. It didn't have anything in it and looked like Taylor's bath water after a day roping cattle.

"What is that?" Taylor asked, staring down at the tray.

"Beef broth. And you have some little gelatin squares. It's strawberry, I think. And some tea. Do you like sugar in your tea, honey?" the nurse asked, trying to be cheerful.

Taylor frowned at her. Sylvia busied herself with Taylor's food tray, tucking the napkin into her hospital gown and testing the temperature of the broth.

"It's not too hot, honey. This will be good for you. I haven't had a nice cup of beef broth in years." She dipped the spoon in the bowl and held it up to Taylor's lips. "Here you go, sweetheart. We'll do this slowly."

"I don't want any," Taylor said through clenched teeth.

"Ms. Fleming, you really need to eat something. The sooner you can eat solid food, the sooner you can get rid of the IV," the nurse said. "We need you to regain your strength."

"I don't want any broth," Taylor said, closing her eyes and turning away from the spoon.

"We can start with one of these little cubes of Jell-O," Sylvia offered, cutting a piece and holding it up.

Taylor tossed a glare at her mother.

"Would you like chicken broth instead?" the nurse asked, trying to be helpful.

"No. What I want is to get out of this bed and get dressed. I want a greasy cheeseburger and a large pop. I'll tell you what you can do with this tray."

"Taylor!" her mother interrupted abruptly.

"How do you expect me to get my strength back by feeding me dirty water? Bring me a steak, well done."

"Ms. Fleming, you have to work up to that. Your body has been through a traumatic ordeal. You have to take it slowly. Your digestive system may not be fully functional yet." The nurse gave her a sympathetic pat. "Don't worry, honey. By next week, we'll have you eating lots of things. The hospital fixes a lovely meat-loaf and mashed potatoes on Fridays and chicken fried steak on Monday. Just be patient and you'll be eating everything in sight in no time."

Taylor glared up at the nurse's patronizing tone.

"I don't plan on being here long enough for meatloaf day," she declared.

The nurse looked at Sylvia. Sylvia shook her head, as if discouraging her remarks.

"Well, I don't. I'll be home by tomorrow." Taylor fixed her with a determined stare.

"Honey, you may be here a little longer than that," her mother said in a kind voice. "But they'll take good care of you. You don't need to worry about the ranch. Your father has already talked with Cesar and Lexie. They can cover the work just fine. You just rest and get better."

Taylor didn't like the nurse's condescending attitude but from her mother it was worse. She was not going to lay there and be treated like an invalid. She was going to be up and back to work in a day or two, three at the most. She was not going to be stuck in a bed. She was not.

"Good morning," a man said, opening the door and striding in. He was tall and distinguished looking, slightly graying at the temples. His white lab coat was neatly buttoned and he wore a pair of shiny black cowboy boots. The name embroidered above the coat pocket read Dr. Elvin Potter, MD. He checked the chart he was carrying and smiled at Taylor. "How are you feeling, Ms. Fleming? How is the pain? Have they been keeping up with that for you?"

"It hurts like heck," she replied.

He laughed and unpinned a safety pin from his lapel.

"Tell me if you feel this, Ms. Fleming," he said, touching the pin point to the bottom of her feet.

"Ouch," she grimaced.

"Good. How about this one?"

"Ouch, yes," she replied, flinching at the pinprick.

He reattached the pin to his lapel then examined under the bandages.

"We'll be able to get the casts on later today. The swelling looks better. You'll be more comfortable with the casts on." He patted her leg and wrote something on the chart.

"Can I go home today?" Taylor asked.

"Not today," he replied, still writing.

"Tomorrow?"

"No. I don't think so, Ms. Fleming. We don't want to rush it." He didn't look at her. He seemed determined to keep his eyes off of Taylor's stare.

"When?" she insisted.

"It's hard to tell. You had a nasty accident. We had to put six screws in your left leg. You have to take it easy for a while. Your right leg wasn't as bad but it needs time to heal as well." He took a small flashlight from his pocket and leaned down to examine Taylor's eyes. "How's your head. Any headaches? Blurred vision? Light-headedness?"

"No," she replied, wondering why he was checking her eyes

when it was her legs that had the bandages.

"She was a little confused yesterday," her mother offered.

"That was probably the anesthesia wearing off." The doctor listened to her heart and lungs with his stethoscope. "I don't think the concussion was very severe."

"What concussion?" Taylor asked.

"Can you cough for me?" he asked, ignoring her question.

She gave a small cough which sent a shooting pain down her legs.

"Sounds good. Your lungs are clear." He draped the stethoscope around his neck and felt her abdomen. He seemed pleased with his examination and went back to writing in her chart. "Are you eating a little, Ms. Fleming?" he asked, looking down at her tray of uneaten food.

"When they bring me something to eat, I'll eat it," she replied.

Dr. Potter narrowed his focus and continued writing.

"Try to eat a bite or two. I need to see if your bowels are working." He closed the chart and turned to leave. "Let the nurse know if you need anything."

"Doctor," Taylor called. "When will I get to go home? Two days, three?"

He thought a moment then turned back to her.

"Ms. Fleming, you will need hospitalization and skilled nursing care for several weeks, maybe months. You were very lucky. Your legs will heal. After rehabilitation you should get back complete use in both of them. But you can't rush the recovery. You can't walk on them. No weight-bearing action of any kind. You can't take a bath or a shower by yourself. You can't even go to the bathroom without help. You'll need daily injections to combat blood clots for weeks as well as antibiotics for infection. You can't cook for yourself. You can't drive or shop or even brush your teeth unless someone is here to help you. You'll tire easily and you'll be moody. You have to accept that for now you are like a newborn baby. You will have to rely on help for everything you do." He fixed her with a stare that froze Taylor with the reality of her existence. "I'm sorry. But for a while you are in bed and in bed you will have to stay. In a few days or weeks, maybe you can work up to some mobility in a wheelchair but your legs have to stay elevated. I'm sorry but the best thing you can do is relax, cooperate and let the nurses take care of you." He turned and walked out of the room, leaving her with his words echoing through her mind. The nurse followed him, closing the door behind her.

Taylor turned to her mother for verification. The look in her eyes told Taylor it was true. The doctor had given an accurate description of her life and what she could expect for the immediate future. For Taylor, the news seemed to be getting worse by the hour. What started as confusion and pain had progressed through embarrassment, humiliation, disillusionment and now anger. She slowly turned her gaze out the window as one tear rolled down her cheek. She couldn't stop it and this vulnerability only added to her frustration. Taylor Fleming didn't cry. That wasn't her style. She always choked back whatever was wrong and kept a certain confidence in her voice and in her actions. She closed her eyes, pinching out the last tear.

"Honey, you'll be fine in a few months. Doctor Potter told me so." Sylvia spoke softly. "He is a good doctor. He told us you were very lucky and you would have the complete use of your legs again. Don't worry, honey. Your father and I have every confidence in him and his medical abilities. We're right here for you. You don't have to eat beef broth if you don't want to today," she said, applying the best of her mothering skills and soothing words.

"I hate this," Taylor said quietly. She looked frightened and defenseless.

"I know."

"I really hate this," she repeated, swallowing hard to hide the fear that threatened to erupt in loud sobs.

"I know, dear. But your father or I will be here every day to visit you. And I'm sure your friends will come visit you, too."

"I don't want anyone to visit me. Don't you understand, Mom. I don't want to be here." She looked away, the anguish festering in her soul.

Sylvia's chin quivered as she stared at her daughter.

"I wish I could take you home, honey. But I can't. I don't know anything about medicine or broken legs. I couldn't give you the injections or do your physical therapy. We have to trust the people who know how to take care of you. I feel terrible about it, honey, but you know I couldn't lift you or turn you, not since my surgery. I don't think I could even carry a pan of water to bathe you." Tears ran down Sylvia's face as she lowered herself into the chair next to the bed. "I wish I could take care of you, honey. I wish I could take you home right now, just like I did when you were a little girl. But I can't. I'm so sorry," she said through her tears.

"I know," Taylor said, touching her mother's hand as she clutched at the sheet. "I know, Mom. I know you can't do it. Don't cry. I'll be okay." Taylor forced a smile for her mother to see. "You go on home, Mom. You have been here for three days. You go home and rest."

"No, honey. I'm not leaving you. I want to stay. You might need something." Sylvia jumped to her feet, returning to her post as mother-protector.

"It's okay, Mom, I have all these nurses just waiting to wash me and stick me and feed me. You go on now. I think I'll take a nap for a while." Taylor nodded and squeezed her mother's hand. "I'm getting a little tired." She felt her eyes growing heavy.

"Are you sure, honey. I don't mind staying here with you. Really I don't."

"Yes, I'm sure. I may sleep all day. You never know." Taylor smiled weakly. "Call me tomorrow." Taylor closed her eyes and was soon asleep.

Sylvia collected her things, kissed Taylor on the forehead and tiptoed out of the room, pulling the door shut behind her.

Chapter 6

Taylor slept most of the day, not waking up until her dinner tray was set on the bed table. It was chicken broth and green gelatin cubes and a Popsicle. She ate part of it, still grumbling about the liquid diet she was forced to accept. Her legs still throbbed but the doctor was satisfied the swelling would not be a problem and had the inflatable air casts replaced with rigid plaster ones that ran from mid-thigh to her toes. It was after seven when Taylor heard the clomping footsteps coming down the hospital corridor and the brim of a cowboy hat peeked around the door.

"Hey, daughter," Grier said, looking in cautiously. "Are you decent?"

"Heck, no, Dad. When have I ever been decent?" Taylor replied.

"You've got a point there," he said, laughing as he entered the room.

"How are things going?" she asked, reading his nervous face. She knew her father hated hospitals. The thought of his only daughter lying in a bed with casts on her legs must be pure torture for him. A bead of sweat formed on his upper lip as he stared at her legs.

"Cesar said that heifer you wanted him to keep an eye on still hasn't calved. He brought her up to the corral last night." Grier tried to keep his eyes off Taylor's casts but it was a struggle.

"Good. If it's a bull, I want to take a look at it. We may want to keep him. I'll decide once the heifer calves."

"Yeah, we'll take a look at it." Grier took off his hat and fidgeted with it, trying to hide how uncomfortable he was. "Cesar's whole family said to tell you hi. He's really sorry about your accident."

"Did they get the fence fixed?" she asked, concerned over what she hadn't been able to do while stuck in the hospital.

"Yep. New posts. New wire."

"Good," Taylor took a deep breath as a shaft of pain shot up her leg. She tried not to grimace but it was hard to hide it. "Anything else?" she asked, shifting in the bed to help dissipate the pain.

"Did your mother tell you the refrigerator in the medicine shed went out? Compressor's shot."

"Which one? The big one or the little one?"

"The big one," he said.

"Did we lose the medicine in it?"

"No. One of the guys noticed it in time. I've got a new one in the back of the truck. I need to get it home before long. We filled the old one with ice to keep the stuff cold."

"You better go then," she said, knowing he was hoping this news would free him to leave.

"Yeah, I guess I better." He carefully placed his hat on his head and settled it down tight. "You need anything?" He looked around the room. "How about some magazines?"

68

"I don't need anything, Dad. What I need is to go home but I can't talk the doctor into agreeing to that."

"I heard. I hate to hear you'll be stuck here for three months."

"Three months?" she gasped. "Who told you three months?"

"Your mother said the doctor told her you'll need round-the-clock help until your legs heal and you get your strength back. She's pretty upset that she can't do it. I reminded her about her back surgery and told her she'd only end up hurting herself more. She can barely get up out of her chair sometimes."

"Yeah, I know. She can't take care of me. I don't want her to hurt herself. You tell her I said not to be upset about it."

"Too bad we don't have a nurse in the family to take care of you at home. If you need to be branded or hog-tied we've got the manpower for that," he chuckled.

"Yeah," she replied, laughing softly.

"I better go," he said. "You call me if you need anything, Taylor. You hear me?" Grier came to the side of the bed and looked down at her, his eyes moist and sorrowful. "Anything at all, you call me." He squeezed her arm then swallowed back a lump that rose in his throat.

"I will Dad. Don't worry about me. Tell Mom I'll be fine," she replied, watching him leave.

The door to the room had no sooner closed than it opened again. Lexie strode in, carrying her hat in her hand and a bouquet of wildflowers that looked like she had hand-picked them on the way to town.

"Hey, you're awake. How about that?" she said through a sympathetic smile. Like Grier, she was uncomfortable in hospitals but she hid it better than he did. She had showered, put on clean jeans and shirt, combed her hair and even polished her boots. Taylor considered herself lucky. Lexie didn't do that for just anyone. The last time she brushed the cow piles from her boots was for one of the ranch hand's wedding, something Lexie thought she ought to do since she was giving the bride away.

"Hey," Taylor said with a groan, trying to pull herself up. She couldn't find a comfortable position and it was starting to show.

"You all right?" Lexie asked, watching Taylor's struggle with the bed.

"Oh, sure. I'm just dandy," she replied, grimacing.

"You need some help?" Lexie stuffed the flowers in a plastic cup and tossed her hat on the chair. She tried to support Taylor's shoulders but it was no use. There was no finding a comfortable spot.

"I wish I was home in my own bed," she said, thrusting her head back against the pillow.

"I wish I could help you, kiddo. But I don't know anything about nursing." Lexie looked genuinely sorry for Taylor. "Nursing a calf, yeah. But not a human."

"Yeah, Dad was just here. He said the same thing. He said if I needed roping or hog-tying, we've got the manpower for that." They both laughed.

"Yep," Lexie teased. "We could put you in a squeeze chute and give you those shots. Stab you right in the rump. We could do your nursing just fine," she added, throwing her head back and laughing wildly.

Taylor narrowed her eyes. "Hey, that's a good idea, Lexie."

"What, stab you in the rump?" she asked, still laughing.

"No. A nurse to take care of me at home, at my house. Yeah. If I had a nurse to give me my injections I could go home and recover in my own bed. I bet I'd recover a lot faster if I was at home, not cooped up in here. Fresh air is good for you when you're sick. I've heard medical experts say that. Haven't you?" she asked, her enthusiasm growing for the idea.

"I guess so but you aren't sick, Taylor. You're injured. Broken legs aren't considered sick, I don't think."

"Even better."

"I don't know," she said, not sure if she should agree with Taylor's plan or not.

"I wonder who you ask about getting a visiting nurse."

"I have no idea. The hospital, I guess. They sent Harvey home with that broken collarbone and had a nurse come out and check on him for a couple weeks."

"I remember that. He said he had orders from the doctor for what the nurse was supposed to do. He said he didn't have to do anything. The hospital handled it all."

"Taylor, this isn't the same. Harvey could walk on his own. All the nurse had to do was help him rehab his arm. You can't do anything. You can't even pee on your own."

"I'm going to learn to use that bedpan on my own," Taylor insisted.

"You can't cook for yourself."

"Since when did I do much of that?"

"How are you going to get up and down the stairs to your bedroom? Drag yourself?"

"There's a bedroom and bathroom downstairs too. It's a bigger room than my room upstairs. I could have my bed moved down there." Taylor had all the answers and nothing was going to stop her. "I bet the floor nurse will know who I talk to about making arrangements to go home."

"Probably," Lexie replied skeptically. "Taylor, I think you better wait a while before you plan on going home. You might do more damage than you already have."

"I'll be fine. The hard part is over. I already have the casts on and I'll have this IV out soon. They want me to eat broth to get my strength back. It looks like dirty water, Lexie. Can you believe they think I'll get better eating broth?"

"Tell them you need a steak," Lexie said with a chuckle. "Nice aged Angus T-bone steak."

"I did. They said broth was better for me."

"I'll bring you a cheeseburger as soon as the IV is out. How's that, kiddo?"

"You can bring it to the house in a couple days. I plan on

being home before you know it."

Lexie frowned but didn't say anything. She wanted to help but she also wanted Taylor to stop talking about going home. Lexie had always tried to protect Taylor, even when she was an awkward teenager and dabbled in her newfound sexuality. Whether it was out of loyalty to the family or unrequited love, Lexie was and always would be Taylor's personal guardian angel. When she heard about Taylor's accident, she practically beat the land speed record to get to the hospital. Taylor might not have been able to see it but there was the slightest glisten in Lexie's eyes as she gazed down at her casts.

"Visiting hours are over," a voice said over the hospital speakers.

"I guess I better get going." Lexie saw that Taylor was still focused on her plans to go home.

"Yeah. Thanks for coming, and thanks for the flowers. I didn't think you were a flowers kind of person."

Lexie blushed. She settled her hat on her head to hide her red face and the smile that curled her lips.

"See ya," she said, tipping her hat as she walked out into the hall.

The door was barely closed when Taylor pushed the call button to summon the nurse, her eyes bright with her scheme.

Chapter 7

The small town of Harland, Texas, was big enough to hold all the necessities of life including a bank, post office, restaurants, several churches, gas stations, a VFW, a five-and-dime, three bars and even a backstreet brothel. It was also small enough to have a courthouse that closed during the lunch hour, bingo for entertainment on Saturday night and all the gossip its residents could handle. It was a cow town, born behind the dusty cattle drives that ran north to Dallas. Its main street had only been paved for a dozen years. The school, which served the western half of the county, didn't have a performing arts building until last year, an addition that was shared by the Future Farmers of America club. Its members routinely brought home top honors at the annual competition. FFA blue ribbon-winning heifers, bulls, sheep, goats and horses roamed the local ranches like tumbleweeds. The sign on the front door of the high school read

Congratulations to the Fair Winners—Stomp your boots before entering. Cowboy hats had to be banned from classrooms because they blocked the view of the blackboard. It wasn't only high school boys who sat around the lunchroom and discussed their pickup trucks and roundup. The girls had their own stories of roping a stubborn calf or scrambling to get the hay in the barn before it rained. Living in ranch country meant learning the ways of ranching. Teenagers could ride and rope before they could drive. But not Jen Holland. She was raised in cattle-rich Texas but she didn't know an Angus from an Angora.

Jen pulled into a parking space in front of the bank. She sat for a minute, leaning her head against the back of the seat and trying to calm her shaky nerves. She closed her eyes and concentrated on one of her sculptures. She could see every curve and bend to the metal, every welded joint and dramatic feature. She forced her mind to that place where she felt accomplished and confident in her work. She needed that comfort and reassurance right now. She needed to know she was not what Rowdy said about her. She finally climbed out, ready to conduct her father's business. The county clerk's office was on the second floor of the courthouse and the sign on the door announced they were closed until one o'clock for lunch.

Jen hadn't even thought about lunch. Her stomach was still churning from her visit to Glen Haven, the nursing home at the edge of town. It was the only facility within sixty miles that had an Alzheimer's unit. It had been a tough sell but she, with the doctor and the sheriff's assistance, had convinced her father life would be simpler and more comfortable if he was closer to town. At first he shouted angry, hateful things that brought Jen to the brink of tears. But she knew better than to buckle under his endless barrage. She smiled and kept her tone soft and encouraging, the way she would reassure a frightened child on their first day of school. Finally Rowdy's eyes moistened, realizing he couldn't fight it any longer. He stared off into space, leaving his care and decisions for Jen to handle. He had a vacant look in his eyes as if surrendering the fight for his freedom.

The sheriff had suggested Jen stop at the clerk's office first with a tone that meant he knew something she didn't and she probably wasn't going to like it. But now she had to wait while the county clerk had lunch before she could find out how much trouble her father had created. Jen checked her watch. She had twenty minutes to kill and she wasn't going to do it pacing the green and tan hall on the second floor of the courthouse.

She collected her sunglasses from the visor of the van and headed up Beller Street, the bright blue skies warm on her face. Beller was the main street that ran from the feed store on one end of town to the Methodist church on the other. Micah Beller wasn't some brave historic figure or financial guru who gave his name to the town's main drag. He was the owner of the paving company from Wichita Falls who offered to pave the main street of Harland with a new and experimental material as a test of its durability if the town agreed to name the street after him. It was a no-brainer. The Harland City Council had no trouble agreeing to the offer. Little did Mr. Beller know, the Main Street signs were being stored in the basement of the town hall, waiting for that time when they could be reposted.

Jen strolled the sidewalk, window shopping and enjoying the warm breeze. She didn't mind the hot Texas summers. Even as a child, she liked to feel the hot sun on her face. Her tan proved she still enjoyed a walk in the sun though her work kept those times short. Jen noticed the painting on the side of the Ziegler's Furniture and Appliance store. The two-story brick building's mural depicting a cattle drive in the late 1800s still had bright blue skies, billows of dust and tumbling sagebrush in brilliant colors and artistic detail. The name J. M. Holland was still fresh and clear on the bottom corner of the wall. It had been four years since Jen painted the mural, a commissioned job that helped with expenses during a particularly thin month. It also led to two other jobs in town, one she accepted, one she did not. But she was never much on painting water towers.

She studied the painting, looking for signs of wear or flaking. She had used a good primer and top quality paint. It should be around a good long time. Her eyes flowed over the details of her work, stopping at the tree set on a hill. You had to be looking for it but it was there, a little girl on a swing. Jen pulled a cautious smile as she stared at the child, her long blond hair flowing behind her as she gleefully pumped the swing. Jen swayed slightly as she watched the child, as if it were her suspended on the swing, floating back and forth on a carefree summer day. She could almost smell the sage and buffalo grass blowing across the prairie. The low mooing of the cattle and the wrangler's whistles to keep them doggies moving veritably called out to her from the paint and brick.

Jen stared at the mural, her eyes mesmerized by the bright colors and tranquil setting. She stood with her hand on the wall and closed her eyes, hoping to revisit that child and that happy innocence. In her mind's eye she could hear a man calling to her, calling her name and urging her to swing higher. His voice was kind. She couldn't see his face but he was there, just out of view, over the hill. Jen could almost hear the little girl giggle as she swung higher, her bare feet reaching for the sky as she soared upward. The man watched the child with a gentle fondness, one that drew her closer to the painting. Jen reached out and touched the little girl she had painted. The man's voice called to her again. It was Rowdy's voice, a kinder, softer Rowdy. It was a daddy's voice. Jen pulled her hand away and continued up the sidewalk. She wished she hadn't stopped to look at the mural.

Jen walked to the end of the block, crossed the street and returned to the courthouse. She had made a mental list of all possible reasons the sheriff thought she should stop at the clerk's office. It included everything from unpaid parking tickets to illegibly signed documents but nothing prepared her for what the clerk disclosed behind his office door.

"Ms. Holland, we've been trying to work with your father for a couple years now but he just hasn't taken our warnings seriously. I'm very sorry. Rowdy has been a resident of the county all his life. That's why we tried to be lenient."

Calvin Henry was the recently reelected county clerk. He had been clerk for twenty-three years and if there was something to know in Harland, he knew it. He wore western style slacks, black cowboy boots, white western shirt with a string tie and a Stetson hat big enough to topple a coat tree. His office walls were covered with photographs of thoroughbred horses, his passion.

"I'm afraid I don't understand," Jen said. "This paper says my father hasn't paid his property taxes in three years. How can that have happened? First of all, my father would never intentionally not pay his taxes. He is well aware of the value of land. And second, why was he allowed to get so far in arrears? Why wasn't this addressed the first year or even the second? But three?" Jen looked over the document Mr. Henry had handed her, her frown intensifying by the second.

Mr. Henry leaned back in his leather desk chair, folding his hands behind his head.

"We have done everything we know to do to get him to take care of this. Registered letters, phone calls, personal visits. You name it, we've done it. The registered letters come back unaccepted. His phone has been disconnected. He won't answer the door. I have to tell you, if your father's ranch was any bigger, we would never have let it go so long. The penalty charges alone on a big spread would be astronomical and almost impossible to pay. But we were prepared to give him one more chance but now . . ." he said, leaning forward and resting his hands on his desk.

"Now what?"

"I understand your father has moved to Glen Haven." Mr. Henry looked at Jen sympathetically.

"News travels fast in a small town." Jen sighed, knowing

Rowdy's business was now fodder for every back fence gossip monger.

"We really have no choice. I'm very sorry."

"No choice for what? Do you want to prosecute him too?" she asked, a subtle edge to her voice.

"No. That wouldn't get us our money. We don't want any harm to come to your father, Ms. Holland. The fair and equitable thing to do is a sale."

"My father doesn't have anything to sell so he can pay this amount," she said, pointing to the figure at the bottom of the second page. "Neither do I for that matter."

"No. You don't understand, Ms. Holland. I meant sell your father's ranch, the Little Diamond. We are prepared to auction it," he said as he looked at his calendar. "On the twenty-ninth of next month."

"You can't do that," Jen declared angrily. "My father won't be ready to sell his ranch by then. He's barely able to remember what month it is."

"I'm sorry but the petition for foreclosure has already been filed. And your father doesn't have to be there. In fact, it would probably be better if he wasn't. All you'll need to do is remove his personal items from the house by that date. I'll be in touch with you if anyone wants to view the house and property prior to the sale. We encourage potential bidders to see what they are getting into before they bid. I'm sure some of his neighbors will take a serious interest in his property. It's small by ranch standards but it has a good stream and adequate pastureland."

"You're serious," she scowled. "You really plan on selling my father's ranch right out from under him while he's in a nursing home."

Mr. Henry gazed over at her. His face told Jen all she needed to know.

"Unless you can pay your father's taxes I'm afraid we have no choice. If you'll read the county laws, you'll see we are within our rights to liquidate property to pay past due taxes. We owe it to the other citizens of the county who do pay their taxes on time. They have a right to expect fair treatment. If we don't collect from Rowdy Holland, other residents will refuse to pay as well. They'll figure if he can get away with it, so can they. Can you pay your father's taxes, Ms. Holland?"

"I already told you, I don't have any way to pay this. I'm a freelance artist. I don't make this kind of money."

"Oh, yes. I remember. You painted the side of the appliance store. I like it. The cows look almost real." He gave a patronizing smile.

"Mr. Henry, I'm starting work on a commission job. It isn't huge but I will be able to start making payments by the first of the year. I'm sure I can get this caught up within a year or two."

"I neglected to mention, come November, a mill levy will increase property taxes for next year. That will mean an additional eighty-six dollars on your father's property taxes. Of course, that's for the amount due in December. So by the time you would make any payment at all, the outstanding balance due will be more than shown on that paper. That is what is due today. And then there is the penalty. County tax penalty is six percent per month, Ms. Holland." Mr. Henry seemed bent on piling on as much bad news as possible.

Jen stared at the paper. She wasn't reading it but she couldn't look Mr. Henry in the eye. It was too painful. Her day was on a fast track to heartache. She had already convinced her father he needed to live in a nursing home, in essence committing him to living behind locked doors. Now she was faced with the imminent sale of his ranch on the courthouse steps, the home she remembered as a little girl. If things could get any worse, she didn't want to know it.

"Mr. Henry, I'm on my way over to the bank. I feel sure my father has funds in his account and as soon as I can petition the bank to add my name to his checking account, I'll be able to write a check to you."

He was already raising his eyebrows in doubt.

"Perhaps you should have a talk with customer service at the bank," he offered, escorting her to the door with a patronizing pat on the shoulder. She wasn't sure why she was getting the bum's rush out the door but like the sheriff, Mr. Henry seemed to know something she didn't. "By the way, Ms. Holland, in case you are thinking of selling his property on your own, there is a lien against the deed. You couldn't sell it without coming through this office."

"Mr. Henry, I don't plan on selling anything. And you shouldn't either. I'll be back." Jen walked out of the office door and crossed the street to the bank. The ten minutes she had to wait to see the customer service manager gave her plenty of time to digest the reality of what the county clerk had said. She expected her father to have problems with his finances, perhaps an overdue bill or two. But she certainly didn't expect the loss of his ranch . . .

"Hello, Ms. Holland. I'm Evelyn Treemont," a woman in a black and white dress said, greeting Jen with a pleasant though reserved smile. "Won't you come in?"

Jen sat in the chair strategically placed at the exact corner of the desk. She wondered if it was meant to keep the customer teetering on tenterhooks. Evelyn closed the door and took her seat behind the desk.

"What can I do for you today?" Evelyn had a smug tone.

"I assume you know who I am and why I am here. I need to have my name added to my father's checking account so I can pay some of his bills for him." She placed the paper Rowdy had signed on the desk. Evelyn looked at it then brought his account up on her computer screen.

"Well, let's see," she said, setting a pair of granny glasses on the end of her nose. "Holland, Holland. Here we are. Ralph D. Holland," she said, glancing over at Jen for verification. Jen

80

nodded. The woman checked the paper again then typed something. "I see one other name on this account. Beatrice Arlene Holland."

Jen's eyes widened at the mention of her mother's name.

"That's my mother. I'm surprised my father didn't have her name removed after they divorced. She passed away several years ago."

"I'm sorry to hear that, but no, it's still here. But I see no problem. It looks like we could add your name to the account if you'd like, Ms. Holland." There was something in her voice that sounded cautionary.

"That's why I'm here. My father isn't able to take care of his affairs right now. I'll need some checks printed with my name on them also."

"Well," Evelyn said carefully, still scanning Rowdy's account.

"How long will it take to have some checks printed?" Jen asked, growing impatient with the woman's stalling tactics.

"Ms. Holland, I'm sure you would like to help your father. I know I would if it was my father. I'd be glad to add your name to the account but there isn't anything in it. In fact, your father has over three hundred forty-five dollars worth of overdraft charges that we can't get him to pay. We have frozen his account. We won't be able to issue any checks to you until that amount has been paid."

"Three hundred forty-five dollars?" Jen gasped in horror. "My father is overdrawn three hundred forty-five dollars? My father has never been overdrawn in his life. He has always been a good businessman and a successful rancher. He may not be as big a rancher as some but he could *always* pay his way." Jen was growing angry at what this woman was suggesting. Rowdy had been extremely careful with his money, that she did know. He was almost miserly in his approach to money. He also took a great deal of pride in his financial independence. "You must not be looking at the right account. He must have a savings account.

Just transfer the money into his checking account and pay the overdraft charges. I'll authorize it."

The woman was already shaking her head slowly and sympathetically.

"I'm sorry but Mr. Holland only has the one account. He doesn't have one at the credit union either. We've already checked."

"But how about his social security check? Isn't it a direct deposit?"

"Yes. But with his utilities being automatically deducted and the checks he continues to write, the overdraft charges just keep growing. We haven't been able to convince him to get these charges caught up."

"So on the first of the month, his next social security check should take care of those fees, right?" Jen suggested.

"I imagine that Mr. Holland's check will go directly to the nursing home. That is what usually happens in cases like these."

"Cases like these?" Jen asked, straightening her posture.

"Yes. Cases where the patient doesn't have financial resources to pay his room and board or the ability to handle his own affairs. I'm sure Glen Haven has already forwarded a request for that. It was probably part of the papers you signed when he was admitted."

Jen wanted to jump to her feet and defend her father's honor. But she was smart enough to know the woman was probably right. Automatic payment was the only way Glen Haven could ensure her father's expenses were paid. In the confusion and stress of admitting Rowdy to the nursing home, she somehow remembered something mentioned about social security.

"So, we'd be happy to add your name to the account but I'm afraid all that would do is make you liable for the overdraft fees. Are you sure you want to do that, Ms. Holland?"

"Absolutely, I want my name on my father's account," she declared, pulling her checkbook from her purse. This woman wasn't going to intimidate her into avoiding her father's trouble. "How much is the total of the overdraft charges?"

"Three hundred forty-five dollars and eighty cents," the woman replied, reading it from the screen.

Jen wrote out the check and placed it on the desk.

"Now you may reopen my father's account," she said and walked out the door.

Jen returned to the courthouse but Mr. Henry was in a meeting and she was forced to sit in the hall and wait. While she waited, she tried to calculate how much cash she could put her hands on but no matter how she figured it, she couldn't come anywhere close to what she needed to pay Rowdy's taxes, let alone the penalties. Paying off his overdraft charges had put a strain on her checking account as it was. She would have to wait on the oil change on the van and repairs to the dryer. It was summer. She could hang her clothes outside to dry. And she could get a few more months out of the air conditioner in the van. The leak wasn't that bad. But how was she going to keep the Little Diamond from falling to the auctioneer's gavel? She wondered how much the interest rate was on a personal loan. Then she remembered she was still paying off her new welder. If she returned it she wouldn't have the monthly payments but then she couldn't build the sculptures for the Merrill town square and she couldn't afford to give up that job.

While she sat planning and calculating, a constant stream of people came and went from the offices up and down the corridor. A woman came out of the county health department across the hall and pulled at the door but it didn't latch. Through the open door Jen could hear someone talking. It sounded like the woman was arguing over the telephone with someone who wouldn't take no for an answer. Jen didn't mean to eavesdrop but she couldn't help it. The woman in the office was practically screaming into the receiver to make her point.

"If I had one, I'd tell you," she said in no uncertain terms.

"What do you think? They grow on trees? This is Harland, not Dallas. We don't have resources like that."

Jen forced her attention to her car keys, trying to ignore the woman's private conversation.

"Last time we had a CSN to do that kind of around-the-clock, live-in care was six years ago. I know it's only for a couple months," the woman continued. "No, she isn't available either. She retired."

Jen couldn't help hearing the term CSN. It struck a deep chord. CSN, certified skilled nursing aide. She stared out the window at the end of the hall, a blank expression on her face. She could remember the conversation with her mother's doctor like it was yesterday.

"If your mother is serious about being at home, you should be aware she'll need a nurse's aide, a skilled nurse's aide, Ms. Holland. Maybe not now, but eventually. She may only need occasional visits from aides at first, but before long she will need more. She'll need around-the-clock care. There will be things you won't be able to do for her. She may have to accept an assisted living center, a hospice facility."

The doctor's words still rang in Jen's ears. She closed her eyes and sighed.

"Ms. Holland," Calvin Henry said, standing in his open office door. "I see you're back. How did it go at the bank?" There was a smug look on his face as if he already knew.

"I imagine you have a pretty good idea how it went, Mr. Henry," she said, taking a seat.

"Like I said, if you would have your father's personal things out of the house soon, we can go ahead and start allowing bidders to take a look around," he said, setting the folder containing the papers about Rowdy's property aside as if business with Jen was finished.

Jen didn't need him to sugarcoat the news but she at least expected a respectful attitude from the man.

"How much do I need to pay to stop the sale?" Jen heard herself ask.

"How much?" He looked at her as if it was a worthless question.

"Yes. How much would it take to stop the sale and keep strangers from trespassing on my father's home?"

"Why, all of it, Ms. Holland." He gave a small chuckle. "We need the entire amount to settle this matter. I told your father that. He thought he could pay twenty dollars and that would take care of it. That isn't the way this county does business."

Jen allowed her eyes to drift out the window for a long moment.

"If I agree to pay it off before the sale date, will you refrain from sending people out to see the property?" she asked in a solemn, almost reverent tone, her eyes still watching the skies outside the courthouse.

"How do you plan on doing that?" He leaned back, rocking his leather desk chair as if he was mocking her question.

"Will you?" she repeated, snapping a sharp look at him.

"I'll tell you what. I'll give you three days to come up with a proposal on how you'll pay this off. I won't post the sale notices until then. But three days is all I can offer, Ms. Holland."

"That will be enough," Jen replied.

She shook his hand and walked out into the hall, gripping her car keys so tight they were cutting into the palm of her hand. She went to the window and stared out at the trees, their branches gently waving in the summer wind. At that moment she didn't know who she disliked more, Taylor Fleming for dragging her into her father's affairs or herself for not doing it sooner. Either way, playing the blame game wasn't going to help anything. The fact remained Rowdy needed help and she wasn't going to turn her back on him. For better or worse, he was her father and she was his one and only child, adopted or not. Jen squared her shoulders and dropped her keys into her purse. She turned on her heels, strode down the hall and through the door that read

County Health Department.

"Excuse me," she said to the woman behind the desk. "I understand you are looking for a CSN."

The woman looked up from her paperwork curiously.

"A CSN?" Jen repeated confidently.

"Yes. Actually, we aren't but the discharge planner in the home care services at the hospital is."

"What does the job involve and how much does it pay?" Jen asked with cold dispatch.

"I'm sorry but do you know what a CSN is, miss?"

"A certified skilled nursing aide."

"Do you know a CSN who might be interested in interviewing for this position?"

"Yes. Me."

"You are a CSN?" the woman asked cautiously.

"Yes. I'm certified and have four years of experience. I took my training in Austin at Memorial Hospital."

"Really? Are you presently employed," the woman asked, her interest growing in Jen.

"I'm not working as an aide right now but my certification is still active." Jen took her ID and certification card from her wallet and handed them to the woman. "Is this job here in Harland?"

The woman began typing things into her computer, taking information off Jen's ID. She didn't answer Jen's question until she had found what she was looking for on her computer.

"Here it is," she said finally, pointing to the screen. "Jen M. Holland." She looked over at Jen. "It doesn't say what the M is for."

"Marie," Jen replied. It had been a long time since she had spoken her birth mother's name.

"Oh," the woman said, going back to reading. "Well, it looks like it's all in order. Yes, you are a CSN, Ms. Holland."

"Did you think I'd make it up? I expected you to check."

"You just never know," the woman said, jotting something on a sticky note then handing it to Jen. "That is the person you need to call for an appointment. Her name is Mrs. Hunter. They do their own screening. We just provide names for them to contact. I'll fax her your certification information. That should save some time. I understand this job is going to be available right away. You might want to call today."

"Are there any other applicants for the job?" Jen asked, wondering if the woman would admit what she had overheard.

"Well, no. You are the only one for this kind of work. They need a live-in caregiver."

"May I call Mrs. Hunter from here?" Jen asked, seeing no reason to wait.

"That's fine," the woman replied, dialing the number then handing the telephone to Jen.

Within a few minutes Jen had an appointment at the hospital to meet the discharge planner and had a general rundown of the kind of duties required. General patient care included checking vitals, daily injections, light housework, cooking for herself and the patient but with no dietary restrictions, occasional shopping for groceries and prescriptions, the normal things Jen would expect and had done before. She was promised a private bedroom and bath, a few hours free per week so she could visit her father in Glen Haven and the best news, a bonus if she could start immediately. Jen agreed to meet the patient and the family before making a decision on taking the job. If they didn't approve of her, she won't be hired since this was a private duty assignment paid for by the patient's insurance with the extra paid by the patient. The amount wasn't enough to buy a house on South Padre Island but it was enough to raise Jen's eyebrows. It was enough to pay Rowdy's county taxes and penalties.

"I'll be glad to meet with the family today, if that is all right with them." Jen didn't mean to sound pushy but the three-day grace period Mr. Henry had allowed was running. "Four o'clock is fine," she agreed to the woman on the telephone. "Thank you. I'll come by your office now."

By the time Jen got to her van and backed out of the parking space she was wondering what had happened. In the space of a few hours she had put her father in a nursing home, spent most of her money on his debt at the bank, made a promise to the county clerk she wasn't sure she could keep and had an interview for a job she never wanted to have to take again. She came to Harland for the day and it looked like she was staying for the summer. So long as she had time to work on her sketches for the Merrill sculptures she didn't mind. But it was the first time in years she would be working to the tune someone else was playing. As an artist who worked on commission, she was her own boss. She got up early, worked when she felt like it and occasionally worked through the night if the mood struck her. She also loved every minute of it. Now she was going to be catering to someone else's needs and whims. But the money was good, good enough to catch up her father's debts and leave some to support the rest of her summer. She had no doubt she could do what was expected of her. When she settled into her nursing mode, doing the job would become automatic.

After an interview with the discharge planner at the hospital, Jen was sent to room 211 to meet the patient she would be taking care of for the next eight to twelve weeks, a patient with two broken legs who refused to spend her recovery in the skilled nursing unit of the hospital.

"Stop back here and I'll have the paperwork ready for you to sign," Mrs. Hunter said, walking Jen to the elevator. "You'll need to get a list put together of home equipment you'll need. As soon as the doctor signs off on it, we can get those things ordered."

Jen was surprised how quickly everything was coming back to her. The lingo, the terms—it was like she had never been away from it.

"I hope the interview goes well," Mrs. Hunter offered a bit

nervously. "I don't want to influence you but you really are the only available and qualified applicant. If you don't take the job or the patient doesn't accept you, she's going to have to stay in the skilled nursing unit for at least two months. And that idea isn't going to sit well at all."

"Sounds like a pretty stubborn patient," Jen replied.

"Yes, she most definitely is that," Mrs. Hunter agreed, raising her eyebrows dramatically.

The elevator opened and Jen stepped in, self-assured and optimistic about her meeting with the patient. As the door closed, she realized she didn't know the patient's name. She knew it was a woman. She had heard reference to a she. She knew everything else about the case, medical history, age, doctor's orders, everything but the name. If it was mentioned she hadn't heard it. She gave a quick thought to going back to the office and asking but the patient was expecting her now and showing up late wouldn't help instill trust. Jen placed a confident yet pleasant smile on her face and opened the door to room 211. The curtain was pulled halfway down the track, exposing only a pair of cast-covered legs supported in slings.

"Are you back already?" a voice behind the curtain grumbled. "I told you, I'll let you know when I'm ready for my bath."

Jen recognized that voice and it did *not* bring a smile to her face.

"I'm not your nurse, yet." Jen quipped but remained hidden behind the curtain. The shocking reality of who was on the other side of the curtain brought her day to a screeching halt.

Suddenly the curtain flew back and Taylor Fleming was scowling at her.

"What are you doing here?" Taylor asked gruffly, holding on to the trapeze bar above her head.

Jen chuckled, slowly at first. But soon she was laughing hysterically, tears rolling down her face.

"I should have known. The way my day has been going, it

couldn't possibly have been anyone else," she said through her laughter.

"What's so funny?" Taylor demanded, trying to pull herself up in bed. She didn't want to be the butt of anyone's joke and certainly not Jen Holland's.

"I should have known this job was too good to be true." As much sympathy as Jen had for Taylor's accident and her broken legs, she still found the irony hilariously funny. She continued to laugh, as much at herself as anything.

"Job? Are you the one here about the nursing job?" Taylor asked, her forehead growing more furrowed by the moment.

Jen nodded, still chuckling softly and wiping the tears that ran down her face.

"Yes, Ms. Fleming, I am your CSN while you recover from your broken legs. By the way, I am sorry about your accident. But don't you see how funny this is?" Jen giggled, trying to hold her laughter in check.

"No. I don't find this funny at all," Taylor replied. She grabbed the telephone on her bedside table and dialed Mrs. Hunter. "I need another aide," she demanded, her eyes on Jen but her anger directed at the person on the other end of the line. "This is *not* going to work. Find someone else."

Jen had brought the shock and humor of the moment under control. The cold hard truth of the matter remained. In spite of their brief but abrasive past, Taylor represented a job and money Jen desperately needed.

"Surely you can find someone," Taylor said with a scowl.

Jen came to Taylor's side and took the telephone from her hand.

"It'll be fine, Mrs. Hunter," she said into the receiver. "Yes, I'm sure we can work it out. Thank you." Jen hung up the telephone.

"What are you doing?" Taylor tried to reach for the receiver but Jen moved it out of reach. "I don't want to work anything out."

"I'm a CSN, the only one in the county, as far as I can tell, who is available as a live-in caregiver. And you need a live-in caregiver who is a CSN. You have two choices Ms. Fleming. It's me or the skilled nursing unit. That's your choice." Jen didn't want to admit she needed the job more than Taylor needed her skills. For Taylor, there was a second option. For Jen, there wasn't.

"I thought you were a welder." Taylor tossed out the words as if they were an insult. "I don't need a welder. I need a nurse."

Jen took her certification card from her wallet and tossed it on the sheet that was covering Taylor's lap. Taylor examined it then handed it back with a snap of the wrist.

"If you are a nurse, how come you make those metal things?"

"I have four years' experience as a nurse's aide. I don't use it but I have the skills you'll need so you can live at home while you recover from your accident. Do you need me to demonstrate? Do you want me to take your blood pressure or change your sheets, Ms. Fleming?" Jen couldn't help but sound a bit condescending.

"No, I don't need you to do anything." Taylor heaved a disgusted sigh. "I need a home care nurse. That's what I need."

"Ms. Fleming," Jen started again in a softer voice. "I know I'm probably the last person you wanted as a caregiver and I must admit, you aren't my favorite person right now either. But I really don't think you have a choice. If you are willing to give me a try, I think we can make this work. I really am a good nurse. We just have to ignore the other things. We'll be just a patient and a nurse. That's all. That's the way we have to look at it." Jen was using her best diplomacy and it seemed to be working. At least Taylor had leaned back on the pillow and wasn't screaming at her anymore.

"Are you sure you know how to take care of someone? I mean, the doctor said I needed injections everyday. Can you do

91

that?" Taylor asked.

"Sure. I'll wear my welding hood."

Taylor hesitated, trying to decide if she could accept Jen or not. She desperately wanted her independence back and it was entirely possible Jen was the only way she could have that. She accepted Jen's handshake tentatively. It was firm but soft and gave Taylor a strangely secure feeling.

"Okay," Taylor said, nodding in agreement. "We'll see how it goes."

"And we won't mention cattle rustling. Agreed?"

"Okay."

"I'll let Mrs. Hunter know. We have a lot to do to get things ready for you to go home."

"I want to go today," Taylor added.

"Are you planning on sleeping on the floor?" Jen asked. "If not, we have to get a hospital bed, a lift, a commode, a wheelchair, lots of things that will allow me to care for you at home. And we can't order them until the doctor signs off on them. So first thing I have to do is have a look at your house and see what we need. And then the equipment has to be delivered and set up. Once I have your house ready, then you will go home, probably transferred in an ambulance. And I will need some of my things from my home in San Antonio." As Jen listed what had to be done, Taylor's face began to melt.

"Can't I just go home and we'll get that other stuff later?" she asked. "Maybe I won't need all that stuff."

"I can't lift you, Ms. Fleming. And I can't carry you. You can't put any, and I repeat, *any* weight on your legs. That means you can't stand up. Until you've been stuck in bed with casts on your legs, you can't understand how many things you can't do for yourself. That is where I come in. I will take care of you but I am not superwoman. I will need all that equipment, and probably more, to do it. So it will be a couple of days before you can go home and that is assuming everything goes like it should."

"Hello, honey," Sylvia said, pushing the door open. "Oh, you have company." She smiled politely at Jen then went to give Taylor a kiss on the forehead. "Do you want me to come back later, honey?"

"Mom, this is Jen Holland," Taylor said, giving her mother an opportunity to absorb that bit of news. "Rowdy Holland's daughter."

"Oh," Sylvia stammered, not sure if she should be surprised or not.

"Hello, Mrs. Fleming," Jen said, shaking her hand.

"Jen is going to be my CSN," Taylor added.

"That's nice, dear. But what's a CSN?" Sylvia asked, studying Jen up and down for signs of what that might be.

"I'm a certified skilled nursing aide, Mrs. Fleming. I'll be taking care of Taylor while she recuperates."

"Oh, so you'll be taking care of Taylor while she's in the skilled nursing unit," she offered.

Jen looked at Taylor with raised eyebrows.

"Jen is going to be my caregiver at home. I'm going to do my recuperating in my own house. I'm not going to the skilled nursing unit."

"Now, honey, we talked about this. Remember the doctor said you will need around-the-clock care and injections and rehabilitation. You can't go home just yet, sweetheart." Sylvia patted Taylor's shoulder as if she were appeasing her. "I know you want to go home but—"

"I talked to the doctor. He said if I had a qualified aide I could go home. And Jen is a qualified aide. She will do everything the doctor orders. With her help, I can be at home until the casts come off and I rehab my legs. I won't have to stay here." Taylor sounded completely convinced this was the right thing to do.

Sylvia didn't know what to say. She looked at Jen for verification and to Taylor to see if she was serious.

"And the insurance will cover almost all of it. They like

93

patients to go home. It costs less than staying in the hospital. But you have to do something for me, Mom."

"Sure, honey. What is it?"

"You need to take Jen by my house so she can see what kind of hospital equipment we'll have to get. She can use my bedroom upstairs. I'll use the one downstairs."

"Are you sure this is a good idea, Taylor. I mean I'll be so happy you are home so long as you are getting the best care possible."

"I'll take good care of her, Mrs. Fleming. I promise you." Jen supplied a reassuring smile. "Patients usually recover quicker and easier in their own surroundings, if that's any consolation to you." Jen touched Sylvia's hand.

"Okay, I guess." Sylvia looked worried but she didn't say anything else. Taylor was already smiling at the idea she would be home soon.

"I need to go sign some papers and talk with your doctor's nurse. I'll be back later," Jen said, leaving Taylor and Sylvia to discuss the plans. As soon as Jen was out of the room and the door had shut, Taylor pushed the button for the nurse.

"You can come take this bedpan now," she said when the nurse replied. "My butt is getting sore."

Chapter 8

Jen went about preparing for Taylor's move home. It required doctor's orders, rental equipment, supplies and a trip to San Antonio so she could pack what she needed to be away from home for two months. If ever she was thankful she had a van, moving her clothes, personal effects, necessary art supplies and a cat to Taylor's was the time. She desperately wanted to load up her welder and some materials so she could begin work on her projects but she didn't have room and she doubted she would have the time. She did bring a few boxes of art supplies to work on her sketches for the sculptures.

Every time Jen stopped by the hospital to talk with Taylor or the nurses about her discharge, Taylor greeted her with a hopeful expression and the same question. Is it time to go home yet? Jen stopped listing what she had accomplished and what was still left to do. It was easier and quicker to just say soon. It took three days and a dozen calls to the medical equipment rental company to get everything they needed set up and in working order. Taylor was ready to bite someone's head off when Jen opened the door to her hospital room Tuesday morning.

"Good morning," Jen said cheerfully, tossing her purse on the chair and opening the curtains. The light streamed in, filling the room with warm sunshine.

"Yeah, yeah. It is for some people," Taylor grumbled, pulling herself up by the trapeze bar and shifting her weight.

"What's the matter? Aren't you ready to meet the day?" Jen asked, looking at her breakfast tray. She refrained from saying it looked gross.

"See what I mean?" Taylor muttered, also looking at the tray. "What is this supposed to be?"

"I thought I ordered scrambled eggs and ham."

"Oh," Jen muttered, examining what had happened to the eggs on the plate.

Taylor slid the rolling table aside, tired of looking at it.

"Tomorrow I'm ordering Cheerios," she said, still not happy with her position in bed. She fought with the bar, shifting and fidgeting until she was comfortable.

"Can I help you?" Jen asked, adjusting the sheet for Taylor.

"Yes, you can. You can finish with the planning and the paperwork and get me home." Taylor was adamant.

"Well, I was going to suggest we move you home today, but if you are dead set on having hospital Cheerios tomorrow I guess we can wait." Jen was busy stacking and refolding the towels on the chair.

"Today? Now?" Taylor asked, her eyes wild with excitement. "Why didn't you say so? Let's go. Back my truck up to the door and get me loaded." Taylor sat up and tossed the sheet aside, ready to make her getaway that very second.

"Now hold your horses, Ms. Fleming," Jen said, putting the sheet back across Taylor's lap. "We are waiting for the doctor to sign the orders and then we will call for the ambulance transfer. It will take an hour or so to get it all set."

"The heck it will. Call the doctor. Call the ambulance. You can get an ambulance here in three minutes if you dial nine-one-one." Taylor was reaching for the telephone, straining against the slings supporting her casts. "I'll dial," she added.

"No, you are not dialing nine-one-one. Don't make me sorry I told you before we had the details finalized." She pushed the telephone out of reach. "Now, lay back, take a deep breath and relax. I'll be back in a few minutes." Jen went to the door then looked back at Taylor. "Maybe you should eat some of your breakfast. It's good for you." Taylor crossed her arms over her chest and scowled at her.

Taylor was fit to be tied by the time Jen and the nurse came in her room with the discharge papers in hand.

"What took so long? You said an hour. It's lunchtime already."

"Are you ready to go home, Ms. Fleming?" the nurse asked, setting her clipboard on the bed table.

"I'm ready." Taylor tossed the sheet on the chair and raised the head of her bed all the way up. "Let's go."

"We need to go over some things before we release you," the nurse said, leafing through several pages of routine discharge orders.

"Oh, no you don't. I have a nurse to take care of all that. All I need is to get in the ambulance and head east. Where do I sign?" Taylor took the pen from the nurse's hand and reached for the papers. Jen nodded at the nurse, giving her permission to ignore the long explanations and warnings. Taylor signed. Jen signed. The nurse signed. And just like that, Taylor was free, ready to go home at last. It had been a week and she was more than ready. She was beyond anxious. If she was a child, it would have been Christmas.

"Did you bring her something to wear?" the nurse asked Jen.

"Yes, I have a shirt and I brought a sheet."

"Don't I get clothes?" Taylor asked. "Maybe sweats or something?"

Jen and the nurse looked at Taylor skeptically.

"There is no way we can get anything over those casts, Ms. Fleming," Jen replied, taking the shirt out of a tote bag. "I bought you an oversized T-shirt that will cover you pretty well. But underwear and sweatpants would just be in the way. They'd be more of a nuisance than anything. We'll use sheets or towels as lap covers." Jen knew Taylor was going to demand some sort of modesty but this was the best she could offer. Taylor's privacy was going to take a backseat to her need for nursing help.

Fortunately Taylor didn't blush every time she was exposed to the world. It took a few days but she had learned to accept help on and off the bedpan and with her bed bath. She wasn't happy about it but the alternative was disgusting. She hadn't wet the bed since she was four and she wasn't starting now.

"Okay, I can live with a T-shirt then." Taylor knew better than to argue on this one.

While the nurse went to see what was delaying the ambulance, Jen helped Taylor change from the hospital gown into the T-shirt.

"I can get you some of these gowns if you'd like to wear them. They're easier to manage." Jen pulled the shirt down over Taylor's head.

"No hospital gowns," Taylor replied stiffly, leaving no doubt about it.

Jen couldn't help but notice Taylor's breasts were firm and round, not at all the breasts of a rough and ready thirty-six-year-old cowgirl, but more the breasts of a twenty-something woman.

"Okay, T-shirts then." Jen smoothed the shirt down Taylor's back and patted her shoulder. "Look at it this way. Think of all the money you will save on summer clothes this year." She offered a small smile.

"I don't buy summer clothes. I wear jeans and shirts." Taylor chuckled. "Can you see me wearing short shorts, a halter top and flip-flops while roping a steer?"

"Um, no. Definitely not you."

The attendants loaded Taylor into the back of the ambulance for the ride home. When they arrived and backed up to the porch, Sylvia came out to greet Taylor and held the door while she was rolled inside. No sooner had Taylor been transferred into the hospital bed than her mother began hovering, adjusting the pillows and sheets while the EMTs attached the sling supports to the bed frame. Taylor tried to help but there was little she could do and it frustrated her. She was moved, positioned, fluffed, supported and covered as if she was a porcelain doll. The ride from the hospital to the house was long and uncomfortable for her. Her legs ached. Her back was sore. She was grumpy. And she was tired of being fussed over. She wanted to throw a saddle over Coal and take a ride, the sun warming her face as she galloped across the range. But that wasn't happening. Instead, she was forced to suffer the indignity of being dressed in a skimpy T-shirt that refused to stay down below her waist while a group of strangers arranged her life to their liking.

Jen checked her blood pressure and pulse as the EMTs finished settling Taylor into bed.

"Deep breath, please," Jen said as she placed the stethoscope on Taylor's chest and listened closely. She checked the position of her legs and adjusted the slings. "Can you move your toes for me?" she asked, feeling the temperature of Taylor's toes where they protruded from the end of the casts.

"Hey," Taylor scowled. "Don't do that."

"Do what? I'm checking your toes for signs of blood restriction. I need to make sure the casts haven't gotten too tight from swelling." She touched the toes on her other foot.

"I told you, don't do that," Taylor yelled, grabbing the trapeze bar over her head.

"Do your toes hurt? Are you in pain when I touch them?" Jen touched them again.

"No, damn it. Stop." Taylor said, gnashing your teeth.

Jen assumed they would have a minor problem or two to work out but this simple act of touching her seemed to infuriate Taylor, something Jen didn't expect.

"I'm sorry, Ms. Fleming but I am going to have to be allowed to touch you if I am going to take care of you," Jen replied sharply.

Sylvia smiled at Jen.

"Taylor is very ticklish on her feet, honey. She always has been." She patted Jen's arm as if to make her point and stop Taylor's torture.

"Oh. I'm sorry." Jen smiled. "Then we know you have good circulation, right?"

"My circulation is just fine, thank you. Now leave my feet alone." Taylor held tight to the bar and leered at Jen until she moved away from the foot of the bed.

"I'll remember that," Jen replied as she made notes on a clipboard. "Okay," she said, setting the clipboard aside. "I need to check for bedsores."

"I don't have any."

"I didn't say you did. But I have to check and show proof you were delivered to home care without any. The EMTs will be witness to my findings."

"Swell," Taylor scoffed.

"Can you pull yourself up with the bar so I can see your back?"

Taylor did as requested, holding her back off the bed while Jen examined her.

"Good. You can lay back now. I need to check your bottom."

"Why?"

"Because I do," Jen replied with the same tenacity Taylor displayed.

"My bottom is fine. If I had any bedsores, the nurse who gave me a bath this morning would have said something."

"I have to look anyway." Jen placed her hands under Taylor's hips, poised to roll her over when Taylor was ready to cooperate.

"I'm tired. I need a nap," Taylor replied, pulling the sheet up around her shoulders.

"That's fine. You'll be able to take a nap in just a few minutes, Ms. Fleming. But first I need to check your bottom. Now please roll to the side for me." Jen kept her hands cradled under Taylor's hip, ready to help.

"Come on, honey," Sylvia said, trying to offer assistance. "You can do it. We'll help you."

"Why not?" Taylor scoffed. "My privacy is shot to hell anyway." She grabbed the bed rail and pulled herself onto her side, exposing her bottom for examination. "Have at it, everyone."

"Thank you. You can roll back now," Jen replied.

"Are you sure you don't want to take pictures for posterity?" Taylor asked, still holding herself on her side.

"No. That won't be necessary. You don't have any sores. But believe me, Ms. Fleming, if you did I'd be documenting them with photographs." Jen eased her onto her back.

"You aren't taking pictures of *my* bottom."

"I'm not taking the blame for someone else's negligent nursing care either." Jen signed the release form and thanked the EMTs for their help then escorted them to the back door.

"Good luck, miss," one of the EMTs said, chuckling softly. He tossed his glance toward the bedroom. "You're going to need it," he whispered.

"Thank you, gentlemen," Jen said, ignoring his comment.

When she returned to the bedroom, Sylvia was going around the bed, tucking in the sheet and arranging the medical equipment as if it were furniture out of place. Jen smiled to herself and didn't say anything. She knew Sylvia was only trying to help. She didn't know the lift needed to be accessible from the middle of the bed, not the far corner of the room. And the commode didn't need to be near the bathroom door. It would only serve its purpose when Taylor was able to get out of bed with help and that wouldn't be for a few days.

"Mom, will you stop fussing?" Taylor said as her mother took her second trip around the bed, tucking and smoothing.

"I want to help, honey. Ms. Holland can't do it all."

"Please, call me Jen, Mrs. Fleming," Jen said warmly. "And I am capable of doing everything Taylor needs. You can depend on it."

"And you are to call me Sylvia," she replied, smiling back at Jen. "I know you can do it, Jen. I never doubted it for a minute. Do you think I'd leave my baby with you if I didn't think she was in good hands?" Sylvia patted Taylor's face and finger-combed her hair again.

"Mom, go home. I'm all tucked in. Your work here is done. I bet you've been here cleaning and arranging things since the sun came up. You need to go home and rest." Taylor squeezed her mother's hand. "Call me later and I'll let you know what kind of pie you can make me."

"How did you know I was going to make you a pie? Did your father tell you?" Sylvia wrinkled her forehead, irritated her secret was out.

"No, Mom. No one told me, but what did you make when Lexie broke her arm last year? And what did you make when Cesar's granddaughter had her appendix out last month? Face it, Mom. You bake pies instead of sending greeting cards. You could single-handedly put Hallmark out of business."

"Well, I have half a mind not to make you one," she mused, feigning anger.

"Pecan, Mom. Or banana cream. Your choice." Taylor gave her mother a wink.

It was the first time Jen had seen Taylor's brighter side and she noticed it brought a sparkle to her eyes and dimples to her cheeks.

"Oh, pecan. That sounds good. I bet your father would like one of those too." Sylvia picked up her purse and headed for the door, wrestling with the decision of which pie make. "Do you like pecan pie, Jen?" she asked from the doorway.

"You don't have to make anything for me, Mrs. Fleming, but thank you."

"It's Sylvia and do you like pecan pie, dear?" she asked in a serious tone.

"You better answer or she'll never leave," Taylor offered.

"Yes, ma'am. I love pecan pie," Jen replied.

"And banana cream?" Sylvia added.

"Um," Jen said hesitantly, not wanting to sound disagreeable.

"Coconut cream?"

"Yes, coconut cream." Jen smiled broadly.

"I'll have Cesar drop off two pies in the morning," she called as she strode out, slamming the screen door as she left.

"Thank you, Mrs. Fleming," Jen called after her. "Sylvia," she corrected.

"She'll make all three. You watch," Taylor declared, holding onto the bar and shifting her weight.

"Why would she make three pies for the two of us?"

"Because that is what she can do. She can't help take care of me. Her back won't let her. She had surgery on it twice. But baking is something she can still do. So, when she wants to help someone, she cooks. When my cousin accidentally shot himself in the foot last year she sent a four-course meal to the house then made his favorite dessert every day for a week. He gained ten pounds."

"I can understand her wanting to help and making pies, but three?"

"She'll have half of each one wrapped in freezer paper. You watch." Taylor heaved a sigh and stretched her shoulders.

"Are you stiff?" Jen asked, noticing her grimace.

"No. I'm fine."

"Uh-huh." Jen was looking over the list of orders from the doctor. "I know I'd be stiff if I was laid up with my legs in casts."

"I'm fine, Ms. Holland. Don't patronize me."

"I'm not patronizing you. I was just suggesting it wasn't uncommon for someone in your situation to feel confined and stiff."

"My situation? You mean trussed up like a Thanksgiving turkey?"

Jen chuckled then continued reading the papers.

"By the way, please call me Jen. According to these orders, you didn't have your LMWH this morning."

"What the heck is LWMH?" Taylor asked.

"LMWH," Jen corrected as she checked all the papers. "Low molecular weight Heparin."

"You mean the shot?"

"Yes," Jen replied, looking up at Taylor to see how this would be accepted.

"Maybe the doctor decided I don't need it. I'm pretty healthy."

"It isn't about being healthy. It's about keeping blood clots from forming, especially in the leg you had surgery on. Inactivity makes you a prime candidate for that kind of thing. Here it is," she pointed to the note on the page. "They thought you'd be home by noon and I am to give you the a.m. shot as soon as you get settled. I'll be right back."

"Oh, boy," Taylor said, "I can hardly wait."

Jen returned with a small plastic tray, an alcohol swab and a disposable syringe already filled with medicine. She went into the bathroom and washed her hands then slipped on a pair of disposable gloves.

"This works best injected into the fatty tissue on your tummy," Jen said, opening the swab.

Taylor had already raised her shirt. There were several puncture wounds in her abdomen.

"Keep in mind I'm rating the nurses who stab me," Taylor advised, watching Jen get things ready. "So far I have had one spear chucker, an ice fisherman and several dart throwers." She leaned her head back and waited.

Jen wiped the area and administered the injection with a quick sure stroke.

"Ouch," Taylor yelled, flexing her muscles.

"Don't tense up like that."

"Let me stab you with an ice pick and see if you tense up," Taylor frowned as she lowered her shirt and rubbed her stomach.

"Are we going to have this each time I have to give you a shot?" Jen asked, cocking an eyebrow at her.

"Yes, we are, especially if you are planning on having the needle come out the back of my shirt."

"Ms. Fleming, are you a big baby?"

"I beg your pardon. I'm not a big baby. But you stab, I complain."

Jen tossed the syringe and the gloves in the trash as she rolled her eyes at Taylor.

"Well, at least we got you home without complaints," Jen muttered as she went into the kitchen to start lunch.

Chapter 9

Sylvia visited or called every day, bringing something as her way of helping. Sometimes it was a pie, sometimes a salad, sometimes an artfully arranged relish tray full of the healthy things Jen told her Taylor should have. Lexie checked on Coal and the heifers Taylor had in her corral. Grier came to keep Taylor up on the news and problems of the ranch. Jen knew he wanted to comment on how much easier it was not to have Rowdy's vandalism but she was grateful Grier showed restraint. He did ask how Rowdy was doing in the nursing home and Jen assumed he was genuinely interested. But since the nursing home requested she allow her father some time to adjust, she didn't have much to offer. As far as Jen knew, Rowdy was eating well, socializing with the other residents and not giving the staff any problems. For that she was thankful. She did look forward to visiting him, hoping they could have a nice conversation even if it was brief.

Rowdy wasn't much for small talk but she was anxious to show him the sketches she was working on and hoped he would show some interest in her work.

Taylor was happy to be home but being cooped up in a bed wasn't what she had in mind when it came to regaining her freedom. Dr. Potter was right. Moody was an accurate description of Taylor. Some days she was more cranky than moody. Jen had moved a portable television into the room but Taylor spent most of the day flipping through the stations, making fun of the ridiculous choices for daytime viewing.

Jen made a chef salad for their lunch, encouraging Taylor to eat a balance of vegetables and protein, something the doctor insisted she do.

"You need to eat all the veggies," Jen said, coming to collect Taylor's tray. "The doctor was very adamant about that. Your body can't heal correctly if you don't eat well."

Taylor picked a carrot out of the bowl and popped it in her mouth.

"Okay. I did," she said, going back to skipping through the stations.

"You didn't eat half of your lunch."

"And I didn't do anything to make me hungry either. It isn't very strenuous just lying here."

"But—" Jen started.

"I don't want it." Taylor gave a decisive stare.

"Okay." Jen didn't feel like arguing about it. "Do you need anything for pain?"

"No." Taylor kept her attention on the screen.

"Call me if you need anything." Jen carried the tray to the kitchen.

Within a few minutes Taylor drifted off to sleep, still holding the remote. Her body still required an occasional nap, something Taylor seldom did during her busy days. When Jen came to check on her, she carefully removed the remote from her hand

and pulled the sheet up around her shoulders. It was a hot out-side but with the air-conditioning on in the house, she didn't want Taylor to get chilled.

She went back to planning a week's worth of meals and check-ing what she would need at the grocery store. Sylvia had offered to shop for her since she had to go to the store herself. The freezer was full of beef, no doubt prime, aged and tender, but Jen intended on adding chicken, fish and other healthy dishes to the menu. She wasn't a gourmet chef but she could hold her own when it came to creative and tasty meals without breaking the budget. Jen also noticed the refrigerator was full of pop and even some beer. Jen was just waiting for Taylor to demand a beer with her lunch. The doctor had said no alcohol and limited amounts of soft drinks. Lots of milk, water and fruit juice were his recom-mendations. Jen had a feeling this was going to be a problem.

Jen had gone upstairs to put away a load of laundry when she heard a scream and Taylor cursing. She ran down the stairs and into her room.

"What's wrong?" Jen yelled, her eyes as big as plates. "Are you all right?"

"*What* is that?" Taylor demanded, staring at the black furry lump lying on the valley between her knees.

Jen came to the bed and looked.

"Picasso, what are you doing in here?" Jen stroked the black cat and picked it up, hugging it lovingly. "You are supposed to stay in the mudroom."

"You brought your cat?" Taylor grumbled, glaring at the animal.

"Yes," Jen held the cat in her arms like a baby, scratching its tummy.

"Don't you think you should have asked first? I don't like cats."

"I did ask. If you'll remember I asked if you had any allergies or were opposed to domesticated animals," Jen replied, refreshing Taylor's memory.

"I don't remember that."

"I most certainly did. It was the day we discussed where to put the hospital bed. And you said so long as you didn't have to take care of them you didn't care what animals I had, so long as it wasn't a skunk."

"Cats are finicky. I don't like them. You can't train them to do anything."

"You can too train them." Picasso was purring so loud Jen had to raise her voice to be heard. "Picasso can do a trick."

"What?"

"Well it isn't really a trick. But he sleeps in the sun spots," Jen announced.

"Sun spots?"

"Yes, you know. When the sun shines in between the blinds or curtains and makes a spot on the floor, he sleeps in those. That's probably why he was on your bed. See the light coming through the window?"

"Well, un-train him."

"I'll put him in the mudroom."

"Why not put him outside? That's where cats belong."

"I would but this house is new to him so I'm letting him get used to it first. I don't want him running off and getting lost." Jen headed out the door with the cat.

"That would be a real shame," Taylor muttered sarcastically.

"I heard that. He won't be any trouble. He never has accidents in the house and he has been fixed so he is always a gentleman. And I couldn't very well leave him in San Antonio alone, could I?"

"Is this the only domesticated animal you have?"

"Yes. Picasso is a black Persian. You won't even know he's here."

"Too late. I already know," Taylor muttered to herself, trying to go back to sleep.

It took a few days before Jen and Taylor got used to the routine and each other. Taylor had trouble asking for help with the bedpan but Jen reassured her it was just part of life and no big deal. Embarrassing Taylor was the last thing Jen wanted to do. After several days of boredom, Taylor began to look for things she could do in the confines of her bed. She polished her boots, repaired the toaster, helped peel potatoes, balanced her checkbook, read about the history of Appaloosa horses, tinkered with the laptop computer, made lists of things she would do the minute the casts were off and harped on why she couldn't get out of bed yet. Finally the doctor approved orders that allowed her to be out of bed and in a wheelchair for a few hours at a time. With the help of the lift, Jen was able to transfer Taylor into the wheelchair for rides around the living room and dining room, her cast-covered legs sticking out like cannons on a colonial frigate. The first thing Taylor wanted to see was the corral and Coal. She settled for watching him from the window as he pranced around the corral. The wheelchair wasn't as comfortable as being in bed but Taylor didn't dare say anything about it for fear that bit of freedom might be taken away.

"If we could get the lift into the living room, couldn't I be on the couch for part of the day instead of in bed?" Taylor asked, rolling herself through the living room.

"We can try it but only if it gives you enough support. We don't want any pressure on your legs. I can prop a bunch of pillows under the casts."

"I can't spend all my time in that bed," Taylor explained, not doing a very good job of hiding her growing frustration.

Jen understood how difficult it was for Taylor to spend hour after hour in a hospital bed staring at the ceiling.

"Just a minute. Let me move the furniture so I can get the lift in here then I'll help you onto the couch."

Taylor rolled her wheelchair back out of the way and watched as Jen rearranged the furniture. It aggravated her not to be able to help. She never had to rely on someone else to do the lifting and moving. She was a self-reliant woman who could do that for herself, that is until now. She wanted to be out of the bed but she didn't want to make heavy work for Jen. For a brief moment she wished she hadn't mentioned it.

"Okay, let's try this," Jen said.

"I'm ready." Taylor removed the armrests and tossed them aside, anxious for this to happen. Jen maneuvered the lift into position and transferred her from the wheelchair to the couch. With carefully placed pillows supporting her head, back and the huge casts, Taylor settled into the cushions.

"Do you need anything? Are you comfortable?"

"I'm fine. No, wait. Can you bring me the green tote bag hanging on the hook in the mudroom, please? It's the flat one with the horse on it." Taylor asked as she adjusted the pillow behind her head.

"Okay," Jen replied, moving the lift out of the way. She returned with the bag and set it on the floor next to the couch. "Here's the remote," she added, placing it on Taylor's lap. "Call me if you need something." Jen went into the kitchen, leaving Taylor to her new location.

Taylor was already digging in the tote bag, her eyes bright and eager as she brought out a coiled leather lariat. It was dirty and well worn but she was excited to have the feel of it in her hands. She adjusted the loop and was tempted to circle it over her head but realized the lamp and vase of flowers Jen had placed on the table would be in her direct line of fire. She flipped the loop over her feet, playing with it happily, lassoing first one foot then the other. Picasso came to watch. He jumped up on the coffee table and sat on his haunches, inspecting each toss and deciding if he should attack the rope.

"Hey, Angus. Maybe you could run across the room and I could practice lassoing you," Taylor said, eyeing the cat.

"I don't think so," Jen said with a scowl, returning to the

living room with the blood pressure cuff and Taylor's chart. "Do we have to have that smelly old rope in the living room? I'm sure it isn't sanitary," Jen said, waving Picasso off the table.

"Smelly old rope?" Taylor replied with dismay. "This is not a smelly old rope. This is a hand-braided leather lariat made in Brazil. This old rope is worth more than this couch."

"Good for it," Jen stated, unwrapping the cuff.

"Do you know how these are made, Ms. Holland?"

"No." She held Taylor's arm under hers and secured the Velcro wrap around her bicep.

"It takes weeks to make one. They have to cut and stretch the strips of leather then braid it then stretch it again. After all that they bury it for a couple weeks to age the leather. Then it's stretched one last time. This is a work of art. It's crafted by masters. You should appreciate that," Taylor added as Jen hooked the stethoscope in her ears and pumped up the cuff.

"Shh," Jen said, listening intently.

"What's the matter? I thought you liked western art," Taylor argued.

"Hush. I'm trying to get a reading. If you don't stop talking I can't hear." She frowned at Taylor and took the blood pressure again.

"Fine," Taylor replied and heaved a sigh. "I don't need my blood pressure taken every two seconds anyway," she muttered.

Jen scowled up at her and continued pumping the bulb, squeezing the cuff even tighter.

"Ouch," Taylor yelled.

"Now will you hush?"

Taylor closed her eyes in surrender. When Jen finished taking her blood pressure, she took Taylor's pulse, temperature and noticed her respiration. She recorded the vitals on the chart then checked Taylor's toes for color and mobility.

"There. All finished," Jen said. "Now you can talk."

"I don't have anything to say," Taylor grumbled, pushing her arms into the couch to raise herself to a sitting position.

"Here. Let me help you," Jen said, coming to her side.

"I can do it," Taylor groaned as she scooted her bottom backward to the end of the couch.

"I know you can, but—" Jen's arms were out and ready to offer aid. Taylor's hand suddenly slid off the edge of the couch. Jen caught her just as she was about to fall over the side and onto the floor. "I've got you," she said reassuringly. Taylor grabbed onto Jen's shoulders for support. Jen wrapped her arms around Taylor and pushed her back onto the couch. "You okay?" she asked anxiously.

"My leg is falling and I can't stop it," Taylor said, frantically reaching for the cast.

"I've got it. I've got it." Jen caught her leg just as it was about to hit the floor. She cradled it in her arms and gently placed it back on the pillow. "There," she said through a relieved sigh. "Now when I say let me help maybe you'll listen."

Taylor didn't say anything. She didn't want to admit she couldn't do even the simplest task for herself.

"We need one of those bed rails they put on the side of the bed for toddlers. The ones that keep them from rolling off at night." Jen was talking and adjusting the pillows under Taylor's legs. She didn't notice Taylor's scowl. "They slide right under the mattress," Jen continued. She glanced up at Taylor and saw her frown. "What? Are you all right?"

"I am *not* a toddler. I don't need to be kept from rolling out of bed." Taylor stared at her angrily. "I just lost my balance. I could have caught myself."

"You would have been on the floor if I hadn't caught you," Jen replied, glowering right back at her. "Your stubborn pride is going to land you right back in the hospital if you don't give in and let me help you. That is what I am here for. If you fall and rip those screws loose, you'll be back in surgery and another week in the hospital before you know what happened." Jen stood up and placed her hands on her hips. "And I have news for you, Ms. Fleming. This is my job and I know the phone number for the ambulance department. I'm telling you right now, you even breathe funny and I'm on the phone to them. So don't push it."

"I am not a toddler," Taylor repeated. She knew Jen was right. As a hired nurse's aide, she was in complete control and it made Taylor furious. She may have to give in to her but she certainly didn't have to like it.

"All right, you're not a toddler. I'm sorry." Jen collected the chart and supplies. "Do you want apple juice or milk?" Jen asked, replacing the equipment in the pouch.

"Neither. How about a—"

"Don't say Coke," Jen interrupted. "You need some nutrition and that isn't it."

Taylor wrinkled her brow and crossed her arms. "What makes you think I was going to say that?"

Jen gave a cockeyed smile and headed for the kitchen.

"Juice?" she repeated.

"NO."

"Suit yourself."

"Iced tea," Taylor called.

A minute later Jen returned with a frosty glass and handed it to Taylor. There was a sprig of mint and a wedge of lemon on the rim of the glass. Taylor took a long drink then immediately frowned up at Jen.

"Hey, this isn't iced tea. It's apple juice." She made a ghastly face.

"It won't kill you." Jen turned back for the kitchen.

"I'd still rather have iced tea."

"Water is better for you than all that caffeine," Jen replied without looking back.

"What about a cold beer with lunch?"

"In a couple months you can have one," Jen shot over her shoulder and kept walking.

"Can't you forget you're a nurse for a minute? What about sympathy for the patient?"

Jen turned around and strode back to the couch. She stared down at Taylor authoritatively.

"Letting you have pop, beer and junk food isn't sympathy. I don't care what you eat or drink, Ms. Fleming. When your legs heal you can have beer and pretzels for breakfast for all I care. But while I am responsible for your recovery you will eat what the doctor recommends and you will drink what I provide. Alcohol doesn't mix with your medicine and your bones won't heal properly without adequate vitamins and protein in your diet. But I think you already knew that. If you don't like it, the phone is behind you and the number for the skilled nursing unit is on the pad. And I'm sure they have a nice room for you with a lovely view of the picnic table. Now shut up and drink your apple juice."

Jen took a deep breath, squared her shoulders and returned to the kitchen. Taylor raised her eyebrows but didn't say anything. She knew she had been chastised. She took another sip from the glass, having forgotten it was juice. She made a face but the taste wasn't as bad as she thought it would be. She sipped again.

"I suppose a fifth of Jack Daniels is out of the question?" Taylor yelled, trying to get in the last word.

The kitchen door slammed shut.

"I guess it is," she muttered, taking a long drink of juice.

A minute later the kitchen door opened again.

"You've got company coming up the drive," Jen announced.

"Who?"

"It's a white pickup truck with chrome bed rails."

"Dad," Taylor said.

"There's somebody with him."

"Mom?"

"I don't think so. I can see two hats in the cab," Jen replied. She went to the dining room window and watched as the truck pulled up to the back porch. "It's Lexie."

"She's probably going to check the heifers." Taylor tried to see out the window but she didn't have a view from the couch.

"Your dad is carrying a box of ledger books." Jen went to the back door to greet them.

"Good." Taylor sat up as straight as she could manage and secured the sheet over her lap, anxious to do some ranch business even if it was from a reclining position. "Hey, Dad," she said brightly. "What's up?"

"Are you feeling up to looking over some figures with me?" Grier set the box on the coffee table and tossed his hat on the chair.

"You bet. Let's see what you've got," Taylor replied, grabbing one of the books from the box.

"A-One and T-bone are above last year's numbers. Tolerance and Viking sired pretty well but Shiloh and Captain Jack are down, especially Jack." He pulled up a chair and looked over Taylor's shoulder as she reviewed the columns of figures.

"If he's not producing we can't afford to keep him out there." Taylor and Grier were engrossed in ranch talk. Jen had overheard some of it before but she didn't understand it. Rowdy had never explained much of the cattle business to her, saying it was a man's job. Jen made Grier a glass of iced tea then made one for Lexie and headed to the corral.

"Lexie, how about some iced tea?" Jen called, holding the glass over the top of the fence.

"Sure," Lexie replied, rubbing her gloved hand across her forehead. She gulped down the glass and handed it back. "Thanks."

"You're welcome." Jen watched as Lexie walked among the cows, their middles wide with calf. "What are you looking for?"

"These eight haven't had their first babies yet. They're a little overdue so we want to keep an eye on them. Hey, there's a new one." Lexie grinned as she stared into the open-sided shed at the far side of the pen. In the back corner of the shed, blocked by its mother, a wobbly-legged black calf stood nursing from its mother's swollen teat. The calf was still shiny and moist from its birth. Lexie squatted down and peered into the shed, not wanting to get too close and scare the baby away from its first meal.

"Where?" Jen asked, trying to see.

"In the back," Lexie said, pointing between the cows. "Come around to this side."

Jen moved to the other side of the corral and jockeyed for a view into the shed.

"Oh, Lexie, look at her. Isn't she cute?" Jen hung her arms over the top of the fence and watched as the baby balanced on new legs and suckled.

"That isn't a she. It's a he, a baby bull and he isn't cute. He's prime Black Angus beef. That little fellow is money in the bank." Lexie's critical eye was sizing up the calf for quality and weight.

"Well, he may be but he's still cute," Jen teased, smiling warmly at the baby.

"Don't let Taylor hear you say that. She says they aren't cute, they're just mini-steak burgers." Lexie laughed.

"You and Taylor have to learn to soften up. Baby animals are all cute."

"Not all of them. Baby rattlesnakes are still rattlesnakes."

"True," Jen agreed, wrinkling her nose.

"Maybe we'll have a couple more of these heifers give birth by tomorrow."

"Please don't ask me to help deliver cows," Jen mused. "Taking care of Taylor is enough."

"I bet that's right. She isn't exactly cooperating, is she?"

Jen just smiled.

"Taylor isn't very good at watching the world go by," Lexie added with a cockeyed grin. "Telling her she can't do something will make her madder than a bull with two cinch straps."

"I noticed that."

"Is she giving you the business?"

"Not really. She's just having a little trouble accepting that she can't do everything she wants to right now." Jen wondered how much Lexie really knew about Taylor.

"Hang in there," Lexie said, settling her hat back on her head. She looked over at Jen. "Taylor has trouble asking for help. She's just afraid."

"Afraid of what?" Jen asked skeptically. "I don't think that woman is afraid of anything."

"She's afraid of losing control."

"Ah, I'll remember that."

"I think she trusts you. She'd never let you take care of her if she didn't."

"Sometimes I'm not so sure," Jen admitted carefully.

"You call me if she gives you any trouble," Lexie added, coming through the gate and latching it behind her.

"Then she'll listen to you?" Jen asked.

"No. But maybe the two of us can hold her down." Lexie patted Jen on the back, offering support for the task ahead of her.

"You all set, Lexie?" Grier called, loading the box into the truck.

"Yep," she replied, climbing in the cab.

"Call me if you need anything, Jen," Grier said, his eyes full of concern for his daughter. He shook Jen's hand then slid in the cab and slammed the door.

"Thanks," Jen said, smiling at them. "Taylor will be fine, really. Don't worry about her. I'll take good care of her."

Grier tipped his hat, a gesture Jen read as his confidence in her ability. Lexie did the same, adding a small smile.

"Remember what I told you, Jen," Lexie said.

Jen waved then went inside. She couldn't decide if Lexie's advice shed new light on Taylor's gruff behavior and brash language but Lexie had Taylor pegged pretty well. She was definitely one woman who didn't like to ask for help.

The next morning, like every morning, Jen brought a basin of water into the bedroom for Taylor to wash herself. Jen washed her back but Taylor insisted she could do the rest. She was tired of feeling like a piece of glass. She was also tired of having to ask Jen for everything she needed, from a glass of water to using the commode.

"Since I am able to be up and in the wheelchair part of the time, I want to take my own bath," Taylor announced.

"You do, mostly." Jen checked the temperature of the water and placed the clean towel and washcloth on the edge of the bed.

"No. I want to go in the bathroom and take a bath."

"You know you can't get your casts wet."

"But I could sit in the wheelchair and wash. I could actually run the hot water myself and brush my teeth in the sink instead of spitting in a cup. This bed bath routine is getting old."

"Okay, we can do that." Jen saw no reason why Taylor couldn't at least use the sink. Picasso had wandered into Taylor's room and sat on the floor, washing his face.

"Too bad I can't just wash like Angus does," Taylor mused.

"His name is Picasso and yes that would be an asset, I guess." Jen pushed Picasso toward the door with her foot. "You go on out and leave Taylor alone," she said, giving him a stern look. Instead of leaving the room, the cat walked between Jen's legs and jumped up on the bed before she could stop him. He stuck his nose in the basin of water, taking a tentative lick.

"Picasso, get down," Jen scoffed.

"Don't you give him anything to drink?" Taylor asked, watching the cat lap up the warm water.

"He has a dish of water in the mudroom next to his food."

Taylor grabbed Jen's hand to stop her from taking him down.

"He's thirsty. Leave him alone," she demanded. "I bet his water dish is empty."

"I just filled it."

"Is it cold water? Some animals don't like cold water."

"Picasso has never turned his nose up at fresh cold tap water before." Jen propped a hand on her hip. "He's just curious. He's also a bit stubborn, like a certain other person I could name. Picasso knows he isn't supposed to be in here."

"I bet he drinks toilet water," Taylor said, eyeing the cat as he continued to take occasional licks from the basin.

"That's gross." Jen wrinkled her nose. "My cat does *not* drink toilet water. What do you think toilet lids are for?"

"That's enough, Angus. You'll bloat." Taylor flicked her finger in the water, splashing a few drops in the cat's face.

"His name is not Angus. It's Picasso."

"He doesn't look like a Picasso. He looks like a Black Angus."

"He has long hair," Jen argued. "Angus cattle have short hair."

"Pablo Picasso was bald."

"Only when he was older." Jen was surprised Taylor knew anything about Pablo Picasso.

The cat carefully walked the length of the bed, sniffing and inspecting Taylor's casts. He jumped over one leg and sat between her feet, continuing with his bath. Taylor wouldn't let Jen remove him, saying she wanted to see who would finish their bath first, the cat with his rough tongue or Taylor with her rough washcloth. It was a tie. As soon as Taylor finished washing and rinsing, the cat stopped as well. He curled himself into a ball and settled in for a nap.

"Tomorrow we'll try using the sink for your bath, if you still want to," Jen advised, coming to take away the basin of water. "I'll be back to get Picasso in a minute."

"Naw. Leave him. Gives me something to aggravate."

"You leave him alone or no wheelchair time for you." Jen smiled at Taylor, pleased she had at least accepted the cat and was ready for some good-natured teasing.

The next morning Jen positioned Taylor's wheelchair next to the sink, just as she wanted.

120

"Do you need any help?" Jen asked, running a sink of water and testing the temperature.

"I've got it," Taylor replied, removing the armrests on the wheelchair. She had accepted help from the nurses at the hospital, her mother and from Jen to do even the simplest task. Today she was going to wash herself in her own bathroom. It was a small triumph for independence but a triumph nonetheless. "You can go have a cup of coffee or read the paper or something. I can do this by myself." She waved Jen out.

"Are you sure?" Jen looked like a mother bird afraid her baby would crash on its first flight from the nest. "I can sit on the side of the tub in case you need me."

"Nope. I can do this. Where's my toothpaste?"

"Right here." Jen set it next to the toothbrush. "Here's a glass if you need it," she added, straightening everything so it was in perfect position. "Anything else?"

Taylor rolled herself backward and held the door open.

"Yes. You, out."

Taylor pointed and closed the door after Jen reluctantly left. After only a few minutes Jen was back at the door, knocking softly.

"How's it going? Anything I can do? Do you need me to do your back?"

"Nope." Taylor had washed her arms and face and was working on her chest. She was dripping all over the floor, splashing soapy water on everything from the mirror to the ceiling but she was doing it without help. She hummed "The Eyes of Texas Are Upon You" as she washed her crotch then each side of her bottom, tipping from side to side, her heavy casts making it difficult to reach. She dipped the towel in the sink and rung it out then used it like a wet rope to wash her back, pulling it back and forth. She finished by brushing her teeth and combing her hair. She pulled a clean shirt over her head and placed a clean towel over her lap for modesty before replacing the arm rests. Her arms were heavy and she was exhausted from the bath but she was also proud of her newfound independence. She rolled herself to the door and opened it to find Jen waiting just outside.

"How did it go?" Jen asked, maneuvering the wheelchair out of the bathroom.

"Fine. There's nothing to this bathing thing," Taylor replied proudly.

"Uh-huh," Jen said, noticing the wet floor and the pile of sopping wet towels in the corner. "I see that."

"I can almost take care of myself, don't you think?" Taylor sounded dead serious, like a child who had run through a sprinkler on a hot summer day and assumed she was ready to join the Olympic swim team.

"Come on Wonder Woman. It's time for your shot," Jen said, smiling to herself.

Chapter 10

A week had passed and Taylor still fought with the couch cushions and pillows to find a comfortable position. Either her body was two inches too long or the couch was shrinking. She always found it a perfect fit before, flopping down on it after a hard day's work. But since she broke her legs nothing felt comfortable. The casts refused to give even a fraction of an inch so she was left to make do with a dull ache in her stiff legs, a sore back and a perpetual desire to scratch an itch deep beneath the plaster.

"Here, watch something educational," Jen teased, handing Taylor the remote after she got settled on the couch.

"Oh, goodie. I'm just in time to watch Sesame Street." Taylor rolled her eyes.

"Would you like milk and cookies while you watch Sesame Street?" Jen asked as she headed to the kitchen.

"If I watch reruns of *Gunsmoke* do I get a shot of whiskey?"

Jen just shook her head. The front doorbell rang telling Taylor whoever it was didn't know to come to the back door. No one used the front door. Why it was put there was anyone's guess. It was on the opposite side of the house from the driveway, the corral, the kitchen and anything else Taylor found important. The only thing the front door had going for it was the huge cottonwood tree that shaded it nearly year-round.

"I'll get it," Taylor called sarcastically.

"Very funny," Jen quipped, going to answer it. She unlocked the dead bolt and opened the door, her eyes widening. Taylor couldn't see who it was but she could see Jen's smile. "Hi, Kelly. What are you doing here?"

"Hey cutie. How's it cooking?" The voice was strong and deep for a woman.

"I got your message. I'm on my way home from the conference in El Paso so I'd thought I swing by and see if you needed some company. You sure are out in the sticks." Kelly laughed. "Is this even on the map?"

"Come on in," Jen said, holding the door for her. "Come meet Taylor," she added, noticing Taylor watching intently over the back of the couch.

"Hey, Taylor," Kelly called, waving at her. Taylor instantly recognized her as the woman who had accompanied Jen to the Rainbow Desert.

Jen led the way into the living room where Taylor held out her hand to Kelly. Kelly shook it with a strong and dominating grip, something Taylor didn't usually fall victim to.

"Gosh, what happened, Taylor? Horse throw you or something?"

"Trailer accident," Taylor offered but Kelly had already turned her attention back to Jen.

"How long are you going to be out here in no-man's land?" Kelly asked, giving the room a quick scan, noticing the cattle-rustic decor and the leather furniture.

"I'm Taylor's nurse while she recuperates."

"You're really living out here?" Kelly asked in a softer but critical tone.

"Taylor needs round-the-clock care. She can't do much without help."

"Sure, I understand. But do you get time off for good behavior? You know, a night off now and then," she asked, winking at Jen.

"I'm her caregiver, Kelly," Jen replied in a quiet but firm voice. "Come on upstairs. I'll show you some sketches I'm working on for the job in Merrill. I'm going with a historic theme." Jen took Kelly by the arm and led her up the steps.

"Historic?" Kelly asked, wrapping her arm around Jen's shoulder. "That sounds great."

Taylor watched until they disappeared. She leaned out as far as she could without falling off the couch. She muted the sound on the television, straining to hear the conversation from Jen's bedroom but the voices became too soft to hear. She cleared her throat loudly but it had no effect on the women or their upstairs rendezvous. Taylor's curiosity was killing her. She never considered herself the jealous type. After all, it wasn't her place to be jealous. Jen was just her nurse. Besides, what was there to be jealous of? Kelly's eyes were too deep and her lips were too full. She didn't have much of a shape, either, that Taylor could tell right off the bat. Nope, no tits to speak of, she thought. What Jen saw in her was anybody's guess. But Taylor wasn't jealous. She was just curious. She was curious how anyone could take a gorgeous woman like Jen to a nightclub but never dance with her. How could she sit next to Jen, an intelligent, vibrant woman, and spend all her time talking with people across the table? That night Taylor hadn't been able to take her eyes off Jen and she didn't even know her name.

Taylor could hear their voices growing louder as they

descended the stairs.

"Would you like something to drink? Iced tea? Lemonade?" Jen asked, leading Kelly into the living room.

"Sure. Iced tea, two sugars." Kelly was still chuckling at whatever they had been talking about upstairs.

"How about you, Taylor? Juice?" Jen asked.

"Iced tea," Taylor said, testing to see if Jen would allow it. She didn't want to be treated like a child in front of this woman and being offered apple juice would only emphasize that.

"Okay," Jen replied after a slight hesitation. "Sugar?"

"No." Taylor had no idea why she said no. She always took sugar in her tea and her coffee and anything else that would support it. Just because Kelly took sugar didn't mean she couldn't.

"Why don't you visit with Taylor while I make it?" Jen said.

"Come on in, Kelly," Taylor declared, a sarcastic lilt in her voice. "Have a seat. Take a load off."

"I know it sounds funny but you sure look familiar. Have I seen you somewhere before?" Kelly asked, studying Taylor.

"I don't think so." Taylor wasn't going to admit she was the woman causing the nuisance at the Rainbow Desert. "You live in San Antonio?" Taylor asked, determined to drive the conversation in a new direction.

"Yes."

"What do you do in San Antone?"

"I own a bed and breakfast."

"Wow, a B&B. That sounds interesting. What part of town?"

"The King William historical district."

"Nice area. Do you back up to the Riverwalk?"

"No. We're across the street from the Riverwalk."

"We?" Taylor asked.

"I have a business partner. She and I co-own it."

"So she runs it and you run off?" Taylor couldn't refrain from the glib remark.

"I've been in El Paso for an innkeeper's conference."

126

"Here we are," Jen said, carrying a tray of glasses into the living room. Taylor and Kelly both reached for the magazines to clear the coffee table at the same moment, tugging them in opposite directions. Taylor won, tossing them under the table. She patted the table for Jen to place the tray. Jen handed Kelly a glass and a napkin then handed one to Taylor with a straw in it. She spread a towel over Taylor's chest to catch the drips, a gesture Taylor instantly disliked. When Taylor tipped the glass to sip from the straw she dribbled down her neck and onto the towel.

"Would you like to sit up a bit?" Jen asked, blotting up the spill.

"Yeah, I think so. Here, you hold this. I'll do it." Taylor handed Jen the glass and sunk her fists into the couch to pull herself upright.

"Wait. Let me help you," Jen said, setting the glass on the tray.

"I can do it," Taylor insisted.

Jen stood at the end of the couch and locked her arms under Taylor's armpits, ready to pull her back against the end.

"Let me do that, Jen," Kelly said, jumping to her feet. "She's too heavy for you."

Taylor glared up at Kelly, the venom in her eyes hard to hide. Kelly pushed Jen aside and took the same position, grabbing Taylor under the arms and hauling her backward in one easy motion.

"There you go, Taylor. All set," Kelly said, patting her on the head.

"I could have done it," Taylor muttered. "I'm not completely helpless. We folks out here in the sticks can do a few things for ourselves."

Jen just smiled and handed Taylor her glass then repositioned the towel across her lap, only making Taylor's humiliation worse. She had been reduced to being placed on the couch and bibbed while she drank through a straw. Taylor drank the entire glass in one long gulp and replaced it on the table.

"Thanks," she said, sounding like a cowpoke finishing a shot of whiskey at the local saloon.

"So, was it a runaway trailer?" Kelly asked, looking Taylor's casts up and down.

"It rolled down an embankment on me."

"Wow. I bet that hurt. Shouldn't you be in a hospital?"

"I was for a few days."

"If it weren't for Jen, you'd still be in the hospital, right?" Kelly suggested.

"I had to have someone who could administer the injections for me and help me use the equipment."

"Injections? You mean you get shots?" Kelly grimaced.

"Yes. Twice a day," Taylor said, wondering why she was telling this woman so much of her personal business.

Kelly chuckled then reached over and touched Jen's arm.

"So, how does it feel to stab ass?" she asked. "Does Taylor like it?"

"Kelly," Jen said sternly.

"Little medical S&M?" Kelly mused in Taylor's direction.

"To tell the truth, I love it. If my legs weren't broken, I'd break them just to get Jen to stab my ass," Taylor declared.

"That isn't funny," Jen leered at both women.

"Come take a walk with me, Jen," Kelly said, setting her glass on the tray and standing up. "Just for a few minutes."

Taylor looked over at Jen to see if she planned on accepting Kelly's invitation.

"You could manage without her for a little while, couldn't you, Taylor?" Kelly asked, taking Jen's hand and leading her toward the back door.

Taylor wanted to say no. She wanted to cut Kelly off at the knees, telling her Jen was her nurse and she might need her. But she couldn't do that. It was up to Jen to decide if she wanted to

128

go with Kelly.

"I need to talk with Jen about some business details. You don't mind, do you?" Kelly added.

"That's up to Jen," Taylor replied. "I can manage."

"Good," Kelly acknowledged, pulling Jen along.

"We'll be right back," Jen said, looking back apologetically.

"Take your time."

Taylor turned her gaze out the window, straining to see them as they walked across the yard. Kelly had slipped her arm around Jen and rested her hand just below her waist, her thumb hooked inside Jen's jeans. When they walked out of Taylor's view, she was frantic for them to cross in front of the other window. But when they didn't, she leaned as far out as she could, hoping to get another glimpse of them. Taylor leaned forward and back, searching both windows for a view. She wished she could reach the wheelchair so she could roll herself out onto the porch. She lunged at it but it was too far away. She strained again to see out the window. She had to accept Kelly and Jen knew each other and probably well. After all, they had gone to the bar together and had left together. She wondered where else Kelly's hands had touched Jen's body. Had they spent long hours in the moonlight, clinging to each other until their energy was spent and their needs were satisfied. Taylor couldn't see them or hear them but it didn't matter. She was scowling at the way Kelly was probably touching Jen and the way Jen allowed it.

"I can't be gone very long," Jen said as they headed for the pasture gate, Kelly's arm draped around her shoulders. "Taylor might need me."

"She'll be okay for a few minutes. We need to talk."

"About what?"

"What do you think? I can't believe you took this job way out here in this godforsaken place without even asking me."

"It's only for a couple of months. And since when do I ask your permission about a job?" Jen scowled. She wasn't happy with Kelly's question or her domineering arm around her shoulder.

"You don't. I'm sorry. But I thought we had an understanding." Kelly opened the gate and held it for Jen then closed it behind them.

"It's a long story, Kelly. I needed this job and I wanted to be near my dad. He's in a nursing home in Harland."

"I didn't know your dad lived around here. You never mentioned it."

"He was a cattle rancher."

"How is he?" There wasn't much sincerity to Kelly's question.

"Okay, I guess. Now, what did you want to talk about?"

"What do you mean?"

"You told Taylor you had some business details you wanted to discuss with me. What are they?"

Kelly laughed.

"I don't have any business details—how was I going to get you to take a walk with me? What was I supposed to say? Hey, Taylor, is it okay if Jen takes a walk with me so I can kiss her gorgeous lips?" Kelly took Jen in her arms and kissed her. At first Jen allowed it but as the kiss grew longer and more passionate, Jen pushed Kelly away.

"Stop, Kelly," Jen said, looking toward the house to see if anyone could see them.

"Why?" Kelly replied, still holding her in a firm embrace. "No one can see us, unless you count the cows." She kissed Jen again.

"Kelly," Jen protested, leaning away from her persistence.

"You know you drive me crazy when you act mad like that. Come on, sugar. Tell me I'm bad. Tell me you're going to spank me if I don't behave." Kelly kissed Jen's neck hungrily.

"Kelly, please."

"You aren't still angry with me about that night we went to

that hokey western bar, are you? We'll have to find a different place for when you want to go dancing." Kelly nibbled Jen's neck and blew in her ear, making Jen shiver.

"I wasn't mad at you." Jen didn't lie very well.

"Then why did you suddenly get a headache and want to go home alone. I had plans for us," Kelly whispered, not relinquishing her hold on Jen.

Jen struggled free and headed across the pasture with long strides.

"You were mad at me," Kelly declared. "Why? Because I wouldn't dance with you?"

Jen frowned back at her.

"Don't be silly. I know you don't like to dance."

"Was I supposed to be jealous when you danced with that other woman? Is that what you want from me? Am I supposed to be possessive?"

Jen narrowed her eyes at Kelly. "No one is possessive of me unless I say so, Kelly. And no, I didn't want you to be jealous. All I wanted from you was a little common courtesy." Jen continued across the field.

"Common courtesy? What the heck does that mean? When haven't I been polite to you?" Kelly followed, grabbing Jen by the arm and turning her around.

"That hurts," Jen replied, pulling her arm out of Kelly's grip.

"Talk to me. Tell me what is happening between us."

"What do you think is happening between us?"

"Don't give me that psychological bullshit. Just tell me why you took a job on a ranch in the middle of nowhere without a word of explanation? How am I supposed to know what to think? I thought we had straightened out our problems. I know I did some stupid things but I thought we had gotten back on track. My God, Jen. We've known each other for fifteen years. How can you just move out here and not tell me?"

"I explained. It is only temporary and I needed the job." Jen stared at Kelly to see if she was the least bit curious as to why she needed the job so desperately.

"That doesn't explain why you didn't tell me why you came out here. Don't I have a right to know? All your message said was where you were."

Jen didn't reply. She just shook her head disgustedly.

"When did you plan on telling me?" Kelly continued.

"Okay. Here. Kelly, I'm working as a CSN on a ranch near Harland, Texas, caring for a woman with two broken legs. I'll be here for eight to twelve weeks. I need the job and what's more, I like what I am doing. I'm helping someone who needs me. Taylor trusts me. She accepts me for who I am. She doesn't want to change me."

"She's your patient. She has to trust you."

"Like always, you only hear what you want to hear." Jen chuckled.

"What does that mean?" Kelly snapped.

"Nothing."

"Does this have anything to do with me and Donna?"

Jen didn't answer at first. She wanted to tell Kelly no, her past indiscretions had nothing to do with their present problems. Jen had suspected Kelly hadn't been faithful to their six-year off-again, on-again relationship from the beginning, but she didn't confront her with her fears until she inadvertently overheard a phone message from Donna. Jen also suspected Kelly was once again seeing the woman on the sly. But Jen didn't want to stomp those grapes again. Their tumultuous six years had drained her of any expectations they could ever find long-term happiness.

"It isn't like you to be so unforgiving, Jen. We talked about this. You know Donna didn't mean anything to me. It was just one of those things that happens."

"That's what I thought the first time," Jen snipped.

"It's behind us, sugar." Kelly smiled affectionately.

"Behind? Every time I think it is behind us, it bites me in the rear."

"It's that woman in there, isn't it?" Kelly barked, pointing toward the house. "You like her, don't you?"

"You leave Taylor out of this. This has nothing to do with her."

"The heck it doesn't. I can see it in your eyes. That's why you didn't tell me about taking this job. You've got it made out here. No one to bother you. You and the cowgirl can have a high old time. You didn't think I'd find out." Kelly grabbed Jen and turned her around. "You've been doing the invalid, haven't you? She lays in the bed and you take care of business for her."

"Let go of me," she demanded, glaring at Kelly.

"You have. Good old Jen, the nurse, gets off on sick people."

Jen pulled away and ran toward the house.

"Jen, wait," Kelly called, chasing her down. "I'm sorry. I didn't mean that." She caught up with Jen behind the barn and trapped her against the wall.

"Let me go, Kelly," Jen gasped, struggling to free herself.

"Jen, baby. Let me explain. I was so worried about you. I was frantic to know what happened. I can't stand it when we're like this." Kelly leaned her body against Jen, pressing a hard kiss onto her mouth, a kiss that hurt Jen's lips. Jen tried to escape Kelly's hold on her but it was no use. She was no match for Kelly's strong arms and tall stature. Kelly plunged her tongue into Jen's mouth as she groped her body. Jen tugged at the back of Kelly's shirt to pull her away but Kelly was like a wild animal. She forced a hand down Jen's jeans, scratching and clawing at her soft skin. Jen moaned, trying to scream, but Kelly's mouth covered hers. Jen gouged her nails into Kelly's shoulders but it only incited her more. Jen reached up and grabbed Kelly's hair with both hands, yanking her head back.

"Let me go," Jen screamed as Kelly grimaced in pain. Kelly released her hold on Jen and grabbed for her head, Jen still holding handfuls of her hair.

"Okay, okay. Let go of my hair." Kelly stepped back and rubbed her head as Jen let go, pushing her away.

"It's time for you to leave, Kelly," Jen demanded and headed for the house. She took a few steps then turned back to Kelly. "If you ever do that to me again, I'll snatch you bald-headed. Do you hear me, Kelly? I am *not* your sex toy."

"I'm sorry, Jen," Kelly was still rubbing her head.

"And now that you mention it, I don't think I can be forgiving like I used to be. You aren't the person I want to forgive anymore, Kelly."

"What are you telling me?"

"Oh, Kelly. I don't think you are that stupid. Surely you can figure it out. If you need some assistance, I'm sure Donna will be glad to help you. Where did you drop her off while you came out to the ranch? In Harland at the café or on the square to do some shopping?"

Kelly's mouth dropped. Jen shook her head when Kelly's expression confirmed what she had guessed. Donna had gone with Kelly to the conference in El Paso. For Jen, it was the last straw that killed the relationship once and for all. She was not going to endure Kelly's unfaithfulness any longer. She liked herself too much for that.

"Baby, wait. It truly isn't like that. Donna is just a friend," Kelly explained.

"Please, Kelly. Not this time." Jen turned for the house.

"Jen, we didn't do anything. I swear it. She just helped me drive." Kelly followed her to the porch, waiting at the bottom step for Jen's forgiveness. "You have to believe me, Jen. Donna and I are just friends. There is nothing sexual between us. Not anymore," Kelly argued adamantly.

Jen looked down at her from the top step and pulled at the collar of Kelly's shirt.

"Oh really? Which friend gave you these?" she asked, examining a pair of hickies on Kelly's neck. "I'll tell Taylor good-bye for you."

"Can I at least use the bathroom before I leave?" Kelly asked. Jen crossed her arms and slowly shook her head.

"There's a grove of trees about a half mile down the road. Help yourself."

Kelly glared up at her then heaved a disgusted sigh. She turned and strode off toward her car. Jen waited until she pulled out of the drive and roared up the road, a plume of dust marking her retreat. Jen stood on the porch thinking over what happened. For the first time in her life she had stood up for herself. She had pushed back. For the first time, she had refused to forgive and forget. She and Kelly had some good times over the years but for once, they weren't enough to override the bad and it didn't hurt a bit to let go. She took a deep breath and looked out across the pasture. A satisfied smile settled over her face. Perhaps Kelly was right. Maybe it did have something to do with Taylor. Whatever the reason, Jen opened the back door and went inside with a twinkle in her eye and a renewed sense of self-worth.

Jen closed the back door and went into Taylor's room. When she returned to the living room Taylor was busy watching television. Jen stood at the end of the couch, holding something behind her back.

"That was cute," she said, looking down at Taylor.

"What was?" Taylor asked, flipping to another channel.

"The looks and the attitude. That's what."

"She started it."

"And you just had to finish it."

"What was that bib thing you were doing?" Taylor kept her eyes on the television, trying to act indifferent.

"I was trying to keep you from spilling your glass but I see it didn't work."

"It was too full."

"So you had to drink it all in one gulp?"

"I was thirsty. You don't let me have iced tea very often."

"Well, let's see." Jen's eyes scanned the ceiling. "You've had two bottles of water, a large glass of orange juice with breakfast, a glass of milk and a *full* glass of iced tea. I'm guessing you probably need this," she said, producing a plastic bedpan from behind her back and setting it on Taylor's lap.

Taylor looked at it then back at the television.

"I hate it when you know what I need even before I do," Taylor muttered then snapped off the set. "Can I at least go in the other room? I'd hate for Kelly to come to the door asking for directions and me sitting on a bedpan."

"Suit yourself, Tex," Jen mused, using the lift to maneuver Taylor into the wheelchair. "What makes you think Kelly would need directions?" Jen asked as she helped steer Taylor through the doorway.

"Did you notice which way she turned onto the road?"

"Yes," Jen replied pensively. "She turned right."

"And which way is the highway east toward San Antonio?" Taylor removed the armrests from the chair as they approached the commode.

Jen didn't answer. She knew Kelly was heading back to Harland to pick up Donna.

"I rest my case," Taylor added then gave a victorious cackle.

"I ought to make you do this by yourself," Jen said.

"I can do it," Taylor reassured her.

"Yeah, I know. But then I have to mop the floor so I think I'll help."

"Hey, I'm getting better." Taylor eased herself onto the commode while Jen held the wheelchair. They had learned the wheel locks were no match for the weight of the casts.

"Uh-huh." She walked out of the bathroom, tossing a roll of toilet paper in Taylor's direction. "Call me."

"I'm not a little kid you put on a potty chair in front of the television to potty train," Taylor called.

"Sure you are," Jen replied from the other room. "You get a

surprise if you go potty like a nice girl."

"What kind of surprise? How about a Coke?"

Jen returned to the bathroom, holding the syringe for Taylor's injection.

"I'll give you three guesses," Jen said with a wry smile.

Taylor frowned up at her.

"Sorry," Jen said, touching her shoulder sympathetically. It was the one thing she sincerely wished she could avoid for Taylor's sake but it was for her own good. Jen helped Taylor back into the wheelchair. "Let me see your stomach."

Taylor held up her shirt. Her belly was littered with injection marks spaced out evenly across her abdomen in brutal accuracy.

"Just as I thought," Jen said, examining Taylor's tender stomach. "We need to move to a new location for a couple days. Do you mind?"

"Where?"

"Your hip. There's too much bruising and redness on your stomach."

"Swell," Taylor muttered, rolling to the side so Jen could get at her hip.

Jen swabbed Taylor's hip with alcohol before stabbing the small needle into her white skin. Taylor flinched slightly, hoping she would soon grow accustomed to the sting of it. Like always, Jen patted Taylor's shoulder and gave it a squeeze, her silent apology for the pain she had caused.

"Let's get you into bed. I need you to be on your stomach for a couple hours," Jen said, lowering the bed all the way flat. "I know it isn't comfortable but—"

"I know, I know, relieves the pressure on my back and butt so I won't get bedsores." Taylor didn't mean to sound sarcastic. It just came out. When she was positioned on her stomach and her casts were aligned correctly, Jen covered Taylor's bottom with a sheet. With carefully placed pillows, Taylor was ready for a boring few hours. She couldn't do much but stare at the floor, her head tilted and her arms at her side.

"All set?" Jen asked, returning the lift to the corner.

"Yep," Taylor replied, tugging her T-shirt out of her crack. "You can go call Kelly now," she added smugly.

"What makes you think I was going to call her?" Jen asked.

"I figured you wanted to talk about playing kissy face in my pasture. Isn't that what the two of you did on your little walk? Or was it more than that? You were gone a long time. Plenty of time for a quick roll in the hay."

"We did no such thing," Jen replied angrily and swatted Taylor hard on her bottom.

"Ouch!"

"Serves you right." Jen walked out and closed the bedroom door, Taylor's punishment for the presumptuous comment.

Chapter 11

Taylor had only been home for two weeks and she was show-ing signs of cabin fever, something Jen had been watching for. Depression was always a challenge for patients who had sud-denly lost their freedom and mobility, even if temporarily. This particular day had been a long one for Taylor. She wasn't used to sleeping on her back and the lack of sleep was only making her more irritable. Breakfast hadn't set well. The injection hurt more than usual. She couldn't get comfortable on the couch. Lunch was still churning in her stomach. She felt clumsy and had dropped her water bottle, the remote and a book she was skim-ming and the sheet wouldn't stay across her lap. Picasso sat on the coffee table watching her like she was a freak of nature, exactly the way she felt.

"Take a hike, Angus," Taylor sneered. "Unless you want me to yank your tail."

"Stop that, Taylor. And his name is Picasso, not Angus." Jen was carrying a stack of clean towels to the bathroom. She was humming something cheery.

"But he doesn't look like a Picasso." Taylor glared at the cat, trying to intimidate him off the table. He yawned and licked his lips.

"Nevertheless," Jen replied, disappearing into the bathroom next to Taylor's room.

"Go on," Taylor whispered, giving the coffee table a jolt. The cat jumped from the table onto the back of the couch, using Taylor's stomach as a springboard. "Ouch. You're dead meat, cat." Taylor rubbed her stomach and checked for claw marks.

"Will you leave him alone?" Jen said firmly as she started up the stairs with the rest of the towels.

"He attacked me," Taylor replied. Picasso stretched out across the back of the couch, ready for a nap.

"You poor thing," Jen replied with a scowl. "I'm going to change my sheets so try and behave for a while. You too, Picasso." She disappeared up the stairs.

Taylor tried to find her place in the book but found little interest in it. She tossed it on the coffee table but it slid all the way across and fell off, knocking over a partially filled cup of coffee. The cup struck the leg of the chair, shattering into several pieces and broadcasting the stale coffee across the carpet.

Taylor heaved a disgusted sigh.

"You okay?" Jen called.

"Yep, just dropped my book. No problem." She pulled the sheet from her lap and wadded it up. She took aim and tossed it toward the spill, hoping to soak up the mess she had made but only succeeded in tipping over the floor lamp, adding a broken light bulb to the mess. She grumbled to herself, pulling the coffee table out of the way so she could see the damage she had caused. Taylor had always been the type to close an open cabinet door or secure a loose top. She didn't leave dirty dishes in the sink overnight and cleaned the hair from the shower drain before leaving the bathroom. Having this catastrophe on the living room floor was something she couldn't ignore and her testy mood only made the matter worse.

"Are you sure you are okay?" Jen called from the top of the stairs, hearing the second crash.

"I'm fine. I dropped it again." Taylor refused to admit she couldn't clean up her own mess.

"Must be a big book," Jen called from upstairs.

Taylor assessed the work to be done, growing more frustrated with her incapacity by the second. The wheelchair was behind the couch. She remembered Jen putting it there. If only she could maneuver it around the end and in front, she could pull herself into it, roll over, pick up the broken glass and dab up the coffee. At least it was a plan. She had never transferred herself and the heavy casts into the wheelchair without help but she was determined this was to be the time. She reached over the back of the couch, sweeping Picasso onto the floor, sending him fleeing into the other room. She waved her arm blindly, fishing for the wheelchair.

"Where is it?" she grunted, straining as far as she could reach. "There it is."

She inched the wheelchair along the back of the couch, changing to two hands extended over her head to steer it around the corner. She never thought it would have been such hard work to move one empty wheelchair such a short distance but she was sweating and gasping for breath as she moved it inch by inch. She stiffened, straining to make it turn the last corner. She twisted her body at such an angle that her left leg slipped to the edge of the couch and teetered on the rim of the cushion. Taylor instantly stopped pulling the wheelchair and reached for the cast, leaning to keep it on the couch. But it was too late. The leg did a slow-motion slide down the front of the couch. Her foot hit the floor with a thump. The weight of it and the angle pulled the rest of her body down as well, her right leg sticking up across the cushion. Taylor grimaced in pain, shocked at how easy she had gone from stretched out on the couch to sprawled across the floor. She tried to pull herself back onto the couch but she couldn't find the leverage to hoist the massive casts back up where they belonged. Her right leg began to hurt from being held at an odd angle. She hated to do it, but pulling her right leg onto the floor seemed the only answer. She grabbed a pillow from the couch and tossed it down where the cast would fall then rolled to her left side until she felt the right cast slide down and onto the floor, the pillow muffling the thump.

"Are you playing football down there or something?" Jen called.

"No. I'm beating Angus with a shovel."

"That isn't funny. Leave the book. I'll get it for you in a minute."

"Too late," she muttered to herself.

Taylor lay on the floor, spread-eagle and disgusted with her predicament. She tried again to pull herself up onto the couch but it was hopeless. Her legs simply wouldn't cooperate. She sat up and dragged herself backward, hand-over-rear, toward the wheelchair. Every few feet she had to stop and release her T-shirt from under her bottom as it was pulling at her neck, choking her. Since she wasn't wearing any underwear, her bottom stung from rug burn. She finally caught up with the wheelchair. She wedged it in the corner of the room, flipped up the leg supports and locked the wheels. She positioned herself in front of it, positive she could lift herself up into the seat. After all, she could pull her weight up a rope. At least she could in high school. She could toss a calf on the ground, hold it with one knee and tie its legs in less than ten seconds. Pulling herself up eighteen inches into a wheelchair seat would be child's play. She reached back and grabbed the sides of the chair and pulled but she couldn't get her rear high enough. She took a deep breath and tried again, this time lunging with her upper body as she pulled with her arms. All she succeeded in doing was tipping the chair forward, whacking herself in the back of the head.

"Ouch," she growled, folding her arms over her head, rubbing the pain. Her nerves had taken all they could take. She shoved the chair to the side, banging it into the wall. She shoved it again, this time making a mark on the wall.

"Damn it," she cursed, tears welling up in her eyes from the frustration. Taylor pounded her fists on the casts. She looked for something to throw. She grabbed the wheelchair with both hands and shook it for all she was worth. She pinched her fingers in the spokes but the pain couldn't stop her anger.

"Taylor!" Jen said, standing at the bottom of the stairs with an armload of sheets. "What happened?" She dropped the sheets and ran to Taylor's side, kneeling next to her. "Are you all right?" Her face went white and her eyes filled with fear. "What happened down here?" She looked around the room. "Why didn't you call me when you fell?"

"I didn't fall," Taylor pulled her fingers out of the spokes then gave the chair a last shove.

"It sure looks like you did. Do your legs hurt? Can you feel your toes? You didn't put weight on your legs, did you?" Jen scrambled to check the color of Taylor's toes and the way the casts looked. She touched Taylor's forehead, checking for a fever then checked her pulse.

"I'm fine," Taylor declared, pulling her wrist away. "I'm not sick. I'm just fine."

"Did you feel anything snap?" Jen frowned at her.

"Stop it. Stop it," Taylor screamed, her anger beyond control. "Leave me alone. I don't want any help. I have to do it myself," she yelled, her eyes red and swollen.

"Taylor, what's wrong? Why are you acting this way?" Jen tried again to take her wrist.

"Acting what way?" Taylor asked, giving a defensive stare.

143

"You mean clumsy and stupid and awkward and dependent? That's me. Good old Taylor, the freak on the floor who can't even get up without help. Hell, I can't do anything for myself. Why not just put a diaper on me and put me in a crib? Then I couldn't make more of a mess for you to clean up," Taylor shouted. "Maybe you should just set me in the bathtub then you can hose me down like a dirty dog." She ripped at her shirt, pulling at the neck.

"Taylor, stop it," Jen said, grabbing her hands.

"I shouldn't be wearing this. I don't need any clothes. I just spill on everything I wear. I can't even hold a glass without dumping it on myself." She tugged at the shirt, making a red mark on her neck.

"Taylor," Jen demanded angrily. "Stop it. You're going to hurt yourself." She grabbed Taylor's wrists and folded them across her chest to restrain her.

"I probably couldn't even do that without help," she replied, trying to pull away as tears rolled down her face. Her voice cracked and her chin quivered as she fought to get her hands free.

"Taylor, listen to me," Jen said, trying to calm her. "Taylor, stop fighting me and listen. It's only temporary. You're going to be all right."

"I don't care. I don't care." She tried to turn away and hide her face. Tears were streaming down her cheeks and it only made matters worse. Taylor wasn't and never had been a crybaby. She was the gutsy type. Tears showed vulnerability and a weakness in her character and she hated it. She also hated Jen seeing her this way.

Jen released her hold on Taylor's wrists and wrapped her arms around her, pulling her close.

"I care," Jen said. She could feel Taylor's sobs against her shoulder. She held her tight and rocked her gently. "I care."

Taylor first fought against Jen's hold on her then succumbed to it, holding onto Jen as the body-wracking sobs took over. She needed Jen's warm embrace as much as she had ever needed anything. She had endured all the disappointment, frustration and feeling of helplessness she could for one day. Perhaps it had been coming since she woke up in the hospital and saw her legs in slings or just since she returned home and realized her predicament. Either way, Taylor needed to cry and cleanse her feelings once and for all.

Jen knelt next to her, cradling Taylor in her arms and whispering to her.

"You don't have to do this alone. I'm right here for you. I don't mind, Taylor. I don't mind at all. Let me take care of you." Jen cooed reassuringly as Taylor cried. "We can do this together. You tell me what you need and I'll do it. Whatever it is, I'll help you." She stroked Taylor's hair as she held her.

Taylor gave a shudder as the tears subsided and she regained her composure. Jen gently wiped away her tears. There was a certain softness to Jen's touch and in her voice that told Taylor it would be okay. Jen brushed the hair from Taylor's face and smiled at her with the look of confidence and understanding.

"Jen, I'm sorry. I don't know where that came from," Taylor said, lowering her eyes as a blush of embarrassment covered her face.

"Shh," Jen replied, dabbing away the last trace of Taylor's tears. "It's all right. I understand. I don't think I could have lasted as long as you did without doing that." Jen raised Taylor's face and smiled at her. "That's all part of the shock to your system. Post-traumatic stress," she said in a forgiving voice. "I should have expected it."

"I didn't." Taylor was still embarrassed, medical reason or not.

Jen sat down on the floor next to Taylor just like two old friends sitting on a porch swing.

"We'll get you through this. I promise," Jen said softly, putting her hand on Taylor's.

Chapter 12

Tuesday morning brought a heavy rain that turned the air thick and the skies dark. Taylor rolled her wheelchair aimlessly through the living room and dining room, making figure eights among the furniture. The empty days were rolling by and she was bored. By afternoon, the skies had cleared and the air was summertime fresh but she was stuck in the house, her cast covered legs bumping into everything in the room. She wished she was outside. She snapped on the television but before it even came into focus, she turned it off and tossed the remote on the couch, too restless to watch it. She rolled over to the window and gazed out at the corral where Coal was munching hay. He looked as bored as Taylor did. She wished she could take a ride on him if even for a few minutes. Or even stroke his shiny coat. But she knew the wheelchair couldn't maneuver through the soft dirt around the corral. For a fleeting moment she wondered if Coal would fit in the mudroom. She raised the window a few inches and whistled at him, the whistle he knew meant Taylor was watching. The stallion raised his head and gave a deep whinny then bobbed his head.

"Hey, Coal. You're getting fat, you lazy thing you." She laughed then closed the window. She rolled into the kitchen and opened the back door, staring out into the yard, hungry for the time when she could throw open the screen door and stride out into the sunshine.

"Do you want to come out onto the porch for a while?" Jen asked, noticing Taylor at the door. She was kneeling by the porch.

"What are you doing in the dirt? Did you fall?" Taylor asked, straining to see what she was doing.

"I'm planting some flowers. I can't believe you don't have anything in bloom around here." Jen was digging at the soil with a trowel. She was wearing green and pink flowered garden gloves and a pink visor pulled down over her forehead. But Taylor didn't notice the visor or the gloves. All she could see was the white short-shorts and bright blue halter top she was wearing. The spaghetti strap that tied at the back of her neck seemed loose and allowed a wonderful view of Jen's cleavage.

"Who has time for gardening? Besides, it gets too hot for flowers," Taylor said, raising herself in the wheelchair so she could get a better look.

"Not if you plant the right kind and water them," Jen continued scratching at the earth while Taylor watched. It wasn't polite to stare but the sight of Jen's firm round breasts bouncing with every stroke of the trowel was more than Taylor had the strength to ignore.

"Are we going into town to buy flowers?"

"I already did. I got them when I went to the grocery store yesterday."

"And where was I?" Taylor asked, trying to remember where

she was when the flowers were purchased.

"You were sleeping. Lexie came over and sat with you while I ran to town and back." Jen kept digging as a trail of sweat ran down her neck and took dead aim on the valley between her breasts.

Taylor couldn't help herself. She slowly drew her tongue across her upper lip as the bead of sweat descended into Jen's halter top and disappeared.

"Maybe I will come out on the porch for a little while," Taylor offered, her eyes stuck on Jen's front. She pushed herself through the door before Jen could climb to her feet and help.

"Wait a minute. Let me hold the door for you," she said, clapping her muddy gloves together and climbing the steps.

"I got it," Taylor said with a grunt as she rolled the bulky chair over the threshold. Jen grabbed one side of the chair and pulled, easing her to a spot on the porch where she had a view of the flower bed as well as the corral.

"Do you need a pillow or anything?" Jen asked, wiping the back of her glove across her forehead, leaving a muddy smear.

"No. How about you? You look like you could use some water," Taylor replied, staring up at her. "I'll go get you some." She turned the wheelchair toward the door but bumped into the rocking chair, whacking it against the window, nearly cracking the glass. Jen grabbed the back of the chair, stopping it from striking the window again.

"You stay here," Jen announced. "I'll get the water." She adjusted Taylor and locked the wheels. She went inside and returned with two bottles of cold water. She handed one to Taylor then tried to open hers but her hands were too sweaty to turn the cap.

"Here," Taylor said, trading Jen for her opened one.

"Thanks," she said, taking a long drink.

"Slowly. You're in Texas. Don't tank up on cold water too fast. You'll get a bellyache."

"I'll remember that, doctor," Jen replied, pouring a dribble of the cool water down the back of her neck before going back to gardening. Taylor immediately noticed the cold water caused Jen's nipples to harden, their erection clearly visible through the thin fabric of the halter top.

"I should have brought my sunglasses with me," Taylor muttered to herself, her eyes following Jen's cleavage relentlessly.

"What did you say?"

"Nothing," Taylor replied, forcing her gaze out across the yard.

"You can't be out here very long. The heat isn't good for you," Jen said, once again digging and bouncing. "It might be too taxing on your system so soon after surgery."

"I know," Taylor said, catching another look at Jen's breasts in her peripheral vision. "I don't think I could endure very much of this."

Taylor turned her attention and her gaze toward the corral. Coal was standing at the gate as if he expected her to come let him out. He snorted his insistence.

"Sorry, Coal. I can't come over there, boy. You'll have to get along without me for a while."

"He is a gorgeous animal," Jen said, looking over her shoulder at him.

"Yes, he sure is. Just ask him. He'll tell you." Taylor laughed, giving a whistle. Coal whinnied long and loud in reply, pacing back and forth. "Think you're hot stuff, don't you, you old glue pot." Taylor gave a different whistle and he backed up several steps. She gave a hand signal and he stopped immediately, lowering his head.

Jen watched, cheering his antics and laughing as Taylor made him perform.

"Did you teach him all that?" Jen asked, still kneeling by the porch.

"Sure. It isn't hard. He's a smart animal. He isn't used to not being ridden. He probably doesn't understand why I won't come out there and saddle him up."

"I think he does. Animals have a way of understanding. Take Picasso. He knows when I'm not feeling well."

"That cat doesn't know which way is up," Taylor chuckled.

"He does too," Jen declared defensively. "He is just as smart as that horse of yours." Jen looked over at the window where Picasso was inside sitting on the sill. A fly landed on the outside of the glass just inches from the cat's face. He sprang at the bug, hitting the glass and falling to the floor. Taylor and Jen could hear an angry meow from inside.

"Yeah, right. Smart cat," Taylor agreed with a grin.

Jen grinned and went back to her digging. There was a scratch at the door and the sound of a lonesome meow.

"Hey, Angus, want to come outside?" Taylor called, reaching over and flipping the screen door open. The cat meandered out, barely clearing the door before it swung shut.

"Pay no attention to her, Picasso. She's just grumpy because she can't go play with her horse." The cat rubbed itself against the wheelchair then sauntered down the steps and stood watching Jen before wandering off to do what cats do.

"I know what that cat is thinking."

"What's that?" Jen grunted as she removed a large clump of roots from the flower bed.

"Angus is thinking you're making him a cat box right outside the back door. He can't wait to christen it."

"He's not thinking that at all. She has never dug in my flower beds or used them as a litter box. He's too refined for that." Jen sat back on her heels and gazed over at the cat as it dug at the corner of the house where she had already planted flowers. "Picasso, stop that," Jen ordered. Taylor laughed wildly.

"I rest my case."

"I'd rub your face with mud, smarty pants, but I'd just have to clean it off." Jen scolded in Taylor's direction.

"Admit it. You like the name Angus."

"I'll do no such thing."

"Call him," Taylor suggested teasingly. "Go ahead. Call him by name and see if he responds."

"Okay," Jen said, sitting up and clearing her throat. "Here, Picasso. Here kitty, kitty." She added a few kissing sounds, trying to coax the cat out of the flower bed but without results. "Picasso, come here kitty," Jen patted the ground next to her but the cat looked over indifferently.

"My turn," Taylor announced.

"He won't come to you. Your casts scare him."

Taylor gave a sharp shrill whistle and snapped her fingers.

"Here, Angus. Come here. Angus," she called, her voice light and friendly.

The cat looked over at Taylor and meowed then strolled over and climbed the stairs, waving its tail contentedly. Taylor reached down and patted the cat's head then looked up at Jen with a raised eyebrow.

"Picasso, you are a traitor," Jen quipped and went back to gardening.

Picasso crouched then sprang onto Taylor's lap, purring loudly and demanding to be petted.

"Hey, I don't like cats," Taylor said, waving at it.

"You should have thought of that before you claimed him as your own."

"I'm not claiming him. I'm just naming him." Taylor leaned back as far as she could and gave the cat an awkward pat on the back. "Go play, Angus." She pushed at the cat, hoping it would hop down and slink off into the bushes. Instead he circled on Taylor's lap, making biscuits on her stomach before curling up for a nap.

The sound of a honking horn and a cloud of road dust attracted their attention. Lexie waved as she roared up the drive pulling a horse trailer. She stopped near the porch with the back of the trailer facing the steps. She climbed out of the truck grinning like a Cheshire cat.

"Hey, Lexie," Taylor said.

"Hi, Lexie," Jen offered, sitting back on her heels and brushing the dirt from her gloves. "What's up with you?"

"I've got something to show you," she said with a grin so wide it looked like it might hurt.

"Did Patsy have her colt?" Taylor asked happily as Lexie unlatched the trailer gate. "Let's have a look at it."

"She's got a keeper, Taylor. I'm telling you, she's got a keeper," Lexie said proudly. She carefully backed a Palomino mare out of the trailer and tied her to the side of the door.

"Where is it?" Jen said, leaning around the side of the trailer and peering inside. A small animal sat in the front corner of the trailer, its spindly legs folded under its tiny body. "Oh, Lexie, isn't he the cutest baby horse you have ever seen," Jen mewed, smiling affectionately.

"It's a she and yes, I think so." Lexie stroked the mare's nose. "You're a good mother, Patsy old girl."

"Is she pale or does she have Patsy's coloring?" Taylor asked, squinting to see into the darkened trailer.

"Oh, Taylor, she's so cute. She is a golden yellow with a tiny little white tail," Jen related in a hush, as if it were a baby napping.

"Let me bring her out," Lexie said, stepping into the trailer. She picked up the colt, wrapping her arms around the animal's little body. The mare whinnied as Lexie set her baby beside her. The foal gave a tiny nicker.

"You're right Lexie. That's a keeper." Taylor smiled at the little animal, unable to hide her fondness for the baby. The foal had completely captured Taylor's heart, just like all the new horses on the ranch did. The baby nuzzled its mother, searching for her teat. Its stubby little tail twitched nervously until it found the nourishment and began to suckle.

"Isn't that the sweetest thing you ever saw, Taylor?" Jen said, a twinkle in her eye as she watched the mother and her newborn.

"I have to admit, a brand new foal is pretty special."

"Baby cows are cute too," Jen offered.

"If they're small enough, they are," Lexie muttered.

"No kidding," Taylor agreed, glancing up at Lexie.

"What do you mean if they are small enough? Bigger calves are cute too." Jen looked over at Taylor curiously.

"Ranchers like small calves."

"I hate to sound dumb but why do you want small calves? I thought the idea was to make big fat cows to take to market."

"When the calves are too big, they run the risk of damaging the mother during birth," Taylor explained. "If we aren't around to see the cow is in distress we could lose the baby and the mother. Small calves mean less risk at birth, especially with heifers. We don't want their first baby to be their last."

"They'll grow fast enough," Lexie chuckled.

"I guess I never knew that but it certainly makes sense," Jen replied, returning her attention to the colt. "What did you name Patsy's baby, Lexie?"

"I haven't decided yet. Any suggestions?"

"I've never named a horse before. Seems like a pretty big responsibility."

"It's like naming anything. You just pick something," Taylor advised.

"I think that's something Lexie should do. But she is the most precious little thing I ever saw, you little yellow thing, you." Jen smiled adoringly at the tiny horse.

"You just named her," Lexie said, looking at Jen with a broad grin. "Amarillo."

"Amarillo?"

"It's Spanish for yellow. That's perfect."

"Good name, Jen," Taylor agreed.

"Hello, Amarillo," Jen said tenderly.

"She'll be a fine-looking animal in a year or two. You'll want to ride her."

"I don't know about that," Jen said, suddenly returning to her gardening.

"I guess I better take Patsy and Amarillo back home," Lexie said, carrying the colt into the trailer and placing it in the bed of straw. She led Patsy into the other side of the trailer and tied her reins to the post.

"Thanks for bringing Amarillo over," Taylor said. "Patsy did a good job."

"Yes, thanks, Lexie. She is wonderful," Jen added.

"Talk with you later," Lexie said, climbing in the truck and pulling away. She honked then disappeared down the road.

"Geez Louise. It sure is hot," Jen said, dabbing the back of her hand across her forehead. She stretched and straightened her posture, her halter top straining to hold her breasts in check. "I think you better go inside. I don't want you to get too hot." Jen shaded her eyes from the sun and looked up at Taylor.

"No doubt about it. If I stay out here, I'm definitely going to get overheated," Taylor said, raising her head as if she was staring out across the pasture but her eyes were not following. They were on Jen's top. The way the perspiration glistened on Jen's smooth legs all the way up to the hem of her short shorts was a view to die for. Taylor needed to go inside, that was for sure. She realized she was feeling better when even the hint of a woman's nipples through a halter top raised her blood pressure.

"I think I'll go throw some cold water on my face," Taylor said, steering herself through the door. She gave a last look at Jen's suppleness then closed the door, heaving a desperate moan. "Yep, that is definitely a hot view."

Chapter 13

"Taylor," Jen said, gently shaking her shoulder. Taylor had been napping on the couch, a restless night without sleep catching up with her. "Taylor, you've got company."

Taylor blinked awake, prepared to tease Jen about bothering her beauty sleep.

"Hi, Taylor," Amber said, rushing to the couch and hugging Taylor carefully. Her eyes gave a pained expression of sympathy. "We heard you had an accident and came to see how you're doing."

Taylor looked over Amber's shoulder to see Sonny, Nancy and AJ, all standing in a row like pallbearers, their faces drawn with worry.

"Hi, babe," Nancy said, also coming to administer kisses and hugs.

"Hey, what are you all doing out here?" Taylor pulled herself up to a sitting position, trying to come to her senses.

"You look so tired," Nancy said, running her hand through Taylor's hair.

"Come on in and sit down," Jen said, motioning them toward the chairs.

"Look at those huge casts," Amber declared. "We were so worried. How did it happen?"

"Flat tire on the horse trailer," Taylor replied, growing accustomed to relating the story. She had learned to shorten it to a few manageable phrases. "It slipped down the ditch and rolled over on me."

"Oh, ouch," Sonny said, reaching down and rubbing her own shins. "I thought you might have gotten kicked by some hot babe." She winked then laughed wickedly.

"No, that's more your style," Amber teased, giving Sonny a playful shove.

"Taylor, if you don't need me, I think I'll go water the flower bed." Jen said, making sure Taylor's sheet was in place and her casts were properly supported. "Call me if you need me. There's pop and lemonade in the fridge if you all want anything. Help yourself."

"Okay, thanks," Nancy said, smiling at Jen and watching her leave the room. As soon as Jen was out of sight and they heard the back door close, all eyes were on Taylor with wide curiosity and surprise.

"Wow, Taylor," Sonny said, flashing a grin. "That's the blonde from the bar. How did you talk that cutie into taking care of you? I may have to break something myself."

"Yeah, not bad, you lady-killer," Amber agreed, winking at Taylor. "Does she give you bed baths?"

"I bet Taylor has her washing lots of things," AJ giggled.

"Stop that," Taylor insisted. She frowned at them and what they were suggesting. Taylor used to participate in good-natured ribbing and off-color jokes but when it came to Jen, she didn't like it at all. She found their insinuations offensive. "It's nothing like that. Hush. She'll hear you."

"Oh, come on. Don't tell me you two haven't, you know," Sonny said, raising her eyebrows.

"No," Taylor declared adamantly. "She is my nurse. She is a certified aide and that is all."

"She can aide me anytime." Sonny looked out the window, leaning forward and hoping for a glimpse of where Jen had gone.

"Sonny, you had your chance with her. Remember, you danced with her but let her get away," AJ reminded her.

"Taylor," Amber said in a soft whisper, leaning over to her. "What kind of candy is the nurse? You know, candy. SweeTart? Jawbreaker?"

"Will you stop it?" Taylor demanded. "Jen is a CSN and a darn good one. She is taking care of me while I recover. Now shut up about it." Taylor scowled at them. "I'd still be in the hospital if it wasn't for her." Her sudden protective attitude surprised even Taylor. She had no idea why, but defending Jen to her friends seemed like the right thing to do.

"I'm sorry," Amber said apologetically. "We didn't mean to make you mad. We were just having fun. You know how we are."

"Yeah, sweetie. We didn't mean anything by it," AJ added. "I'm sure she is a wonderful nurse's aide. Pay no attention to us. We are all goofs. Really, we are happy you have a nice nurse."

"I can't wait for you to get better," Amber said, rubbing Taylor's arm. "You owe me a dance as soon as you are back on your feet, okay?"

"Sure, Amber. You keep practicing," Taylor smiled at her. "I'll be fine. The doctor said after rehab, I'll be good as new."

"We'll have a party for you at the Rainbow," Sonny said.

"Yeah, a party," Nancy agreed happily. "You know how they have coming out parties? Well, we can have a coming off party."

"I'll make you a cake in the shape of a cast," Amber offered.

"No, make it in the shape of her cowboy boots. She won't

want to even think about these casts," AJ declared. "We want Jen to come too. Really."

"I thought I'd bring you all some drinks before I go outside. It's a long drive from San Antonio," Jen said, carrying a tray from the kitchen. They hadn't heard the back door open and everyone immediately blushed bright red at the thought that Jen was nearby and had probably heard their teasing and lusty insinuations. Jen set the tray on the coffee table. "Lemonade?" she said lightly as if nothing had happened.

The women sat silently for a long moment, quietly sipping lemonade, their eyes lowered with embarrassment. Jen smiled at Taylor, winked and went out to water. She had gotten in the last word without saying a thing.

"Yep, a darn good nurse," Taylor muttered, smiling to herself. At that moment all Taylor could think of was Jen's soft skin and the way it looked in the halter top. She hated to admit it but yes, she wanted a taste of that sweet candy.

"You must like nurses. Isn't that what Trish was?" Nancy asked.

Taylor looked over at Nancy, her mind slipping back to a radiant redhead with green eyes, something she hadn't done in a long time.

"I remember Trish," AJ declared, smiling at Taylor. "She wasn't a nurse, Nancy. She was a fireman, or is it firewoman? Whatever happened to her?"

"I don't know. I heard she moved to Dallas or somewhere," Taylor replied as she tripped down memory lane. Everyone saw the smile grow across Taylor's face. They also saw the moment it changed to a stunned and hollow expression.

Taylor had met Trish Watkins at the Rainbow Desert the first year it opened and fell for her so fast and so hard, the thud could be heard all the way to the Rio Grande. Trish had batted her long eyelashes at Taylor and she was a goner. A forty-two-year-old ex-Navy captain, Trish could dance, flirt, kiss and lick her lips in all the right ways. Taylor spent many a late night driving between the Cottonwood Ranch and San Antonio to woo the redhead with the seductive eyes and dazzling smile. Trish was soft-spoken and attentive. She hung on Taylor's every word and dressed just the way Taylor liked. She was a quick study, eagerly learning all the things that melted Taylor's heart into butter. Trish was a lesbian's dream. Great looking, great lover and faithful to the end. But unfortunately for Taylor, the end did come. Trish was satisfied with a six-month relationship and nothing more. Like all her courtships, Trish liked them short and sweet, something Taylor wished she knew ahead of time. But it might not have made any difference. Taylor had fallen victim to Trish's charm. She didn't know why Trish preferred to avoid long-term devotion but the reality of it smacked Taylor so hard she couldn't see straight. For over a year Taylor refused to date or even dance with anyone, coming to the Rainbow Desert to only drink and dream. For a while she blamed herself. She had fallen in love too soon and too hard. Trish had mentioned a long list of past girlfriends—she met all of them for the first time at the bar. But Taylor didn't read the warnings. She assumed the other women just failed to measure up. She never thought she too would end up at the bottom of Trish's list of conquests.

"I remember her," Sonny said, smiling at the floor. "I was a day late on that one. You got there before I did."

"Next one's yours," Taylor offered with a wink.

"I think I already missed a good one," Sonny replied, casting her eyes out the window to where Jen was watering the flowers. She looked over at Taylor, reading her expression. Taylor only stared at her, the smallest glint in her eyes.

After Taylor's friends were satisfied she was in good hands, it was hugs and kisses all around for Taylor and Jen before they headed back to San Antonio.

"Do you mind if I go to town this afternoon?" Jen asked after carrying the tray of glasses to the kitchen. "I want to visit Dad."

"Sure, go ahead. I'll be fine. Take as long as you want. Tell Rowdy hi for me."

"I will but your mother is coming over to sit with you. I'll only be gone a couple hours."

"I don't need a babysitter."

"Taylor, I'm not going unless she can be here in case you fall," Jen said, giving a decisive stare.

"My mother can't pick me up and she couldn't operate the lift either."

"All she'd have to do is call for help. Lexie said she may stop by to check on the horses anyway. So your mother comes for a visit or I won't go. You decide."

"She may not be available. This might be her bridge club day."

"I already asked her. She was thrilled to do it. I think she looks at it as an opportunity to offer hands-on help. Don't disappoint her."

Taylor finally nodded in agreement.

"I'm here," her mother called brightly, opening the back door.

"In here, Mom," Taylor replied, not liking the idea she needed watching.

"Hi, Sylvia," Jen said, hugging her. "You look nice."

"This is my brand new pair of capri pants and I just love them. I never liked that length on me before but these are so comfortable. How is my daughter today? Did you sleep well last night, honey?" she said, babbling on like she was meeting a long lost friend.

"I'm okay, Mom. How are you? How's Dad?" Taylor asked.

"We're just fine." She petted Taylor's head softly then arranged her sheet, tucking it in the edge of the cushion.

"I guess I'll get ready and head into town. Do you need anything from the store, Sylvia?" Jen asked.

"I don't think so, dear. I just went into town yesterday. If I think of anything, I could call you on your cell phone, couldn't I?"

"Absolutely. Please do. I have to go right by the grocery store. How about you, Taylor? Do you need anything?"

"Chiliburger and onion rings?" Taylor asked calmly but with a strong suspicion Jen was going to tell her she couldn't have it.

"Yes, well . . ." Jen said, clearing her throat. She hurried upstairs to get ready then headed for town. It was the first time since she had convinced her father to live in the nursing home that she had gone to see him. The staff was cautiously optimistic he was ready for guests. Jen was excited at the thought she could finally sit down and have a nice conversation with him. She bought him a new pair of pajamas and slippers, hoping it would please him. She took her sketches and planned all the things they would talk about. Even though it would be a brief visit, as the staff recommended, she wanted it to be pleasant.

Jen parked in the visitor's parking lot, checked in at the nurse's station then headed down the hall to Rowdy's room, the third door on the right. She knocked on the door and peeked in. He was sitting in a chair with the television on, his head nodding. She entered the room and knelt at his side, touching his arm gently.

"Hello, Dad," she said softly.

He opened his eyes and looked at her with a confused stare.

"It's me, Dad. It's Jen." She gave him a hug and a kiss on the cheek.

He continued to stare as if he didn't yet recognize her.

"How are you feeling today?"

"Jen," he said as if trying out the name.

"Yes, Daddy. It's Jen." She brushed his thin hair back from his forehead and smiled at him.

"What day is it?"

"Thursday, Dad. It's Thursday, the sixteenth."

"Thursday," he repeated, a vacancy in his eyes telling her it didn't matter.

"What did you have for lunch today?" she asked, trying to bring him to reality.

"I don't think we've had lunch yet." Rowdy's eyes searched the room for something familiar.

Jen knew he had eaten lunch. It was two o'clock. But she didn't push it.

"I'm sure you will soon, Dad."

"What's in the sack?" he asked, noticing the parcel she was carrying.

"I brought you some new pajamas, Dad. I know you like the ones with snaps instead of buttons." She pulled out the navy blue pinstripe pajama shirt and held it up for him to see. He stroked the sleeve, his frail and weathered fingers caressing the fabric.

"Are there pants too?" he asked.

"Sure," she reassured him and pulled them out. "I brought you a new pair of slippers, too."

"I don't need slippers," he replied, frowning at her extravagance. "I've got slippers."

"I know but those are too big for you. I don't want you to fall." Jen patted his arm then opened the box. She looked down and noticed his slippers were on the wrong feet. "Let me put these new ones on for you, Daddy. I think you'll like them. They have nice thick cushions in them."

Rowdy watched as she changed his slippers, making sure they were on the right foot.

"There. How do they feel?"

"Are they new?" he asked, studying them. "These aren't mine. Whose slippers are they?"

"Yes, they're yours. I got them at Culmer's here in town. I can exchange them if they don't fit." Jen checked the fit and was satisfied they were the right size. "I brought you some candy, Daddy." Jen handed him a small white sack, hoping he would leave the new slippers on his feet and ignore them.

He opened the sack and fished out one of the candies, popping it in his mouth.

"They're lemon drops," he declared, his eyes lighting up. He tilted the sack to Jen and offered her one, something that surprised her. She didn't particularly care for lemon drops but she took one to please him.

"Thank you, Daddy."

"Did it rain today?" he asked, working the candy around in his mouth.

"No. It's hot outside. It may rain tomorrow, I heard. The ground sure could use some rain. Have you seen the flowers in the garden, Dad. They're lovely. I saw them when I came in. Would you like me to walk you down to the recreation room to see them?"

Rowdy looked at her curiously as if he didn't understand.

"Would you show me your garden, Daddy?" she asked in a different tone.

Jen accompanied Rowdy toward the recreation room, her arm locked through his. He squeezed her hand as they walked the hall, his steps hesitant and stiff.

"How are you this fine afternoon, Mr. Holland? You've got a pretty escort there," one of the nurses said with a smile as she pushed a wheelchair past them.

Jen smiled in return but Rowdy paid little attention. They crossed the dining room and into the recreation room where a group of residents were clustered around a piano singing tunes from the Fifties.

"Look, Dad. Why don't you join in the sing-along?"

He shook his head and kept his eyes on the windows that looked out onto the garden. An oscillating sprinkler was dousing the flowers, splattering the window as it completed its circle. Jen stood next to him, allowing her father to use her arm for support.

"It takes a lot of water to keep them blooming. Did you know that?" he asked, his eyes marching up and down each row of blooms.

"I'm sure it does, Dad. They are so lovely. I wish my garden looked this nice." She wrapped her arm around his waist. She noticed he was thinner than she remembered and his stooped posture made him seem shorter. "Do you know what the little yellow flowers are, Dad? I don't recognize them."

"Yellow bells," he replied, studying them.

"That's right," she agreed, rubbing his back. "I still have that gardening book you gave me. I use it all the time."

"When did I give it to you?"

"High school graduation. You sent me to the botanical gardens in Galveston. Remember? You gave me a round-trip ticket and a room at a hotel right on the beach."

"Galveston," he repeated, trying to resurrect a memory of that time.

"I learned how to prune roses." Jen gave his hand a squeeze.

"Do you have roses, Jennie?" It was the first time in years he called her by name and it touched her deeply. "I like roses in a garden."

"Yes, Daddy. I have yellow tea roses and a red climber that grows up over the garage. I had over three hundred blooms on it this year. It was spectacular. Maybe next year you could come see it."

Rowdy continued to watch the sprinkler make its sweep across the flower bed.

"Three hundred roses," he muttered. "That's a nice climber. Do you water it, Jennie?"

"Yes, Daddy. Just like you told me."

Rowdy lost interest in the garden and turned around, ready to return to his room.

"Do you need anything, Dad?" Jen asked, holding his hand as they slowly made their way down the hall. "Do you want anything special? Maybe some of those cookies you like? The

164

coconut macaroons."

"I don't need anything," he replied. "The food is good. I had chocolate cake. Do you like chocolate cake?"

"Yes. Momma used to make good chocolate cake," Jen said but immediately wished she hadn't mentioned her mother. She held her breath over what Rowdy might say.

"Bea made pie, not cake," he said harshly as he entered his room. He sat down in his chair and glared up at Jen. "She made chocolate pie."

Jen didn't want to argue with him. It didn't matter.

"She wouldn't make chocolate cake for me," he continued, seemingly lost in his memory of that time over thirty years ago. "I asked her but she wouldn't make it. Lemon cake. She made lemon cake. I hate lemon cake." He wrinkled his nose and looked to Jen for agreement.

"But you like lemon drops, Dad," she said, handing him the sack of candy.

"The hell I do. I hate lemon." He scowled at her and threw the sack across the room. "I told you. I hate it." Rowdy grabbed the arms of the chair and leaned forward, a vengeful fire in his eyes. "Don't tell me what I like."

"I didn't mean to upset you, Daddy." Jen picked up the strewn candy as best she could and dropped it in the trash.

"Why did you bring up your mother? You can't do anything right. I don't want to hear about her."

"I know, Daddy. I'm sorry," she said in a calming voice.

"I don't want to hear anything about her," he continued, staring out the window as if he was in a daze.

"Shall I put your new pajamas in your drawer for you?" Jen could see Rowdy was irritated and she wanted to defuse his tirade before it got any worse.

"I don't need any new pajamas. My pajamas are fine."

"Okay, Dad." Jen left them over the foot of the bed.

"Bea never made chocolate cake," he insisted. "I don't want

you talking about her. You hear me?"

"Yes, Dad," She didn't want to make him mad but it didn't seem to matter what she said. He was fueling his own fire.

"You go on home," he said, flipping a hand at her.

"I wanted to show you the sketches for the sculptures I'm making." She pulled the stack of pictures from her tote bag.

"I don't want to see them. You need to leave," he insisted, raising his voice.

"I wanted your opinion on what kind of cattle I should use," she said, trying to divert his attention.

"I said go home," he yelled, standing up and glaring at her. He waved his arms at her, shooing her toward the door. "I want you to leave right now. And don't come back. Go on," he grumbled.

"All right, Dad. Calm down. I'll go," she said, collecting her pictures and purse.

"I don't want any pie, Bea. I want cake." He scowled at Jen with a vacant yet angry look in his eyes.

"Mr. Holland, is everything all right?" a nurse asked, coming into the room.

"I want her to go home and leave me alone," he said, pointing a finger at Jen.

"Calm down," Jen said in a soothing voice. "I'm going, Dad." She looked at the nurse, conveying her concern for her father's sudden flare up.

"Mr. Holland, it's all right, honey. Sit down," the nurse said.

Jen waited in the hall, clutching her tote bag as she listened to the nurse trying to calm Rowdy enough so he would sit down. Jen closed her eyes, hoping the tears welling up wouldn't spill out and run down her face. She didn't know what happened. The visit started innocently enough. Rowdy was a little disoriented but she expected that. She knew better than to bring up her mother. She reproached herself for ruining their conversation. She hadn't had a chance to show him her work. She hadn't told him she loved him either. Jen wanted to go back in his room. She wanted to give him a hug but she knew he didn't want that. It would only reignite his anger.

"Bye, Dad," she muttered under her breath.

The nurse came out of the room, pulling the door shut behind her.

"He'll be all right, miss. He's going to take a little rest," she said, patting Jen's arm sympathetically. "Don't worry, honey. He'll be fine."

"I didn't mean to upset him," Jen replied.

"I know. Sometimes it takes the slightest thing. We'll keep an eye on him. By dinner time he'll be back to his old self." She smiled reassuringly. "He won't remember who he was upset with."

"I don't know about that."

"Just give him some time, honey."

"Will you call me if he needs anything?" Jen asked.

"Of course we will. We'll take real good care of him."

"Thank you," Jen replied. "Tell him his daughter said good-bye." She started up the hall then looked back. "Will you tell him I love him?"

"I will, honey. I will."

When Jen returned to the ranch, Sylvia was sitting in the living room watching soap operas and writing thank-you notes for anniversary gifts she and Grier had received.

"Hello, honey. How was your trip to town?" Sylvia asked, closing her stationery box.

"Fine." Jen carried several sacks of groceries into the kitchen. "You should see the peaches at the IGA. They're huge." Jen pulled one from the sack and held it up. "Would you like to take some home with you?"

"Thank you but I got a bushel of them the other day. Aren't they nice?" she said, coming into the kitchen. "Grier loves peach marmalade with his toast. Cesar's daughter-in-law makes the best marmalade you've ever tasted. She won a blue ribbon for it at the fair last year. I'll send some over for you all."

"That would be wonderful," Jen replied, emptying the sacks and putting away the groceries. "Taylor would love some, I'm sure. I'm not much of a cook."

"I don't know about that. Taylor looks like she has been eating pretty well." Sylvia touched Jen's arm and whispered. "Taylor can't cook worth beans. She never took the time to learn. She was more interested in riding a horse than baking a pie." She chuckled.

"Well, I can't bake a pie either," Jen admitted. "How is she, by the way? Did you get along okay?"

"Yes. She's fine. We didn't have any trouble. Lexie stopped by. She helped get her onto the commode then Taylor wanted to get in bed." Sylvia's eyes saddened. "I sure wish I could help take care of her. She looks so helpless with those big casts on her legs."

"You don't have to," Jen replied, noticing Sylvia's disappointment. She gave her a reassuring hug and smiled warmly. "That's what I'm here for. You make her a pie. I'll do the nursing things. By the way, where is she? Sleeping?"

"Yes. We played gin rummy and she suddenly got very tired."

"Is she sick?" Jen asked instantly.

"No," Sylvia chuckled. "She was losing big time. I skunked her six hands running."

"Oh," Jen laughed.

"How about you, honey? You look tired or something. Are you all right?" Sylvia studied Jen's eyes.

Jen didn't want to admit it took most of the trip back to the ranch to get over the mood her father had put her in.

"I'm fine, Sylvia. But thanks for asking. It has just been a long day."

"You have to take care of yourself, honey. What would we do if you got sick?" Sylvia smiled fondly at her. "If you don't need me anymore, I think I'll go home and see what Rita has made for dinner. I'm so glad we hired her to cook all the meals. I'm not much of a cook anymore."

"Wouldn't you like to eat with us? I'm making beef and noodles."

"That sounds wonderful, but no. If I'm not there to call Grier in for dinner, he'd work with those cows until midnight. I remember one night he and Taylor were in that barn pulling calves until the wee hours of the morning. I had to take a thermos of coffee and a box of sandwiches out to them or they never would have eaten." She sighed reflectively. "Tell Taylor I'll call tomorrow." Sylvia collected her things and left Jen waving from the back porch.

Jen finished with the groceries then went to check on Taylor. Her head had slid off the pillow and she was snoring. Jen carefully eased her head back onto the pillow and straightened the sheet over her. She checked the color of her toes and peeked at the top of the casts. Satisfied that Taylor was okay, she tiptoed out of the room, pulling the door shut behind her.

"Hey," Taylor said sleepily. "You back?"

"Shh, go back to sleep," Jen replied in a whisper.

"I'm awake." Taylor stretched and raised the head of the bed.

"I didn't mean to wake you. I'm sorry."

"I'm glad you did. If I nap too long I won't sleep tonight. How was your dad? How was the trip to town?"

"I brought you some peaches and a new kind of whole grain bread. You said you didn't like that last kind I got."

"Great. How was Rowdy?"

"Did you know they have a sing-along every Thursday afternoon at the nursing home? The activities director plays the piano in the rec room and everyone joins in." Jen laughed. "You should hear them. I've never heard such caterwauling in my life."

"Jen, how was you father?" Taylor persisted.

"Let's just say Rowdy was Rowdy," she replied. Jen picked up a box of tissues that had fallen on the floor and placed it on the bed table then turned to leave but Taylor grabbed her hand, stopping her escape.

"What happened?" Taylor asked, still holding onto Jen's hand.

"Nothing." Jen diverted her gaze. "Everything went fine, just fine." The muscles in her jaw rippled.

"Really?" Taylor asked, trying to see Jen's face. She pulled her closer.

"I have to start dinner. Do you want green beans or carrots?" Jen tried to pull away.

"I want you to tell me what's wrong, that's what I want." Taylor took Jen's other hand and turned her toward the bed. "What happened, Jen? Is Rowdy okay?"

"Oh, Rowdy is fine. He's shaved and clean and wearing the new clothes I got him. He is eating well and has good color. He hasn't looked so good in years."

"And?"

"And he still—" Jen started but a lump rose in her throat and her eyes glistened with tears.

"He still what?" Taylor held tight to Jen's hands.

Jen slowly looked up woefully.

"He still hates me."

"No, he doesn't. He doesn't hate you. You're his daughter. He might not like being in the nursing home but surely he knows he's better off there where he has a clean bed and hot food. He'll get over you putting him there. Give him some time."

"He doesn't need any time. He loves it there. He has women hovering over him, taking care of him and cooking for him. He doesn't have to lift a finger. He doesn't hate me for putting him there. Actually, he thinks it was his idea to move to Glen Haven. He has a private room because no one can stand to share a room with him. He's in seventh heaven." Jen stiffened her posture. "That has absolutely nothing to do with the way he feels about me."

Taylor pulled Jen down to sit on the edge of the bed next to her.

"What did he say?" she asked, stroking Jen's arm softly.

Jen hesitated as if even thinking about it was too painful.

"Jen?"

"He told me to get out of his room. He told me to get out and stay out."

"Why?" Taylor asked with a frown.

"I have no idea. I gave him a hug. I brought him a new pair of pajamas and some hard candy he likes. I hoped we could have a nice conversation. I wanted to tell him about the sculptures I was working on for Merrill's centennial but as soon as I mentioned my mother he didn't want to hear it. He stood up from his chair and started screaming at me. He didn't want to see me. I thought they were going to have to sedate him."

"Jen, I'm so sorry. I know you were looking forward to seeing him." Taylor squeezed her hand.

"The nurse said most of the time he is fine. He has small episodes like that but they don't have any trouble with him. He just sits there, watching TV and visiting with the other residents. He doesn't try to walk off."

"What brought on his flare-up against you?"

"Taylor, he has always felt that way about me. It isn't anything new. I just thought maybe, with the senile dementia, maybe he'd be different. Maybe he would have changed or at least forgotten he hated me. I just wanted to be able to talk with him without him telling me how much of a disappointment I was."

"If you'll excuse me saying so, he's freaking crazy. I have no idea how you could possibly be a disappointment to anyone. You are a nurse and an artist. You're smart and creative. You're beautiful and funny." Taylor smiled broadly, hoping to brighten Jen's spirits. "How could he not be proud of you?"

"Because he is Rowdy Holland. That's how. When I was

about five, he thought I should learn to ride a horse. He said if you live in Texas, you have to know how to ride. He thought I should have been born with that skill. He set me up on this huge horse. It was probably just an average-size horse but when you are five, all horses are huge. I was scared to death. I remember screaming and holding onto the saddle horn with a death grip. The horse was just standing there and I was hysterical. He told me to hold on to the reins and to sit up straight. I was crying and screaming for my mother to take me down. He wouldn't hear of it. He climbed up behind me and gave the horse a kick in the sides. That horse took off like a shot across the field, galloping at full speed. I was so scared I couldn't breath. I just closed my eyes and held on. He turned around and galloped back, bouncing me up and down in the saddle so hard my bottom was sore. He held onto the reins but he didn't hold onto me."

"Did you fall off?" Taylor asked with dread.

"No. But I wished I had. I thought if I fell off at least I wouldn't have to ride anymore." Jen heaved a reflective sigh. "When he stopped, my mother took me down and sent me in the house. They had one of their big yelling matches over that. He said I was an embarrassment if I wouldn't ride a horse."

"You were five, for heaven's sake. And not everyone in Texas can ride a horse. Believe it or not, my mother can't ride a horse. She's afraid of them too," Taylor offered in defense.

"I bet you could ride by the time you were five."

"Actually, I was three but everyone in the county says I was born on a horse. Dad tells everyone my first diaper was leather and had stirrups. I don't understand why your father thought you had to ride a horse if it scared you."

"I have no idea. I have no idea why he thought my scholarship to the University of Texas was a waste of time just because it was in art either."

"What about your nurse's training? He must have admired that."

"I doubt it. He wanted to know why I couldn't make up my mind what I wanted to do. I didn't tell him I took the nursing courses so I could take care of mother when she got so sick. She wanted to be at home and she couldn't afford a home nurse so I did it." Jen lowered her eyes as her mind wandered back to those years.

"How long was she sick?" Taylor asked tenderly.

"About five years. She might have survived another few years but she had a stroke."

"I'm so sorry, Jen."

"It was a blessing. She was practically bedridden. She was in constant pain and was losing weight." Jen smiled at the ceiling as if comfortable with her mother's passing. "Cancer is a cruel taskmaster."

"Sounds like you were a brave and caring daughter."

"Yeah, well. I'm batting five hundred. Dad doesn't think so."

"You're batting more than five hundred. You're taking care of me and doing a great job." Taylor touched Jen's cheek. "That has to count for something."

"Thank you, but my father—"

"Your father has senile dementia. He can't remember what day it is. Don't let what he said today upset you." Taylor studied Jen's face. "I have to ask you something, Jen. It may not be any of my business but why did you take this job as my caregiver? I asked the social worker at the hospital and she told me you walked in and offered to take it. Why? I mean, our first two meetings weren't exactly the stuff friendships are made of. Did it have anything to do with Rowdy?"

"I needed a job," she replied. "And you needed a nurse."

"But you are an artist, a good artist. Why did you need to take a job as a CSN in Harland? You live in San Antonio. Surely you could find work there."

"I needed a job that would pay me well and right away."

"Rowdy?"

Jen nodded.

"Bad?"

Jen nodded again.

"IRS?" Taylor asked carefully.

"Property taxes. Three years and penalties."

"Did you get it taken care of?" Taylor asked cautiously.

"I will."

"Jen, let me help," Taylor insisted. "Let me pay it off."

"Absolutely not," Jen replied in her most adamant voice. "This is my responsibility. And besides, it is almost caught up. By the time you are recuperated, I will have paid Mr. Henry the last payment."

"Let me advance it to you now."

"No, Taylor. I won't hear of it. Not another word about it."

"Do you need me to keep the casts on longer so you can earn more? Would that make a difference?"

"No, I'll be fine. And you couldn't wait one second longer than you have to anyway," Jen replied with a chuckle.

"Probably not," she muttered.

"But thank you for the offer."

"Does your father know what you are doing? Does he know you are paying off his debts?"

"No, I don't think so. He doesn't understand his financial situation. If he did, I'm sure he would have paid it himself. He was very careful about money. I know you don't think he was much of a rancher or a father but in his day he was."

"I'm sure he was. I heard he had a small operation but he had some of the best beef cattle to come out of the county. He was well-liked by his fellow ranchers."

"He was a kind and gentle man but that was years ago. That was before he and my mother divorced. I hardly know him anymore."

"I bet the split between them was hard on you."

"I was very young but I do remember we had some nice times

together. They reconciled a few times but it was brief."

"They couldn't have children of their own?" Taylor asked.

"No. And I think each one blamed the other. He wanted a son so he would have someone to take over the ranch. She wanted a daughter to dress in frilly clothes and show off to her friends. They spent their time together picking on everything. If she made chicken for dinner, he'd want hamburger. If he brought her candy, she'd want flowers." Jen shrugged. "By the time I came along, I think their marriage was already gone."

"Maybe they thought you'd be the tonic they both needed."

"Maybe. Or Mother needed someone to be on her side. I think I remind Dad of their marriage and how it fell apart."

"You can't think you are responsible for their divorce, Jen." Taylor offered softly. "That had nothing to do with you."

"I know. But I certainly didn't help it. I was like a pebble in Rowdy's shoe. I just rubbed him the wrong way."

"Did it have anything to do with you being gay?"

Jen smiled reflectively.

"That was the cherry on the top. After he found out I had an art scholarship, which he thought was a waste of time, and then split my attention with nurse's aide training, he didn't need much to find my life completely useless in his eyes."

"But you are a wonderful artist. Has he ever seen your work?"

"I've sent him clippings and pictures but he never mentions it and after seeing the inside of his house, I bet he never even saw them."

"I can guess what it looks like. I've been up to the door a couple times. He's never let me in but I could see inside. It looked kind of messy." Taylor picked her words carefully, not wanting to hurt Jen's feeling further.

"Messy?" Jen scoffed and shook her head. "I went inside the day I signed him into the nursing home. He needed some clothes and pajamas and his personal things. I hadn't been in the house in several years. He would never answer the door when I

175

came to visit. He'd tell me later he wasn't home but I knew he was in there, watching from the window. Well, when I opened the door, I thought I'd made a mistake. I thought I was in the wrong house. It looked like a storage shed full of trash. I could barely get in the door. He kept every piece of paper and box and empty container he ever had. Every dish and pan and glass in his kitchen was covered with crusty grease and food. Taylor, I was so shocked. I never thought he'd let his house get that bad. I took one look and ran out. I didn't even look for clean clothes. I knew he wouldn't have any. All the clothes I saw were in disgusting piles. There were mouse droppings and cobwebs everywhere. I didn't go past the living room and kitchen. I have no idea where he slept. I couldn't get down the hall to the bedrooms."

Taylor held Jen's hands in hers securely, hoping to console her.

"I'm so sorry, Jen. I had no idea."

"I haven't been able to go back over there. I know I should but I just can't."

"You don't need to go over there. It isn't anything you need to do right now. Someday he may want to go back there. He may get better and be able to live by himself again." Taylor had no idea why she said that. She wasn't a nurse or a doctor but she knew Rowdy Holland wasn't ever going to be well enough to live by himself. But she also didn't want Jen to wrap his problems around herself so tightly that they suffocated her. She wanted to help Jen. She wanted to protect her from this never-ending pain Rowdy was causing. "Someday I'll go with you."

"I'll be all right. I'll just have to wait until I'm ready." Jen blinked away a tear. She gave a small smile and stood up.

"When you go back to see him, you'll see. It'll be just like old times. He'll be anxious to see you. He'll ask where you've been and why it's been so long since you came to see him."

"So, do you want green beans or carrots?" Jen asked, regaining her composure.

"You are going back to visit him, aren't you?" Taylor asked, trying to read Jen's face.

"I don't think so."

"Jen, don't let his condition get in the way of seeing your father. You know you want to go back."

"What I want isn't at Glen Haven, Taylor. That isn't my father." She went to the door then looked back. "I'll let you know when dinner is ready."

Chapter 14

"Jen," Taylor called from her room. It was sometime after midnight and the house was dark. The only sound was the rhythmic tick-tock of the grandfather clock in the hall. Taylor didn't want to bother Jen. She had learned to manage the bedpan during the night. She could slide it under her rear and out again without spilling a drop. Jen insisted it was okay to call her for help but Taylor wanted to regain some shred of dignity. But tonight was different. She didn't need the bedpan. That wasn't what was bothering her. This was a pain in her leg, a pain unlike anything she had ever felt before. It wasn't a bone pain. That she had learned to recognize. This was a muscle pain, a deep and gripping pain. This was a charley horse from hell and she couldn't do anything about it. If she had a saw, she would gladly cut the cast from her leg, even if it meant taking the leg off with it.

"Jen," she screamed through gritted teeth, the pain growing stronger with every second. She could hear footsteps coming down the stairs.

"What's wrong?" Jen said, frantically turning on the light and rushing to her side. "What happened?" She stared at Taylor's face, instantly reading the anguish in her eyes.

"My leg," Taylor grimaced, writhing in pain. She twisted in the bed and reached for the cast on her left leg.

"Describe the pain to me, Taylor," Jen demanded as she went to the foot of the bed and held the cast in her hands. She examined Taylor's toes and grabbed them to check their temperature.

"It hurts. Like a charley horse." Taylor winced, turning on her side to get away from it.

"Just this one?" Jen asked, checking the other toes.

Taylor nodded, her eyes closed tight and her teeth clenched.

"Did it hurt when you went to bed?"

Taylor shook her head violently.

"It just started. It woke me up. It's killing me, Jen. It hurts so bad. We've got to get the cast off. I can't stand it." Taylor gasped, grabbing the pillow behind her head as tears rolled down her face and onto the pillow.

"It's a muscle contraction, Taylor. A cramp." Jen lowered the bed all the way down. She tossed the sheet aside and sat down next to Taylor, pulling her shoulders up into a sitting position. "Sit up, Taylor."

"I can't. I can't."

"Yes, you can. We're going to stretch it as much as we can. Come on. Sit up." Jen helped her up, wedging herself behind Taylor for support. She wrapped her arms around Taylor's chest and hugged her. She could feel every muscle in Taylor's body taut from the pain. "Lean forward, Taylor. Lean over. As far as you can go."

Taylor fought against Jen's hold, the pain controlling her mind and her body.

179

"I can't," she said, gripping the sheet with both hands and stiffening. She cried out loud, great sobs consuming her.

"Yes you can," Jen replied in a soothing voice. "I'll help you. We need to stretch the back of your thigh. Lean with me, Taylor. Lean," Jen said, coaxing her forward as she pressed against her back. "Now back then forward again," she said reassuringly. "Easy. Back and forward." She continued to rock Taylor forward, bending her at the waist until she felt her body begin to relax in her arms. "That's it."

With slow but steady pressure, Jen continued to bend Taylor forward, stretching her hamstring and working the constricted muscles. Jen could feel Taylor's body dripping with sweat through her shirt.

"How's it feeling?" Jen asked.

"Better," Taylor replied, her breaths short and labored from the strain, perspiration running down her face.

"We should do this every night before you go to bed," Jen said, finishing a few more reps, easing Taylor forward and back with gentle pressure.

Taylor heaved a great sigh of relief as the pain subsided.

"I'm sorry I had to wake you up but I couldn't move."

"That's what I'm here for." Jen replied, still sitting behind Taylor and holding her up in a sitting position. "How's it now?"

"Much better. Thank you," Taylor declared. "I didn't mean to act so stupid about it." She lowered her eyes, well aware of what she had done in the throes of pain.

"You didn't act stupid," Jen said softly. "You were in pain. I'd probably do the exact same thing. It's okay. I don't mind." She released her hold around Taylor's chest. "Let me get you a clean shirt. That one is all sweaty."

"That's okay. I've taken enough of your night's sleep."

"Baby blue or white with a horse on it?" Jen asked, holding up two T-shirts from the drawer and ignoring Taylor's remark. "You'll catch a chill if we don't change it."

"Blue, I guess." Taylor reached out to take it, prepared to change her own shirt.

"Just a second," Jen said, going into the bathroom and returning with a wet washcloth and towel.

"I can do this. You go on to bed. Thank you for your help."

"Shh." Jen pulled the sweaty shirt over Taylor's head and tossed it in the hamper. She washed Taylor's back and shoulders. When she moved to the front, she sat down on the side of the bed, giving the job her full attention. She rubbed down each arm and back up then moved to Taylor's chest, wiping the washcloth over each breast with tender strokes. All the while Taylor sat watching, studying Jen's face as she performed her nursing chores. Jen took the towel from over her shoulder and dried Taylor's body. "There. Don't you feel better?" Jen asked, tossing the washcloth and towel into the hamper as well.

She reached for the T-shirt and placed the neck of it over Taylor's head, as if she was dressing a child. The arms came next but before Taylor slipped an arm in the sleeve, Jen looked up at her. Their eyes met and froze Jen where she sat. For a long moment they sat gazing at each other, not a movement between them. Slowly Taylor reached up and brushed a lock of hair that had fallen over Jen's face. Jen didn't move. She sat holding the shirt around Taylor's neck.

"Let me help you put your shirt on," Jen said finally, her eyes still on Taylor's.

"You don't have to be a nurse all the time. I can do some things for myself," Taylor replied, folding another lock of hair over her shoulder.

"I know. But this is what I'm paid to do." Jen felt a tingle that made the hair on the back of her neck stand on end as Taylor touched her. She shivered deeply.

"Your shirt is sweaty too," she said, hooking a finger in the neck of Jen's nightshirt. "We should change it. You can wear one of mine."

"I'll be all right," Jen replied, another shiver sending a blush over her face.

"You'll catch a chill if we don't change it," Taylor said, pulling at the hem of Jen's shirt.

"No, wait," she stammered.

"Hands up," Taylor said, pulling against Jen's refusal.

"Stop. I'll change upstairs," she argued, pulling her shirt down.

"Let me guess. Nurses don't take off their wet shirts in front of their patients, right?"

"I can change my shirt by myself."

"And I can't?" Taylor chuckled.

Jen realized she didn't have an answer.

"If you are embarrassed, say so," Taylor said.

"No, I'm not embarrassed," she replied hesitantly.

"Then hands up."

Jen sat on the bed for a long moment then raised her arms. Taylor peeled the damp nightshirt over her head and tossed it aside. Jen sat with her eyes lowered. She knew Taylor was staring at her. She could feel it. She could also feel her nipples harden.

"See how easy that was?" Taylor said quietly, unable to look away from Jen's perfectly formed breasts.

Jen sat motionless while Taylor's eyes drank in every curve and soft line of her shape. Jen knew it was only fair. Taylor had been exposed to examination so often her modesty was surely long gone. As a nurse, Jen had seen many naked patients. Some gorgeous bodies with tanned muscles and well-toned shapes. Some pale, old and fragile bodies of ill patients barely clinging to life. She never thought much about her own, not when she was consumed with caring for the sick and infirmed.

"Here," Taylor said, pulling her own shirt off and slipping it over Jen's head. She guided Jen's arms in the arm holes and settled it down over her body. "Now you're ready for bed."

"I'll get you one," Jen said.

Taylor grabbed her hand to stop her from standing up.

"I don't want one. I'll just use the sheet."

"But," Jen started to say.

"I really don't want one," she whispered. "I usually sleep naked."

Jen smoothed the sheet across Taylor's lap as she sat next to her.

"Are you ready for bed now?" Jen asked, desperate to keep her eyes off Taylor's firm round breasts and her patch of dark pubic hair. For some strange reason, this wasn't the body of a patient. It was Taylor's body, the body of a gorgeous, desirable woman.

Taylor adjusted the hem of Jen's shirt.

"Are you?" Taylor asked in soft tones.

"It's almost one o'clock. You need your rest." Jen couldn't keep her eyes from meeting Taylor's. There was a warmth about them tonight, a warmth that was inviting and gentle.

"I'm not tired," Taylor replied, resting her hand on Jen's thigh. The touch made Jen moan ever so slightly.

"Do you need a drink or something?"

"No," Taylor replied in a warm whisper. "I don't need anything. I'm very happy just sitting here like this." Taylor squeezed Jen's thigh slightly.

"I'm glad your leg isn't bothering you anymore. You should have called me sooner." Jen wasn't aware of it but she was ever so slowly leaning forward, her upper body moving closer to Taylor's.

"I didn't want to get you out of bed. I bet you were all cuddled up, sound asleep." Taylor rubbed Jen's leg tenderly.

"And I'm sure I look like a witch. I ran down the stairs without even combing my hair." Jen ran her fingers through her hair in a veiled attempt at straightening it. Taylor took Jen's hands and folded them across her lap.

"You look wonderful. You aren't capable of looking like a

witch."

"Thank you but you should see me when I've been painting." Jen chuckled quietly. "I look hideous."

"Do you get paint on your face?"

"Oh, yes. And in my hair. The last mural I did I had a big smear of red paint right across my face from cheek to cheek. I looked like a clown." She wiped two fingers across her face.

"Like lipstick gone bad?" Taylor asked through a chuckle.

"Exactly." Jen joined in the laughter. "And it wasn't even my color."

"Oh, wow. Ugly lipstick gone bad."

"Very ugly."

"What color do you wear? I take you for a pink?"

"It's sort of a berry color. It's called Santa Fe Rose."

"I like the sound of that. But I haven't seen you wearing much makeup since you came to work. Why not?"

"I don't wear it while I'm working. It's too hard to keep it looking fresh when I'm sweating and lifting and all."

"I guess that would make it wilt a tad. Besides, you don't need makeup. You look wonderful without it."

Jen blushed and lowered her eyes.

"I don't agree with you but thanks anyway," she replied.

Taylor cupped her hand under Jen's chin and raised her face.

"It wasn't an idle compliment. You are beautiful. I love to see sexy women in makeup and tight jeans but you are breathtaking without them," Taylor said, smiling softly at her.

"And you're an expert?" Jen asked, her eyes sparkling as she gazed at Taylor.

"You bet I am. Who do you think I was trying to see at the Rainbow Desert that night?" Taylor replied, guiding Jen's face closer to hers. "You are the one I was straining to get another look at and no one was getting in my way."

"You sound pretty sure of yourself."

"I know what I like," Taylor whispered, her lips just inches from Jen's.

"And what is that?"

"Women artists who wear Santa Fe Rose lipstick, right here," Taylor replied then pressed her lips to Jen's. She held her chin as they kissed a brief but meaningful kiss.

"I'm not wearing lipstick," Jen said softly, reveling in Taylor's touch and gaze.

"Consider this practice." Taylor folded her arms around Jen and drew her close, kissing her again.

Jen sat stiffly, pressing her hands into the bed to keep her weight off Taylor as they kissed. It was an awkward position at best.

"What's the matter?" Taylor asked, feeling Jen's resistance. "Am I doing something I shouldn't?"

Jen leaned back, pulling out of Taylor's embrace.

"This could be dangerous," Jen warned.

"I know," Taylor said with a coy smile.

"For several reasons."

"I may have casts on my legs but not on my lips." Taylor leaned forward, trying to kiss Jen again.

"Stop, Taylor. Please." Jen stood up and folded the sheet across Taylor's shoulders, covering her naked and tempting body. "You need to go to bed," she said nervously.

"I am in bed," Taylor grinned, pushing the sheet down to her waist. "And so were you."

"I mean go to sleep," she corrected, draping it back over her shoulders.

"I told you, I'm not tired." Taylor pushed it down again.

"It's late. You need rest to keep up your strength." Jen pushed Taylor's shoulders down on the bed and covered her again.

"I don't need any rest," Taylor argued, sitting back up in bed and grabbing for Jen's hand. "Why don't you sit and talk with me. We can talk about lipstick. I don't wear it but you can tell me all about the different colors." Taylor patted the bed next to her.

"I need sleep and so do you. Now you lay down." Jen pushed her shoulders back against the bed and tucked the sheet in around her as if it would somehow hold her down. "Good night." She hurried out the door and closed it, leaving the light on.

"Hey," Taylor called, sitting up again.

The door opened a few inches and Jen's hand slid inside, flicking off the light then closing the door again. Taylor could hear footsteps going up the stairs. There was a hesitation then the footsteps descended a few steps. After a moment, Jen continued back upstairs. The telltale creak of the headboard meant Jen had climbed into bed. Taylor folded her hands behind her head and smiled at the ceiling. There was no way she was going to sleep tonight, not with Jen's gorgeous body sleeping directly above her like a gossamer vision. Taylor may be incapacitated with thirty-pound casts on her legs but she still had feelings and yearnings, yearnings that weren't used to being ignored. Even with tangled hair and sleepy face, Jen Holland was the most beautiful woman she had ever seen. Her kiss set fire to something in Taylor she had never felt before. She didn't know what it was but she liked it and she knew she would spend the rest of the night reliving it.

Chapter 15

"Do you want to go into town or something for a couple hours?" Taylor asked after hanging up the telephone and rolling herself into the dining room. Jen was standing at the dining room table, arranging papers and juggling sketch pads.

"Why? Did you need something?" she asked, trying to find enough room to spread out her work.

"No. I don't need anything."

"Here, hold this for one second," Jen said, handing her a box of charcoal pencils. Taylor obliged, rolling as close as she could to get a look at Jen's work.

"I just thought since Lexie was coming over you might want some time off. She'll be here for a couple hours. Coal is expecting a visitor."

"Coal is expecting a visit?" Jen asked curiously.

"Yes, an Appaloosa mare. Heavy date," Taylor said, giving a

187

crooked smile.

"Oh, stud service heavy date," Jen teased.

"Yes, but don't tell him. If he knew I was getting paid for his services, he'd want half." She picked up one of the sketches and held it up for examination. "I like this one. What is it?"

"It was supposed to be a cactus. But I'm not sure about that one. It leaves something to be desired."

"I still like it," Taylor said, setting it back in its place. "So, do you want some time away from here?"

"I do have some errands I could run. When is Lexie coming over?"

"Any minute. That was her on the phone. She just picked up the mare and is on her way."

"I will if you promise to behave yourself. Remember, absolutely no weight bearing on your legs of any kind. That means you stay in the chair or on the couch, period." Jen narrowed her eyes at Taylor. "Promise?"

"Scout's honor," Taylor replied. "Besides, when it comes to breeding horses, they pretty much do it by themselves."

"Yes, but you have to promise me anyway."

"Fine, I promise. I will not help Coal pork the mare."

"That's disgusting," Jen said.

"If you knew how much Coal's stud fees were you wouldn't say that. His grandfather was a grand champion. Coal has sired some expensive horse flesh."

"Is he a gentleman about it?" Jen teased, as she began stacking her supplies.

"Sure. He's a Fleming. We are all polite to our dates," she mused. "No, I take that back, T-bone has a mean streak. For a registered Black Angus bull, he acts more like a Brahma. He doesn't like to be kept waiting."

"And how about you?" Jen asked with a chuckle, filling two cardboard boxes to overflowing. "Are you patient?"

"I'm learning to be," Taylor replied, her eyes scanning Jen's

188

backside as she picked up a box. "Here, put that box on my lap," she said, patting her thighs. "I'll carry it."

"I will not," she scowled. "It's way too heavy."

"My legs aren't broken up here." Taylor followed her into the kitchen and watched as Jen stacked the boxes in the mudroom. "I could've held it in my hands," Taylor argued.

"Thanks but it's all done." Jen smiled and patted Taylor's shoulder as she headed for the stairs. "Be right down."

Lexie honked the horn as she pulled into the yard and stopped next to the corral. Taylor rolled herself out onto the back porch and watched as Lexie unloaded the mare and led her into the corral. She gave the skittish animal a few minutes to get acclimated before opening the gate and allowing Coal to enter.

"Nice looking mare," Taylor called, trying to see between the truck and trailer.

"Susan said thanks. She's glad we agreed to bring the mare over here. She backed her flatbed truck into her corral and put a ten-foot hole in the fence. Ripped three posts right out of the ground," Lexie chuckled. "Wonder if she's any relation to Rowdy," she added, yelling across the yard.

Before Taylor could chastise Lexie for her comment, Jen stepped out on the back porch. Her face told Taylor she had overheard Lexie's joke.

"I'm sorry, Jen," Lexie stammered. "I've got a big mouth." She lowered her eyes.

"That's okay, Lexie," Jen replied, though it was obvious her words had hurt.

"She didn't mean anything by it, Jen," Taylor added, touching Jen's arm softly.

"I know." Jen smiled back at Taylor. "Rowdy's reputation follows him everywhere."

Lexie came to the porch, still red-faced.

"I'm really sorry. If you want to slap me or something, I'll understand."

Jen descended the three steps and smiled at Lexie.

"No, I don't want to slap you," she said softly. "I know how much work and aggravation my father cost you. It's okay." Then Jen gave Lexie a serious scowl. "But I will slap you both if I get back and you have allowed Taylor to do anything stupid. You both know her limitations." Jen laughed. "I sound like I'm leaving a first-grader to watch a kindergartner."

"Hey, I'm the first-grader here," Taylor declared.

"No, you are not," Lexie scoffed. "I'm the first-grader. You're the snot-nosed kindergartner. I'm in charge."

"I'm leaving. You two can argue about it as soon as I'm out of the driveway. And remember, Lexie. No beer for Taylor. She just had her injection." Jen tossed back a disciplinary stare then climbed in the van and pulled away, waving out the window.

"Good, she's gone," Taylor said brightly.

"Don't go getting me in any trouble here," Lexie replied.

"I have a job for you and we'll have just enough time to finish before she gets back."

"What kind of job? Does this have anything to do with your legs and you getting out of that chair?"

"No, you're safe. I'm not doing anything I shouldn't," Taylor replied, rolling herself inside. "Come on."

Jen went to the grocery store, the hardware store, the gas station and treated herself to lunch in town. She went by Glen Haven to check on her father but he was napping. She decided it was just as well she didn't wake him. She called twice to check on Taylor, both times concerned that it took her four rings to pick up.

"Don't you have the cordless phone in the pouch on the side of the chair?" she asked when Taylor answered breathlessly.

"I guess I put it down on the table," Taylor replied, seemingly distracted.

"Are you getting along okay? How are your legs? Any pain?"

"Nope, I'm fine."

"How is Coal?" Jen teased. "Is this date going well?"

"Yep," Taylor replied, not offering much conversation.

"Do you need anything?" Jen asked, trying to determine if Taylor was all right.

"Don't need a thing. Take your time."

"Okay," Jen heard the line click. "I guess she was finished talking," she muttered to herself. She stopped at the feed store and bought Picasso a bag of cat food then headed back to the ranch, still curious why Taylor seemed distracted and indifferent to her call. She pulled into the yard and parked next to Lexie's truck.

"I'm back," she called, carrying her purchases in the house. Lexie strode into the kitchen smiling a guilty smile. Taylor came rolling in behind her. Both of them had devious looks in their eyes and it didn't go unnoticed by Jen.

"Hi," Taylor said quickly.

"Hi," Lexie said in the same artificial tone.

"What?" Jen said, looking at them warily.

"What what?" Taylor asked, straightening the sheet across her lap.

"If ever anyone looked like the cat that swallowed the canary, it's you two." She placed her hands on her hips. "What have you been up to?"

"Nothing," Lexie offered, trying desperately to look innocent.

"Yeah, nothing," Taylor agreed.

"I better load up the mare and head back. I'm sure Coal has taken care of business. I heard them snorting at one another." Lexie took her hat from the kitchen counter and pulled it down tight on her head.

"Thanks," Taylor said, following her to the back door.

"No problem." Lexie tossed a look at Jen then pulled the

door shut behind her.

"Why do I feel like you did something against the doctor's orders," Jen suggested, studying Taylor for clues.

"I didn't do anything against the doctor's orders. Believe me." Taylor turned her chair and went back into the living room. "I'm innocent," she added as she rolled away.

"That is debatable."

"I heard that. And if you don't behave, you won't get to see your surprise. So there."

Jen came to the doorway and looked at Taylor skeptically.

"What surprise?" she asked.

"Oh, you'll see."

"When is this surprise happening, if I dare ask?"

"After dinner."

"Oh, geez. I forgot to defrost anything," Jen gasped and went to the refrigerator. "It's after six and I don't have anything out."

"Don't we have leftovers or something?"

"No, that's what we had last night," Jen searched the refrigerator for anything she could call dinner. "How about salad and"— she kept searching—"baked potato royale?" she asked hopefully, holding up two potatoes.

"What is baked potato royale?"

"If you give me twenty minutes, I'll let you know." Jen went to the sink and scrubbed the potatoes. Taylor rolled herself into the kitchen and took them from her hands.

"I want a bologna sandwich and an apple," she said, dropping the potatoes back in the bin.

"That isn't enough for dinner." Jen opened the freezer, looking for something she could defrost in the microwave.

"Yes, it is. I want a sandwich, with mustard, of course. I'll help make them."

"Are you sure? I'm sorry, Taylor. I shouldn't have gone to town today. I didn't get all my chores finished and now you have to eat a cold sandwich for dinner," Jen said, scolding herself.

"I like bologna."

"But you need something healthy. Bologna isn't very good for you."

"My legs won't fall off, believe me. It's okay," Taylor smiled reassuringly. "I won't fire you for missing a meal."

"Are you really sure you don't mind?" Jen began making the sandwiches, her face filled with guilt.

"I really don't mind. Besides, now you can see your surprise sooner."

"Are you going to tell me what you and Lexie have been up to?"

"Okay," Taylor said, unable to wait another minute to show Jen what she had done. "Come on." She waved for Jen to follow.

"Where are we going?" Jen helped roll the wheelchair, waiting for Taylor's directions.

"Down the hall," she said, pointing toward the storeroom.

"In there? If this is to show me some new saddle or box of steer horns you've put in that room, forget it. I don't want to see it. That room is a disaster. I'm surprised it doesn't walk on its own." Jen said, hesitantly rolling her toward the closed door. "There isn't room for us in there anyway. It is full to the ceiling."

"Not anymore, it isn't," Taylor said, reaching over and opening the door. She pushed it open and rolled herself in. "This is now officially the Jen Holland art room."

Jen gasped as she looked through the door. The room that had been home to whatever Taylor couldn't bring herself to get rid of was now empty of everything but a spare dining room table, an adjustable chair, a floor lamp and a bookshelf. Clothesline rope had been strung from one corner of the room to the next with clothespins to hold Jen's art work. A piece of paper hanging from one of the clothespins read WELCOME TO JEN'S STUDIO.

"I figured you needed a place to put your art stuff where you didn't have to keep picking it up all the time. You can spread out

in here and just leave it. Close the door and come back later."
Taylor rolled out of the way so Jen could see it.

"Oh, Taylor," she grinned, rubbing her hand over the table.
"This is wonderful. How did you do all this? Did you carry all
this on your lap like I told you not to do?" She frowned at Taylor.

"Nope, I didn't. Lexie did the carrying. I had her store it all in
the barn. I didn't even know half the stuff that was in here. I
found my extra saddle blanket though."

Jen hugged Taylor around the neck and gave her a big slob-
bery kiss on the cheek.

"Thank you." Jen grinned, smiling wildly. "What a nice thing
for you to do. I don't think my art room at my house is this big."

"I should have done it earlier but I was busy being an ass-
hole," Taylor replied.

"No, you weren't. You were just getting used to your casts."
Jen stroked Taylor's face. "This is wonderful. I was having such a
problem keeping my work organized. I didn't know what I had
done and what I hadn't. Thank you. You are so thoughtful. And
you were going to let me feed you a bologna sandwich. Now I
really feel bad about not defrosting anything."

"Don't worry about it."

"I can't wait to set up my stuff." Jen hurried out of the room
on her way to the mudroom.

"Wait a minute. Come back in here," Taylor called. She
opened the closet door and pointed to the boxes of Jen's art supplies stacked neatly on the floor. "You mean these?"

Jen's smile broadened.

"You thought of everything." Jen set the boxes on the table
and began setting up her supplies. "Since I have to make a sketch
from every angle for each sculpture I end up with a lot of them.
This will be perfect."

"Give me something to stack over here in the bookshelves,"
Taylor said, looking in one of the boxes. "What is this?" She
pulled out a naked wooden doll with moveable limbs. She shook

it, making the arms and legs flop.

"It's a fully articulated and poseable manikin," Jen explained. "And don't break it, please."

Taylor stopped playing with it and set it on the shelf. She picked through the art supplies, examining each item. She tried out a few, making a squiggle here and there on a scrap of paper. "I don't see any crayons in here."

"I don't think I have any."

"How can you be an artist without crayons and white paste? You know, the kind in a jar you have to smear on with a stick."

Jen chuckled.

"I had the box of forty-eight crayons when I was a kid," Taylor announced.

"Wow, forty-eight. You must have whined a long time to get those."

"Yeah, but Sandy Stern had the huge box of sixty-four." Taylor gave a crooked smile. "And she never let me forget it, either."

"You can only color with one at a time, Taylor," Jen said in a maternal voice.

"Didn't you ever try holding a whole fist full and rub them across the paper all at once? Makes a great rainbow."

"Rainbow, eh?" Jen smiled.

"Yes. Every lesbian has to be able to make a rainbow on her paper by first grade," Taylor advised with a knowing grin.

"And if they can't?" Jen teased. "What happens? They lose their membership card?"

"No. They have to wear bows in their hair until they can."

"I wore bows in my hair until junior high school," Jen declared.

"I bet you did," Taylor smiled. "What color? Pink?"

"I had a whole shoebox full. I had a different color bow for every outfit. My mother made them. She bought a huge package of plain hairclips then yards and yards of ribbon to make the bows. She made little ones and big ones—you name it and I had a hair bow to match it." Jen laughed at the memory. "Didn't you have hair bows?"

"If I did, I prefer not to remember it." Taylor frowned.

"I bet you looked cute with little pink bows in your hair," Jen teased, pulling up tufts of Taylor's hair.

"Quit it," Taylor scowled, trying to act mad.

"And curls. I bet you had lots of curls, bouncy cute curls everywhere."

"And I hated them. Naturally curly hair and a cowboy hat are worst enemies."

"I love your hair. Reddish-brown and curly. What more could anyone want?" Jen arranged a few curls into Taylor's short hair. "Were you able to draw a rainbow very young?"

"If you mean how young was I when I knew I was a lesbian, I think I always knew but it wasn't until I was about fifteen or so that I really knew. How about you?"

"I was a late bloomer. I didn't realize what the funny feelings meant until I was in college," Jen related.

"How did you find out?" Taylor asked, running her hands through her hair to discourage the curls Jen had placed.

"I had a roommate who was gorgeous. She was tall and had gorgeous skin and a figure to die for. I couldn't keep my eyes off her. I almost flunked out first semester because I spent more time with her than on my studies."

"Was she gay?" Taylor asked.

"Heavens, no. She dated the captain of the football team and was the freshman homecoming queen. She was forever sneaking guys in the dorm after hours and telling me to go sleep in the lounge. Like an idiot, I did it, thinking she'd like me if I agreed. She was the one who flunked out after just one semester. It's a good thing. I almost lost my scholarship over swivel hips. That's what I called her. She could definitely swivel what her momma gave her. She was the one who opened my eyes to my gender identity though."

"Sounds like my kind of woman," Taylor teased, flashing a big grin. "What's her phone number?"

"I told you, she wasn't a lesbian," Jen replied.

"Maybe not yet, but you know what they say. We're always looking to recruit."

"Taylor," Jen scoffed.

"You're right. She'd probably be more work than she's worth." Taylor winked.

"Who was your first? I can't imagine there are very many openly gay women in Harland, Texas."

"You'd be surprised. There are probably half dozen ranches in the county owned and operated by gay couples. Susan and Kitty have been breeding and selling horses for thirty years. They're the ones who owned the Appaloosa mare bred to Coal. They both have been openly gay since they bought their ranch. I dare anyone to cross their paths. They are the salt of the earth, give you the shirt off their back but don't mess with them. They are both crack shots and could take you off a horse at fifty yards with a BB gun."

"And there's Lexie," Jen suggested diplomatically.

"Yeah," Taylor replied with a small smile. "I wondered if you knew."

"I'm just guessing."

"Lexie knew she was gay all her life. I think she had her first date with a woman when she was fourteen. She's a good cowhand though. She knows all there is to know about calving. She's saved many a calf for us. She's the one who helps me decide which bulls to keep."

"She likes you," Jen offered. "I mean, she sure seems concerned about your legs."

"She has always been there for me. She's twenty years older but she understands a lot about me. I can talk to her."

"She's tough on the outside but I bet she is like a big teddy bear on the inside."

"I'll have to tell her that," Taylor chuckled. "She thinks she's got the roughneck-Tex thing working for her."

"So do you, the roughneck-Tex thing," Jen said, looking over at Taylor.

"No, I don't," she replied, lowering her eyes as she blushed.

"Who was it who wouldn't ask for help the first two weeks she was home with thirty pound casts on her legs?" Jen said coyly.

"Yeah, well," Taylor stammered, still blushing.

"You still haven't answered my question," Jen said.

"What question?"

"Who was your first?" Jen asked.

"Pearl Nesbitt. Pearly Mae." Taylor tossed her head back and laughed.

"Okay, let's hear it." Jen announced, pulling up a chair and facing Taylor.

"You don't want to hear this," Taylor replied with a frown.

"Sure I do. After all, I've helped you on and off a bedpan. There can be no secrets between a nurse and her patient," Jen added, giving Taylor a gentle push.

"Just remember, you asked. Well, Pearl was several years older than me. She lived over in Federal. Her daddy had a goat ranch and she drove an old Jeep, one of those old army surplus ones. They used it on the ranch to round up the goats. On weekends she'd drive over to Gilbert's Crossing. That's a stone bridge across the river about fifteen miles south of Harland. She'd bring a blanket, hang her clothes over the bumper and sunbathe along the bank of the river. Sometimes the river would be up high enough so you could jump in off the bridge. They had signs up saying it was against the law to jump but no one paid any attention to them. The signs were used as clothes hangers while folks went skinny dipping. Well, this one Saturday afternoon it was hot, scorching hot. I didn't go down there very often but it had rained and the river was deep enough for a swim so I decided to go on down. I had to finish my chores first so by the time I got there, all the other kids had left. I was hot and dirty so I stripped out of my clothes and jumped in. It was so cool and nice. I was floating along when I looked up and saw this face staring down at me from the bridge. It was Pearly Mae Nesbitt. The most gorgeous woman I had ever seen. Of course, I was only sixteen. My experiences were pretty limited. Pearly asked me if I minded if she joined me. She was sweaty and had driven all the way down there from Federal, a good forty miles away, so I said sure."

"Were you naked?" Jen asked.

"No, I had my underwear on. I had my period so I figured I better keep them on. I have no idea why. The water was filthy, all brownish-green. How we kept from getting sick is anyone's guess. So, Pearl disappeared behind a tree. The next thing I knew, this golden-tanned body was jumping in right next to me. She had long legs that wouldn't quit and the biggest bush I had ever seen. She was kind of flat-chested but at that age, I wasn't sure where my preferences were when it came to the female body. Anyway, she came up behind me and bumped me. She said it was accidental but I didn't care. Whatever the reason, she had touched my ass and I was on fire." Taylor gave a cockeyed smile.

"What happened next?"

"Are you sure you want to hear this?" Taylor was surprised at herself for admitting so much of a subject she didn't usually talk about. She had never been the kiss-and-tell type.

"Come on, you can't stop now. I have to hear what Pearly Mae did with her flat chest and bushy mound." Jen giggled.

"Let's see. Where was I? Oh, yes. Pearl and I swam around for a while, you know. Small talk about where we lived, what our folks did, what kind of music we liked, stuff like that. I was going to be a junior in high school. She was a high school dropout. That was about as much as we had in common. Other than we couldn't keep our eyes off each other's tits."

"And yours are very nice," Jen teased.

"Mine aren't big but both of Pearl's together didn't make one of mine. Actually, as I think back on it, I got gypped." Taylor chuckled.

"Go on."

"Well, I had never been with a woman before. I had never been with anyone before. I had watched the bulls riding the cows and knew what was supposed to happen between a boy and a girl but with a woman, I had no clue. I thought maybe we were supposed to just kiss and look."

Jen laughed hysterically.

"I soon found out Pearl knew way more than I did. She used the excuse she wanted to show me her necklace to get real close to me. It was a small necklace so I had to practically touch her to see it. I think she used that ploy before. Anyway, I swam over and looked. While I was looking at the necklace, she had her hands on my back. I could feel them sliding down toward my butt. The more her hands slid, the more I studied the necklace. I was looking that thing over like a jeweler examining a rare diamond. I couldn't wait for her hands to grab my ass. My nipples were pressed up against hers and I could hardly breathe. Finally her hands were cupped around my bottom and I felt something inside of me start to burn like a branding iron. I had no idea what it was. Then Pearl started pulling my panties down. Her nails were skittering down my butt and making me groan like a heifer in heat. I didn't know what I was supposed to do. So, like an idiot, I kept examining the necklace. It was a gold heart with a red stone in the middle. I could see that tiny red chip in my sleep for weeks after that."

"Okay, okay. So she got your panties down. Then what?" Jen was snickering.

"That pair of Fruit of the Loom went down stream and are probably somewhere in the Gulf of Mexico, washed up on some deserted beach in the tropics. As for me, I was being held in Pearl's skillful hands, her incredible bush pressed up against mine and rubbing for all we were worth. She was kissing my neck and pushing her breasts, tiny as they were, against mine. Well, needless to say, my nipples were harder than acorns. Then," Taylor declared, waving her hands across the air like announcing something important. "Then Pearl did it. She kissed me right on the mouth. She put her tongue in my mouth and she had me weak in the knees."

"And?" Jen urged, eager to hear more.

Taylor lowered her eyes and chuckled sheepishly.

"That's pretty much it. Before she could do anything else, I had my first orgasm right there in the river with Pearly Mae's tongue in my mouth and her hands on my ass. It happened so fast I didn't know what hit me. She had to hold me up. I think I broke the chain on her necklace because the next thing I knew, something gold disappeared down the river."

Jen chuckled behind her hand.

"That's it?" she asked.

"Yep. First times are always the best." Taylor laughed but for a strange instant she felt as if she had been unfaithful to Jen. It had been years ago and she hadn't seen Pearl Nesbitt since but somehow Taylor wished she hadn't allowed Pearly Mae to touch her, not with Jen Holland waiting for her in the future.

"Now don't laugh, but at sixteen, I probably still thought you could get pregnant by kissing."

"You're kidding," Taylor mused. "Kissing? What did you think the guy was doing with his equipment? Exercising?"

"I had no idea. I had never seen a man's equipment until I was in college." It was now Jen's turn to blush.

"Wow, talk about a sheltered life. I caught my first glimpse of a man's penis when I was about six. The ranch hands are always taking a leak behind the barn or in the brush. They don't care where they pull it out. They aren't embarrassed about it either."

"I didn't live with my father so I didn't get a chance to see anything by accident."

"Did you blush the first time you saw one?" Taylor chuckled.

"I didn't blush but I dropped a full pan of hot water all over the floor. I began my nursing training my senior year at college while I was finishing my fine arts degree. I was supposed to give my first bed bath for a grade and I thought my patient was a woman. When I pulled back the curtain, this hairy, fat man was lying there—and I do mean hairy. He didn't even have his hospital gown on. He tossed the sheet off and just grinned at me." Jen shook her head as she remembered the event.

"Now there's a gross image for sure."

"No kidding. But I did it. It took a while and I'm sure I was beet red with embarrassment but I gave him a bath. And I mean a bath everywhere. My instructor was standing there and she was glaring at me. I knew I wouldn't pass her class if I didn't do it right."

"Did the patient cooperate?"

"He wasn't a patient. I found out later he was an orderly the teacher had conned into doing it. I was so mad. He never let me live that down." Jen rolled her eyes and went back to emptying the boxes.

"How about your first time?" Taylor asked cautiously. "I told you mine. Now you tell me yours."

"I don't think so." Jen arched an eyebrow at her.

"That's not fair. I told you what I did with Pearly Mae."

"That's different," Jen said, keeping her eyes on the contents of the box.

"No it isn't."

The telephone rang in the living room, bringing a look of relief to Jen's face.

"I'll get it," she said, going to answer it.

"Timing is everything," Taylor called after her, steering her chair out the door.

"I wasn't going to tell you anyway," Jen teased, grinning back at her.

"Someday you will," Taylor whispered to herself.

Chapter 16

Jen switched off the lights in the living room and headed for bed. Taylor had already been helped into bed and Jen spent a few minutes on the finishing touches on one of the sketches. Before she went up the stairs she stuck her head in Taylor's room to see if she needed anything, the light from the hall dimly lighting the room. She could see Taylor sitting stiffly in the bed, throwing one shoulder then the other.

"What are you doing?" Jen asked with a chuckle. "Are you doing the shimmy?"

"I'm trying to adjust the ridge in my pillow," Taylor replied, grimacing with determination.

"Here, let me smooth it for you."

"No, don't do that." Taylor leaned back, protecting her pillow from being fluffed.

Jen placed a hand on her hip and scowled through her laughter.

"Why not? That's my job. I'm a certified skilled pillow smoother."

"And a darn good one too." Taylor went back to rubbing her back against the ridge. "But my pillow is personal. No one removes the lumps in my pillow unless I say so."

"Oh, really?"

"You bet. You don't understand the relationship between a person and their pillow ridge."

Jen cocked an eyebrow at Taylor.

"I don't remember pillow ridge rubbing on the doctor's orders."

"If it wasn't there, it should have been."

"Would you like to be alone with your pillow ridge?" Jen teased.

"No. It isn't doing anything for me anyway." Taylor reached around and mashed the pillow between her shoulder blades then returned to rubbing against it.

"Taylor, what is wrong? Does your back hurt? Do you need me to rub it?" Jen stood at the side of the bed, reaching for Taylor's shoulders.

"It doesn't hurt," she replied, adjusting it again. "It just itches like crazy." Taylor gritted her teeth as she worked at satisfying her itch.

"Why didn't you say so?" Jen pulled Taylor forward. "Let me see?"

"I can get it," Taylor argued, rolling her shoulders.

"Yeah, yeah. I know. You can take care of yourself but you're going to let me see where it itches or I'm going to hog-tie you." Jen raised the back of Taylor's shirt. "I don't see anything."

"Well, it itches anyway so move so I can rub it," Taylor said anxiously.

"Where?" Jen ran her hand over Taylor's back.

"In the middle."

"Here?"

"Lower. Yes, right there." Taylor gasped, sucking air as Jen's fingernails found the spot that was driving her crazy.

"Here?" Jen asked, scratching carefully.

"Harder. Scratch, scratch, scratch," Taylor said, closing her eyes and sighing with satisfaction. "Yes. Lots of that."

Jen kept scratching as Taylor's muscles relaxed at the sheer pleasure of it.

"Yes, oh yes." Taylor moaned like she was having an orgasm. "I hate to say it, Jen, but you are better than a pillow ridge."

"I won't tell anyone," Jen replied with a giggle. She gave a last scratch then patted Taylor's back. "How's that?"

"Heaven," Taylor replied as she sighed and smiled up at Jen. "You're hired."

"I thought I already was." Jen pulled Taylor's shirt down in back and adjusted the sheet.

"That was for medical reasons. This is for pure pleasure." Taylor caught Jen's eyes in a soft gaze.

"So I shouldn't cut my fingernails?"

"Leave them long. Job security." Taylor took one of Jen's hands and examined her nails. "They are perfect."

"Maybe I should add these to my resume," she said, smoothing a stray lock of Taylor's hair.

"Don't do that. I don't want anyone else to know you have great scratchers. You never know when some pervert might hire you and expect you to scratch their back for reasons other than an itch."

"Oh, really?"

"Yeah. People expect all kinds of things from fingernails." Taylor gently sat Jen on the bed next to her, still holding her hand.

"They didn't tell me that in nursing school." Jen was lost in Taylor's big brown eyes. For the first time since Jen came to care for Taylor, she felt the nurse in her waiting outside while the woman in her gazed into Taylor's soul.

"Maybe you should go back for a refresher course," Taylor whispered as she drew Jen's hand to her lips and kissed each fingertip.

"Maybe." Jen's breath caught in her throat as she felt Taylor's soft lips against her skin.

"Maybe I could help you with home schooling."

"I'd like that," Jen replied dreamily. "Yes, I'd definitely like that."

Taylor pulled her close, their faces just inches apart.

"There may be long hours and lots of homework," Taylor added as her lips pressed against Jen's forehead.

"I'm sure it'll be worth it," she whispered.

"Put yourself in my hands," Taylor said just above a hush then took Jen in her arms and kissed her. It was a long and wonderful kiss, one that curled Jen's toes and made her yearn for more. Taylor tightened her embrace, their mouths hungry for the taste of each other.

"Should we be doing this?" Jen muttered as Taylor painted kisses down her neck.

"Absolutely," Taylor said as she moved to the other side.

"But your legs." Jen's eyes closed as Taylor's kisses swept across her neck.

"Forget my legs," Taylor replied, unbuttoning the top of Jen's blouse.

"I don't want to hurt you."

"I promise. You won't hurt me, Jen." Taylor kissed her again, drawing her onto the bed with her.

Jen tried to hold herself off Taylor's chest but the tantalizing touch of her lips made it hard not to throw herself on top of Taylor and demand more. She sighed as Taylor licked and explored the waiting skin between her breasts.

"Relax," Taylor whispered as she finished unbuttoning Jen's blouse, exposing her bra.

"I am," Jen muttered as she forced herself to breathe. As the woman in her came alive, it was becoming harder for her to keep herself from falling across Taylor.

"Put your arms up here," Taylor said, positioning her arms on the pillow.

"I can't. I'll fall on you."

"I want you to," Taylor urged. "I want to feel you against me."

"No. I shouldn't." Jen looked down at Taylor with her nurse's eyes.

"Shh," Taylor replied, pressing her fingertips against Jen's lips. "Don't talk like a nurse tonight. Tonight you are just Jen and I am just the one who wants to touch you."

"Shouldn't we wait?" Jen asked breathlessly as Taylor cupped her hand over one of her breasts, feeling the lace-covered nipple as it hardened.

"I can't wait." Taylor kissed Jen softly.

Jen's mind was a mixture of emotions. The nurse in her was screaming to stop, telling her Taylor was a patient, an injured, convalescing patient in her care. This was as unorthodox as it got for a nurse, not to mention Taylor's legs were still fragile. She shouldn't do anything that might jeopardize their healing. But the woman in her wanted Taylor's touch. She craved it. She needed it more than she wanted to admit. There was a softness to this hard working, hard-living woman that intrigued her. It was an attraction Jen couldn't ignore. Whether it was her help-lessness or her courage or her brash independence, Taylor held the key to their night together and Jen desperately wanted her to unlock that door. Jen couldn't fight her yearning any longer. She was ready for Taylor and what's more, she needed her. Since that first gaze into Taylor's big brown eyes at the Rainbow Desert, Jen knew she wanted this moment to happen.

"Do you really want me to wait?" Taylor spoke so softly it sounded like a summer breeze flowing over Jen's body.

"No," Jen replied, lowering herself against Taylor's breasts. "I don't want to wait. I can't." Jen pressed her lips to Taylor's, kissing her urgently, demanding Taylor's tongue in her mouth. Jen stretched out next to Taylor, searching for a position that was comfortable but allowed them to touch and kiss without putting pressure on Taylor's legs. Finally, Taylor threw the sheet back and guided Jen to sit across her lap, straddling her hips. She slipped Jen's blouse off her shoulders. Taylor reached around and released her bra with one quick flick and pulled the straps down, exposing Jen's breasts with their small, dark nipples. Taylor held them in her hands, feeling them harden as she massaged them in her palms. Jen arched her back as she felt her body tingle, waves of goose bumps covering her skin.

"You have the most incredible skin," Taylor said, looking up at Jen and stroking her softly.

Jen sighed deeply, a sigh that was a soft surrender to Taylor's touch.

"I could spend all night touching you like this," Taylor whispered.

"Am I too heavy on you?" Jen asked, holding Taylor's hands against her yearning breasts.

"No, never," Taylor replied, sitting up and taking one of Jen's breasts in her mouth.

Jen groaned as Taylor's tongue flicked and massaged the nipple to full erection. Jen cradled Taylor's head in her arms as a shaft of electricity ran down her body. She desperately wanted to close her legs as her womanhood pulsed but she was sitting astride Taylor, her relentless touch enough to make her scream.

"Taylor, you have to stop," she gasped. But Taylor didn't stop. She moved to the other breast, tugging at the nipple with playful bites and nips. Jen's body stiffened and her thighs flexed as Taylor brought on a fresh round of tingling throbs between her legs. Taylor released the button on Jen's shorts and unzipped the fly. She slid her hand inside, cupping her fingers over Jen's damp panties. Jen pulled Taylor tighter to her breast as her body went into a spasm. Her legs twitched and pressed against Taylor's hips as the hot flood of passion took control of her every move. Taylor could feel Jen's urgency and pushed past her panties, curling her fingers over her mound and taking the nub between her fingers. Jen responded with deep throaty gasps as she jerked in rhythm to Taylor's strokes.

"Don't stop. Please, don't stop," Jen said mindlessly as her abdomen contracted and her legs stiffened, squeezing Taylor like a vice. Taylor didn't stop but plunged her fingers deep inside Jen's hotness. With slow but deliberate thrusts, Taylor delved deeper, feeling Jen's contractions. Jen couldn't speak. Her heart was pounding and her body jerked as wave after wave grew from deep inside only to rush out in a fiery explosion. Taylor felt Jen's chamber close around her fingers as she continued to move in and out. Jen gave a great shudder that started in her toes and moved up her body until every muscle had flexed and released. Sweat glistened on her skin as she clung to Taylor, gasping for breath. Taylor held her in her arms as she rode the last waves of her orgasm then leaned back against the pillow, pulling Jen down on top of her. Jen rested her cheek against Taylor's chest, listening to her heart. It was pounding as hard as her own and it was a reassuring feeling. They lay in each other arms for a long time, Jen cuddled against Taylor as she stroked her back.

Taylor sighed and closed her eyes as she held Jen in her arms. Something wonderful had happened. Jen had come into her life and filled a void, a void Taylor didn't think she would ever fill. Until now, she had been satisfied with the lust-driven one-night stands that sailed in and out of her world. But she couldn't deny it. Jen was different. She was special. Jen's body could start a flame burning in Taylor with just a toss of her silken blond hair. Even the sight of Jen napping with Picasso on her lap brought a smile to Taylor's face. As surprising as it was, Taylor knew she would never look at love and commitment in the same casual way again. She wanted her arms around Jen, protecting her and keeping her safe. She wanted Jen to find comfort in her arms and to rely on her for everything she would ever need.

"I can't wait for these casts to come off." Taylor sighed, kissing Jen softly.

"I know, sweetie. Me, too."

Chapter 17

For days Jen tried to ignore what had happened between them and not let it get out of control but it was difficult. Taylor's smile and soft gaze followed her everywhere. As much as Jen's professionalism conflicted with her emotions over their passionate evening, it was clear Taylor had no such inner turmoil. She couldn't be happier with what they had shared.

"Lexie called," Jen reported, sticking her head in the bathroom where Taylor was finishing with her sink bath. "She said she's fixing some fence not far from here and she'd ride on over around ten to feed Coal and check his shoes."

"Okay, good."

Taylor pulled her T-shirt over her head and tucked it in around her thighs. "I'll sure be glad when I can wear all my clothes again, not just the top part."

"I know." Jen smiled and helped guide the wheelchair

through the door. "But you have a cute little tush so don't be embarrassed."

"Hey, I'm not embarrassed. My rear just gets cold." Taylor gave the wheels a strong spin and sent the chair sailing toward the door. She steered herself into the dining room and sat facing the kitchen, waiting for Lexie's arrival.

"Do you need anything before I go take my shower? I need to wash my hair," Jen asked.

Taylor just grinned at her.

"Behave yourself," Jen called as she started up the stairs.

Taylor smiled to herself, happy with the image of the water droplets running down Jen's supple skin. Although she was anxious for Lexie to come take care of Coal, a job she desperately wished she could do herself, Taylor hoped Jen would finish her shower first. Something down deep was hungry for a kiss and a few minutes of her warm touch.

"Anyone here," Lexie called from the back door.

"Come on in," Taylor replied, checking to see if she was discreetly covered.

Lexie was the most modest person Taylor ever met. She blushed bright red when one of the ranch hands came out from behind a tree having forgotten to zip himself up. She absolutely couldn't function if she thought her jeans weren't pulled up in the back covering her crack as she sat in the saddle.

"Hey, kid. You're looking good." She came over and shook Taylor's hand, giving her a hearty slap on the back. Lexie didn't hug. It wasn't in her nature.

"How are things going? Did all the orders get sent out?" Taylor was anxious for news about the ranch. Her sense of isolation was growing even though she spoke with her father every day.

"Yep, your dad and Cesar have everything under control."

Lexie sat on the arm of the couch, her cowboy hat in her hand as she told the news from the ranch. She was wearing her leather chaps and her silver spurs that jingled with every step. She looked like she had already worked a long, hard day, her boots and chaps covered with a thin layer of dust.

Jen came bouncing down the stairs, towel drying her hair and humming. She was dressed in a pair of tight-fitting jeans and a sleeveless shirt that was tied in a knot at the waist.

"Hi, Lexie," Jen said.

"Hey, Jen," Lexie replied, her eyes instantly finding the gap in her shirt where two buttons were undone.

Taylor noticed as well, her eyes riveted to the exposed cleavage. Jen continued to towel dry her hair with one hand as she subtly buttoned her shirt. She noticed Taylor's hungry stare and wondered if she would have rebuttoned her shirt if Lexie wasn't there.

"Did you bring Coal's shoes?" Taylor asked, needing to change the subject.

"Yep. I'll take care of him for you," Lexie replied, looking at Taylor. Lexie saw something in the way Taylor and Jen gazed at each other that brought a smile to her face. "Tell me what you want done."

"Come on," Taylor said, rolling her chair toward the back door as if she was taking long purposeful strides. Lexie followed, listening to Taylor's instructions.

"Taylor, you stay on the porch, do you hear me?" Jen called, as she headed back upstairs to brush her hair. "I don't want those casts covered in dirt."

"Yes, mother," she scoffed.

Lexie laughed and gave Taylor a playful poke.

"She's sure got your number, doesn't she?" Lexie teased, opening the door for Taylor then helping her over the threshold.

Taylor had to admit Jen could read her like a book. It gave her a warm fuzzy feeling to know Jen cared.

"Be sure you check Coal's teeth. I haven't done that in weeks. And pinch to see if he has good hydration," Taylor said.

"Taylor," Lexie interrupted, placing her hat on her head and settling it down tight. "I know how to take care of a horse." She patted Taylor on the shoulder and headed for the barn, her spurs jingling as she walked.

"The tall bin is the oats and there's a jug of molasses on the window sill," Taylor called, not willing to give up control completely.

Lexie nodded without looking back, her hat brim bouncing up and down.

Taylor rolled herself to the corner of the porch closest to the corral and watched anxiously for Lexie and Coal to appear. It was a long agonizing few minutes.

"Everything all right?" she yelled when they didn't appear quickly enough to satisfy her curiosity.

Finally Coal came trotting out of the barn and circled the corral, his tail flagging behind him proudly. He made several turns around the enclosure, bobbing his head as if he knew Taylor was watching. Lexie came out into the middle of the corral with a bucket of tools and waited for the stallion to satisfy his need to frolic. Taylor watched intently, scrutinizing every move they made. When Lexie was finished she returned the tools to the barn and slipped a headstall and pair of reins over his head. She swung the corral gate open and led Coal toward the porch. As they neared, Taylor's eyes grew brighter and wider. She smiled broadly as the Appaloosa neared, the muscles of his sleek body rippling in the Texas sun. Lexie handed Taylor the reins, knowing she needed to touch her horse.

"Hey, Coal," Taylor said, her smile so wide it squeezed a tear out of each eye. She cleared her throat and blinked them away as she patted his long nose and scratched his chin. He stood absolutely still as she held his head in her arms, rubbing her face against his. "I wish I could ride you, boy. But I can't. Not yet. But soon. We just have to be patient."

Lexie watched, the moment touching even her crusty exterior. She adjusted her hat, pulling the front down to protect her eyes even though they were standing in the shade.

"You want me to saddle him up and ride him a little?" Lexie asked, feeling sorry for both Taylor and her horse. Offering to ride him seemed like the best way to help.

Taylor wiped her hand across her eyes and forced a hearty grin.

"Yeah, that would be great. You'd like that, wouldn't you, Coal?" She combed her fingers through his forelock.

"Leave it to you two to find a way for Taylor to play with her horse," Jen said, coming out onto the back porch. She stood behind the wheelchair, her hands on Taylor's shoulders.

"Taylor's half horse herself," Lexie joked.

"I'm beginning to see that. And a stubborn one as well." Jen watched the horse apprehensively.

"Lexie's going to ride him. He needs the exercise." Taylor handed the reins back to Lexie and gave Coal a pat.

"I'll bring the saddle out here. You hold him," Lexie pushed the reins back at Taylor and headed for the tack room.

"Come touch him, Jen," Taylor suggested kindly. "He'll let you pat his face. It's real soft right here." She demonstrated.

"That's okay," Jen replied, folding her arms across the chest.

"Jen, really. He may be big but he's very gentle."

"Taylor, you play with him. I have things to do inside." Jen turned to open the door.

"Wait," Taylor said, taking her hand. "Are you still afraid of horses?"

"No," she replied hesitantly. "I'm not afraid of them. I just don't love them like you do."

"Is this because of what your father did when you were a child?"

Jen didn't answer. She stood staring at Coal, mesmerized by his sheer size. Her mind was in another place and another time.

"Just touch him. I promise, he won't hurt you." Taylor spoke softly, trying to reassure Jen's hesitancy.

"But—" Jen stopped, her eyes growing larger as Taylor slowly pulled her toward the horse.

"I won't force you. All you have to do is reach out and touch his nose. It feels like velvet." Taylor shortened her hold on the reins and pulled Coal's head down so he didn't look so overwhelming. She stroked his nose to show Jen how she should do it. "Like this."

Jen slowly reached for his nose, her body stiff with fear.

"Good boy," Taylor cooed, keeping Coal calm as Jen's hand moved ever closer. Finally she extended two fingers and touched the soft skin between his nostrils. He blew a snort, fluttering his nostrils and making her pull her hand away. "That's it. Try again. He does that because it tickles."

"Oh, great. You've got me tickling a horse. He isn't going to like me at all."

"Sure he will. He only does it once in a while. He isn't as ticklish as I am."

Jen tried again, this time applying her whole hand to his long snout. She gave a few awkward strokes, keeping her arm extended and her body well back.

"Okay. I did it. Can I go inside now?"

"No. Actually, I need you to hold this for a second." Taylor handed her the reins.

"I can't do that, Taylor," she said, her eyes again wide. "I can't hold him."

"Please, just for a minute. I've got to move a little. I'm getting stiff."

"Taylor, can't you wait for Lexie to hold him?" Jen argued, stepping back.

"What if I'm pinching a nerve or something?" Taylor replied, still holding the reins up for her to take.

"Oh, geez," she gasped, taking the very end of the reins by two fingers. "I don't know how to do this."

"That's fine just like that," Taylor said, releasing the reins and shifting her weight. She pushed herself up by her arms several times to find a comfortable position. By the time she was finished, which she prolonged as much as possible, Jen had secured her hand around the reins and was holding them at her side.

"Do you need help?" Jen asked.

"I've got it. How are you doing?" She looked up at Jen but didn't reclaim the reins from her.

"Here we go," Lexie called, carrying a saddle over her shoulder. "I thought I'd never find the blanket." She dropped the saddle on the ground and arranged the saddle blanket over Coal's back. He stood absolutely still, just as Taylor had trained him to do. Taylor watched, her eyes helping with every move. She could saddle a horse in her sleep but watching someone else do it was hard. She wanted to be the one to buck the heavy saddle over his back and tighten the cinch. She wanted to be the one who stepped into the stirrup and swung her leg over the saddle, hearing the leather creak under her weight. She wanted to be the one who pressed her knees to his flanks and urged him up to a gentle trot. But that wasn't happening. It was Lexie who got to feel the saddle and Coal's broad back against her jeans. And for that, Taylor was uncontrollably jealous. It only lasted a moment but Jen could see it in her eyes. Jen patted Taylor's arm, rubbing it tenderly as they watched Lexie step up on Coal and turn him toward the pasture.

"Be back in a little while." Lexie pulled her hat down tight. She sat comfortably in the saddle as Coal trotted eagerly toward the open spaces beyond the corral. He seemed anxious for the ride.

"He is a handsome horse, Taylor. I have to give you that." Jen watched as they moved effortlessly across the field.

Taylor didn't reply, holding her emotions tight. She squinted into the morning sun as if it would hide her quivering chin. Jen knelt next to her chair and smiled softly at her.

"Soon, sweetheart, soon," she said, touching Taylor's face. "I can just see you sitting up there on him. I bet you look so good in denim and leather," she added with a wink.

Taylor chuckled, looking over at her.

"Not as good as you do, I bet," Taylor replied.

"I'm not exactly the chaps kind of girl."

"I'm sorry but I really hate Rowdy for what he did to you. I wish he had never set you on a horse like that. All it did was scare you away from a wonderful experience. Riding a horse can be very peaceful, even if all you do is walk around the yard. It gives you a sense of independence and freedom you can't get behind the wheel of a car." Taylor turned her gaze toward the pasture where Lexie and Coal were trotting across the horizon. "A horse's power is something to admire. And when you are sitting on his back, it's like riding on a pair of wings. They share their power with you."

"I'm sorry too," Jen said, also watching the horse and rider. "I wish I wasn't such a disappointment to you. I know how much horses and cattle are a part of your life."

Taylor instantly snapped a harsh look at her.

"You are *not* a disappointment to me, Jen. Never think that. I don't care if you ride a horse or ride a rocking chair, you could never be a disappointment to me." She squeezed Jen's hand firmly. "Yes, I love animals. But that isn't all I love." Her voice was suddenly soft. "I love you too."

Jen looked at her with wide eyes, surprised at Taylor's confession.

"You heard me," Taylor continued. "I love you."

"Oh, Taylor," Jen gasped.

"Did I say something I shouldn't have?"

"No, it's just—" Jen looked away.

"I did. I said something wrong." Taylor's face turned to shame.

"No, you didn't. I am very flattered. Really I am. Thank you."

"But?"

Jen lowered her eyes as if trying to decide how to explain.

"You're in love with someone else. Is that it?" Taylor declared resolutely. "Is it Kelly?"

"Taylor, it isn't unusual for patients to become infatuated with their caregivers, especially when the assistance required is of such an intimate nature." Jen had taken on a clinical tone. "I should never have allowed the other night to happen. That was the last thing I should have done. I'm a nurse. I knew better. But you caught me at a weak moment." Jen gave a gentle smile. "But that doesn't excuse what I did. I'm so sorry, Taylor. I should have never allowed you to make love to me."

"Are you saying you don't love me?" Taylor looked at Jen with hopeful eyes, begging for Jen to confess she did indeed love her.

"Please, Taylor." Jen said, standing up, putting space between her and Taylor's touch. "It was wrong. I blame myself."

"Jen," Taylor interrupted and reached for her.

"Forgive me," Jen said then hurried toward the back door.

Taylor spun her wheelchair around and blocked the door.

"Jen, please don't run away from me. You know I can't chase you. Talk to me." Taylor touched Jen's arm. "I'm the one who should be sorry if I said something you didn't want to hear. I didn't mean to rush you. I understand it came out of the blue and you weren't prepared for me to say that. You aren't ready. Believe me, I understand."

Jen turned to Taylor and gazed into her eyes, reading her guilt and apology. Jen's eyes looked past Taylor and suddenly widened.

"Taylor, look," she gasped, pointing toward the horse wandering across the yard, dragging his reins. It was a small pinto with a black saddle and bridle. He seemed happy to graze on the grass next to the porch, unaware he wasn't tied to anything.

"Hey, Tum," Taylor called, giving a whistle. The horse

looked up at her then went back to munching the grass. "Lexie didn't get him tied to the fence," she chuckled.

"Is he going to run off?" Jen asked anxiously.

"No. Tumbleweed Fleming will only go where there's grass. He's too old to run off."

"Should I call Lexie to come back and get him?"

"He'll be all right. Hey, Tum," she called. He ignored her, a fresh clump of grass holding his complete attention. "Do we have any carrots in the hydrator?"

"I think so. Should I get some?"

"Just one," Taylor advised.

Jen went inside and returned with a carrot, handing it to Taylor.

"Go stand at the bottom of the steps and hold it out to him."

"But . . . Taylor . . ."

"Just stand there and hold it out. Don't drop it. When he sees it and starts to come to you, back up. He'll follow you right up to the railing. Then you can grab his reins and tie him to the post."

"Taylor," she whined.

"Jen, he will not hurt you. Just hold the carrot out and he'll walk right over to you. You can stretch your arm all the way out if you want to. If you don't, he's going to eat your flowers." Taylor pointed to where the horse was moving closer and closer to the tasty petunia blooms.

"Oh, gosh," she muttered, nervously stroking the carrot and deciding if she could save the flower bed. "Are you sure he won't attack or something?"

"Tumbleweed is an ex-rodeo horse. He was trained to stand still and not move. He's very gentle. Most of the kids on the ranch have learned to ride on him. If you think he is coming too close, just say stand and he'll stop right where he is."

Jen watched as he nibbled closer to the row of flowers. She took a deep breath and cautiously descended the steps.

"That's it," Taylor said with soft encouragement. "Now hold

it out."

Jen extended her arm as far as it could reach, shaking the carrot nervously at the end of her hand.

"Here, Tumbleweed. Would you like some carrot?" she asked in a scared voice.

"Hey, Tum," Taylor called and whistled when he didn't respond to Jen's words. He finally looked up, his ears twitching and his nostrils sniffing the wind. "Come on, Tum."

"Here, Tum." Jen urged, her eyes as big as saucers. He tried to bob his head but he had stepped on his reins. "Oh, Taylor. He's going to hurt himself."

"Naw. He's okay. Call him and wave the carrot. He'll step off of it."

Jen waved the carrot at him and he walked toward her, his nose extended and eager for a taste.

"Tum, no. Not so fast. Stop. Taylor, what do I say?"

"Tum, stand." Taylor gave the order and the horse stopped immediately, his nose still sniffing the aroma of the carrot.

"I forgot what to say," Jen said, once again holding the carrot out to him. "How do we start him again?"

"Tum, come," she said then gave a whistle.

He continued toward Jen and the carrot, her expression growing more terrified as he neared.

"Tum, stand," Jen ordered, her voice shaky but adamant.

"Good," Taylor said with a smile.

Once Jen was happy he had stopped and she was ready, she called him again. It took three times but finally Tum was close enough to nibble the end of the carrot.

"Now back up," Taylor said. "Walk him to the railing."

Jen took a step backward and Tum followed, his teeth chomping at the carrot.

"He's eating it too fast," she said, holding it by two fingers.

"Let him have it," Taylor advised. "Now pick up the reins and tie them to the post."

"Oh, Taylor, I don't know about this," Jen said as she squatted and grabbed for the reins. She missed on her first attempt but finally snagged one. She quickly wrapped it around the post and stepped back. She hadn't taken a breath in over a minute and her face was pale.

"Good job," Taylor declared happily.

"He isn't as big as Coal, is he?"

"No. He's only about fourteen and a half hands."

"How big is Coal?"

"He's a good sixteen and a half or seventeen hands. He's a big boy," Taylor acknowledged.

"Yes, Coal is one big horse. That's for sure."

"I like tall horses. It allows me to see over the top of the herd. Lots of cowhands like tall horses. It's easier to keep things under control."

"Maybe that's why I have a cat," Jen joked.

"Maybe you should have started out on a smaller horse."

"Maybe so. My father's horse was a giant. At least as a kid I thought it was."

"Tum is a little small for a ranch pony but he's so good-natured we hate to give him up. Lexie is using him until Patsy's colt is weaned."

"Amarillo?" Jen asked.

"Yes."

"That is the cutest little colt I have ever seen." Jen smiled fondly as she remembered the tiny animal.

"I'm sure Lexie will be glad to show her off anytime you want to see her. You'd think she was a grandmother or something." Taylor laughed, looking across the field for signs of Coal and Lexie. They had rode out of sight.

"Should I get Tum another carrot or maybe an apple?"

"No. He's too fat as it is. Maybe you could put some water in a bucket for him though."

"Okay," Jen said, going to fill a plastic pail.

"Not too much. He'll bloat. About a third of a bucket is enough."

Jen carried it from the faucet, slopping and splashing water along the way.

"Where do I put it?"

"Right in front of him. He'll find it."

She set it as close as she dare. Tum tried to slurp at the water but his reins were tied too short.

"He can't reach it. I tied him too tight," Jen said, noticing him strain against the strap.

"Could you hold the reins while he drinks?" Taylor asked, reaching over, ready to untie them.

"I guess so," she replied. Jen held the reins while Tum drank. When he finished, he shook his head, rattling his harness but Jen held on.

"Pat his neck," Taylor suggested. "Then he'll know you're his friend."

Jen gave his neck an awkward pat, keeping a safe distance from his side. He bobbed his head, turning to see if she had anything else to eat.

"No, Tum," she said, stepping to the side and away from his curious tongue. As she moved, she didn't realize she was pulling at his reins and he turned with her, circling toward her. The more she moved, the more he followed, imprisoning her in a continuous circle. "Tum, no, wait," she said, pushing back at his side.

Taylor laughed so hard she wasn't able to help stop him from circling around her.

"Tum, stop. Stand, Tum, stand," Jen said frantically.

"He won't stop while you're pulling him," Taylor managed to say through her laughter. "You look like you are dancing with him."

"Stop him, Taylor," Jen said with a worried frown as she continued to back in a circle.

"Walk in a straight line, Jen. Stop circling."

Jen started across the yard, looking over her shoulder as she went. She held the reins out to the side and Tum plodded along behind.

"Now turn just a little," Taylor called, watching Jen with a smile. "Make a big circle."

Jen did it, keeping a brisk pace so she wouldn't feel like she was being overrun.

"Now what?" she asked, keeping one eye on Tum and one on where she was going.

"If you want to stop, say stand at the same time you stop walking."

"Tum, stand," Jen ordered and stopped in her tracks. The horse stopped and stared at her. "Hey, he did it." Jen grinned over at Taylor.

"Now what are you going to do?" Taylor asked as if she was a teacher.

"Tum, come," she said, giving a whistle of her own as she started walking again. "How about that?"

"Try turning the other way."

Jen was soon leading Tum in figure eights and circles all around the yard, proudly displaying her newfound ability. Taylor sat on the porch, praising her efforts and laughing hilariously at their fun. Twice Jen stopped and patted Tum's neck, something he graciously allowed her to do without fuss.

"Are you having fun?" Taylor asked, noticing Jen's broad and satisfied smile.

"Yes, I am. Can you believe I am actually leading a horse?"

"Next time you stop to pet him, touch his saddle. Grab the saddle horn."

"Why?"

"Just to get a feel of it."

"I know what a saddle feels like, Taylor."

"Okay," Taylor acknowledged, not wanting to push it.

Jen looked back at Tum's saddle then over at Taylor.

"Will he stand still if I touch it?"

"If you tell him to, he will."

"Tum, stand." Jen waited until she was sure he had stopped completely. "Should I drop the reins?"

"No, toss them over his neck. He'll stay there. Come around to his left side, Jen." Taylor watched intently, leaning forward as if she was ready to race to Jen's side if she needed her. "Pat his neck and tell him he's a good boy," Taylor added calmly.

Jen took a deep breath then carefully draped the reins over Tum's neck. She patted his neck, stroking him gently.

"Tum, you're a good boy. Yes, you are. You're going to let me touch your pretty saddle, aren't you? Yes, Tum. You're a good boy." Jen eased her way closer, continuing to stroke his neck with one hand as she reached out and touched the saddle with the other. She folded her fingers around the saddle horn, her eyes darting back and forth between his neck and the saddle. "Good boy, Tum. Good boy," she cooed, calming herself as she reassured the horse. Tum's back wasn't much higher than Jen's armpit, so she could see over him, a reassurance in itself. She stroked the leather seat, feeling the tooling and stitching.

"You don't have to keep patting his neck. He knows where you are. He won't move. If he takes a step, just remind him to stand." Taylor's voice was kind and supportive. "Touch the stirrup, too."

Jen examined the saddle from swell to cantle, touching the stirrup and feeling the leather laces strung from the conches.

"You are such a good boy, Tum. Yes, you are," Jen muttered warmly.

"Jen," Taylor said softly. "He won't move one inch if you want to sit on him. All you have to do is hold onto the saddle horn and put your foot in the stirrup." She said it carefully and gently, not wanting it to sound like she had to do it. But Taylor wanted Jen to know it would be all right if this was the time to try.

Jen looked over at Taylor, searching for the confidence she needed to accept the challenge and climb onto Tum's back.

"It's up to you, sweetie," Taylor added. "You don't have to. But I want you to know he will let you and he won't move." Taylor knew how hard this moment was for Jen and what memories were fighting within her. "I'm right here for you, Jen. Right here."

"Oh, Taylor," Jen whispered, the fear of her childhood screaming in her ears. "I want to but—" She looked back at the saddle, her hand stroking it like a family pet.

"When you are ready, sweetie," Taylor said. "We've got all day. He will keep standing there as long as you want him to."

Jen took several deep breaths, calling up her courage and wrestling her fears back into the past where they belonged. She desperately wanted to do this. For herself, for her father and for Taylor, she wanted to do this.

"Lexie is taller than me. I won't fit in the stirrups. I won't be able to get my leg over." Jen wasn't sure why she said that. If it was an excuse not to try, she wished she hadn't thought of it. It was a feeble excuse at best.

"Lift the stirrup and shorten the buckle. It's real simple to do." Taylor explained. "If you can strap me into the lift, you can shorten a stirrup."

Taylor wished she could get her wheelchair down the steps and do it for her. Before Taylor could explain further, Jen flopped the stirrup over the saddle and made the adjustment then looked back to Taylor as if she now faced the moment of truth, all obstacles conquered.

"Now what?" Jen asked, swallowing hard.

"Put your left hand on the saddle horn and your right hand on the back of the saddle," she instructed. Jen did it, her knuckles white from the grip. "Now, just slip your left foot into the stirrup and pull yourself up." Jen hesitated for a long moment.

"Take your time, baby," Taylor offered.

"Ready or not, Tum. Here I come. I'm going to do it," Jen muttered. She raised her leg and stuffed her foot into the stirrup. She stood there a long second, planning her vault into the saddle. All at once she did it. She stood up in the stirrup as she pulled at the saddle then swung her leg over Tum's back, settling into place. She held onto the saddle horn with both hands, sucking in a long, desperate breath as she came to rest. She finally looked over at Taylor, her face as white as a ghost. Taylor smiled proudly, applauding Jen's accomplishment. Jen slowly sat up straight in the saddle, holding tight as a smile grew across her face.

"I did it, Taylor. I got up here all by myself." Jen laughed. "Geez, I sound like a little kid."

"I think that is the bravest thing I ever saw anyone do, Jen," Taylor declared, cheering and applauding.

"I don't know how I'm going to get down but I'm up here."

"Hold the reins, sweetie. You'll feel more secure if you hold onto his reins."

Jen kept one hand on the saddle horn and took the reins in the other.

"Yep. Just like that," Taylor said, smiling proudly.

"Tum, you are a good, good boy," she said, reaching down and patting him. He hadn't taken a single step.

"Do you trust Tum now?" Taylor asked.

"Yes, I do. He's so sweet."

"Do you want him to walk a few steps? Remember, you know how to start him and to stop him."

Jen blew a mouth full of air.

"Whoa, I don't know," she said, her voice nervous again.

"He will do the exact same thing as when you were walking in front of him. He will stop when you say stand and he will start when you say—" Taylor hesitated, not wanting to say the word that would make him take a step until Jen was ready. Jen looked over at her, tightening her grip on the reins and the saddle horn.

"Come on, Tum," Jen said carefully, coaxing him into motion. She gave a soft whistle, her mouth too dry to give a loud one. Tum took a step, jolting Jen in the saddle but she held on, her shoulders rolled forward protectively.

"All right, Jen. Way to go," Taylor announced enthusiastically.

Jen couldn't look up. Her attention was on the back of Tum's bobbing head as he plodded across the yard in slow but steady steps. Her legs were locked around his middle and her toes were turned inward, spearing his flanks. Jen Holland looked scared to death but she was riding a horse and she had done it all by herself. She had adjusted the saddle, stepped up on his back and urged him forward. No one, not even Rowdy, could take that moment away from her or diminish its greatness. Taylor smiled broadly at Jen's courage to do it all alone.

"Tum, stand," Jen said, trying out the command to make sure she was still in control. He stopped. She gave a satisfied smile. "Okay, Tum. Come on, let's go," she said, whistling at him.

"If you press your knees into his middle with the command, you don't need the whistle," Taylor offered.

"I like the whistle." Jen sat a little straighter and prouder. "You whistle for Coal. I'll whistle for Tum." She grinned over at Taylor.

Jen walked Tum around the yard, stopping and starting him a dozen times. Taylor instructed her on how to sit and hold her legs in the stirrups to make the ride more comfortable. She wasn't ready to gallop across the range but slowly Jen was able to release the saddle horn and hold onto the reins alone. Taylor explained how to lean the reins against his neck to make him turn and how to guide him with her legs. Tum obliged by walking in a measured pace like a circus horse around a ring.

"Look." Jen pointed toward the pasture gate. "Here comes Lexie and Coal."

"You're fine. Don't get down. Just sit there," Taylor advised as Coal trotted across the yard, blowing air through his nostrils and jerking his head against the reins.

"How did he do?" Taylor called.

"He'd like to take off across the field," Lexie replied, guiding him to the porch. "He's full of vinegar today. You sure need to get back in the saddle, kiddo."

"Yeah, I know."

"Look at you," Lexie said, grinning at Jen. "You look mighty smart up there on old Tum."

"He has agreed to let me ride him," Jen said confidently.

"I think that's a great idea. Anytime you want to ride, you just call and I'll toss a saddle on him."

Coal's energetic hijinks had stirred Tum's attention. He crow-hopped to the side, making Jen grab for the saddle horn.

"Stand, Tum. Stand," Jen said in a firm but kind voice. He stopped and gave his head a shake.

"That's the way, Jen," Lexie said with a chuckle. "Don't let him get away with that stuff." She nodded her respect. "Want me to turn Coal out, Taylor?" she asked as Coal jerked his head and danced in a circle, too excited to stand quietly. Lexie sat in the saddle with the skill of a veteran horsewoman, allowing him to stomp and express his frustration at the short ride.

"Yeah, that's fine," Taylor said. "Behave yourself, Coal. It won't be too much longer."

"Be right back." Lexie gave Coal his lead and let him gallop toward the pasture gate, his tail and mane standing full to the wind.

"And before you even ask, no, I don't want Tum to run across the yard like that," Jen said, watching Coal's spirited flight.

"Next time," Taylor mused.

Jen guided Tum to the porch and stopped him at the bottom of the steps.

"Thank you," Jen said affectionately. "You have no idea how

much I appreciate what you did for me today. This was very important to me."

"I didn't do it, Jen. You did it all. You are the one who climbed up on that horse without anyone helping you. I am very proud of you." Taylor reached out and rubbed Tum's nose. "I can't wait for you to tell Rowdy. He'll be very proud of you too. I'm sure of it."

"I hope so. I really hope so. I'm going to see him next week. While you're at the doctor's office having x-rays and getting your casts off, I'm going to the nursing home." Jen's blue eyes flashed brightly and she reveled in her accomplishment.

Chapter 18

"So you think you're hot stuff, don't you?" Taylor teased. Jen's satisfied grin at overcoming her fear of riding a horse had lasted well into the evening.

"Yes, I do," she replied, setting Taylor's dinner on the table then swinging her hips as she returned to the kitchen. "I rode a horse all by myself and I didn't fall off."

"We'll have to get you a cowboy hat and chaps to wear next time."

"And you're sure there will be a next time?" Jen brought her plate to the table along with a bottle of ketchup.

"Absolutely." Taylor applied a ribbon of ketchup to her french fries. "Once you've been in the saddle, there's nothing like it. Well, almost nothing." She dipped one of her fries then held it up for Jen. "I can think of one or two things just as nice." She winked at Jen.

"And what would that be? Roping a steer?" Jen teased. She opened her mouth and took the french fry then wiggled it between her teeth.

"Oh, yeah. I forgot steer roping. Three things then," Taylor agreed happily.

"Taylor!" Jen scoffed, scowling at her. "You rate me with roping a steer? Shame on you."

"We ranchers have our priorities, you know." Taylor leaned over and puckered her lips, expecting a little peck.

"I'm not kissing you until you tell me I'm way, way better than roping a steer," Jen replied, acting indignant about it.

"Do you mean I have to make that decision now? I may need time to think about it."

"Taylor Fleming." Jen glared over at her. "You better tell me right this second or tonight your injection goes right in your keister. No more gentle tummy sticks. I'll haul off and give you such a stab you won't be able to sit on that cheek for a week," Jen squinted at her.

"Okay, let's see here. Jen Holland. Steer roping. Jen Holland. Steer roping," Taylor said, balancing one hand then the other. "Then there's calf branding. That's a goodie too." Taylor shook her head and smiled as she pondered.

"That's it. Stab city for you." Jen went back to eating.

"Could I have a day to think it over?" Taylor asked with a grin.

"No, you may not. It's too late. You had your chance." Jen took a delicate bite and chewed slowly, rolling her eyes to the ceiling. "I don't wish to discuss it further."

"Oh, you don't," Taylor teased, reaching over and poking Jen in the ribs, making her flip a french fry onto the floor.

"Quit it," Jen giggled, reaching for the fry but Picasso got there first. "I'm trying to eat."

"You think so?" Taylor did it again. This time Jen whacked her elbow on the edge of the table, stinging her funny bone.

"You better stop or you'll be sorry, Taylor Fleming," Jen scolded.

"Or what? You already plan on shoving that needle to the bone. What else could you do? Break my legs?" she joked.

"How about this?" Jen declared, wiggling her fingers in the air above Taylor's toes. "How about fair play? You tickle. I tickle." She raised an eyebrow.

"No, Jen. Don't you dare," Taylor replied, holding up a stern hand. "That isn't allowed and you know it."

"Oh, it isn't?" Jen inched her hands closer to Taylor's toes. Taylor stiffened and frantically released the wheel locks, backing away from Jen's fingers.

"Jen, don't do it. I'm warning you." Taylor rolled herself backward across the room, bumping into everything in the way. Jen followed, her fingers wiggling like angry spiders, a devilish look in her eye.

"You're daring me?"

"I didn't dare you," Taylor replied, trying to keep a safe distance between her exposed toes and Jen's fingers. "I warned you not to do it."

"You did too. You said don't you dare." Jen cut off her retreat at the couch, trapping her in the corner. She knelt in front of her and moved maniacally closer.

"Jen, this isn't fair. You have me at a disadvantage and you know it." Taylor turned her chair first one way then the other to keep her feet away from Jen's waving fingers.

"You tickled me and I believe in reciprocity. I think I'll start with your right foot." She looked down at Taylor's toes as they wiggled for mercy. "First the little one. No, I'll do them all at once."

"Jen, no. I'm telling you. Don't do it." Taylor looked genuinely worried, a frown covering her forehead.

"Then the left one, toe by toe," Jen said slowly and fiendishly.

"Jen!" Taylor yelled, sucking in air as she feared the worst.

233

Jen cackled, sounding like a witch ready to toss a bat's wing into the cauldron. She was being as dramatic as possible, the anxiety of it obviously more torture for Taylor than the actually tickling. Jen held one of the casts around the ankle, ready to apply Taylor's punishment. But before she could tickle even one toe, Taylor grabbed the lariat she had left on the floor by the couch and tossed a loop over Jen, trapping her arms at her side.

"Taylor," Jen squealed as she drew up the slack on the rope. "Let me go."

"I don't think so." She laughed triumphantly.

"Let go. I wasn't really going to tickle you." Jen struggled to free herself but Taylor kept a taut line on her.

"I'm not sure I believe you." Taylor pulled Jen toward her, slowly closing the distance between them.

Jen finally quit struggling and allowed her to pull her in.

"You stinker, you," she chuckled.

Taylor kept the rope tight around Jen's arms until she had her sitting on her lap. She then loosened it and lifted it over her head.

"I guess I was wrong," Taylor said softly, running her fingers through Jen's hair. "You are much better than steer roping."

"I'm glad you finally think so," Jen whispered, draping her arms around Taylor's neck. "I'd hate to have to wait for spring roundup to get another chance at you."

"You won't have to wait," Taylor replied then pulled Jen to her and kissed her.

"Remember earlier today you asked me if I loved you," Jen said softly.

"Yes, I remember."

"Ask me again."

"I don't want to rush you, Jen," Taylor replied.

"Ask me," she repeated, gazing deep into Taylor's eyes.

Taylor smiled slowly, enjoying the tenderness in Jen's blue eyes.

"Do you love me?" she asked in a whisper.

"Oh, yes. I do love you, Taylor. I thought I shouldn't allow myself to have these feelings for you. I thought it would be wrong for us to fall in love when you are the patient and I am the nurse but I can't help it. I love you so much. All I think about is being in your arms. I need you, Taylor, like I have never needed anyone in my life."

Jen responded with urgent kisses of her own, devouring Taylor's mouth, eagerly taking in her tongue. Through their frenzied moans and sighs, their hands were groping for nipples and breasts. At the same time, they tugged at each other's shirts.

"Yours first," Taylor muttered, not wanting to waste a moment of their kiss.

"No, yours," Jen argued, smothering Taylor's mouth with her own again and again. "I need yours off. I need to touch you."

"Knock, knock. Anyone here?" Lexie called from the back door.

Taylor gasped, rearranging her shirt while Jen did the same and scrambled off Taylor's lap.

"In here," Jen replied, wiping her mouth and straightening her hair. She put on a smile and tried to look innocent. Taylor tugged at her shirt, trying to cover herself.

"Get my towel," she whispered urgently, pointing to her lap towel that had been pushed to the floor. Jen quickly grabbed it and spread it across Taylor's lap just as Lexie strode into the room.

"Good evening, troops," Lexie announced, studying their strange expressions. "Did I interrupt anything?" She gave a coy smile.

"No, I was just showing Jen how we rope a steer," Taylor said, pointing to the rope at Jen's feet.

"Yes, Taylor was showing me how to rope," Jen agreed.

"Good," Lexie replied, trying to hide a snicker. "But next time you are teaching Jen something you might want to close the curtains," she added, pointing to her truck just outside the window. Taylor and Jen both immediately blushed bright red.

"I was just—" Taylor stammered, trying to find some excuse for what Lexie probably saw.

"Here. Sign these, motor mouth," Lexie said, chuckling. "Your dad asked me to bring them over. He's over at Cesar's trying to figure out why the straw count is off by a couple hundred."

"What are these? Registration papers?" Taylor asked, taking the brown envelope from her and pulling out a stack of papers.

"Yep. He's sending them in tomorrow."

"What's a straw?" Jen asked.

"A tube of bull semen," Taylor replied, looking over the papers. "A-One's straws are worth five grand a pop."

"Wow. Each?" Jen replied, completely surprised. "I bet my dad never bought any of those."

Taylor smiled up at her.

"Hey, it sounds like a lot but if you get a bull calf out of a champion like A-One, he'll grow up to be worth a lot in stud services or for semen collection," Lexie offered. "By the way, that bull calf you wanted us to watch is filling out nicely. I think he's got the looks you want, Taylor." Lexie had gone into her ranch talk.

Jen took this opportunity to clear the table then go upstairs for a shower. She knew she carried the aroma of her horse ride, leather and sweat.

"You two have fun talking about bull semen. I'm going to take a shower," she said, starting up the stairs.

"Sorry I came busting in on you tonight, Jen," Lexie said.

"That's okay," she replied. "Taylor was getting overheated anyway." She winked then hurried up the steps.

"Hey," Taylor grumbled in the direction of the stairs but it was too late. Jen was gone. Taylor looked up at Lexie and was greeted with a wide grin. "Oh, shut up."

"I didn't say anything," Lexie declared, trying to keep from laughing out loud.

"Get me a pen so I can sign these."

Lexie produced one from her shirt pocket. Taylor quickly scribbled her signature and returned the papers to the envelope.

"Here," she said, pushing it at Lexie. "Now you can go and take that stupid grin with you." Taylor rolled herself into the kitchen and opened the back door.

"You know, I have to say I did like the shirt thing you two were doing," Lexie said as she walked out the door. She turned back to Taylor, unable to control her laughter any longer. "Yep, I'll have to remember that move." She laughed so hard tears rolled down her cheeks.

"Very funny," Taylor replied and closed the door. When she got back into the dining room, Lexie was standing at the window, still chuckling at her. Taylor flipped her the bird then closed the curtains. Lexie pulled away, honking her horn just so she could tease Taylor one last time. Taylor couldn't help but smile. It wasn't a tragedy that Lexie had seen them kissing and groping. Embarrassing for Jen, perhaps, but they were adults and they weren't hiding anything. At least now Taylor didn't have to stumble over her words to explain to Lexie how she felt about Jen.

Taylor went to the stairs and listened. She could hear the shower running. That meant she had about ten minutes before Jen would be finished. Taylor knew her evening routine. She would shower, blow dry her hair, dress in her robe, the one with the pink rosebuds on it, then come bouncing down the stairs to watch some television. And ten minutes was just the right amount of time for Taylor to get ready for her, if she hurried.

Taylor wheeled herself from room to room as she made preparations for Jen's return then went into her bathroom for a quick sink bath of her own. She worked like a woman possessed and finished just as Jen opened the bathroom door at the top of the stairs.

"What happened to the lights? Is the power out down there?" Jen asked, buttoning her robe as she descended the stairs.

"Nope, but we're having candlelight tonight," Taylor said, waiting for her at the bottom of the steps.

"Is Lexie still here?"

"No." She smiled and took Jen's hand. "I thought we'd try this again but with the curtains closed."

"Oh, Taylor, look at this," Jen gasped, looking into the candle-filled living room. "When did you do all this, sweetheart?"

"I'm lucky. You take long showers." Taylor led her into the room. Jen followed, looking at the cozy love nest she had created. Taylor had arranged every pillow and cushion she could find into a palette on the floor then covered it with a blanket. Two wine glasses filled with apple juice were waiting on the coffee table and there was something soft playing on the stereo. Candles flickered from every table, bathing the room in a sensual glow.

"What is this?" Jen asked, picking up a dish of lemon wedges. "Are we having iced tea?"

"I didn't have any smelly potpourri stuff so I made some."

Jen took a whiff and closed her eyes, sighing at the sweet aroma.

"That's lovely, Taylor. What is it? What did you put on the lemons?"

"Vanilla. But I can take it away if you don't like it," Taylor replied, ready to do whatever Jen asked of her.

"It's wonderful. Thank you. You went to a lot of work, didn't you?" Jen came to Taylor and kissed her cheek.

"Could you do one little thing for me?"

"What is it, pussycat?"

"Help me with that," Taylor said, pointing to the lift hidden in the corner. "I want us to be down there on the floor, together.

I want you in my arms and I want to feel your body against mine."

A twinkle came to Jen's eye.

"Yes, I most certainly can," Jen whispered then scurried over to get it. The time it took to scoop Taylor from the wheelchair, roll her into position and lower her onto the palette couldn't diminish their excitement and anticipation. As soon as she was arranged and supported on the floor, Jen was at her side, her robe open and her body molded against Taylor's as they kissed.

"You don't know how much I wish I could run up those stairs to you," Taylor said, her hands flowing over Jen's back.

"Do you know how many nights I stared at the ceiling, trying to figure out how to get you up there?" Jen replied, licking Taylor's neck then nibbling at her ear. She pulled Taylor's shirt over her head and tossed it aside. Taylor peeled Jen's robe off her shoulders in a slow striptease.

"Tonight we will be together. Tonight all my wishes come true."

"And what wishes are those?" Jen slipped her hand down to Taylor's mound and tugged at her hair.

"Tonight it is just us, two women in love. Not a nurse and a patient. Tonight I am whole and strong for you," Taylor whispered. "And tonight you will feel a hot Texas wind caress your body."

"Melt me, baby. Melt me." Jen wrapped a leg over Taylor's hips, opening herself to Taylor's touch.

"I want to taste you, sweet woman," Taylor whispered as she applied kisses down Jen's neck and across her shoulders. Jen moaned and arched her back as Taylor's tongue found her nipple.

"I want that too." Jen could barely speak. The time for conversation was over. Her body was demanding more. She wanted to feel Taylor's hot breath on her tender folds. She wanted to scream out in ecstasy as Taylor drew every drop of passion from her body. She wanted to lay in Taylor's arms as sweat covered their bodies and their hearts pounded in unison.

"Come up here," Taylor said, guiding her to kneel straddling her head, facing the casts. Jen took her position, gently offering herself to Taylor. The first hot touch of Taylor's tongue sent a shiver through her and she groaned guttural sounds.

"Oh, baby," Jen gasped, her body tingling. She leaned forward onto her hands and knees.

Taylor folded her arms around Jen's hips and pulled her closer, her tongue as artistic as Jen's skillful hands. Jen gently pushed the casts apart just enough and lowered her mouth onto Taylor's waiting nub. Taylor gasped, tightening her grip on Jen's hips. She hadn't expected Jen to make love to her. More often than not, she was the one who made love to women but went home without. She learned to not always expect reciprocation. With Jen's hot breath heating her dormant volcano, it wouldn't be long before Taylor felt an eruption that was going to blow the roof off. Taylor tried to concentrate on what she was doing but it was hard. She wanted to take care of Jen's need but her own growing spasms blurred her mind. She felt her tongue swell in her throat and she could barely breathe. Taylor held tight to Jen as she felt her own orgasm nearing. She increased her pace on Jen's throbbing spur, forcing her tongue to complete its task before she had to scream out in ecstasy.

Jen moaned and flexed in response to her own orgasm. Taylor wanted to take her mouth away long enough to tell Jen to hurry but she knew better than to deny someone their pleasure at a crucial moment. Instead she dug her fingers into Jen's hips, holding on for dear life. The harder she held to Jen, the faster Jen's tongue flicked. Sweat was running down Taylor's forehead. Hold on, she told herself. Hold on just another minute. Don't climax. Please, wait. But she couldn't contain the powerful shockwave racing to the surface. Taylor curled her toes into a tight ball and her bottom clenched as her orgasm exploded within her. As the hot passion roared through her body, she extended her tongue deep into Jen, feeling her chamber contract and her nub pulse wildly. Jen kept her mouth against Taylor until she felt her body relax. Taylor groaned, dropping her exhausted arms and struggling to catch her breath. Jen crawled up next to Taylor and cuddled against her side.

"Oh, sweetheart. I've never felt anything so incredible in my whole life," Jen cooed. "I felt like you were a very part of me."

Taylor held Jen against her, kissing her temple.

"Please don't laugh, but that was a first for me," Jen sighed, nuzzling Taylor's neck.

"I'm not laughing at anything, baby." Taylor heaved a satisfied sigh.

"I read in a magazine that is supposed to be better than sex on satin sheets."

"Sweetheart, for a minute you had me forgetting I had casts on my legs." She hugged Jen close.

Chapter 19

Taylor wanted to sleep on the floor with Jen in her arms all night but her casts wouldn't cooperate. Jen finally convinced Taylor to sleep in her room, even though they couldn't both fit in the single hospital bed. Jen used the lift to transfer her to the bed then kissed Taylor good night.

"See you in the morning, sweethcart," Jen whispered and turned out the light. Taylor assumed Jen would go upstairs to bed but she slept on the couch, curled up with the blanket they had used, a contented smile on her face. She wanted to be near Taylor.

"I sure wish Taylor's big bed was downstairs," Jen muttered to herself just before she fell asleep.

The next morning, Jen peeked in Taylor's room as the sun rose over the pasture. Taylor's eyes were already open and waiting for her. Taylor held out her hand and Jen came to her, inching her way onto the side of the bed.

"Hello," Taylor said, kissing her. "How did you sleep?"

"I slept away from you, that's how I slept and I didn't like it." Jen stroked Taylor's arm, remembering the passion and the tenderness from last night.

"I didn't like it either. I missed you." Taylor pulled Jen against her.

They snuggled together watching the sunrise climb across the bedroom window. No sooner than the sun's rays found their way onto the bed than Picasso jumped up and wedged his way between them, searching for sunshine.

"Hey, Angus. You want up here too?" Taylor teased, stroking his fluffy tail.

"Picasso," Jen corrected, pretending to be critical.

"Angus, she just doesn't understand." Taylor formed a tuft of fur into a point on the top of his head.

"What if I called Coal spot or pebbles?" Jen asked, watching Taylor play with the cat's ears.

"He'd ignore you. He's stubborn. He won't answer to anything but Coal. I tried changing his name a few years ago. I thought it ought to be something more macho, after all he is a registered Appaloosa stallion. I tried Cherokee and Sergeant and half a dozen others but he just stood there like a dope until I called him Coal."

"He looks like a Coal though. It is just right for him. He doesn't need a big name. He's big enough."

"I hate to break up this happy family but if you'll excuse the expression, nature calls, sweetie," Taylor said, kissing Jen then pulling back the sheet so she could take care of business.

Jen hopped up and helped her with the bedpan.

"I'm sorry, babe. Why didn't you say something?" Jen apologized.

"I just did," she winked. "Go get dressed and I'll take care of this." Taylor waved her out.

"I'll go fix us a special breakfast then you can help me with some sketches. I want your opinion. I need to get them finished."

Picasso stood by the dining room table while they ate then followed them into the art room, waiting for some attention. When it didn't come soon enough to his liking, he jumped up on the work table and walked across the sketch Jen was working on.

"Get down, Picasso." Jen scowled, pushing him back with her elbow.

"He won't get down until you call him Angus."

"His name is going to be mud if he doesn't quit clawing up the pictures," Jen advised, trying to work around him.

"So, you and Kelly," Taylor said casually as she sat at the table trying to draw a horse's head.

"Uh-huh," Jen replied, working studiously.

"Have you known her a long time?"

"Uh-huh." Jen held up the sketch, examining it.

"How long?" Taylor asked, not satisfied with her answer.

"I met her at college." Jen went back to work on the picture.

"More than just a couple years then, right?" Taylor suggested.

"Yes." Taylor couldn't see the smile growing on Jen's face over her curiosity.

"Do you two go to the Rainbow Desert often?"

"No. Kelly doesn't like to dance. She'd rather go to the movies. Actually," Jen said, looking up, "the only reason we were at the Rainbow Desert that night was because I won a bet." She raised her eyebrows as if it was something sinister.

"What kind of bet?"

"We were in her spa and she bet me she could stay under water longer than I could."

Taylor tried not to imagine what they were doing under water.

"Kelly is a smoker," Jen chuckled. "It wasn't even close. I won hands down."

"Sounds like you spend a lot of time together then, right?"

Jen placed the sketch pencil on the table, pushed her chair back and turned to Taylor.

"Okay. Let's have it. What is this all about? I know you aren't just making casual conversation. So what are you trying to ask?" Jen folded her hands in her lap, waiting for Taylor's explanation.

"I have no idea what you are talking about." Taylor adjusted her lap towel, diverting her eyes from Jen's stare. "I was just asking about you and Kelly. I thought we could have a nice conversation about something other than my casts and your cat's attitude."

"Taylor Fleming, you are a big fibber," Jen replied. She gave Taylor a kiss on the cheek then went back to work.

"I am not a fibber. You're the one being evasive and devious. I just asked a simple question and you didn't answer it," Taylor declared.

"Which question? You asked a dozen questions all about the same subject." Jen finished with the sketch then clipped it on one of the clothespins strung on the rope. "I'll tell you what. You may ask one more question about Kelly but only one." Jen held up a finger. "Anything you want to know. Just remember you only get one question."

"And you'll answer it truthfully?"

"If I know the answer, I will. But after that, the subject of Kelly is closed."

"Any question, eh?" Taylor muttered, her mind searching for the perfect question that would satisfy her curiosity about Kelly and Jen. Her first impulse was to ask if she and Kelly made love on a regular basis or just after trips to the Rainbow Desert but she knew that sounded tacky. She furrowed her brow as she thought.

Jen looked over at her, poised for the question.

"Yes?" she said, studying Taylor's expression.

"Don't rush me. I have to think about this," Taylor said. She found the limits Jen put on her curiosity a problem. "One?"

Jen nodded.

"Anything?" Taylor added.

Jen smiled and nodded again.

"Yes, Taylor. Any one question you want to ask."

Taylor opened her mouth as if she was ready to ask her question then closed it and thought some more.

"Do you want me to help you?" Jen teased.

"No," Taylor snipped. "I can do this by myself, thank you very much."

Jen sat staring at her, trying to keep from snickering. Taylor wrenched her face one way then the other as she plotted her question. She hadn't hid her feelings for Jen and she wanted to know how much competition Kelly represented. Taylor wanted to know if she could count on Jen and their growing relationship after her recovery. Or if once she was back on her feet Jen would return to Kelly and whatever life they had before the accident. Taylor couldn't imagine how she could find out everything she wanted to know in just one question. But maybe she didn't need to know the details of Jen and Kelly's relationship. Maybe it didn't matter. That was their personal history just as Taylor's past was her personal history. Taylor couldn't change what happened last month or last year. All she could do was trust her heart from this moment forward.

"I have my question ready," Taylor said finally.

"I'm listening," Jen replied, leaning back and giving Taylor her undivided attention.

"Where shall we spend Valentine's Day, your place or mine?" Taylor asked, looking deep into Jen's eyes.

Jen sat motionless as she considered the question, her eyes searching Taylor's. She slowly smiled.

"Yours," she replied softly. "Your bed is more comfortable than mine." Jen reached over and gave Taylor a kiss. "Taylor, there is nothing between Kelly and me that makes any difference. Not anymore."

"I'm glad," Taylor replied, touching Jen's soft cheek. She sighed, relieved, and returned to her doodling. "This looks more like a goat than a horse," she said, holding it up and tilting it from side to side.

"Here," Jen said, taking it and adding a few lines here and there. She then handed it back.

"Wow, baby. That is amazing. How did you do that? It's a horse." Taylor admired it proudly.

"All it takes is four years of college and a scholarship. Sometimes I wonder if I wasted the alumni's money."

"No way. You have a talent. I can't wait to see the sculptures." Taylor tossed her pencil on the table and Picasso chased it down, batting it between his front paws.

"Angus," Jen scolded.

"Ah-ha," Taylor gloated. "You finally know his name."

The telephone rang before she could rub it in. "I'll get it." Taylor maneuvered herself through the door and picked up the telephone on the fourth ring, trying to control her laughter. "Hello," she said, watching Jen chase the cat off her work table. Her sketches were flying in all directions as Angus scampered across them.

"Is Ms. Holland there?" a woman said in a business voice.

"Just a minute. I'll get her."

"If it's for me, take a message," Jen called from the other room.

"Can I take a message? She's busy wringing her cat's neck," Taylor joked.

There was a hesitation on the other end of the line.

"Are you there?" Taylor asked.

"Yes, but I really need to talk with Ms. Holland."

"Can I have her call you?" Taylor inquired.

"Who is it?" Jen called, finally coming into the living room carrying an armload of sketches. "Bad kitty," she scowled in the cat's direction as he wandered between her legs, trying to make

247

nice.

"This is Mrs. Thelman. I'm the administrator at Glen Haven nursing home," the woman said to Taylor.

"It's Glen Haven, a Mrs. Thelman," Taylor announced, covering the receiver with her hand and checking Jen to see if she wanted to answer it.

"I'll take it," Jen said, piling the papers on the dining room table. "Just a second."

"She's coming. The cat's been thrown down a well." Taylor teased and held the telephone out to Jen.

"Taylor Fleming, that isn't nice," Jen whispered, tugging a lock of Taylor's hair. "Hello, Mrs. Thelman."

"Ms. Holland, Dr. Rodriquez asked me to call you and advise you your father has had a small episode this morning." The woman's voice was hesitant.

"Yes," Jen replied, not sure what she was trying to tell her. She knew patients like her father would have some days when they seemed more rational than others and some days when they would regress dramatically. Tiny strokes in his brain, a common problem for dementia patients, were often the cause. "I understand he had one last Tuesday also." She tapped Taylor on the shoulder and pointed toward the cat, crouched and ready to jump on the table. Taylor rolled her wheelchair toward him, taking aim at him and his intention to have his way with the sketches one more time.

"Dr. Rodriquez has transferred your father to the hospital."

"What exactly did the doctor say was wrong?" Jen asked with growing concern.

"I'm not sure. He has asked me to contact you but that is all I know." The woman had chosen to play dumb and Jen didn't appreciate it. She felt sure the administrator knew every detail of every patient in the nursing home. It was her job. Jen wasn't buying her uninformed responses.

"Is the doctor at the hospital now?" Jen asked. Taylor noticed her expression and came to her side.

"Yes, I think so. Your father was transferred about an hour ago," Mrs. Thelman replied.

"Did they take him to the hospital in an ambulance?"

"Yes, we always transfer our patients by ambulance. We have no other way of moving them. Don't worry, honey. Medicare will take care of it."

"I wasn't worried about that. But couldn't you give me some idea of what happened to my father? Did he fall? Did he pass out? What?"

"I'm sorry but I really don't know. I know they had oxygen on him in the ambulance. The nurse on his floor said they had a heck of a time getting him to leave it on his nose." She gave a small chuckle.

"I'm sure they did," Jen said. The idea he was at least awake and arguing with the ambulance attendants seemed like some reassurance. She was sure Rowdy was confused and probably belligerent at the sudden chaos of being transferred by ambulance. "I'll come right away." Jen hung up, her mind a scramble with thoughts of what could be wrong.

"What is it, sweetie? What happened to Rowdy?" Taylor asked in a concerned tone.

"They had to take dad to the hospital. The administrator doesn't know why or if she does, she isn't telling me. She did say he was fighting with the nurses over leaving the oxygen on his nose for the ride to the hospital. I feel sorry for him. I'm sure he was very confused about the whole thing. It's hard to reason with a patient like him and explain what is happening."

"Call the hospital and talk to the doctor," Taylor suggested. Jen stood staring out the window, seemingly unable to focus on what she needed to do. "Do you want me to call?" she said softly, taking the receiver from Jen's hand.

"What? No, I can do it," Jen replied, coming back to reality. She dialed the hospital, a number they had memorized because

Taylor's doctor was in the physicians' pavilion attached to the hospital building. "Rowdy Holland was transferred by ambulance from Glen Haven nursing home about an hour ago. Could you tell me if he is in a room or still in the ER?" Jen asked the operator.

She waited while the woman on the other end searched.

"Rowdy Holland?" the operator asked curiously.

"I'm sorry. His name is Ralph Holland," Jen corrected. "Rowdy is his nickname. Dr. Rodriquez is the admitting physician."

"I don't see anyone by the name Holland. Are you sure about the name? I have a Ralph Desmond and a Ralph Smith."

"No, I'm sure. Holland, like the country." Jen was growing impatient. How could a hospital misplace a patient? "Maybe he hasn't been entered into the system yet."

"Just a moment." There was a long silence then the operator returned to the line. "Oh, yes. Here it is. I'm sorry but we don't enter deceased transfers into the patient list."

"Deceased?" Jen gasped then dropped the telephone. Her face went white and she fell to her knees, unable to stand.

Taylor grabbed the receiver.

"There must be a mistake. Are you telling us Mr. Holland is deceased?" she asked, ready to scream profanities at the thoughtless and insensitive operator.

"Yes. He passed away about forty minutes ago. The doctor entered the cause of death as myocardial infarction. We are trying to notify his next of kin. Do you know how to contact a Jim Holland?"

"It isn't Jim Holland," Taylor replied angrily. "It's J M Holland, Jen Holland and you have just notified her."

The operator stammered an apology.

"Tell the doctor Mr. Holland's daughter will be there within the hour." Taylor hung up and turned to Jen as she sat crumpled on the floor, the news sinking in. Taylor pulled Jen onto her lap and held her in her arms as the tears flowed. "Oh, baby, I'm so, so sorry," she whispered, rocking Jen as she cried. Jen held tight to Taylor as she cried long and loud. The shock of hearing her father had died had ripped their day apart. Everything stood still. The air refused to move. The only sounds in the house were Jen's sobs and Taylor's soft whispers of support and comfort. Taylor called for Lexie to come to the house. She didn't explain why. It didn't matter. She knew she would come. Lexie roared up the drive and ran in the back door, breathless from her scramble to get there.

"What happened?" she asked cautiously, seeing Jen still crying in Taylor's arms.

"We need you to take us to the hospital. Jen wants to see her father," Taylor advised. "Rowdy passed away this morning." As she said it, she stroked Jen's hair softly.

Lexie gasped in horror.

"Oh, Jen. I'm so sorry. He was a damn good rancher. Don't worry. We'll take care of you." Lexie touched Jen's shoulder sympathetically then loaded Taylor into the van and drove them to town. At first Jen thought she could go inside alone but the closer they got to the hospital, the tighter she clung to Taylor's hand.

"It's all right, sweetie," Taylor said, touching her face gently. "I'll go with you. They have ramps and I can get out. I don't mind. You don't have to do this by yourself."

Jen didn't reply. She closed her eyes and leaned against Taylor's shoulder until they pulled up to the emergency entrance and waited for help unloading Taylor's wheelchair. Together they went to the information desk. Dr. Rodriquez came to meet them and offered his condolences.

"I'm very sorry about your father, Ms. Holland. He had some chest pains this morning after breakfast. He was transferred to the hospital but he suffered a heart attack in the ambulance. They tried to resuscitate but—" He stopped and shook his head regretfully. "There wasn't much they could do."

"I wanted to tell him about riding the horse," Jen said quietly, lowering her eyes as tears again filled them. "I wanted him to know."

"He knows, Jen," Taylor said, squeezing her hand. "He knows."

"Would you like to see him, Ms. Holland?" the doctor asked respectfully, wrapping an arm around Jen's shoulders. She nodded slightly then looked down at Taylor to make sure she would come with her.

"Yes, we would," Taylor replied, taking charge for Jen. The doctor rolled Taylor's wheelchair into the emergency room and up to a closed door.

"I thought you'd like to see your father in here," he said, opening the door. Jen slowly raised her eyes and looked in. Her father was lying on a bed, covered to the neck with a white sheet. He was shaved, clean and pale. His thin white hair was combed straight back. He looked like he was sleeping. Jen stood in the doorway, staring at his lifeless body. She wanted to go in and take his hand. She wanted to tell him good-bye and that she loved him but she couldn't move. She just stood there and trembled.

"Jen, are you all right?" Taylor asked, noticing the color drain from her face. "We don't have to do this."

"I have to," she said with a weak voice. She entered the room and walked to the bed. She placed a kiss on her father's forehead then turned and ran down the hall and outside. When Taylor made her way to the parking lot, Lexie was doing her best to comfort Jen.

"Are you okay, baby?" Taylor asked, wishing with all her heart she could stand up and hold Jen in her arms, protecting her from this pain.

"Rowdy wanted to be cremated and his ashes scattered at the Little Diamond," Jen said, trying to find composure. "Who do I tell?"

"It's already taken care of," Taylor reassured her. "The doctor told me Rowdy left a will and told the nursing home what he wanted. He didn't want you to have to do it."

"I'll have to go pay the funeral home," Jen said, her mind now clinging to details.

"Jen, he already paid for it. Years ago. Rowdy told the director at Glen Haven and she checked with the funeral home. It was the one thing he seemed sure of, in spite of his waning memory. He didn't want to worry you about it. He didn't want to be a burden to you." Jen found it strange he paid for his own funeral but forgot to pay his taxes.

Lexie drove Jen and Taylor home, Jen's mind spinning with thoughts of her father, his ranch, his funeral, their life together and the moments they had missed. During the next few days Taylor stayed close to her, offering a kiss and reassuring touch whenever it seemed Jen was so lost in her grief she couldn't find her way back. Jen would occasionally stare out the window, sometimes smiling reflectively, sometimes preoccupied with a serious thought.

"I'm going for a walk," Jen announced from the kitchen doorway. "Will you be all right for a little while?"

"Sure, sweetheart," Taylor replied, looking up from the newspaper. "Anything I can do?"

"No. I just need a little fresh air." Jen offered a weak smile.

Taylor rolled herself to the window and watched as Jen crossed the yard and entered the pasture. She wondered if Jen knew she was headed toward her father's ranch. It would take all day to get there on foot but the corner of the Little Diamond was exactly in line with the point on the top of the barn. Taylor had seen it in an aerial photograph and found it coincidental that her house, barn and a corner of the Cottonwood Ranch that touch the Little Diamond all formed a perfectly straight line. If Jen needed to get away from her thoughts and memories of her father, Taylor wondered if she knew she was headed right toward the ranch she had worked so hard to save.

Jen strolled the pasture for over an hour, resting under a tree for some shade before returning to the house.

"I'm back," she said, taking a bottle of water from the refrigerator.

"Are you okay?" Taylor asked, wheeling herself into the kitchen.

"Uh-huh," she replied, taking a long drink. "And yes, I know. It's Texas, so don't tank up on water. I'll get a bellyache." She rubbed Taylor's arm as she passed her on her way to the dining room. She stopped in her tracks, staring at the gray plastic box on the table.

"The funeral home brought that by a little while ago," Taylor offered. There was no way to soften the fact that Jen's father was in that box, a plastic bag of ashes that would fit in two hands.

Jen's eyes remained riveted on the box. She walked to the table but didn't touch it.

"Are you sure you don't want a memorial service?" Taylor asked gently.

"No. Rowdy didn't want any service. He was very adamant about it. He just wanted his ashes scattered on his ranch. That's all."

"Memorial services are for the living, Jen. It's how you say good-bye and how you start to heal." Taylor wrapped an arm around Jen's waist.

"No. No memorial service. Daddy didn't want one." Jen took a last look at the box then went upstairs to wash.

The next morning Jen finished her chores for Taylor, administering her injection, helping her into her wheelchair and taking her vitals, all by nine o'clock. While Taylor was sifting through the mail in the living room, Jen took the box from the dining room table and headed for the back door.

"Hey, where you going?" Taylor asked.

Jen stopped but didn't turn around.

254

"I thought I'd take a drive," she replied, hugging the box to her chest. Her voice was shaky and Taylor could tell she was close to tears.

"Sweetheart, wait. Don't you want me to go with you?" Taylor came into the kitchen and reached for her arm.

"You don't want to do this, Taylor." Jen didn't look at her.

"Jen, look at me. Of course I want to do this with you. I'll do whatever you want me to do. Don't you understand? You are not just my nurse. I know I don't look like it with these logs on my legs but I want to help you. I can't even dress myself right now but someday I will. I want to be the one you run to, Jen. I hate it that I can't take care of this for you," Taylor said. "I feel so impotent."

"No," Jen argued, looking back at her. "You are wonderful. You are so courageous. I envy how strong you are."

"If you don't want me to go, just say so. I'll understand if this is something you want to do by yourself."

"There is nothing I want more than for you to go with me. I didn't know how to ask you," Jen replied, a scared look in her tear-swollen eyes. "I'm not sure I can do this by myself."

"Where are you taking Rowdy? Do you have a place in mind?"

"I'm not sure. Somewhere out in the pasture. Will I be able to drive my van out there?"

"I think so. Maybe not everywhere but most of it is like Cottonwood, relatively smooth range. Over time the cattle wear paths between the grazing sections and you'll be able to drive those like dirt roads."

"Can we go now before I change my mind?" Jen asked, wiping a tear.

"Let's go," Taylor replied.

Taylor got situated in the back of the van and gave Jen directions. She knew all the short cuts and back roads to get to Rowdy's property without going around by way of the county road.

"Turn down there, just past the cattle guard," Taylor said, straining to see out the windshield.

"The gate has a lock on it," Jen said, slamming on the brakes as she rumbled toward the gate.

"It's not locked."

"I can see the padlock, Taylor. We have to go around." Jen put the van in reverse and started to back up.

"No, wait. Pull up to the gate," Taylor declared. "Barely bump it."

Jen looked back at her skeptically.

"It isn't locked, Jen. Trust me."

Jen eased up to the steel gate and tapped it with the bumper. Nothing happened.

"Do it again, a bit harder." Taylor squinted at the gate.

Jen gave it another tap and the gate swung open.

"We were forever losing the combination or the key so we jury-rigged it. This path runs right onto Little Diamond property when you cross the stream. I think your dad knew it and used this gate too. One of those secrets no one discusses." Taylor winked.

"Should I close it?"

"Naw. We'll get it when we come out."

They crossed a rickety timber bridge and climbed a hill that overlooked the open pasture. Jen stared out at the patches of wildflowers filling the pasture with lavender and gold. A pond glistened in the sun, water lilies skirting its shore. An old windmill spun in the breeze, squeaking at every turn.

"There you go," Taylor declared. "The Little Diamond Ranch."

"I don't remember this view. Isn't it pretty?" Jen rolled down her window and took a deep breath. "Smell the flowers."

"You wouldn't have any flowers if there were cattle up here. Angus just love tender little blossoms." Taylor chuckled.

"Then I'm glad Dad didn't have any."

"Now where?"

Jen heaved a sigh and tapped her fingers on the steering wheel.

"I have no idea. I've been thinking about it for two days. I guess I'll just have to drive around and look."

Jen headed across the pasture, steering around trees, downed logs and rocks. It was a rough ride, bouncing Taylor back and forth in her wheelchair. They crisscrossed the pastures from one end of the ranch to the other for over an hour. Jen occasionally got out and looked at the open spaces but nothing seemed right. Nothing looked like the place where Rowdy should rest. Taylor tried as best she could to point out various spots. They visited the creek lined with scruffy trees and a bald rise with a granite outcropping. They even drove along the property line where Rowdy had repeatedly cut the fence. Jen headed back for the center of the pasture, frustrated and angry with herself for her indecision. She drove to the top of the hill and parked under a huge cottonwood tree, looking for shade.

"I'm so sorry, honey. I know I am being silly but I have no idea what place to pick. According to the will, I'm supposed to know where he wants to be. But he never said a word to me about it. I bet it was just one of those things he thought he told me but forgot." Jen leaned her head back against the seat and closed her eyes. "I don't know what to do."

"Where was his favorite place?"

"I don't know. He never mentioned any place on the ranch that was special to him."

"Where is your favorite place then?" Taylor asked, reaching up and rubbing Jen's arm.

"I only lived here a short time as a child. I don't remember much. I do remember swinging in a big tree. Dad cut a piece of barn board and hung it from a branch one summer. I do remember that. It was one of the few things I remember we did together."

"Where was that tree?"

"I have no idea. I was very young. All I remember is it was high up on a hill but that isn't much to go on."

"Oh, sweetheart. It's exactly enough to go on," Taylor said proudly. "There is only one place on the Little Diamond that has a tree large enough for a rope swing that is on a hill." She pointed out the windshield at the tree they were parked under. "This has to be your tree."

Jen gasped and sat up.

"You mean I was sitting here and didn't even know it? We've driven past this tree a half a dozen times in the past hour."

"Do you think this is where Rowdy would like to be?" Taylor asked softly.

Jen climbed out and stood looking up at the huge tree with its massive branches. She could see a frayed piece of rope knotted around a branch. A smile slowly grew across her face.

"It's the perfect place," she said. Jen opened the side door and maneuvered Taylor to the opening so she could see. Taylor handed Jen the box containing Rowdy's ashes.

"Will you open it for me? Please," Jen asked as she stared at the box, suddenly unable to face the duty she had come to perform. "I don't think I can do this alone."

"All you have to do is ask, sweetheart." Taylor opened the lid and pulled out the plastic bag containing the ashes. Jen immediately felt tears filling her eyes. Taylor opened the bag and held it up for Jen but her hands were shaking too much to hold it. Jen looked at Taylor, tears rolling down her face. She shook her head then threw her arms around Taylor's neck, burying her face in her shoulder. Taylor kissed Jen's cheek then turned the bag, emptying the ashes to the breeze.

"It's all finished, sweetheart," Taylor whispered as the bag emptied and Rowdy's ashes had fallen over the hillside. She replaced the bag in the box and handed it to Jen.

Jen walked under the tree and stood looking out over the field, clutching the box to her chest. This was Jen's moment to reflect and to grieve. Taylor didn't interfere. She waited for Jen to return from that faraway place where children go when they lose a parent, even an adoptive one. He may not have treated Jen with as much kindness and compassion as some fathers but he was her daddy. For all his shortcomings, he was the one who brought her back to Harland and the one she would miss. She stood under the tree, silently watching as the wind feathered the ashes out in an ever widening arc. Finally Jen bent down and pressed her fingertip to a speck of Rowdy's dust and touched it to her tongue.

"You'll always be with me, Daddy," she whispered then climbed in the van. She sat for a long moment then sighed deeply and turned to Taylor. "I have to do one more thing while I'm out here. Would you come with me?" Jen looked at Taylor, her expression even more apprehensive than it was about spreading the ashes.

"Sure, baby. What is it?" Taylor agreed immediately.

"You don't have to go in if you don't want to. I mean, this is something I shouldn't ask you to do. I'll understand if you say no," Jen insisted.

"Sweetie, I'll do anything," Taylor replied tenderly.

"I have to go in the house." Jen swallowed hard as if just mentioning it was a horror she could barely face. "I have to make sure the utilities are turned off. I can't face going through it right now but I'll keep getting bills if I don't turn them off. They have a minimum charge even if no one is living there."

"All you have to do is call the utility companies and tell them," Taylor said, offering a reassuring smile for Jen.

"I know. But I have to do this. Besides, I want to see what is waiting for me. I don't know if I can salvage the house or not. Dad left it to me but it may be too far gone."

"But you have the land. That will always be there."

"I thought it might make a great place for an artist studio."
Jen chuckled at the idea. "Dad would have a fit if he knew I was
thinking about turning his cattle ranch into an artist retreat. He
would never have approved of that."

"You do what Jen Holland approves of now."

Jen started the van and headed for the house. She pulled up to
the back door and turned off the engine. They sat for a long
moment, staring at the door and what they both knew was waiting inside. Finally, Jen attached the planks to the back of the van
and rolled Taylor onto the porch. She unlocked the door and
pushed it in, the stale, musty smell of a closed up house flowing
out to greet them.

"Whew," Jen scoffed, wrinkling her nose as the smell of
garbage added to the stench. "I need to open some windows, big
time."

"Or remove the roof," Taylor muttered, rubbing her nose as
the smell watered her eyes.

Taylor rolled herself inside, Jen helping her over the threshold. They were stunned as they stared into Rowdy's world.
Stacks of newspapers and magazines formed a barrier between
the living room and the dining room. Piles of trash, boxes of
junk and mountains of dirty clothes littered the floor. Every
chair and table was piled with refuse. Coffee cans with cigarette
butts and tobacco juice covered the tables. Unopened mail was
everywhere, used as coasters for cans of tamales and soup with
their lids peeled open. A footstool was piled with aluminum foil
TV dinners, half eaten and covered with bugs and mouse droppings. The kitchen counters were piled high with dirty dishes
and pans. Several cardboard boxes were filled with empty beer
cans. Muddy footprints created a trail from the door to the
kitchen and back, leading off toward the bathroom and bedrooms down the hall. The path between the piles of debris was
narrow and perilous. The ceiling was stained with water leaks
and the wallpaper was peeling back, strips of it hanging like

drapes.

Jen didn't say anything. There was nothing she could say, no words for the ghastly horror of the way her father lived. She pushed open the door to his bedroom and groaned. The sheets on the bed had been white, she assumed, but were now stained a dirty brown. Clothes were strewn over every piece of furniture, doorknob and door, all of them smelly mud-covered rags.

"I don't think I want to know what this looks like," Jen said, carefully pushing the bathroom door open a few inches and looking inside. "Oh, gosh. Nope. I don't." She gagged and pulled it shut again.

Taylor was poking through a box of tools and leather tack on the dining room table. She lifted out a pair of cattle horns that had been sun-bleached to a bright white.

"I don't think there is anything here worth keeping," Jen said, pushing through a stack of old magazines with one finger.

"It looks like he kept everything he ever had." Taylor brushed off her hands, trying to remove the rust.

"It's a condition called hoarding. I had no idea it was this bad."

Jen moved string-tied bundles of old newspapers to make a path down the hall.

"Be careful down there," Taylor warned. "Watch where you step. I see some nails on the floor."

"There can't be much down here. I hate to think what nasty things are hiding in the bedrooms," she said as a stack of magazines tipped over and cascaded across the room.

"This house is an accident just waiting to happen," Taylor muttered to herself.

"You be careful yourself."

Jen made it to end of the hall, a stack of boxes growing up the wall between two doors. She looked inside one of the boxes filled with canceled checks and papers, most of them yellowed with age.

261

"I found Dad's filing system," she called as she gingerly plucked a check from the box. "He bought fourteen bales of hay from your dad in Eighty-one and paid twenty-four dollars and fifty cents."

"Wow. That's a bargain. That's the year Dad changed over to round bales."

"There's a note scribbled at the bottom of the check. It says Grier won't deliver them." Jen chuckled.

"We never delivered hay." Taylor laughed too. "But I bet Rowdy tried to talk him into it."

"I'm sure he did." Jen returned the check to the box and wiped off her hands. She suddenly burst out laughing as she opened another box.

"What did you find?"

"You know the tags that are stapled to the back pocket of new jeans? Well, he saved them. This is a whole box of tags from clothes. There's flannel shirt tags, a denim chore coat tag, wrappers from underwear and even the little hanger thingies from pairs of socks."

"Maybe he kept them in case he needed to return them," Taylor offered.

"Thank you, sweetheart, but I doubt there was any logical reason he would keep them."

"Just trying to help." Taylor came to the head of the hall. "Are you sure you want to go through anymore of this today. We can have a dumpster put out in the yard. When I'm back on my feet we can get it cleaned out room by room."

"I just want to look in the bedrooms. Who knows? Dad may have a cow hidden in here. It'll only take a minute."

"Okay. I'll be right here if you need me."

Jen opened the door that used to be her mother's sewing room. She remembered it had floral wallpaper and white eyelet curtains at the two windows, curtains her mother made with meticulous attention to the tiny stitches. She also remembered there was a single bed with an iron headboard painted white. It was where guests would stay. The only guest Jen could remember was Grandma Holland who came for Christmas the year before Jen and her mother moved away. The only thing Jen could recall about her grandmother was her teeth that she kept in a glass more than in her mouth and the white handkerchief she tucked in the belt of her flowered dress. Jen didn't remember playing with her grandmother or receiving any words of encouragement from her. Grandma Holland was a quiet woman who kept to herself. She died a few years later, something Rowdy didn't tell Jen for several years. The door to the sewing room was stuck, the wood swollen at the top. Jen leaned on it, giving it a bump with her hip. It opened a few inches then struck something inside. She stuck her head in the door to see what was blocking it.

"What's in there? More junk?" Taylor asked.

"Looks like it. A stack of boxes tipped over and is blocking the door. All I can see is lots of old clothes and some broken furniture." Jen coughed and gagged. She pulled her head out and closed the door. "It stinks. Musty smell." She coughed and sneezed. "I need to open the windows in there but not today."

"No rush," Taylor offered. "You've got lots of time."

"Be right there. Let me check the other bedroom."

"Which one was yours?"

"This one," Jen replied, pointing to the unopened door. She turned the knob and expected it to be stuck as well but it released without effort. She held the doorknob in her hand for a moment, the door barely open. A sudden flush of memory flowed over her. She wasn't ready to see her room. She wasn't ready to see the room she remembered with gingham curtains and a four poster bed turned into a room full of trash. She wanted her childhood memories to be protected from what she knew was behind this door. She took a deep breath, straightened her posture and slowly pushed the door open. She had steeled herself for what she would find. Jen stood frozen in the doorway. She could neither speak nor move at what she saw. Her hand remained on the doorknob, her knuckles white from her grip.

"Is it full or just half full?" Taylor joked, trying to lighten the horror of what Jen surely found.

Jen didn't answer.

"Jen?" Taylor called cautiously, not wanting to interfere with her memories. "Hey, sweetie. You okay?" she asked, growing concerned at what terrible things she might have found.

Jen stepped into the room and stood staring, her mind swimming in childhood memories.

"Jen?" Taylor called sternly. "What is it?" She plowed her way down the hall, pushing trash and boxes out of the way. She could hear the door to the bedroom close.

"Jen," Taylor yelled as she worked her way along the obstacle course of garbage.

By the time she reached the door she was breathless and dripping sweat from the strain. She carefully turned the knob and pushed it open. Jen was sitting on the side of a four poster bed covered with a white quilt with pink flowers. There were faded pink gingham curtains at the windows. A storybook doll lamp was on the dresser along with a ballerina statue. A child's red felt cowboy hat was hung over the back of a small rocking chair. A wooden rocking horse stood in the corner, a small pink quilt over the back like a saddle blanket. Nothing was out of place. Nothing was littering the floor. Except for the layers of dust, it was as if a child still lived in the room. Jen looked up at Taylor, her face pale and her eyes wide, stunned at what she had found.

Taylor rolled herself inside, slowly turning and studying the row of framed pictures on the wall. The one over the dresser was of a baby with blond ringlets and dimpled cheeks. The baby was happy and laughing at the man holding her over his head proudly. The next picture was of a barefoot toddler in a pair of lacy underpants picking a flower from a flower pot. The pictures chronicled the towhead little girl as she grew through her teen years to young womanhood and on to adulthood. There was a picture of Jen as she graduated from high school and another in her nurse's uniform. Another of her standing next to one of her metal sculptures was in a frame with a newspaper clipping tucked in the corner of the glass. Other newspaper clippings were taped to the mirror in a neat row, some about Jen's artistic accomplishments, others about her scholarships. A snapshot of Jen receiving a check was handwritten across the bottom with the words, Henson Scholarship for Outstanding Art Achievement. Another clipping announced Jen's commission to make the sculptures for the rodeo grounds. Every picture and clipping Jen ever sent her father was preserved and displayed proudly.

"I had no idea," Jen whispered as her eyes flowed around the room. "He never said anything about this."

"How could he possibly tell you? One thing is for sure, sweetheart. Your father loved you more than any father ever loved a child. He was proud of you from the first moment they brought you home. He just didn't know how to tell you." Taylor touched the photograph of Jen and her mother taped to the wall. "Your father owned the braggin' rights on you, Jen. That's for sure." Taylor smiled warmly at her. Jen ran to Taylor and hugged her, a sense of relief and contentment settling over her. She had the one thing she thought she would never have, a father who truly loved her.

Chapter 20

The few days before Taylor's doctor's appointment seemed to take forever. Jen knew she was anxious to get the casts off and nothing seemed more important to them both than that day. Taylor offered support for Jen's grief, trying as best she could to hide her anxiety to be back on her feet. Taylor had flowers delivered from town every day. Jen's favorites—bouquets of roses, daisies and bluebonnets. Taylor tried to ask for as little help as possible. She considered hiring someone to take over her care but Jen wouldn't hear of it. She insisted she was capable of doing her job, a job she did with love and affection.

"Jen," Taylor called from her room. "I could use your help a minute. Are you busy?"

"Yes, I am," she said, walking into the room as she dried her hands on a towel. "I'm getting ready to go into town. I have to leave in ten minutes," she added. "What's up?"

"And just where do you think you are going? What if I need you for something?"

"Sorry but this is important. I'm taking this gorgeous woman rancher I know to see her doctor so she can have her casts removed. She's waited a long time for this and she doesn't want to be late." Jen winked at her.

"Oh, really. And you think you ought to be there when she takes her first steps?"

"I absolutely want to be there," Jen replied, smiling sweetly. "She promised me a big hug and a kiss."

"Sounds like a promise she should keep. I can't think of a more deserving recipient of a hug and kiss than you. I can't tell you how much I appreciate everything you did for me. You got me through this and I can't wait until I'm back on my feet so I can show you just how much." Taylor held out her hand to Jen. When she took it, Taylor pulled Jen onto her lap and kissed her. "So we have ten minutes then." Taylor asked, grinning at her suggestively.

"Nine minutes and no, that isn't enough for what you have in mind," Jen teased and stood up. "Now, what is it you need me to help you with?"

"Pants," Taylor replied, holding up a pair of well-worn gray sweat pants she had cut off to shorts. "I want to wear something over my butt. These are way too big on me and I thought we could get them over the casts. I'm taking jeans and my boots to wear home but would you help me get these on for now?" Taylor tried to hook one leg opening over a foot but she couldn't reach.

"First things first," Jen said, taking the shorts from her and finding the front. "Have you used the little girl's room recently?"

"Yes, I have but thank you for asking." Taylor laughed.

"Okay then. Let me see what I can do." Jen stood at Taylor's feet and slipped the shorts over her casts. They fit fine until they reached her knees then the elastic became stretched to the limit. Taylor raised herself as much as she could while Jen wiggled and tugged them up over her thighs. "It's going to be a tight fit," Jen said, working them up inch by inch. "If the doctor wants them off before he removes the casts, they will have to cut them off."

"I don't care but I don't want to go in there bottomless."

"There, all finished."

"I'm even wearing a real shirt and a bra," Taylor said proudly as she smoothed the front of her pearl-buttoned western shirt. "First time in weeks."

"I like this shirt," Jen said with a smile, adjusting the collar. "This is the one you wore that night at the Rainbow Desert when you stood blocking the doorway."

"It's the one I wore when I saw the woman of my dreams," Taylor offered tenderly.

"It will be our shirt. I can always remember it as the shirt you wore when you told me to f-off." Jen kissed Taylor on the nose.

"You aren't going to let me live that down, are you?"

Jen shook her head.

"So Tex, are you ready to go?" Jen grabbed the tote bag that contained Taylor's underpants, favorite jeans, socks and polished boots.

"I was ready two months ago. Let's go." Taylor made a bee-line for the back door, bumping into every piece of furniture along the way.

"Go sit by the back door and simmer." Jen kissed the top of her head as she slid past. "I'll bring the van up."

"Wait, I have to go potty again," Taylor muttered disgustedly, heading for the bathroom. She stopped and turned around. "No, I don't. Just nerves."

"Baby doll, I hate to throw a wet blanket on you but have you ever considered the doctor may not take the casts off today. The x-rays may show your legs need a bit more time to heal," Jen stated cautiously.

"Don't say it," Taylor replied, clamping her hands over her ears. "I don't want to even think about it. The doctor *is* going to take the casts off today. I'm healed. I'm fine. I get my life back today. Now hurry up. Get that cute little rear of yours out there and back up the van."

"Okay, be right back," Jen replied and hurried out the back door.

Taylor waited nervously on the back porch as Jen backed into position against the steps. Jen maneuvered the wheelchair into the van, locked the chair into place and pulled away.

"By the way, I'm riding in the front on the way home," Taylor announced from the back. "I don't care if my legs have to hang out the window, I'm sitting in front. I'm tired of being cargo."

"Yes, dear," Jen mused.

"And I may stop along the way and neck with my girl."

"Yes, dear," Jen repeated with a brighter tone, looking at Taylor in the rearview mirror and smiling broadly.

Taylor was practically jumping out of her skin be the time she rolled into the doctor's waiting room. The doctor's office was attached to the hospital and when Taylor was told he was running late with an emergency, Jen thought she would need to restrain her. Finally Taylor was called into the exam room. While the doctor examined x-rays and blood tests, Taylor lay on the exam table, rolling her eyes and drumming her fingers on sides of her casts.

"It won't be much longer, sweetie," Jen whispered, sitting in the chair next to the exam table. She reached over and patted her arm, trying to calm Taylor's nerves.

"Looks good, Taylor. Looks real good," the doctor said, slipping the x-rays into the light panel and snapping it on. "You are one lucky lady. Everything knitted well. No infection. No loose pins. The plate looks nice and tight." He gave the x-rays a long look through his bifocals then turned to Taylor with a smile. "So, do you want those casts off or do you want to wear them a while longer?"

"Get these things off, Doc. I've been waiting all day for this."

Taylor sat up and scowled at him.

"I figured as much but I hate to destroy the artwork on your casts. Who did it?" he asked, looking at the designs and sketches covering the white casts.

"Jen did it. She's a great nurse but she's an even better artist. You should see the metal sculptures she does." Jen blushed as Taylor sang her praises.

The nurse handed the doctor the cast cutter. He started on the outside, inching his way down her left leg then up the other side.

"Taylor, I want you to remember your leg muscles haven't been used in a long time. They will have lost a lot of their strength. It'll take a while for you to get back to normal. So easy does it at first. Stay off that horse of yours for a while. You hear me?" He gave her a hard look. "And no calf roping or bull riding or any of that other stuff you do. Your legs muscles have to regain their strength. I've ordered physical therapy three times a week for two weeks. Then I'll reassess."

"I hear you," Taylor said, watching the cutter slowly inch its way up the cast.

"No driving today. You let Jen drive you home. Take it easy the rest of the day."

"You sound like you don't trust me, Doc," Taylor said.

He looked up over his glasses at Jen then at Taylor.

"Aren't you the one who broke an arm two years ago and re-broke it the day after the cast came off?" he asked, starting down the other cast.

"No. I think that was Lexie." Taylor knew good and well he was talking about her. She was also the one who rode Coal during roundup with a brace around two cracked ribs.

"I'm giving Jen some instructions, nonetheless."

Taylor watched anxiously as he made the last few inches of cut. He finally set the cutter aside. There was a stale smell of sweat and plaster as he removed the top of one of the casts but it was still like a dip in a cool stream for Taylor.

"Oh, wow. That feels so good," she said, throwing her head back and sighing deeply. She didn't need to move to feel better. Just to have the cast off was heaven. The doctor lifted the other cast off and examined the scar across her shin where he had pre-formed the surgery. He lifted each leg and pulled away the bottom half of the cast. Taylor could hardly stand the wait while he examined her legs.

"Can you wiggle your toes?" he asked.

Taylor flexed her feet up and down, wiggling her toes. She bent her knees and rolled each leg side to side, a proud smile painting her face. Jen watched intently, she too smiling at the progress.

"Okay, let's see you stand up on them." He helped her down from the table. "No heroics, Taylor. Just stand on them. Lean on the table if you need to."

Taylor eagerly stood up but was surprised at how weak she felt. Her leg muscles flinched as she put her weight on them. She quickly caught herself on the table but was determined to stand up straight. Jen reached out instinctively, ready to catch her.

"Feels a little strange, doesn't it?" he said, stepping back.

"No kidding," Taylor said, bracing herself on the table.

"I want you to use this for a couple days," he advised, handing her an aluminum cane. "You may not think you need it but as your muscles rehab, they'll tire faster. Use the cane for support."

Taylor tried it out. She took one wobbly step, feeling and looking like a newborn calf finding its legs for the first time. She tried another tentative step, using the cane dutifully.

"Good," he said, watching her carefully. "I want to see you in two weeks and I don't want you abusing my handiwork, Taylor Fleming."

"Thank you, Doc," she said, a huge smile on her face. She beamed her independence as she took a few more hesitant steps around the room. She straightened her posture and turned to walk toward Jen, her face bright with confidence. Suddenly her face lost its color and she reached for the table. A deep scowl wrinkled her forehead as she pulled the cane closer, leaning heavily on it.

"Taylor?" Jen said, noticing her strange expression.

"It sure is hot in here," she mumbled, sweat immediately forming on the brow.

"Ms. Fleming?" the doctor asked, looking up as he finished some notes on her chart. He studied her frozen gait. "Are your legs stiff? Do you need to sit down?"

"I don't know," she replied as the room began to spin. She felt a stabbing pain grip her back and send a pain down her legs that took her breath away. Taylor opened her mouth to scream at the surprising and excruciating pain but nothing came out. Her eyes widened as she grabbed her back just below her waist.

"Taylor," Jen screamed, jumping to her feet and reaching for her. The doctor and the nurse converged on Taylor at the same moment but it was too late. Her legs gave way and she crumpled to the floor. Jen caught her head before it hit the floor but she couldn't stop Taylor from falling with a thump. She lay on the floor unconscious, her head cradled in Jen's lap as the doctor examined her.

"Ms. Fleming," he called repeatedly, checking her vitals.

"Taylor." Jen stroked Taylor's forehead, her voice anxious and guarded. She was only a nurse's aide but she had read something in the doctor's face that told her he was concerned. "Taylor," she repeated.

Taylor finally opened her eyes and tried to focus on Jen's face but she was confused.

"Blood pressure is down," the nurse reported, checking it again. "Way down."

"Did she pass out because she stood up too fast?" Jen asked.

"I can't tell." The doctor instructed the nurse to get a gurney for Taylor and some help to lift her.

"I'll help," Jen instantly replied.

"We don't want to twist or bend anything when we lift her," he advised. "Ms. Fleming, can you hear me?"

Taylor's eyes searched for his face and nodded.

"Can you move your legs?" he asked, looking down at her limp legs.

Again she nodded but they didn't move.

"Again, Taylor," he said with a frown. "Move them again, please."

Nothing happened. Taylor looked up at Jen and stared deep into her soul, a terrified look so horrifying it made Jen's blood run cold.

Taylor was quickly swallowed up by the hospital staff, whisked away for x-rays and a MRI. Jen was left to sit and worry in the waiting room for hours. She thought about calling Grier and Sylvia to let them know something was wrong but she wasn't sure what to tell them. Perhaps Taylor had just fainted from a sudden drop in blood pressure as blood surged down her legs and once she regained her senses they would go home. If she had fractured her legs again, she wanted to have more information before she worried them needlessly. Jen sat in the corner chair of the waiting room clutching Taylor's tote bag like holding a teddy bear, desperately clinging to the feel of Taylor's boots inside. She strained at every voice and every door that opened, hoping to hear something about Taylor's condition. Occasionally she walked down the hall to the nurse's station and asked if they had any word on Taylor Fleming but all she received for her efforts were sympathetic apologies and no information. Lunch time came and went but Jen stayed in the waiting room, afraid she would miss the doctor.

"Ms. Holland?" a nurse said.

"Yes," Jen replied, jumping to her feet.

"Doctor Potter said you may go to room one eighteen."

"How is Taylor? Is she all right?"

"I don't know. I'm just passing on a message," she added.

"Okay," Jen said, hurrying down the hall. Jen could barely contain herself as she flew around the corner and passed the nurse's station. She opened the door to room 118 and saw Taylor sitting in the bed in a hospital gown, a sheet covering her legs. "Are you finally ready to walk out of here?" Jen asked, forcing a smile and a chipper tone.

She came to the side of the bed and was immediately greeted by Taylor's blank expression. She slowly raised her eyes to meet Jen's, the tracks of tears clearly visible on her cheeks.

"Taylor, what is it?" Jen asked, dropping the tote bag and taking her hand.

"The MRI showed the cause of Ms. Fleming's collapse," the doctor said quietly, standing on the other side of the bed. "Taylor has had a spinal stroke."

"WHAT?" As a nurse's aide, Jen instantly understood what that meant but she loved Taylor too much to accept it.

"The tests revealed a blood clot," he added, closing her chart and tucking it under his arm.

Taylor closed her eyes as the doctor retold the bitter news.

"No, no. She couldn't have a blood clot," Jen gasped. "I gave her the injections. I never missed even one. She had low molecular weight Heparin twice a day every day since she got home. I was very careful about that." Jen argued her case as if she could undo the news by defending her nursing skills. "And I was very careful about turning her and elevating her legs. We followed your orders to the letter, doctor." Jen frowned at him. "I even made sure she ate a balanced diet, just like you told me."

"It had nothing to do with you. The blood clot could have been caused by the initial accident that broke her legs and was just lying in wait to move. It could have been something she had for years. It's hard to tell. But I feel certain it had nothing to do with the care or the time she spent at home," the doctor said, turning a sympathetic tone in Jen's direction. "When she stood up and took her first steps, the clot migrated. Then boom." He snapped his fingers. The noise made Taylor flinch.

"What are you going to do about it? Remove it by surgery? Dissolve it?" Jen asked, gripping Taylor's hand so tight her knuckles were white.

"As I told Taylor, it was very small and it took only a second to happen, but when the blood clot restricted the blood supply to the nerve, the nerve suffered irreparable damage."

Taylor kept her eyes closed but Jen could see her jaw muscles stiffen.

"Irreparable?" Jen asked cautiously. She knew what it meant but she wanted the doctor to say it. She didn't want to be the one who assumed the worse.

"When a nerve is denied its blood supply it dies." The doctor said it as sensitively as he could. "It appears Taylor's sensory impulses are intact." That statement had all the earmarks of dropping just one shoe.

"But—"

"But Taylor's motor neurons to her legs were damaged," he added.

Jen closed her eyes, unable to accept the statement. She wished she didn't understand the medical jargon. But that wouldn't change the fact. Jen knew exactly what he meant. He had just explained that Taylor would never walk again. She could feel pain in her legs but she couldn't stand up and walk across the room. Taylor was used to chasing calves and saddling a horse and working in the barn. She loved the outdoors, sports, fresh air, grinding through the gears of her truck, dancing until midnight at the Rainbow Desert. But that was all behind her now. Jen looked down at Taylor, her eyes still closed as she sat motionless in the bed.

"Tell him, Taylor. Tell him we did everything just like he told us. You didn't do anything you weren't supposed to do. Tell him, Taylor." Jen's voice broke as she stood watching Taylor, praying she would suddenly throw back the sheet, leap to her feet and stride out of the room. A tear pillowed out of the corner of Taylor's eye and slowly trailed down her cheek. Jen felt her knees go weak and she could no longer stand. She held onto the side of the bed and lowered herself into the chair, a stunned look on her face. She pulled Taylor's hand to her face and kissed it softly. There was nothing that sounded right to say. Nothing could possibly explain how badly she felt for Taylor. Nothing would be enough. She refused to say I'm sorry. It sounded hollow and meaningless. She wanted to hold Taylor in her arms. And even more, she wanted Taylor to hold her as well. Taylor was the one she turned to for a smile and a soft touch. Taylor had been her strength and her courage when Rowdy had died. Taylor was the woman who could caress her body and soul like no other person she had ever known. All Jen could do was stare at her.

"We are going to keep Taylor for a couple days and monitor the situation," the doctor said.

"Okay," Jen replied, her chin quivering.

"Taylor, you let me or the nurse know if you need anything," he said, squeezing Taylor's hand. "I'll be back later this evening to check on you."

Taylor didn't reply. She only nodded slightly. She couldn't even look him in the eye.

"We'll take good care of her, Jen," he said then left them in a cold silence.

Jen carefully sat down on the edge of the bed. She brushed Taylor's hair from her face and rubbed her thumbs across the trail of tears.

"Sweetheart," she said softly. "I am here for you. What do you want me to do?"

Taylor finally opened her eyes and brought them up to meet Jen's. There was a painful vulnerability in them that scared Jen. The Taylor she knew was gone. This was a different person.

"Take me home," Taylor whispered, her voice weak and lifeless.

Jen felt tears welling up in her eyes and she couldn't stop them. She grabbed Taylor and held her in her arms as her sobs overtook her.

"Oh, God, I wish I could," she replied through her tears. "You don't know how much I wish I could."

Taylor's tears mixed with Jen's, the sounds of their crying filling the room. Taylor folded her arms around Jen, tugging at her shirt as her body shook with despair.

"My sweet baby," Jen cried, rocking Taylor in her arms.

Chapter 21

By the time Taylor was released from the hospital and returned home, she had a nearly constant stream of well-wishers and sympathetic friends stopping by the house to hug her and stare at her lifeless legs. Jen stayed in the background, helping where she could but allowing Sylvia and Grier to fuss over her. Taylor had changed. Whether she was in shock or still hadn't accepted the tragic realization she would never again walk out the door on her way to a busy day on the ranch, she was no longer the energized and robust woman Jen remembered that first time she strode into her garage and stared up at her. Jen wanted that Taylor back. Not because she could walk, but because she cared about things. She cared about life and living it. This Taylor was sullen and listless. Her eyes had lost their shine and she hadn't smiled since the day she crumpled onto the exam room floor. Jen didn't expect her to make light of her situation but she did expect Taylor to fight for what she could do, rather than wallow in what she couldn't do. But it was hard to find any brightness in a house where the topic of conversation revolved around Taylor's shortcomings. It wasn't Jen's place to tell Sylvia that Taylor had heard enough pity. She needed to hear something positive. Jen understood this was hard for Sylvia and for Grier. They were grieving just like Taylor was. They had lost something as well. They had lost the part of their daughter that smiled and laughed and rushed off to conquer the world. What was left for them to protect was a broken woman. It took five days before the house quieted down to some semblance of normal. Grier and Sylvia had planned a trip to Cheyenne to a cattleman's conference but they had threatened to cancel it, saying Taylor needed them more. Taylor insisted they keep their reservations. In no uncertain terms, she demanded they leave her alone and go on their trip. Her words were terse, something they assumed was just her way of persuading them to go. But Jen knew better. She could see Taylor was reaching critical mass and was on the verge of imploding. Her parents begrudgingly agreed and left for their trip.

"Your lunch is here on the table," Jen said, coming into the living room. "Don't you want it? I made chicken salad sandwiches, just the way you like it."

"I'm not hungry," Taylor said, staring absently at the television.

"I can put it in the refrigerator and you can have it later."

"I'm not hungry," she repeated.

"Okay. I'm taking a sandwich out to Lexie. I saw her go in the barn," Jen said, seeing if mentioning her name would bring Taylor's attention outside. But she just nodded. "Be back shortly." Jen let her hand stroke Taylor's arm softly.

Jen wrapped a sandwich in a napkin and headed outside.

"Lexie," Jen called into the barn. "Are you in here?"

"Over here, Jen," she replied, coiling a rope into a neat figure eight.

"I brought you some lunch. Chicken salad sandwich. Oh, look," she declared happily. "Do we have a new baby?" She peered over the top rail of a stall.

"Yep, a baby heifer."

"Lexie, look at her," Jen cooed at the tiny black calf, balancing on wobbly legs. "Isn't she cute? Oh, I forgot." Jen chuckled. "Calves are not cute. They are money in the bank." She smiled over at Lexie.

"You learn quick." Lexie returned a half smile.

Jen squatted at the fence and poked a finger through to touch the new baby.

"How is Taylor?" Lexie asked cautiously, a painful sound to her question.

"Why don't you come in and see her?"

"I've got a lot of work out here today," Lexie declared, trying to look busy with the bucket of feed. "Maybe next time."

"Lexie, you need to come to grips with this just like Taylor does."

"I have no idea what you mean. But a ranch doesn't run itself. I've got more work than ever to do now that . . ." Her voice trailed off.

"You mean now that Taylor is in a wheelchair permanently?"

"I didn't mean that." Lexie turned away, hiding whatever her face might reveal.

"Yes, you did. You are mad at Taylor for giving you all this extra work, aren't you?" Jen knew it wasn't true but she wanted Lexie to say so.

"The hell I am," she yelled. "I'm not mad at her. I'd never be mad at her." Lexie emptied the feed into a trough then threw the bucket at the wall. "It's not her fault she can't walk." It was the first time Jen had ever heard Lexie truly angry and she was glad it wasn't aimed at her.

"You know she wishes she could come out here and help you.

She can't even bring herself to watch from the porch. Couldn't you come visit with her a minute?" Jen studied Lexie sympathetically. She knew this was hard on her. Lexie would do anything for Taylor. Watching her go from active, vibrant woman to invalid had to be incredibly painful for her.

Lexie cut the twine on a bale of hay and began splitting the flakes.

"Lexie, she needs you. You are the only one who hasn't been to see her. You are her friend and she needs to know you still accept her for who she is. She is still Taylor, the same funny, smart, attractive woman she always was."

Lexie kept her attention on her work but Jen could see she was fighting her emotions.

"I still love her," Jen confessed. "I will always love her. She doesn't believe me but I do." Jen walked over to Lexie and took her arm. "Do you love her enough to help her through this?"

Lexie looked over at Jen, her eyes narrowed and cutting.

"You have no idea," Lexie replied. "I'd cut off my own legs if I could give Taylor back the use of hers."

"Will you help her?"

"You tell me what to do to help Taylor and I'll do it."

"I want you to saddle Coal and tie him to the back porch."

Lexie stiffened and stepped back.

"No, I won't do that," she replied bitterly. "I'm not going to hurt her like that."

"Please, just do it. I'll take responsibility for it."

"She can't ride her horse and you want me to tie it right there so she can see it. If you'll excuse my expression, Jen, I think you are out of your fucking mind."

"I need you to trust me on this one, Lexie." Jen took one of Lexie's hands in hers and squeezed it. "Please. Just do it."

Lexie scowled at her but Jen could see she was still deciding what to do.

"Coal is her horse. She needs to touch him," Jen explained.

"She needs to know she is still Taylor Fleming, not some freak. I can't wait for her to get so deep inside herself I can't reach her. She has many obstacles ahead of her and there will be all the rest of her life. She has to know she can conquer at least one of them. Lexie, she needs to do this. She may not think so, but she does. Believe me."

"How can you be so sure?" Lexie asked doubtfully.

"If you think I would deliberately hurt her, no, of course I wouldn't. But I'm not going to stand by and watch her waste what's left of her life, either. Am I sure about this? No. My first instinct is to keep her safe and free from any harm ever again. I want to protect her just like you do. But that won't help her. I don't think we have a choice, not if we love her. I don't want her to spend the rest of her life in that living room, contented to let life pass her by. She has so much to give."

"She can't ride her horse. She can't even climb into the saddle."

"You saddle Coal. I'll take care of the rest. Believe me, Lexie. If I knew how to saddle him myself, I would." Jen sounded confident, something Lexie needed to hear.

"Okay," she finally agreed. "I hope she doesn't hate me for this." Lexie said, going into the tack room.

Jen returned to the house. Taylor was in the dining room going through a stack of mail and tossing unopened catalogs into a trash bag.

"Would you like something to drink, sweetheart?" Jen asked, standing behind her and draping her arms around her shoulders.

Taylor shook her head, forcing her attention on her task.

"Iced tea?" Jen joked. "I promise, no apple juice." She stroked Taylor's cheek but felt her lean away from her touch.

"I don't need anything."

"I'm having the hospital bed picked up this afternoon. A few of the boys from the ranch are coming by later to move your bed down from upstairs." Jen wanted to tell Taylor about the equipment available for her but thought better of it. Taylor didn't need to hear about the bath bench for paraplegics or the clothing catalog of easier-to-operate pants and accessories. There would be time for that later. Jen wanted to tell Taylor how much she looked forward to their first night together in the same bed. Lying next to Taylor was something Jen had been looking forward to for weeks. The idea of sleeping in Taylor's arms still sent a tingle down Jen's body that was undeniable. But she knew there would be time for that as well. For now, getting Taylor out of her self-imposed prison was more important than anything else. When she first came home with the casts on her legs, she was angry and stubborn. But now Taylor was indifferent to everyone and everything. "You'll get to sleep in your own bed tonight. I bet you can't wait. Nice, big queen-size bed instead of that little one. I got some new sheets for it. Have you ever slept on satin sheets, Tex?" Jen hugged her around the neck and kissed her cheek.

"No, I like cotton." Taylor showed little interest in the idea or in Jen's deliberate innuendo.

"Cotton is nice but satin is sexy," Jen whispered in her ear. "Just you wait."

"Jen, please, I've got stuff to do," Taylor said, pulling away. "We'll talk about it later."

"Can't you remember how you felt that first night we were together?" Jen asked, kneeling next to Taylor's wheelchair. "That night you said you couldn't wait to touch me and hold me. Your body against mine was the most sensuous feeling I have ever felt. Your hands against my skin were so soft I wanted to stay in your arms all night long. Can't you remember that night? What if we still can have those special moments? Don't you want to know?"

"You mean so what if I can't walk, at least we can still fuck," Taylor replied bitterly. "That would be great for you, now, wouldn't it?" She stared at Jen cruelly.

"I didn't mean that," Jen stammered. "You know I'd never

think that, Taylor." Taylor's words cut through Jen just as Rowdy's words had done. Jen knew Taylor was hurting and like Rowdy, she had to ignore her angry attack though it was still hard to hear. "I love you, Taylor. I want to help you."

Taylor straightened her posture and pulled herself back in the wheelchair, making herself as tall as possible.

"I won't need a CSN this time. I don't need injections to keep me from getting a blood clot," Taylor said coldly. "You are free to go back to your art studio."

"Taylor, do you blame me for this?" Jen asked, placing her hand on Taylor's leg.

"No," she snapped. "I'm the one to blame. I'm the one who changed the flat tire on the trailer."

"You didn't do this to yourself. It just happened. No one is to blame. It was a terrible, terrible accident but only God knows why."

Taylor didn't reply but gazed out the window. When she did, she gasped. Coal was tied to the railing of the back porch only a few feet away. Just as Jen had asked Lexie to do, he was saddled and stood proudly waiting for a rider. Taylor couldn't take her eyes off of him. She dropped the stack of catalogs and rolled to the window. She placed her hand on the glass as if she was touching Coal's long smooth nose. The sight of her horse so captured Taylor she drew in a deep breath that she couldn't release.

"What is he doing out there?" she asked. "Why is Coal tied to the railing? Where is Lexie?"

Jen came to the window and looked out.

"I don't know. When I took her the sandwich she was feeding the heifers. By the way, you've got the cutest new baby calf, Taylor. It's a baby girl. She has the biggest brown eyes." Jen wanted Taylor to argue with her and tell her it wasn't a cute calf, it was just part of the ranch's cash crop. But Taylor just nodded.

"Coal needs to be in the corral."

"Please don't ask me to move him, Taylor. You know he is too big for me to handle." Jen placed a hand on Taylor's shoulder. "It was all I could do to lead Tum around."

"Lexie needs to move him," Taylor said, turning her wheelchair away from the window. She couldn't help taking another look over her shoulder.

"Do you want to call him? I'll open the window," Jen offered, unlocking the window latch.

"No," Taylor replied adamantly. "Go tell Lexie she needs to move Coal out of the sun. It's too hot for him there. He doesn't have any water."

Jen knew that didn't have anything to do with it. Coal had stood in the sun and on hotter days than this many times. And Taylor had ridden him on hotter days as well. Taylor just didn't want to see him, not so close and not with his saddle and bridle on, ready for a ride she could never take.

"Don't you want to come out on the porch and talk to him? I'm sure he misses you."

"Coal needs to learn not to expect me to come out for a ride. The sooner he accepts that, the better off he'll be."

"I'm not sure where Lexie is. Are you sure you don't want to just touch him once? After all, he's right there." Jen looked at Taylor, hoping to persuade her to at least come out onto the porch.

"No," Taylor replied, her gaze once again finding its way out the window and onto Coal's proud stance.

"Okay, I'll go get her." Jen started for the door then looked back at her. "Coal loves you too, Taylor," she said softly then went out to the barn to find Lexie.

"What did she say?" Lexie asked from the far corner of the barn.

"She said for you to move him out of the sun," Jen replied, coming to stand next to her. From the darkened corner of the barn they could see the back porch where Coal was waiting.

"I'm not surprised that was her reaction. I'll move him,"

285

Lexie said with a regrettable sigh.

Jen grabbed her arm and stopped her.

"No. Leave him there." Jen stood watching the house.

"But you said Taylor wants me to move him," she said skeptically.

"That's what she said but that isn't what she wants."

"I'm sorry, but I can't be a part of this." Lexie frowned and looked out at the horse. "If she doesn't want him there, I'll move him."

"No, wait," Jen gasped, noticing the back door open and Taylor sitting in the doorway. "Look," she whispered.

"She's going to call for me to come get him. You watch," Lexie said quietly.

"If she does, don't answer. Just give her a few minutes." Jen held tight to Lexie's arm.

Taylor pushed the screen door open and rolled herself out. She kept her distance from Coal, scanning the yard and the pasture for signs of Lexie or Jen.

"Jen, I can't do this to her," Lexie said, her voice cracking slightly.

"Wait," she insisted as Taylor looked over at her horse. Coal gave a deep-belly whinney and bobbed his head, pulling against the reins to reach Taylor. He jerked against the tether and the reins fell loose from the railing. Coal came to Taylor and nuzzled her. She tried to ignore him but he persisted, nibbling at her shirt and licking her hand.

"Coal, no, get back," Taylor said, tugging at his harness. He shook his head, draping the reins across her lap. Taylor picked them up and looked for someone to help her. "Lexie? Jen?"

"Shh," Jen whispered, holding Lexie back. "Let her hold him."

"Lexie!" Taylor yelled angrily. "Where are you?"

Lexie's chin quivered as she watched Taylor with her horse. She was a tough no-nonsense woman but the sight of Taylor holding the reins of her beloved horse from a wheelchair was even more than she could bear. Tears streamed down Lexie's face. She looked over at Jen for guidance. She wanted to go to Taylor. If holding Coal's reins was too painful for her, she wanted to rescue her.

"She's all right," Jen said, squeezing Lexie's hand. "Give her a chance to do this."

Coal refused to be ignored. He kept nuzzling at Taylor's hand, encouraging her to pet him and scratch his jaw just like she always did.

"Coal, I can't," Taylor said, looking up at him. "Please." Taylor bit down on her lip and blinked away the tears that welled up in her eyes. Coal pressed his face into her chest, rolling her wheelchair backward. Taylor grabbed onto his harness with both hands to keep from rolling back into the window. "Coal, stop," she said angrily. "Okay, I'll pat you one time." She gave his long snout a stroke then another as he stood motionless, enjoying her touch.

Jen smiled over at Lexie, nodding toward Taylor.

"I know, Coal. I know," Taylor sniffled as she continued to stroke his face softly. "I'm sorry but I can't ride you. You don't understand but I just can't. I don't understand it either. But that's the way it is." Coal bobbed his head and stomped his foot nervously, as if he was tired of waiting for Taylor to climb into the saddle. She pulled at the reins to bring him back within reach. "Lexie will ride you, boy. Maybe you'd like to be over at the big house with the other horses." That remark brought a flood of tears to Taylor's eyes. She knew it was best for him but she hated to admit it to him or to herself. She threw her arms around his head and hugged him, sobbing into his mane.

"Come on, Lexie," Jen said, leading the way out of the barn. Lexie followed, wiping the tears from her eyes.

"I found her," Jen called, striding up to the porch.

Taylor quickly pushed Coal away and rubbed her hand across

her eyes.

"Lexie, you need to move Coal out of the sun," Taylor said, turning her wheelchair toward the door.

"Wait, Taylor," Jen said. "You don't need to go inside yet."

"I've got things to do," she argued, fumbling to get the wheelchair out of the way so she could open the door.

"No, you don't," Jen snapped right back at her. "You wait here," she said, slithering by and going inside then closing the door and locking it.

"Hey, I want to come inside," Taylor called, rattling the door-knob. "Jen!"

"Looks like she doesn't want you to go in just yet," Lexie said, chuckling artificially. She didn't know what to say to Taylor. She felt uncomfortable. Usually she and Taylor could joke about anything but this Taylor was different. This Taylor was surly and distant. There was a cold edge to her voice and a vacancy in her eyes that Lexie didn't recognize.

"You shouldn't have left Coal in the sun," Taylor said without looking over at her.

"He's been in the sun before, Taylor," Lexie replied.

"I don't care. He doesn't need to be tied to the porch."

"Why? Because you don't want to see him?"

Taylor turned and cast a callous stare at her. "What the hell do you know about it?"

"I know you love this horse and he doesn't understand why you have ignored him," Lexie replied.

"Sure. Fine. Every day you can bring him over to the porch and I can roll myself out here and pet him for five minutes. Does that make you happy?"

"Is that what you want, Taylor?"

"I want him taken over to Dad's. Let someone ride him. I don't care."

"Since when don't you care?" Jen said, opening the door and pushing the lift out onto the porch.

"Oh, no, you don't. Take that damn thing back inside," Taylor scowled. "You know I can't ride."

"She'll need her legs to hold on," Lexie advised cautiously.

"Not to just sit on a horse you don't," Jen said, maneuvering it to the top of the newly constructed ramp and locking the wheels.

"I am *not* sitting on Coal. So forget it." Taylor rolled her chair back to the corner of the porch. "Take that back inside."

"Are you afraid of him?" Jen asked, looking over at her.

"No," Taylor scoffed. "Of course not."

"Then why won't you just sit on him?"

"You know why?" Taylor replied, resting her hands on her knees. "I can't."

"Says who?" Jen released the straps of the sling and let them dangle.

"My legs, that's who." Taylor stared wide-eyed at the straps that had lifted her in and out of the wheelchair so many times.

"You helped me sit on a horse. You talked me over my fear. Let me help you over yours," Jen said, coming to Taylor's side. "You will not fall. I promise you that."

"I *cannot* ride a horse," Taylor said, her jaw rippling with fear.

"I'll hold him," Lexie offered reassuringly. "He isn't going anywhere." She held the reins and turned Coal to the ramp.

"We will help you, sweetheart," Jen said, kneeling at her side. "All you have to do is let us. You know you want to. Don't be afraid."

"I can't," Taylor said, swallowing back a lump in her throat.

"When I needed your help, you were there for me. You were the strong, courageous woman I leaned on when my father died. Let me be the one you lean on now."

"Jen, you don't know what you are asking me to do."

"Oh, yes, I do. I love you. And I am asking you to love me enough to trust me." Jen placed a hand on Taylor's. There was a kind confidence in Jen's eyes.

"What if I can't do it?" Taylor pleaded.

"Then you'll know you tried."

"But—" she started, her eyes turning to Coal and the saddle on his back.

"Yes," Jen replied with a soft smile. "I want your butt in that saddle. And so do you." Jen saw something in Taylor's face. She didn't say it, but Jen knew this was the time. She kissed Taylor's cheek then rolled her wheelchair into place next to the lift. Taylor didn't argue as Jen hooked the slings under her legs and around her back. She carefully raised Taylor out of the wheelchair and rolled her down the ramp. Taylor held onto the straps, her eyes big and her face pale as she was raised up next to Coal's back. With the skill of a surgeon, Jen positioned her over the saddle. Coal never moved a muscle as Taylor was slowly lowered into place, one of her lifeless legs draped over each side of the saddle.

"Unhook the sling, Taylor," Jen advised.

"I don't know about this. Maybe I'll just sit like this." She held tight to the canvas straps.

"I want to move the lift out of the way so Coal doesn't get hit by it. Just release the hooks. I'll bring it back as soon as you are ready."

"Don't take it too far," Taylor said, nervously releasing first one hook then the other. As her body settled into the saddle, she grabbed onto the saddle horn with both hands. "Wait," she gasped as her body shifted slightly. "I can't pull myself up straight." She leaned forward and grabbed onto Coal's neck.

"I've got you," Lexie said, grabbing one of her legs and easing her up straight. "Sit up, kid. Sit up straight. Square your shoulders over the cantle." Lexie looked up at her, offering an encouraging smile. "That's it."

Jen rolled the lift out of the way, leaving Taylor alone on Coal's back.

"Does it feel different?" Jen asked.

"Yeah," Taylor replied, swallowing hard as sweat formed on

her upper lip. "I think I better get down now."

"How about walking around the yard? Coal will take it slow." Jen smiled up at her.

"No," Taylor snapped immediately. "This is fine. Bring the lift back."

"I'll lead him real slow," Lexie acknowledged.

"I don't need to be treated like a child. Get me down from here."

"You're fine," Jen said, looking up at her.

"No, I'm not. Get me down. I'll fall," Taylor said, scowling down at her. "I can't stop myself if I slide off the side. I'll fall. Get me down. Get me down," she yelled, the veins popping out in her neck.

"Taylor, you are all right," Jen said calmly, touching her leg.

"Jen, I can't do this." Taylor hissed, unable to control her anger or her fear.

"Lexie, help me up," Jen said, reaching for the saddle horn. She strained to get her toe into the stirrup, the height of it above her thigh.

"What are you doing?" Taylor scowled.

"Move your hand," Jen said, grabbing hold.

Lexie gave Jen a boost, pushing her up behind Taylor. She swung her leg over Coal's rump and hitched herself in behind Taylor, folding her arms around her.

"Oh, geez. This is the tallest horse I have ever seen," Jen gasped as she locked her legs around his middle. She wiggled her way up tight against Taylor, their bodies molded together. Jen swallowed hard and refused to look down.

"I've got you now. You can't fall." Jen gave Taylor a squeeze. "Give Taylor the reins, Lexie. We are going for a ride."

"Here you go, kid," Lexie said proudly, holding them up to her.

"No, wait," Taylor argued but her hand took the reins.

"Please, Taylor. Go slow. I'm not used to tall horses." Jen

gave a nervous giggle.

"I don't know about this," Taylor said.

"I do," Jen whispered.

"Are you sure you want to do this, Jen," Taylor asked.

"There is nothing I want more," Jen replied, holding tight to Taylor, her legs locked around Coal's broad middle.

Taylor adjusted the reins in her hand then gave a little whistle. Coal responded with a slow but steady pace across the yard, his long strides surprisingly smooth. Taylor fought the urge to grab onto the saddle horn. Instead, she sat proudly in the saddle, steering him with light neck pressure. It took several circles around the yard before Taylor relaxed into Jen's embrace. Jen could feel her body melt into the rhythmic sway of Coal's walk.

"Are you comfortable?" Jen asked.

"Yes," she replied. "Are you okay?" Taylor dropped her hand and molded it around Jen's thigh.

"I'm fine. And so are you," she added, kissing Taylor's neck. "I'm so proud of you."

"I didn't think I could ever do this again," Taylor said, a lump rising in her throat.

"Oh, sweetheart, I did. You love this too much not to."

"Thank you," Taylor said, squeezing Jen's leg gently.

"For what?" Jen asked innocently.

"Satin sheets," Taylor replied softly. She turned her head to Jen's lips and leaned into them. "And for being here with me."

"I'm not going anywhere, darling," Jen said tenderly.

Taylor gave a whistle and Coal moved up to a soft trot. She steered him through the open gate beyond the corral. Jen held tight to Taylor, as much to reassure herself as for protection for Taylor. They floated across the pasture at an easy lope, the Texas wind in their hair. Jen couldn't see the tears rolling down Taylor's face, tears pinched out by her broad grin.

"Don't worry, Jen. I'll never let you fall," Taylor said.

Publications from
BELLA BOOKS, INC.
The best in contemporary lesbian fiction

P.O. Box 10543, Tallahassee, FL 32302
Phone: 800-729-4992
www.bellabooks.com

ROMANCING THE ZONE by Kenna White. 272 pp. Liz's world begins to crumble when a secret from her past returns to Ashton. 1-59493-060-0 $13.95

SIGN ON THE LINE by Jaime Clevenger. 204 pp. Alexis Getty, a flirtatious delivery driver is committed to finding the rightful owner of a mysterious package. 1-59493-052-X $13.95

END OF WATCH by Clare Baxter. 256 pp. LAPD Lieutenant L.A Franco Frank follows the lone clue down the unlit steps of memory to a final, unthinkable resolution. 1-59493-064-4 $13.95

BEHIND THE PINE CURTAIN by Gerri Hill. 280 pp. Jacqueline returns home after her father's death and comes face-to-face with her first crush. 1-59493-057-0 $13.95

18TH & CASTRO by Karin Kallmaker. 200 pp. First-time couplings and couples who know how to mix lust and love make 18th & Castro the hottest address in the city by the bay. 1-59493-066-X $13.95

JUST THIS ONCE by KG MacGregor. 200 pp. Mindful of the obligations back home that she must honor, Wynne Connelly struggles to resist the fascination and allure that a particular woman she meets on her business trip represents. 1-59493-087-2 $13.95

ANTICIPATION by Terri Breneman. 240 pp. Two women struggle to remain professional as they work together to find a serial killer. 1-59493-055-4 $13.95

OBSESSION by Jackie Calhoun. 240 pp. Lindsey's life is turned upside down when Sarah comes into the family nursery in search of perennials. 1-59493-058-9 $13.95

BENEATH THE WILLOW by Kenna White. 240 pp. A torch that still burns brightly even after twenty-five years threatens to consume two childhood friends. 1-59493-053-8 $13.95

SISTER LOST, SISTER FOUND by Jeanne G'fellers. 224 pp. The highly anticipated sequel to *No Sister of Mine*. 1-59493-056-2 $13.95

THE WEEKEND VISITOR by Jessica Thomas. 240 pp. In this latest Alex Peres mystery, Alex is asked to investigate an assault on a local woman but finds that her client may have more secrets than she lets on. 1-59493-054-6 $13.95

THE KILLING ROOM by Gerri Hill. 392 pp. How can two women forget and go their separate ways? 1-59493-050-3 $12.95

PASSIONATE KISSES by Megan Carter. 240 pp. Will two old friends run from love? 1-59493-051-1 $12.95

ALWAYS AND FOREVER by Lyn Denison. 224 pp. The girl next door turns Shannon's world upside down. 1-59493-049-X $12.95

BACK TALK by Saxon Bennett. 200 pp. Can a talk show host find love after heartbreak? 1-59493-028-7 $12.95

THE PERFECT VALENTINE: EROTIC LESBIAN VALENTINE STORIES edited by Barbara Johnson and Therese Szymanski—from Bella After Dark. 328 pp. Stories from the hottest writers around. 1-59493-061-9 $14.95

MURDER AT RANDOM by Claire McNab. 200 pp. The Sixth Denise Cleever Thriller. Denise realizes the fate of thousands is in her hands.   1-59493-047-3 $12.95

THE TIDES OF PASSION by Diana Tremain Braund. 240 pp. Will Susan be able to hold it all together and find the one woman who touches her soul?
1-59493-048-1 $12.95

JUST LIKE THAT by Karin Kallmaker. 240 pp. Disliking each other—and everything they stand for—even before they meet, Toni and Syrah find feelings can change, just like that.   1-59493-025-2 $12.95

WHEN FIRST WE PRACTICE by Therese Szymanski. 200 pp. Brett and Allie are once again caught in the middle of murder and intrigue.   1-59493-045-7 $12.95

REUNION by Jane Frances. 240 pp. Cathy Braithwaite seems to have it all: good looks, money and a thriving accounting practice . . .   1-59493-046-5 $12.95

BELL, BOOK & DYKE: NEW EXPLOITS OF MAGICAL LESBIANS by Kallmaker, Watts, Johnson and Szymanski. 360 pp. Reluctant witches, tempting spells and skyclad beauties—delve into the mysteries of love, lust and power in this quartet of novellas.   1-59493-023-6 $14.95

ARTIST'S DREAM by Gerri Hill. 320 pp. When Cassie meets Luke Winston, she can no longer deny her attraction to women . . .   1-59493-042-2 $12.95

NO EVIDENCE by Nancy Sanra. 240 pp. Private investigator Tally McGinnis once again returns to the horror-filled world of a serial killer.   1-59493-043-04 $12.95

WHEN LOVE FINDS A HOME by Megan Carter. 280 pp. What will it take for Anna and Rona to find their way back to each other again?   1-59493-041-4 $12.95

MEMORIES TO DIE FOR by Adrian Gold. 240 pp. Rachel attempts to avoid her attraction to the charms of Anna Sigurdson . . .   1-59493-038-4 $12.95

SILENT HEART by Claire McNab. 280 pp. Exotic lesbian romance.
1-59493-044-9 $12.95

MIDNIGHT RAIN by Peggy J. Herring. 240 pp. Bridget McBee is determined to find the woman who saved her life.   1-59493-021-X $12.95

THE MISSING PAGE A Brenda Strange Mystery by Patty G. Henderson. 240 pp. Brenda investigates her client's murder . . .   1-59493-004-X $12.95

WHISPERS ON THE WIND by Frankie J. Jones. 240 pp. Dixon thinks she and her best friend, Elizabeth Colter, would make the perfect couple . . .   1-59493-037-6 $12.95

CALL OF THE DARK: EROTIC LESBIAN TALES OF THE SUPERNATURAL edited by Therese Szymanski—from Bella After Dark. 320 pp.
1-59493-040-6 $14.95

A TIME TO CAST AWAY A Helen Black Mystery by Pat Welch. 240 pp. Helen stops by Alice's apartment—only to find the woman dead . . .   1-59493-036-8 $12.95

DESERT OF THE HEART by Jane Rule. 224 pp. The book that launched the most popular lesbian movie of all time is back.   1-1-59493-035-X $12.95

THE NEXT WORLD by Ursula Steck. 240 pp. Anna's friend Mido is threatened and eventually disappears . . .   1-59493-024-4 $12.95

CALL SHOTGUN by Jaime Clevenger. 240 pp. Kelly gets pulled back into the world of private investigation . . .   1-59493-016-3 $12.95

52 PICKUP by Bonnie J. Morris and E.B. Casey. 240 pp. 52 hot, romantic tales—one for every Saturday night of the year.   1-59493-026-0 $12.95

GOLD FEVER by Lyn Denison. 240 pp. Kate's first love, Ashley, returns to their home town, where Kate now lives . . .   1-1-59493-039-2 $12.95

RISKY INVESTMENT by Beth Moore. 240 pp. Lynn's best friend and roommate needs her to pretend Chris is his fiancé. But nothing is ever easy.   1-59493-019-8 $12.95

HUNTER'S WAY by Gerri Hill. 240 pp. Homicide detective Tori Hunter is forced to team up with the hot-tempered Samantha Kennedy.   1-59493-018-X $12.95

CAR POOL by Karin Kallmaker. 240 pp. Soft shoulders, merging traffic and slippery when wet . . . Anthea and Shay find love in the car pool.   1-59493-013-9 $12.95

NO SISTER OF MINE by Jeanne G'Fellers. 240 pp. Telepathic women fight to coexist with a patriarchal society that wishes their eradication.   1-59493-017-1 $12.95

ON THE WINGS OF LOVE by Megan Carter. 240 pp. Stacie's reporting career is on the rocks. She has to interview bestselling author Cheryl, or else!   1-59493-027-9 $12.95

WICKED GOOD TIME by Diana Tremain Braund. 224 pp. Does Christina need Miki as a protector . . . or want her as a lover?   1-59493-031-7 $12.95

THOSE WHO WAIT by Peggy J. Herring. 240 pp. Two brilliant sisters—in love with the same woman!   1-59493-032-5 $12.95

ABBY'S PASSION by Jackie Calhoun. 240 pp. Abby's bipolar sister helps turn her world upside down, so she must decide what's most important.   1-59493-014-7 $12.95

PICTURE PERFECT by Jane Vollbrecht. 240 pp. Kate is reintroduced to Casey, the daughter of an old friend. Can they withstand Kate's career?   1-59493-015-5 $12.95

PAPERBACK ROMANCE by Karin Kallmaker. 240 pp. Carolyn falls for tall, dark and . . . female . . . in this classic lesbian romance.   1-59493-033-3 $12.95

DAWN OF CHANGE by Gerri Hill. 240 pp. Susan ran away to find peace in remote Kings Canyon—then she met Shawn . . .   1-59493-011-2 $12.95

DOWN THE RABBIT HOLE by Lynne Jamneck. 240 pp. Is a killer holding a grudge against FBI Agent Samantha Skellar?   1-59493-012-0 $12.95

SEASONS OF THE HEART by Jackie Calhoun. 240 pp. Overwhelmed, Sara saw only one way out—leaving . . .   1-59493-030-9 $12.95

TURNING THE TABLES by Jessica Thomas. 240 pp. The 2nd Alex Peres Mystery. *From ghosties and ghoulies and long leggity beasties . . .*   1-59493-009-0 $12.95

FOR EVERY SEASON by Frankie Jones. 240 pp. Andi, who is investigating a 65-year-old murder, meets Janice, a charming district attorney . . .   1-59493-010-4 $12.95

LOVE ON THE LINE by Laura DeHart Young. 240 pp. Kay leaves a younger woman behind to go on a mission to Alaska . . . will she regret it?   1-59493-008-2 $12.95

UNDER THE SOUTHERN CROSS by Claire McNab. 200 pp. Lee, an American travel agent, goes down under and meets Australian Alex, and the sparks fly under the

Southern Cross. 1-59493-029-5 $12.95

SUGAR by Karin Kallmaker. 240 pp. Three women want sugar from Sugar, who can't make up her mind. 1-59493-001-5 $12.95

FALL GUY by Claire McNab. 200 pp. 16th Detective Inspector Carol Ashton Mystery. 1-59493-000-7 $12.95

ONE SUMMER NIGHT by Gerri Hill. 232 pp. Johanna swore to never fall in love again—but then she met the charming Kelly . . . 1-59493-007-4 $12.95

TALK OF THE TOWN TOO by Saxon Bennett. 181 pp. Second in the series about wild and fun loving friends. 1-931513-77-5 $12.95

LOVE SPEAKS HER NAME by Laura DeHart Young. 170 pp. Love and friendship, desire and intrigue, spark this exciting sequel to *Forever and the Night*.
1-59493-002-3 $12.95

TO HAVE AND TO HOLD by Peggy J. Herring. 184 pp. By finally letting down her defenses, will Dorian be opening herself to a devastating betrayal?
1-59493-005-8 $12.95

WILD THINGS by Karin Kallmaker. 228 pp. Dutiful daughter Faith has met the perfect man. There's just one problem: she's in love with his sister.
1-931513-64-3 $12.95

SHARED WINDS by Kenna White. 216 pp. Can Emma rebuild more than just Lanny's marina? 1-59493-006-6 $12.95

THE UNKNOWN MILE by Jaime Clevenger. 253 pp. Kelly's world is getting more and more complicated every moment. 1-931513-57-0 $12.95

TREASURED PAST by Linda Hill. 189 pp. A shared passion for antiques leads to love. 1-59493-003-1 $12.95

SIERRA CITY by Gerri Hill. 284 pp. Chris and Jesse cannot deny their growing attraction . . . 1-931513-98-8 $12.95

ALL THE WRONG PLACES by Karin Kallmaker. 174 pp. Sex and the single girl—Brandy is looking for love and usually she finds it. Karin Kallmaker's first *After Dark* erotic novel. 1-931513-76-7 $12.95

WHEN THE CORPSE LIES A Motor City Thriller by Therese Szymanski. 328 pp. Butch bad-girl Brett Higgins is used to waking up next to beautiful women she hardly knows. Problem is, this one's dead. 1-931513-74-0 $12.95

GUARDED HEARTS by Hannah Rickard. 240 pp. Someone's reminding Alyssa about her secret past, and then she becomes the suspect in a series of burglaries.
1-931513-99-6 $12.95

ONCE MORE WITH FEELING by Peggy J. Herring. 184 pp. A lighthearted, loving, romantic adventure. 1-931513-60-0 $12.95

TANGLED AND DARK A Brenda Strange Mystery by Patty G. Henderson. 240 pp. When investigating a local death, Brenda finds two possible killers—one diagnosed with multiple personality disorder. 1-931513-75-9 $12.95

WHITE LACE AND PROMISES by Peggy J. Herring. 240 pp. Maxine and Betina realize sex may not be the most important thing in their lives. 1-931513-73-2 $12.95

UNFORGETTABLE by Karin Kallmaker. 288 pp. Can Rett find love with the cheer-leader who broke her heart so many years ago?   1-931513-63-5 $12.95

HIGHER GROUND by Saxon Bennett. 280 pp. A delightfully complex reflection of the successful, high society lives of a small group of women.   1-931513-69-4 $12.95

LAST CALL A Detective Franco Mystery by Baxter Clare. 240 pp. Frank overlooks all else to try to solve a cold case of two murdered children . . .   1-931513-70-8 $12.95

ONCE UPON A DYKE: NEW EXPLOITS OF FAIRY-TALE LESBIANS by Karin Kallmaker, Julia Watts, Barbara Johnson & Therese Szymanski. 320 pp. You've never read fairy tales like these before! From Bella After Dark.   1-931513-71-6 $14.95

FINEST KIND OF LOVE by Diana Tremain Braund. 224 pp. Can Molly and Carolyn stop clashing long enough to see beyond their differences?   1-931513-68-6 $12.95

DREAM LOVER by Lyn Denison. 188 pp. A soft, sensuous, romantic fantasy.
1-931513-96-1 $12.95

NEVER SAY NEVER by Linda Hill. 224 pp. A classic love story . . . where rules aren't the only things broken.   1-931513-67-8 $12.95

PAINTED MOON by Karin Kallmaker. 214 pp. Stranded together in a snowbound cabin, Jackie and Leah's lives will never be the same.   1-931513-53-8 $12.95

WIZARD OF ISIS by Jean Stewart. 240 pp. Fifth in the exciting Isis series.
1-931513-71-4 $12.95

WOMAN IN THE MIRROR by Jackie Calhoun. 216 pp. Josey learns to love again, while her niece is learning to love women for the first time.   1-931513-78-3 $12.95

SUBSTITUTE FOR LOVE by Karin Kallmaker. 200 pp. When Holly and Reyna meet the combination adds up to pure passion. But what about tomorrow?
1-931513-62-7 $12.95

GULF BREEZE by Gerri Hill. 288 pp. Could Carly really be the woman Pat has always been searching for?   1-931513-97-X $12.95

THE TOMSTOWN INCIDENT by Penny Hayes. 184 pp. Caught between two worlds, Eloise must make a decision that will change her life forever.
1-931513-56-2 $12.95

MAKING UP FOR LOST TIME by Karin Kallmaker. 240 pp. Discover delicious recipes for romance by the undisputed mistress.   1-931513-61-9 $12.95

THE WAY LIFE SHOULD BE by Diana Tremain Braund. 173 pp. With which woman will Jennifer find the true meaning of love?   1-931513-66-X $12.95

BACK TO BASICS: A BUTCH/FEMME ANTHOLOGY edited by Therese Szymanski—from Bella After Dark. 324 pp.   1-931513-35-X $14.95

SURVIVAL OF LOVE by Frankie J. Jones. 236 pp. What will Jody do when she falls in love with her best friend's daughter?   1-931513-55-4 $12.95

LESSONS IN MURDER by Claire McNab. 184 pp. 1st Detective Inspector Carol Ashton Mystery.   1-931513-65-1 $12.95

DEATH BY DEATH by Claire McNab. 167 pp. 5th Denise Cleever Thriller.
1-931513-34-1 $12.95